THE OFFICE OF LOST AND FOUND

Vincent Holland-Keen is an author, artist and video director currently residing in the North of England. He works for a major metropolitan university as a business analyst/system designer.

The Office of Lost and Found

Vincent Holland-Keen

www.foxspirit.co.uk

First published as an ebook in 2011 by Anarchy Books

conversion by handebooks.co.uk

Second Edition

ISBN: 978-1-909348-87-5

Published by:
Fox Spirit Books
www.foxspirit.co.uk
adele@foxspirit.co.uk

"My name is Thomas Locke. I am a private detective and what I'm about to say may sound strange, but it is absolutely true."

Prelude

He woke up from nothing into a dark room with a single window. A cat figurine sat on the floor next to where he lay.

He stared at the ornament, waiting for his memory to explain the situation, but his memory was gone.

He knew a world existed beyond these walls and he knew it was full of people and places and facts and figures and he knew he must have lived a life there, but the details were lost to him.

He became very afraid. He curled tightly into a ball and closed his eyes and prayed that if he waited long enough, maybe at least his name would come back to him.

A breeze touched his face, followed by a faint scratching at his nose.

He opened his eyes. A piece of paper fluttered weakly on the floor before him. A message was written upon it in thick black ink:

'Your name is Thomas Locke. You work for me now.'

He looked up and around, both hopeful and fearful that the author was here. That was when he saw the shadow within the shadow for the first time.

The Office of Lost and Found

Kathleen Muller almost laughed in disbelief, but the man standing on her doorstep did not look as if he was joking. Despite a pleasant smile, his young face was etched with humourless lines that ran up his brow in pursuit of a receding hairline. No, she must have misheard. He couldn't have said that.

"Come again?" said Kathleen.

"Good morning. My name is Thomas Locke. I am a private detective and what I'm about to say may sound strange, but it is absolutely true. I know your husband was taken from you recently. I was hired to return him home." The stranger triumphantly held up a toaster. "Reincarnation works in mysterious ways."

Kathleen shook her head. She hadn't misheard. She called back into the house.

"Leonard!"

A burly brute of a man appeared by her side. Kathleen put an arm around his shoulder.

"Leonard, dear, apparently you've died and come back as a toaster."

Leonard looked at his wife. He looked at the private detective. Then he grabbed the toaster, dashed it to the ground and came at Thomas Locke with fists raised.

"Hospital's your best bet," said the tramp, nodding as he considered the photo in his dirty hand. "To find the man who can find your man, try the hospital. Remember the hurricane that hit a while back? Story goes that he found the butterfly what started it."

The picture was snatched from him by fingers sheathed in a black silk glove and returned to a black leather handbag.

"The hospital?" queried the lady, the contempt in her voice as barely concealed as the hard-on in the tramp's trousers.

"Yep," said the tramp, shrugging. "Sometimes at the police station and sometimes, not often, he's there."

He nodded toward Kirkfield Towers, a dirty grey tower block overlooking the alleyway. She set off in that direction without further word. The tramp scampered after her, his gaze fixated on the hypnotic swaying of the pert, posh ass hidden beneath the lady's tight, knee-length skirt.

"So what's a little helpful advice worth, Miss? A quid for a cup of tea? A tenner for dinner down the Nag's Head? Heh, maybe you got a little something else for a fella who lives on the streets with only his right hand for company?"

The lady stopped and turned. The tramp's dentally-challenged grin dropped away and the hand he had buried beneath the draw-string waistband of his trousers froze in mid-wank as she pointed a gun at his head.

Thomas Locke lived on the fourteenth floor of Kirkfield Towers. There was a crude sign on his door; a scrap of paper affixed with Sellotape and bearing six words scrawled in black marker pen – 'The Office of Lost and Found'.

The lady glanced at the note and then tried the door handle. The door opened. She slipped through into a squalid apartment. Narrow shafts of light fell through tilted blinds, piercing an oppressive gloom and hinting at precarious stacks of boxed up junk.

A voice cried out from an adjoining room.

"Don't give up on me, Leonard! Come on, hang in there!"

The lady remained motionless for a few moments, staring at the doorway through which the words had come. She took an unsteady breath before approaching slowly; her high heels safely and silently navigated a carpet littered with shadowy debris. She was unaware of movement behind her: the stacks of boxes there one moment and then… there the next, only different - slightly shorter or taller or an inch to the right.

A flash of electric blue greeted her arrival at the doorway. Beyond was a cramped bedroom. Thomas Locke was crouched on the floor with his back to her, his attention focussed on a battered toaster attached to a pair of jump leads.

Another spark and Locke tossed the jump leads aside in favour of a hammer. Two sharp clangs, a screwdriver hastily tweaking this and that and then Locke leaned back, his shoulders tense, his breath held.

She watched. He waited.

Sproing!

A slice of toast popped up from the repaired appliance and the lady jumped. Locke snatched it out of the air, glanced at the browned bread and then whipped his head round to face his visitor.

The lady smiled.

"Your secretary said I should come straight in," she said, lifting a lit cigarette to her lips.

"She should have said I was with a client," replied Locke.

"She must have guessed I could pay better than a toaster."

Locke watched smoke drift up in front of her face.

"I'm afraid I can't help you."

He got to his feet and pushed past her into the room of boxes.

"I haven't told you what I'm looking for."

"You're not looking for anything," replied Locke, rooting through cardboard containers at random. "You're looking to escape, to lose yourself. I can't help with that, but I can call my partner, he handles that side of the business."

Locke's search amongst the boxes unearthed a mobile phone and he lifted it to his ear.

"If you can help me find what I'm looking for I don't need to go anywhere," said the lady, handing over a photograph. "My name is Veronica Drysdale and that is my husband, Vincent. He went missing two nights ago."

Veronica Drysdale sat back on the boxes behind her, crossing her legs and letting the fingers of one hand linger around the hem of her skirt. Locke glanced at the picture. It showed a handsome man of middle-aged years with neat hair greying at the temples. He wore a confident smile and a paisley cardigan.

"Sorry," replied Locke, holding out the photograph, "I'm already on a case."

"If you find him, I can make it worth your while."

"Mrs Drysdale, I'm afraid I'm not in a position—"

"Veronica, please. Just name your price."

She leaned forward to show off her cleavage and teased the cigarette with her tongue. Then she dropped the cigarette and made a show of uncrossing her stocking-clad legs to grind out the butt with her shoe.

"Thanks," replied Locke, "but I'm still paying alimony from my last one-night stand."

The seductress transformed into a petulant schoolgirl and snatched the mobile phone from his hand.

"Then I'll speak to your partner."

'Lafarge' was the name shown on the screen. Veronica's thumb stabbed the 'call' button and she treated the detective to a triumphant grin, which promptly vanished when he dived at her. He grabbed her wrist. She beat a fist against the side of his head. He began prizing her fingers free of the phone. She slashed her fingers across his face. He didn't even flinch.

Then the struggle was over. Locke stepped away with the phone and cancelled the call. The name 'Lafarge' disappeared from the screen. Locke sighed relief.

Veronica glared at him. She made no attempt to straighten her ruffled clothes.

"I have to find my husband, Mr Locke." These words were spoken soprano. They trembled as they passed her lips. "I have to know he's really gone."

Veronica Drysdale's last vestige of composure held the gun in her gloved hands rock-steady.

Locke didn't say anything. He didn't even look at the gun. He just stared back at her in silence.

She pulled the trigger.

Blood burst from Locke's arm, forcing him to drop the phone. He didn't cry out, he just gritted his teeth against the pain.

"As you can see, my aim isn't so good. That's why he got away."

Veronica pulled out another cigarette and squeezed it between her blood red lips. She inhaled an uneven breath and then blew out the smoke. Locke reached down with his good arm and began searching for the phone with his fingers. It lay next to where he'd dropped the photograph. Mr Drysdale was still smiling.

"Maybe you should speak to my partner," suggested Locke.

"Find my husband, Mr Locke, or your partner will find himself working alone."

* * *

Two policemen knelt down in a park-keeper's hut and studied the subject of today's paperwork – a dead man with a septic bullet wound in his stomach.

"I know this corpse," said Inspector Brody. "He sold me my life insurance."

Sergeant Erroll raised an eyebrow. "An insurance salesman?"

His superior nodded.

"Then bang, motive," said Erroll. "Bet you the wife gets a big policy payout. Bingo, prime suspect. This detecting lark is too easy sometimes."

Inspector Brody gave him a contemptuous glance.

"This was a good and decent man, Sergeant. He knew the value of safeguarding your future. You don't have life insurance do you, Sergeant?"

"No, sir. A dead man doesn't need money."

Their conversation was interrupted by the crackling of the Sergeant's radio.

"All units, we have reports of shots fired at Kirkfield Towers..."

Veronica Drysdale staggered through her front door and slammed it shut behind her. She fell against the polished wood breathing heavily. Wild strands of hair stuck to the sweat on her cheeks. She held her breath and listened for sounds of pursuit, but all she heard was blood rushing around her skull and a voice from three nights ago:

"Honey, I'm home!"

She didn't want to remember this. She didn't want to remember him; handsome and dapper in a sleek grey suit, stepping through this same front door and calling out those words. Most of all, she didn't want to remember herself rushing down the stairs and flinging her arms around him with girlish glee.

Veronica tramped into the kitchen. She flicked the lights on and set about banishing her past naivety by preparing a dose of strong, black coffee.

While Veronica waited for the kettle to boil, she set down her handbag and removed her gloves. She tried to concentrate on the here and now and the simple act of retrieving an empty mug from a cupboard, but her mind rebelled, asking if it was only a week ago when her husband interrupted her happy retrieval of washing from the tumble dryer with the proposition that they have sex on the dining table after he had finishing trimming his nails in front of the nightly news? Had she really smiled and said: "Certainly, Darling" in reply?

All too aware the answer to both those questions was 'yes', Veronica switched off the kettle and grabbed a whisky bottle from a cupboard. She filled the empty mug and took a swig before drawing on a hastily lit cigarette.

"Veronica, dear," said her husband, after their intense, post-nightly news intercourse on the dining table, "your post-coital charm lacks only for a cigarette between your sweet lips."

"Then I shall start smoking forthwith, dear," Veronica had replied.

The bitter memory dumped the cigarette into the mug of whisky. Veronica slammed her hands against the worktop, trying to stop the shaking that threatened to loose tears from her eyes and sobs from her mouth.

The doorbell chimed.

"Mrs Drysdale," called a weary voice from outside, "this is the police. We would like to talk to you about various people you may have killed."

With a single, determined sniff, Veronica got a grip on her emotions and departed the kitchen, hurrying up the stairs and into the bedroom.

"We know you're in there, Mrs Drysdale!"

She pulled a large suitcase out of a wardrobe and hauled it over to the window. A sturdy drainpipe ran down the outside, but before could she could attempt escape, another policeman strode into view in the garden below.

"Sir, I see her!" he called out.

Veronica hurried back onto the landing, suitcase in tow. Through the marbled glass around the front door she could see one burly shape joined by a slimmer second. The policemen held a brief conversation before hurrying away. Veronica's hope of a reprieve was swiftly ended by the sound of smashing glass.

Instinct told her to run, but reason demanded to know

where. She tried to think of options, but panic blanked out everything except the consequences. She would be caught. She would be punished. She would suffer for the rest of her days.

But then she forgot all about that, because a piece of paper born on an unfelt breeze was dancing past her feet. It continued on along the landing and then swooped up and stuck itself to the bathroom door.

Inspector Brody lifted one of Veronica's discarded gloves from the kitchen worktop. He ran it across his fingertips and savoured the feel of the silken fabric. Sergeant Erroll fidgeted as he watched.

"Sir, I know we avoid doing things by the book, but isn't fondling potentially material evidence taking things a bit…?" The sergeant's words tailed off when faced with his superior's glare. "How about I go check upstairs?"

He hurried out of the kitchen, leaving Brody to examine the handbag. The inspector tossed tissues, car keys, lipstick and a tampon out onto the worktop, before carefully retrieving Veronica's gun.

She stared at the piece of paper stuck to the bathroom door. It was the same notepaper, the same thick black marker, but this was her bathroom, not 'The Office of Lost and Found'.

Veronica turned the handle and pushed the door open.

Inside, the light was on. Thomas Locke sat on the toilet with the jump-started toaster in his lap, a newspaper hiding his modesty and a thick bandage around his head. Veronica's legs went weak. In the middle of his brow, blood stained the dressing where her bullet had entered his skull.

He looked up.

"My partner and I have reconsidered your proposal."

"But… I killed you."

"Right now that's neither here nor there. Do you still want to find your husband or not?"

Sergeant Erroll took the stairs two steps at a time. He reached the landing and saw Veronica standing in the bathroom doorway with her suitcase.

"Freeze!" he cried.

She quickly stepped into the bathroom and slammed the door shut behind her.

Locke nodded as Veronica drove home the lock.

"Perhaps I should have done that."

He philosophically tore off a couple of sheets of toilet roll.

A bang against the door sent Veronica stumbling backward over her suitcase. The policeman outside rammed the door again, but the lock held.

Inspector Brody walked into the hallway as his colleague appeared at the top of the stairs.

"She's up here!" said Sergeant Erroll. "She's locked herself in the bathroom."

Brody smiled and pulled on one of Veronica's black silk gloves. He slipped her gun into the covered palm.

"Then she's going nowhere."

Veronica jumped at the sound of the gunshot. It was loud and brief. A series of dull thuds followed. She sank down against the side of the bath. She drew her knees to her chest and clasped her hands behind her head.

"I just wanted to be free of him."

Yet she could hear Vincent Drysdale's tuneless singing as he showered. She could hear him calling out to her, asking his dear wife to come scrub his back.

Locke stood, pulled up his trousers and flushed the toilet. The gurgling rumble of plumbing soon gave way to the sound of heavy footsteps approaching along the landing. When they stopped, when silence threatened to return and leave her with only her husband's foul melody, Veronica jumped to her feet and threw open the cabinet above the sink. Her red fingernails sought out a bottle of paracetamol, but that was thrown aside in favour of bleach, which was in turn discarded in favour of razor blades.

"A bullet would be quicker," said Locke, who was now waiting to wash his hands.

Veronica cast him a caustic glance.

A gentle knocking came at the door.

"I'm not here to kill you, Mrs Drysdale," said Inspector Brody. "I'm here for a friend. Veronica… he wants you back."

The packet of razor blades tumbled from her hand into the sink. Locke had to catch her as she fell, the colour suddenly gone from her face. He set her down on the floor next to the suitcase and tried to locate the sense behind her vacant eyes.

"My partner's waiting," whispered Locke. "If you never want to be found again, it'll only take one call."

"He still loves you, Veronica, and didn't you love him too, once?"

She began to shiver. The ghost standing in the bath behind her accepted the wife she'd once been into the shower with a knowing smile.

"You always come when I need you," said Vincent Drysdale.

"No," whispered Veronica to herself, before turning her desperate eyes on Locke. "You say you can find my husband?"

Inspector Brody's foot tapped impatience. The notepaper stuck to the door fluttered mockery. He tore it off and threw it to the floor. This wasn't getting him anywhere. If she wouldn't listen to reason, then to Hell with reason.

Brody lifted the gun and aimed at where he guessed the door's lock would be, but sounds from within stayed his hand. He pressed an ear up against the door and heard a window opening.

Veronica awkwardly manhandled the suitcase out through the bathroom's small window. Locke held his mobile phone to his ear and waited for it to ring. The name on the display read 'Lafarge'.

Unanswered ringing echoed around the Drysdale's kitchen. A black hand reached out and took Veronica's car keys from the worktop.

Inspector Brody was about to shoot his way into the bathroom when the sound of a car engine turning over came from outside.

He ran to the top of the stairs. The front door was open. Brody rushed down the stairs, jumped over Sergeant Erroll's corpse and dashed outside to see Veronica's car tear out of the driveway. Without breaking stride, the policeman vaulted the Drysdale's garden wall and raced over to his own car.

Veronica reached the front door as the policeman sped off in pursuit. Locke ambled up beside her, his gaze repeatedly returning to the police sergeant lying in a crumpled heap at the bottom of the stairs.

Veronica glanced first at Locke, then at the corpse, then at the bloody wound in the centre of Locke's forehead.

"Why aren't you dead?" she asked.

Locke's gaze detached from the dead body and searched the air about her head before he replied.

"Lafarge. He'll keep the police off our backs, but there'll be others."

"My husband has a lot of powerful friends."

"You have no idea. You shot him through here?"

He was at the kitchen door, nodded toward the dining table. When Veronica looked into the room she could see the memory of her husband sitting there, crossing his cutlery on the plate after finishing his meal.

Vincent didn't see her step up behind him with the gun. She pointed the barrel at the back of his head and closed her eyes before pulling the trigger.

The plate exploded in shards of china.

When Veronica opened her eyes, her husband was crawling away along the floor, clutching an ear freely losing blood. Grim determination stole over her face and she pursued him out of the kitchen and on into the lounge. She fired wildly. Plaster exploded from the walls. A picture frame shattered.

The picture still lay on the floor as Locke tracked the chase from two nights ago out through the conservatory and into the back garden. Veronica slowed as she passed. It showed a photograph from her wedding – bride and groom together. Her beaming smile announced it the happiest day of her life. The groom used to smile too, but now he no longer had a head, just a bullet hole. Veronica took care to kick the picture under a sideboard before heading after Locke.

* * *

Vincent Drysdale stumbled across the grass. His wife stood behind him, silhouetted against the light of the house. She fired again. The shot tore through his midriff.

Locke knelt down before a ragged hedge. He examined it, touching the traces of dry blood daubed on the brittle branches.

Veronica advanced as her husband tried to drag himself through the hedge. One more pull of the trigger and he'd be gone for good. Aim for the heart, she told herself. No, he hasn't got a heart. Aim for the head.

He turned to stare back at her along the gun-sight with tear-filled eyes. He wasn't frightened or angry. His face, the face she once loved, expressed only regret; a wish that things had been different. He held out a blood-covered hand.

She stepped forward and took the hand. A hopeful smile touched his lips and she relented. She couldn't do it. She dropped the gun and fell to her knees, embracing the husband she nearly killed.

"No!" exclaimed Veronica, abruptly. "That's not right! That's not what happened!"

"That's why we haven't got much time," replied Locke. "Come on."

He struggled through the hedge and out onto the road beyond.

Inspector Brody pursued Veronica's car down a country lane, the trees speeding past on either side bleached a deathly pale by their headlights.

And then the chase ended. The car in front drew slowly to a halt.

Brody applied the brakes and pulled up a safe distance behind. One hand touched the door release and the other gripped Veronica's gun, ready for when his quarry made a run for it.

But nobody exited the car ahead.

He tapped his fingers against the interior trim. They were playing games, forcing him to make the first move. Brody sniffed. So be it.

He retrieved a torch from the glove box, opened his door and stepped out. He left the engine running, just in case.

The other car remained silent, motionless.

Cautiously, he approached. The flashlight went first, venturing into the dark interior and over empty back seats as Brody kept his distance and the gun trained on his line of sight. The torch glinted off the passenger-side window before revealing the front seats were empty too. Brody stepped forward, finger tense around the pistol's trigger, angling the spotlight down into the foot-wells and then again into the back.

Nothing. No one.

Brody swept the verge with the torch, but was certain no one had left that car.

He took out his mobile phone and speed dialled a number.

"It's me. Something strange is going on here."

Veronica and Locke stood under a streetlight. Locke was staring into space, holding Leonard the toaster under his good arm. Periodically Veronica would look at him, then shake her head.

"I need a new gun," she muttered.

"For they clearly bring you luck," said Locke.

"I thought you said we didn't have much time."

"Time enough to wait."

Veronica looked up and down the street. It was empty; suburbia asleep.

"Why come back and help me?" she asked.

"Lafarge and I had been working on Leonard's case for weeks. You shooting me in the head was the lucky break we'd been after. Let's say I owe you one."

"They said you were crazy."

"I'm just a loose cannon detective playing by my own rules."

"And your partner?"

Long seconds passed before Veronica realised she wasn't going to get an answer. Without thinking, she pulled out a cigarette and lit up. It was almost at her lips when she caught herself. Cursing instincts still slave to her husband's desires, she made to throw the cigarette away in disgust, but Locke grabbed her hand.

"That's what we've been waiting for," he said.

Locke set off at a trot, still gripping her hand. Veronica, confused, let herself be dragged along after him.

"A wisp of smoke is the result of a billion coincidences," he explained. "The beat of a butterfly's wings…"

Two weeks ago in Ecuador, a butterfly alighting on a delicate rose.

"A woman's choice of red underwear."

That morning, Veronica attaching stockings to a crimson garter belt.

"A man happily drinking a wine he's always hated."

That very moment, on the other side of town, Kathleen Muller staring at her husband as he raises a glass to toast their anniversary.

"And, just around the corner…"

A bag lady pushed a pram filled with scavenged trash. Veronica frowned at the sight of a hapless kitten tucked up inside.

"Forty-eight, seventeen, thirty-three, eight," muttered the woman.

Locke greeted her with a smile, but she didn't notice – too busy with her counting and pram-pushing. He walked alongside, scanning the scavenged bric-a-brac. Veronica couldn't guess why he snatched out the dog collar, but the grin on Locke's face suggested this was a vital lead to be followed.

"Here, Benjie, boy," called out Locke. "Heel, woof, bark."

Veronica trailed behind him, wondering why she was following this madman into a misty wood as the hour approached midnight.

A bark in the distance set Locke running. Veronica didn't hurry after him. Her high heels made navigation of the woodland floor treacherous enough at walking pace. When she caught up with him, Locke was using his good arm to dig away the soil around a pale hand sticking up through the earth. A dog hampered his attempts by trying to lick his hands and face until he produced the collar and slipped it around the dog's neck.

"Now go home, boy. Go home, Benjie."

The dog stared at him, barked and then ran off.

Free of interference, Locke continued digging. Veronica edged closer, her shoes unsteady in the mud. The breath caught in her throat when Locke cleared away the dirt covering her husband's face.

"My God," she said, "he is dead."

"We're looking for your husband," said Locke, dismissively, "not a corpse."

"But this is—"

Her protest was cut off by headlights searching through the trees. Locke grabbed her hand and dragged her from the scene.

Inspector Brody's shadow fell over the shallow grave, his car behind him, the engine rumbling patiently.

"Yes, they've been here," he reported into his mobile phone.

The reply was drowned out by the rumble turning into a roar. Brody spun around to see the headlights sweep away, his car turning in reverse before hitting first gear and turning again, leaving the Inspector to watch two red tail lights escape away into the darkness.

The headlights drew expanding circles on the garage door and then went dark as Veronica turned off the ignition. Locke was already out of the car, striding to the front door of the adjacent house with the contents of the glove-box in hand.

Veronica exited from the driver's side and followed, briefly lamenting the filth that now covered her shoes.

"We found him," she said, repeating the point she'd made during their drive. "He's dead. It's over."

One by one, Locke tossed aside Brody's papers until he was left with only a few sweet wrappers between his fingers. He let them go to a capricious breeze that carried them across the small front lawn and into the face of a cheery plaster gnome.

Locke picked up the gnome and revealed a key sitting underneath.

"I think I could enjoy being in prison," said Veronica as she followed Locke up the stairs of Brody's house and into a bedroom. "After him, institutionalised abuse would be a breeze. Or maybe I'll skip the country. Go to Cuba. They don't have an extradition treaty with us, do they?"

Locke didn't answer the question. Instead he began rifling through the inspector's wardrobe.

"You're ignoring me, aren't you?"

He unearthed a security box beneath a false floor and heaved it over to the bed.

"Give me three numbers," he said. "Random numbers. Now. Don't think."

"Err, forty-eight, seventeen, thirty-three."

Locke spun the combination lock three times before hitting the catch. The lid sprung open. Inside was a stack of papers Locke proceeded to examine. Veronica sidled up to him and peered over his shoulder.

"Isn't it about time I paid you for your services?"

She slipped her hands under his coat. His only reaction was to wince when she brushed the bullet wound in his arm.

Veronica pouted frustration, then darted a hand into his pocket and snatched his phone.

"Maybe I should pay Mr Lafarge instead?"

Locke spun around, his eyes wide.

"No!"

"You found my husband," she purred while locating Lafarge's number. "It's only fair someone gets paid."

This time when Locke grabbed for the phone, Veronica was ready. She stepped back and coyly dropped it down inside her top. Locke's dismay was met by a lascivious smile.

"Okay, okay," said Locke. "I do the finding, you can pay me. Lafarge… works differently. He loses things. He takes away, so… he has to give you something in return."

"That sounds like a good deal."

"If someone gave you syphilis would you think that was a good deal? Besides, I haven't found your husband yet."

"But—"

Locke handed her a document from the security box.

"One of your husband's insurance policies. Read the small print."

Veronica, bemused, began reading. Her expression slowly shifted from confusion to boredom and, eventually, to outright disbelief.

"This can't be…"

"Your husband isn't who you think he is, Mrs Drysdale. Come, there's another dead person you need to meet."

Thomas Locke stood on the doorstep of a pebble-dashed semi-detached house with Leonard the Toaster under his arm and Veronica by his side. All trace of her studied poise was gone, stolen away by a senseless series of events that had dragged her through hedges and woods and finally to the door of a stranger's house.

Locke pressed the doorbell. It played 'Greensleeves'.

A large man in a woollen jumper opened the door. He held a glass of wine in his hand. The easy smile on the podgy face suggested it had already consumed a number of refills.

"Hello? Yes?"

Locke didn't answer him. Instead he turned to Veronica.

"Mrs Drysdale, this is your husband. Now I'm done."

He turned and began walking away to the front gate. Veronica grabbed him by the arm. She offered an apologetic smile to the man at the door before hissing at Locke: "that is not my husband."

Locke blinked and turned back to the man in question.

"Have you or have you not recently survived a near death experience?" he asked.

The big man slowly shook his head.

"Oh," said Locke.

Veronica lowered her eyebrows to glare at Locke. His unfocussed eyes darted through recollections to try and find his mistake until a light, chiming voice came from inside the house.

"I think they're here to see me, Gavin. Show them in, please."

Gavin obligingly stepped aside. Locke led the way into a brightly lit living room. Veronica trailed behind, trying not to associate herself too closely with the oddball detective.

They stepped into a semi-circle of people. Some sat on dining chairs, others crammed onto a settee, yet more stood in front of a fireplace bricked up in order to harbour an electric heater. Above them a banner said 'Welcome Home'.

'Get Well Soon' cards lined the mantelpiece, but the centre of attention was a delicately-featured woman of middle-aged years occupying an upright armchair. She smiled at Locke and Veronica.

"Clearly I misread my newspaper," said Locke, solemnly. "It was Mrs Rose, not Mr Rose. I stand corrected. Veronica, this is your husband."

Veronica stared at him, not even considering his lunatic assertion, but trying instead to fathom why she'd followed him this far. Hushed whispers circulated as the guests tried to work out what was going on.

"Mr Locke, isn't it?" asked Mrs Rose, her words soft, but authoritative enough to silence the room. "I think you owe everyone an explanation."

Locke took a deep breath and surveyed his audience, lingering on Veronica longest of all.

"My name is Thomas Locke," he announced. "I am a private detective and what I'm about to say may sound strange, but it is absolutely true. Once upon a time, about two years ago, there was a man called Leonard Muller who tried driving home through a fearsome storm. All he could see were sheets of driving rain, so he didn't see the fallen tree in the road ahead until it was too late. He died that night, but some part of him remained, desperate to make it home. So desperate, part of him did come back… as this toaster."

Locke held up the aforementioned appliance. While he talked, a guest rose from his seat and moved to the door. Locke glanced over at the man and their eyes met, sharing a memory of a beating doled out that very morning.

"Leonard hired me and my partner to find his wife," continued Locke. "We did, but we also found her husband, alive and well, standing next to her."

That husband now stood by the door, grinning.

"I didn't understand why until Mrs Drysdale shot me in the head a few hours later. I travelled that fabled tunnel of light, felt its promise of peace…" Locke's voice trailed off, his eyes closed in remembrance of that moment's respite. "Then I was forced to come back."

Locke's eyes flicked open and he looked about at those in the room once more.

"I came back knowing exactly what kind of life insurance Mrs Drysdale's husband sold."

The door edged open and Inspector Brody stepped inside. The key turned in the lock behind him.

"Elizabeth Rose died of a tragic asthma attack two days ago," continued Locke. "She saw the tunnel of light and was welcomed to the other side by her late Mum and Dad, but in her wake someone else came back. Someone shot dead, but with an insurance policy that promised a new life would be provided in the event of death. Someone like the impostor who now inhabits the body of Leonard Muller."

Locke turned his accusing stare on the man by the door, but it was the Inspector beside him that responded.

"Or someone like me," said Brody.

Veronica looked around at the policeman, registering shock at both his presence and his agreement with Locke.

"Or me," said an old lady on the sofa.

"Or any one of us," said a young man on a dining chair.

"I'm not sure if I'm following this," said a frowning Gavin Rose.

Veronica was about to applaud the one person in the room on her wavelength when Inspector Brody took the confused husband aside and silenced him with a practised sleeper hold.

"I am glad you brought her back to me, Mr Locke," said Mrs Rose, prompting Veronica to feel a chill of recognition. "But she would have returned sooner or later. You've killed people, my love. Me, Inspector Brody's young partner. Mr Locke here seems to have been the lucky one. They're hunting for you, Veronica, and no one else will take you in. No one else can protect you. No one except me."

"No," said Veronica, shaking her head, "I won't go back."

Mrs Rose stood and Brody passed her Veronica's gun.

"Kill me again if it'll make you feel better."

Veronica tried to back away, but Leonard was behind her, blocking her exit. She trembled as Mrs Rose took her hand and caressed it. The gun was pressed into her sweaty palm and her fingers forced closed around the handle. Mrs Rose lifted the gun until Veronica was staring down the sight at the pale woman's forehead. Her finger touched the trigger. If she believed that this was her husband, she also had to believe that killing him again would achieve nothing. He would come back. She would never be free.

Veronica pulled away and bundled past Leonard to the door. He snatched away the key, but she wasn't interested in that. She backed into the corner and put the gun to her temple. This was the only way out; the only escape.

"You have a policy too," said Mrs Rose. "Sooner or later…"

The all-too-familiar stranger opened her arms for an embrace.

A feeling of vertigo sent Veronica's senses swimming. She was teetering on the precipice and all these people were here to watch her fall. All except Thomas Locke. He was whispering to his toaster.

Veronica threw the gun aside and pulled violently at the handle of the locked door.

"Let me out!" she screamed.

Mrs Rose sighed and nodded to Leonard. He held Veronica aside with an arm and slid the key into the lock. When the door opened, Veronica ran from the house, her heels clattering away down the path.

"I'll be waiting," said Mrs Rose softly. Then she turned to the private detective. "There's always a queue to come back, Mr Locke. Those with the cheaper policies, they aren't picky about who they end up as. They don't care too much what state their new body is in."

Locke found himself at the centre of a rapidly diminishing circle of reincarnated vultures.

"Before I vacate this body," he said, taking a firm hold of the toaster, "the real Leonard has a message for his replacement."

This took the form of a wild swing that clubbed the fake Leonard around the side of the head. Locke dived for the door, but Mr Drysdale's clientele were on him before he managed another step.

Veronica slumped against the gatepost. She hugged her knees to her chest and hung her head. A glance back would have shown Locke's hand reach out through the open door. But she didn't look. She didn't see him dragged back inside. She didn't even hear the door slam shut. Veronica was lost to the world around her, trying to find a sanctuary in the depths of her own mind that she couldn't find in the world outside.

But then Locke's cries of pain came and they drowned out the voice inside her head pleading for escape. She covered her ears, but his cries were too loud. She screamed, but when her breath ran out, Locke's torment continued.

Veronica threw back her head and stared up at the sky, at the infinite blackness of sky and stars that told of an endless universe - an endless universe in which he would always find her.

When she looked down again she saw another light, glinting up from her cleavage. It was Locke's phone, deposited there back at Brody's house. Her mind empty and numb, she retrieved it and her fingers began working of their own accord. She selected a number from the address book and pressed the 'call' button.

The phone rang.

And rang.

And rang.

Each ring was swallowed up by the silence of the night before the next came, sharp and insistent, only to be lost again, same as the last.

Veronica lost count of the rings. No voice came from the other end of the phone. It just rang until she pressed the 'cancel' button. By then she had got her reply.

He stood over her.

His shape was that of a man dressed in hat and coat, but it was nothing more than a shape. Within that outline there were no features, only blackness.

"Where can I go?" she asked him.

He said nothing.

"I loved him. I did. He was my everything."

He said nothing.

"Then everything changed. Suddenly. The tumble dryer broke and... why should that change anything? Why should I love my husband one moment and then the next moment...? Ten years and I hadn't thought of anything. Everything in my head came from him. Everything he said, I did. I never thought, I never questioned. I loved him unconditionally, but then the tumble dryer broke and his... his spell broke. Until that moment I didn't exist. I was just a puppet, mindless, empty… happy. Then I wasn't. I woke up. I realised I didn't love him, I hated him for what he'd done to me."

Veronica looked to the house.

"He'll always find me, won't he? In this world or the next, I'll never be free, but… your partner said you could lose things. Lose things so they can never be found?"

Lafarge nodded.

Veronica hung her head and weighed up her options. What was left for her in this world anyway? Everything she'd had, everything she'd known, it was all because of him. There were no options. There was only one way she could be free.

Veronica looked up at Lafarge with the same bitter resolve that had murdered her husband.

"Lose him. Give me whatever you want, but take him somewhere no one will ever hear from him again."

The wind rose suddenly. It howled down the street and bore leaves and debris that forced Veronica to close her eyes. Something fluttered into her face. She clawed it away and the wind dropped.

Veronica opened her eyes. She was alone once more. She looked down at the piece of ragged notepaper in her hand. It was written with that familiar black marker, but this time all it said was: 'Deal'.

Then came the scream.

It was louder and more chilling than anything Locke had managed. Veronica climbed to her feet and looked up the path to the Rose house. The door was open once again. Despite fear driving her frantic heartbeat, she advanced up the path.

She was almost at the doorstep when Leonard staggered out. His scream turned into a whistle and then silence as his mouth closed up, his fearful eyes staring at her before they too disappeared into a blank sheet of skin. He dropped to the ground, convulsing, starved of breath and minutes from death.

Veronica walked on, entering the house and a living room cast in disarray. A dining chair missing two legs stood lop-sided on ragged strips of floral carpet. The banner on the wall was severed, leaving only the word 'Home' remaining. The young man who'd spoken before was now crouched in the corner, hands clutching his head as he muttered to himself and rocked back and forth. The old woman sat pale and still on the sofa. Gavin Rose was still unconscious in the corner, but he had been robbed of clothes.

Veronica stepped over a body holding a knife in its own chest and into a small pile of dust that dispersed under her shoe. A figure, frozen rigid, watched her pass with unnervingly mobile eyes. Another made a grab for her, but without form or substance it passed right through her. Its anguished cry went as unnoticed as its presence.

Locke sat at the bottom of the stairs, tending bruises and bloody wounds. He didn't acknowledge Veronica's arrival. She began climbing the steps.

Lafarge was at the top, still no more than a shadow despite the lights. A guttural cry preceded Brody plunging through the black shape and stumbling down the topmost steps in surprise.

Lafarge moved on. When Veronica reached Brody, he was staring at fingertips disintegrating before his eyes.

"But I'm covered," he said, "I can come back..."

Neither of them believed it. Veronica reached out. When her finger touched him, he dissolved into a shower of embers.

"Veronica!" screamed a voice from up ahead.

She ran into a bedroom where Lafarge held Mrs Rose, his black arm around her throat, tears fluid on her cheeks.

"I loved you," cried Mrs Rose, "yet you called him?"

Lafarge's blackness began to spread. It leaked into the corners of the room, touching the shadows and causing them to grow.

Veronica stared at the woman who was her husband.

"Yeah, I'm a lousy wife. Goodbye, Vincent."

Mrs Rose tried to scream again, but the onrushing blackness filled her mouth, covered her face, consumed everything in the room until nothing was left but blackness.

Kathleen Muller opened her eyes. She rubbed feeling into her face and pulled herself upright on the settee. Sunlight was streaming in through a gap between the drawn curtains. For a moment she thought the doorbell's chime was the remnant of a dream, but then it rang again.

"I promise you, Leonard, if you've forgotten your keys after I've spent the whole night worrying..."

She staggered up to the front door, unlocked it, pulled it open and found nobody standing there.

She tried blinking away her tiredness and leant forward to check if anyone was hiding out of sight. Nope, no one.

It was only when she began to close the door that Kathleen noticed the dented toaster sitting on the doorstep.

From behind a hedge, Locke and Veronica watched Kathleen cautiously pick up the toaster and then, with a last suspicious glance up and down the street, retreat back inside.

"Do you think she'll ever believe it's him?" asked Veronica, standing up and joining Locke in walking back toward the Office of Lost and Found.

"Maybe," he replied, "when he starts burning love hearts across all her toast."

They walked on in silence for a while.

"Did you really find the butterfly that started that hurricane?" asked Veronica.

"I found a butterfly," replied Locke, "turned out it had an alibi."

Veronica nodded.

They crossed a road. They passed shops that had yet to open for the day. Curtains opened as the town started to wake. A milkman waved to them. A dog barked at them. They reached another road and waited for a solitary car to pass by. Veronica spoke again.

"He didn't give me anything, you know. And nothing's different, except of course Vincent's gone. I feel exactly the same."

Locke shook his head with a weary wisdom.

"Appearances can be deceptive." He looked up at a sky of fading orange and burgeoning blue, across which aeroplanes drew lines of white and distant birds circled and flew. "Trust me; once you've met Lafarge, everything changes."

He walked on, but Veronica lingered a moment. She stared upwards and fancied she saw one of those birds swallow up a passing Boeing 747, but quickly dismissed the notion and hurried on after her oddball private detective.

Interlude I

Lafarge stood atop a fire brigade training tower, his black coat blown by a different wind to the one whose chill had Locke huddled down behind the cover of a wall.

"Of all the things you could have given her," said Locke, shaking his head, "how could you give her that without asking me?"

Crime, Punishment and Fiddlesticks

Cross-stitched kittens frolicked with balls of string across the table cloth. The tea tray was polished silver, the china white with painted flowers; pristine save for the milk jug, whose spout was chipped. Mrs Cribbins and Mrs Lonley held cups brimful with tea and sipped delicately with pinky fingers extended.

"I did not say they deserve to be shot," said Mrs Cribbins, firmly, "I just said a fine is no deterrent."

"A bullet in the leg would be a deterrent," said Mrs Lonley.

"Oh, seriously, Agatha, think it through. They get shot in the leg and they'll need medical attention. Who'll pay for that? Us, the taxpayers, that's who. Not to mention the fact that they'll be fouling the footpath with blood as well as their dog's do-do."

"Hmm, you're right, yes. We need a sanitary deterrent. Like cremation. On the spot. Policemen with flamethrowers. Justice served and no expensive corpse disposal."

The two hunchback old ladies hunched up further in fits of giggles. They were watched impassively by a piebald cat sitting on the lap of a third old lady. This old lady was called Mrs Maunley and until that moment she had been twitching aside the cottage's net curtain to steal glances of the street outside. Now she turned on her guests and looked at them over her blue-framed glasses.

"Really, you two, dog mess is no joking matter. Need I remind you of Mrs Gregory?"

Mrs Maunley's friends went abruptly quiet and shook their heads shamefully.

"I still think it was that Hemingway dog," muttered Mrs Cribbins. "He's always letting it run off the lead and—"

"If it was," cut in Mrs Maunley, "he'll get what's coming to him sooner or later. Everyone does."

All three of them nodded sagely at this wisdom and looked to the window. Police tape marked a cordon around the house across the street. A Panda car was parked in the street outside.

"They haven't found her yet, have they?" said Mrs Lonley.

"Not yet," replied Mrs Maunley. "Tell me, do you think that woman out there is behaving suspiciously?"

"What woman?" asked Mrs Cribbins.

"I can't see anybody," said Mrs Lonley, "though I see the Holloways lawn still needs mowing. I told him the other day it was a disgrace—"

"Down the street," snapped Mrs Maunley, "the woman in the long coat and dark glasses. Look, she's turning to go. Have you two not got your long-distance glasses on?"

Mrs Cribbins and Mrs Lonley removed their spectacles and examined them.

"I'm not sure," said Mrs Cribbins, "I'll have to get out my reading glasses to check."

The two old women began rooting through their handbags. Mrs Maunley shook her head, leant down to the piebald cat and whispered in its ear.

"Fiddlesticks, dear, Mummy would like you to do her a favour..."

Veronica Drysdale gave one last, lingering look back at her house and its police tape cordon before striding away.

A wild autumn wind blew the tail of her long coat out behind her and she had to hold her hat to her head to keep it from blowing off. Her pace didn't falter as she traversed direct marketing boundaries; travelling from her 'wealthy executive' postcode, through 'settled suburbia' and 'blue collar roots' into an estate of boarded up windows and empty car parks categorised as 'high rise hardship'. Veronica stopped in the shadow of a decrepit grey tower block and removed her sunglasses to stare up at a window on the seventh floor. The thought that she was returning here again brought a flicker of disgust to her face. She hastily replaced her sunglasses and walked on toward the tower block entrance. At no point during her travels did she realise a little piebald cat was following her.

Behind the glass of the seventh floor window was a room filled with stacks of bric-a-brac. A man lost in his thirties with the frown of a fifty year old sat at a bare wooden table.

His name was Thomas Locke. This was his office. Opposite him sat a young girl wearing the make-up of a fifteen year old trying to look twenty-one.

"How much you want then?" asked the girl.

"Kayla, it's not a question of money," replied Locke.

"Mam said you'd say that. Said you's funny like that. He'll find you anything, she said, but you got to give him something and likely as not he won't take your money. But that's good, 'cos I ain't got any."

The teenager reached down and lifted a battered silver toaster onto the table. Locke lowered his head and shook it slowly.

"Kayla, I'm sorry—"

"How about these then?" She pushed a couple of crumpled tickets across the table. "See my brother's band down the Red Lion. Dead good they are. They're already talking to record companies."

"Listen, Kayla, I don't think—"

"Or I got this too," cut in Kayla, eager to curtail another rejection. She produced a moth-eaten toy rabbit. "It's really Britney's, but Mam said I should bring it. Said you liked weird stuff and..."

She tailed off on seeing Locke's lips readying another apologetic refusal. He was pre-empted by a gust of wind blowing a scrap of paper across the table and into the face of the stuffed rabbit. Kayla glanced at the window. It was firmly shut. Locke snatched the paper and read a few crudely written words. He closed his eyes, crumpled up the note and thrust it into his pocket.

"Okay," he sighed, "what do you want me to find?"

Veronica rapidly exited the lift. The stench from a pool of urine gathered in one corner followed her until the doors closed. Then Fiddlesticks the cat slipped out from the stairwell and took over the pursuit.

The only daylight gracing the passageway came from a small window at the far end. The rest of its length was illuminated by haphazard electrics; lights that hummed, flickered or hung dead and lifeless from the ceiling. Veronica hesitated for a moment as she tried to get her bearings – all of the doors in Kirkfield Towers looked identically uninviting – before spotting the scrap of paper ahead that declared in thick black writing the location of The Office of Lost and Found.

"A man?" asked Locke. "What man? Have you got a name?"

"No," snapped Kayla, "I don't mean like that. I mean like… The guys round here are scum, right? Well, I'd like to meet a guy who's not. I want to meet a guy who's funny and handsome and who might actually, really… love me, you know?"

Kayla's wide eyes radiated an innocent hope at odds with her brash attitude. Locke was lost for words, so he reached into his pocket and crumpled the note more tightly within his fist.

The door burst open. Kayla's cynicism quickly returned with narrowed eyes focussed on the new arrival.

"Good morning, Mr Locke," said Veronica, "your secretary said I should come straight in."

"She should have said I was with a client," he replied.

"A client?" Veronica looked at the toaster, the teenager and then back at Locke. "So which is it? The slut or the toaster?"

"Who you calling a slut, bitch?" spat Kayla.

Veronica drew a gun from her coat pocket and pressed the barrel up against the young girl's forehead.

"Whoever I want, slut. Now get out, me and the private dick need to talk."

Kayla's fists were clenched tight, but her bottom lip was trembling. She looked across at Locke.

"Take your things," he said, "but leave the rabbit and I'll see what I can do."

Kayla managed a brief smile at Locke, before ducking away from the gun, gathering up the tickets and bundling the toaster under an arm. She treated Veronica to a scowl before hurrying out of the door. Veronica kicked it closed behind her.

"I see you've got a new gun," said Locke as the pistol was returned to its coat pocket.

Veronica pulled off her black silk gloves and picked the toy rabbit up from the table.

"The police are still at the house," she said. Her pale fingers lifted the left ear of the rabbit and a red painted nail picked at the few remaining stitches that kept it attached to the head. "I'd have thought they would have finished with the place by now."

Locke shrugged. Veronica put the rabbit back down on the table.

"So what did the slut want?" she asked.

The side of Locke's mouth twitched up into a half smile, then the furrows of his frown deepened and his mouth dropped open to reply with another question.

"How do you go about finding love?"

Fiddlesticks hopped through the cat flap in the front door and returned to Mrs Maunley's living room. The three old ladies were on their third pot of tea when the cat jumped up onto the table, knocked over the milk jug and then began lapping up the spillage as if that's what he'd intended to do all along.

Mrs Cribbins and Mrs Lonley regarded this feline intrusion with disapproval. In contrast, Mrs Maunley leaned forward, her hands two trembling fists tucked under her bosom, her rheumy eyes fixed on the cat, her croaky voice whispering: "Was it her?"

Fiddlesticks stopped lapping milk and stared up at his owner. Mrs Maunley's urgent expression lifted and she very nearly clapped her hands together. Neither Mrs Cribbins nor Mrs Lonley owned a cat, so the look they exchanged was mutual puzzlement at how a cat's look could elicit such a response.

"My, my, look at the time," said Mrs Maunley, adopting a sudden air of forced gravity. "I'm afraid it's time for you to be going, ladies. Same time next week?"

The guests were ushered into the hallway.

"But we've not even finished our tea," said Mrs Lonley.

"You can finish it next time," said Mrs Maunley. "A bit of cling-film, stick it in the fridge, keep as good as new I'm sure." She nodded to the front door. "You know the way from here. My regards to Mr Lonley and Mr…" She waved her hand for an aide memoire.

"Cribbins," said Mrs Cribbins.

Mrs Maunley nodded and smiled, pointed to the door and then hobbled at speed back into the living room. The two remaining old ladies began pulling on their coats as Mrs Maunley's whispers crept out from the living room.

"And you're sure it was her? Where did she go? Should I get the A to Z? Oh, you've got it already. You're so much better at turning the pages than I am anyway. Claws beat arthritis any day of the week, isn't that right, Fiddlesticks?"

Mrs Lonley looked at Mrs Cribbins and both sighed deeply before hurrying from the house.

Veronica and Locke stepped from an anonymous doorway onto a street busied by pedestrians. Shabby storefronts tried to lure in the passers-by with splintered crates of fruit and veg, inflammatory newspaper headlines and neon promises of pizza, curries, kebabs and burgers above windowsills that served as a graveyard for dead flies. Cars crawled impatiently along the road, stopping every hundred metres at another pelican crossing. From a pub across the street came furious shouting. No one paid the commotion any mind, save for the detective and his companion.

Moments later, Kayla stormed out of the building and then turned to hurl insults back at the fat man that followed her. He folded his arms over his ample belly. When she paused for breath, he shook his head and jerked a thumb up the street.

"You should be thankful I'm just firing you and not calling the police," he said. "Now, sling yer hook."

Kayla pouted petulantly and then continued her invective as she walked away. The fat man dismissed this with a wave of his hand and disappeared back inside the pub. Veronica and Locke followed the teenager from the other side of the street.

"That girl doesn't need a man," said Veronica.

"I'd say she needs a new job," replied Locke.

"She needs a swift kick up the arse, that's what she needs."

"Alas I get paid to find what people want," said Locke, "not what they need."

"You get paid in stuffed toys, is that what you want?"

Locke didn't reply. He just pushed Kayla's toy rabbit deeper into his coat pocket.

"Look at her," said Veronica. "Look at the way she walks, the way she swears at passers-by when they look at her. She has relationship issues with complete strangers. You could find her the perfect man and it'd be over in a week, because she'd throw one too many tantrums and he'd be out the door and away."

Locke shrugged.

"You're wasting your time with her," concluded Veronica.

"Right now it's the only job I've got."

"And tailing her? Is this how you expect to find her a man? Is this how you normally find things? I was expecting a bit more method to your madness."

Kayla stopped at a cashpoint machine. A moment of calm preceded a scream and fists battering the plastic screen.

"I find best when I'm not looking," said Locke. "The answer is suddenly there, right under my nose."

Kayla begrudgingly accepted the few notes the ATM was prepared to dispense as another teenager stepped up behind her. He looked a few years older, but with her in heels, he stood a few inches shorter. He slipped a hand over her backside and whispered in her ear. She immediately turned around and pushed him away. He reeled backwards with exaggerated effect and fell to his knees. Still on his knees, he shuffled back up to her with his hands clasped together as if offering her a prayer.

Kayla tolerated this display for a few seconds with hands stiffly on hips before turning around and sashaying away. The money was slipped into a pocket inside her jacket. The guy jumped to his feet and scampered in pursuit, his pleas now more extravagant than ever. Finally, Kayla laughed and let herself be dragged by the sleeve into the mouth of an alley-way. Her back fell against brickwork, his hand fell upon her thigh and they exchanged more words that drew smiles on their faces.

Locke looked across at Veronica. She didn't look back. Stare fixed on the two teenagers, she said: "The answer might be right under your nose, but don't confuse an answer with a dangling gob of snot."

The guy led Kayla deeper into the alleyway. When she grew hesitant, he surprised her with a kiss. This sparked a pubescent passion that accelerated toward consummation up against a dumpster. She panted for breath and struggled to unbuckle his belt. His fingers nimbly unzipped her jacket, fondled her breasts and then swiped the money from her inside pocket.

That pretty much killed any romance the moment had.

Kayla asked what the Hell he was doing and tried to snatch the bank notes back. He pushed her away. She grabbed for the money again and was rewarded with a rabbit punch to the stomach that left her doubled up on the floor, gasping for air.

Veronica's gun was half-drawn when Locke placed his hand on hers.

"Things happen for a reason," he said. "Let's just wait and see what reason lies behind this."

Veronica ground her teeth in frustration as Kayla's attacker disappeared into the crowds of shoppers. She glared at Locke, but his expression was inscrutable. His eyes widened whenever someone passing the alleyway slowed their step on hearing Kayla's sobs. Words of triumph crested his lips when a tall businessman ventured toward the fallen girl, but the ringing of the businessman's mobile phone gave him an excuse to turn a blind eye and continue on his way.

Veronica stepped up the curb and waited for a break in the traffic. She was about to cross when Locke grabbed her arm and nodded his head toward a gray-haired woman in an expensive coat hurrying to the young girl's aid.

"But Kayla's after a man," said Veronica.

"Maybe our Samaritan's got a son," replied Locke.

The woman helped the teenager to her feet while repeatedly asking if she was okay. Kayla answered by snatching the woman's handbag and sprinting from the alleyway.

"Hey! Stop! Stop, thief!" cried the wronged Samaritan.

Veronica cast a baleful glance at Locke.

"You are such an idiot."

They made to take chase, but Kayla was already lost to the crowd.

Mrs Maunley and Fiddlesticks were the only ones to get off the bus, which then rumbled away, leaving them exposed and alone at the edge of waste ground. To their right, surrounded by long grass, sat the shell of a car, blackened by a fire that flared and died months before. Behind them ran a row of semi-detached houses; all abandoned, with wooden boards barring the windows. Ahead lay Kirkfield Towers.

Mrs Maunley reached down and tickled her cat with trembling fingers. "Bad things happen here, don't they, Fiddlesticks?"

The old lady nodded in answer to her own question and began a steady march toward the tower block. Fiddlesticks fell in line beside her.

"She's here!" hissed Veronica. "In the corner."

Locke spared a fleeting glance across the café to the secluded table by the toilets where Kayla was rooting through the stolen handbag.

"Don't draw attention," he advised and turned his attention back to queuing at the service counter.

"Did you know she'd be here?" asked Veronica.

"No," replied Locke. "I just wanted a cup of tea."

Two minutes later, he had his cup of tea and Veronica had a cup of coffee, black. He sought out a free table.

"Shouldn't we call the police?" she asked.

"Why? Do you think she'd go for a policeman?"

"No, because she's a deviant little felon. She should be locked up."

Two mothers vacated a table. Veronica and Locke took their place.

"Maybe she's a victim of circumstance?" suggested Locke. "Absentee father, shoplifter mother, no prospects—"

"And that means she shouldn't get punished for her actions?"

"No, I just thought that you'd know as well as anyone what circumstances can drive a person to do."

"I was never a victim of circumstance, Vincent was. And he got what he deserved."

Veronica grabbed Locke's arm on seeing two police enter the café. Kayla saw them too and surreptitiously slipping the handbag under her table. The policemen remained oblivious to this attention; they were engrossed in a conversation that took them all the way to the counter.

"I thought they'd recognise me," said Veronica, cautiously releasing her grip on Locke.

Her hands shook until she'd retrieved a pack of cigarettes from her coat pocket. She fumbled it open, but found no cigarettes inside, just a photograph.

"Don't say anything," warned Veronica, replacing the photo and slipping the box back inside her coat. Her hands were shaking again. "If she deserves getting locked up, I know I deserve worse."

"That's not for you to judge," said Locke, sipping gently at his tea.

The newspaper had chosen the shiftiest photograph of Veronica Drysdale they could find. Dark make-up surrounded narrowed eyes. Her curled lips were caught swearing death on the photographer if he dared take the shot. No one knew when it was taken, but this didn't matter to the young man studying her picture beneath the one good light in the tower block corridor.

"Are you sure you haven't seen her?" asked Mrs Maunley. "The police think she killed her husband and a young detective. Look again, please?"

The denim-clad youth squinted again at the scrap of paper. The old lady shifted her weight expectantly from one foot to the other.

"I'd swear I haven't seen her, but her face, it's like I recognise it, I've seen it, but where? When? I dunno. She been on TV? Maybe it's that."

"Well, thank-you. You've been most helpful."

"Yeah, sure. Now could you get your cat off my leg?"

"Oh, he just likes you. Fiddlesticks, get down."

Fiddlesticks obliged, but only after a burst of ferocious scrabbling tore open the youth's pocket and allowed a bag of white powder to drop to the floor.

The youth swung a kick at the cat. Fiddlesticks danced clear behind Mrs Maunley and began preening himself. She raised her eyebrows at the boy.

"You want to know about this now, do you?" he asked, snatching up the bag. "Is that your business? Sticking your nose into other people's? Yeah? Well, I got an answer for you all right." He whipped out a combat knife. "This satisfy your curiosity, old woman?"

Mrs Maunley backed away. The youth pushed past her anyway as he headed for the lift.

"No good will come of that one," said Mrs Maunley to Fiddlesticks.

She composed herself, straightening creases in her coat and fussing with her scarf. The lift doors closed on the sneering youth. Machinery groaned as he began his descent, then a sharp crack preceded a screaming chorus of scraping metal and mortal terror. It ended with an abrupt thud seconds later.

"Now, Fiddlesticks," said Mrs Maunley, "which door held this Office of Lost and Found you told me about?"

"Everyone who meets Lafarge becomes a little bit lost," explained Locke. "You slip from people's notice. You become a nondescript face in the crowd, background detail to other people's lives. But some people manage to achieve this quite naturally, so I wouldn't worry about it too much."

He downed the last of his tea. Veronica's coffee remained untouched. She was trying not to stare at the two policemen as they worked through a plate of doughnuts. Despite Locke's words and however much she tried to remain calm and nonchalant, she felt her crimes were plain for all to see.

But no one was looking.

The passers-by on the other side of the window never once turned their heads. Those sat at the surrounding tables were caught up in their own affairs. The policemen had doughnuts to concentrate on. Veronica's paranoid ego cast her as the star of the show, but the rest of the world was treating her like a non-speaking extra, little more than set dressing. She told herself it couldn't last.

Veronica looked over at Kayla. The teenager was half-sitting, half-standing and gathering up the stolen goods, ready to risk the constables' notice with a dash to the exit.

"She's lost too, isn't she?" said Veronica.

"I think we need a new approach on finding her a man," said Locke.

He rose from their table and made his way to the back of

the café. Veronica followed. They passed Kayla en route. The teenager gave no sign she recognised them.

"So what's this new approach?" asked Veronica, joining Locke in front of a door marked 'Staff Only'.

He pulled the toy rabbit from his pocket and fashioned its loose ear into a crude key. He turned it in the lock and opened the door. They stepped through into the Office of Lost and Found.

"I thought we could go see her mother," replied Locke, securing the door behind them and then tossing the rabbit aside.

Veronica nodded without enthusiasm. She walked to the flat door and opened it to find a little old lady standing outside accompanied by a small, piebald cat.

"Veronica Drysdale, I am performing a citizen's arrest upon you for the suspected murder of your husband," said Mrs Maunley.

The handcuffs were slapped on Veronica's wrists before she could register what was happening.

"What the Hell do you think you're doing?" she asked.

A hypodermic needle was jabbed into her leg.

"Okay, you're pissing me off," said Veronica.

She swung her cuffed fists. Mrs Maunley dodged and Veronica toppled against the door frame. She blinked a few times, shook her head and tried to stand up straight again. One of her legs gave way.

Mrs Maunley carefully returned the syringe to her handbag. Veronica ham-fistedly produced her gun, but Locke interceded. He took the pistol from her weakened fingers and tossed it back into the Office.

Mrs Maunley studied the detective over the top of her glasses.

"Young man, I shall assume you were unaware of this creature's crimes and ask you to kindly help me transport her down the stairs." A raised finger pre-empted Locke's reply. "The lift appears to be out of order. Please, hurry along now, I have called a taxi and it should be here any minute."

Locke watched Mrs Maunley hobble off toward the stairs, her cat in close attendance. Veronica was crumpled on the floor, babbling insensibly. He lifted her up over his shoulder and staggered off after the old lady.

* * *

Detective Inspector Edward Forth's excitement at hearing of Veronica Drysdale's capture swiftly gave way to a desperate longing for the end of his shift and a relaxing night spent at home with his wife.

"Once again, Mrs Maunley, thank-you, but we really can take it from here."

"I trust that you will see justice done, Inspector," persisted Mrs Maunley. "That is a dangerous woman."

Veronica didn't look dangerous at the moment. She could barely stand without the assistance of the constables holding her arms. They should have escorted her straight to a holding cell, but they were enjoying Forth's attempts to get rid of Mrs Maunley too much.

"The courts will see her judged, Ma'am," said Forth, "we simply gather the evidence. Though in her case it is pretty clear cut. Was she in this state when you found her?"

"And that place," continued Mrs Maunley, ignoring his question, "Kirkfield Towers, such a hive of crime and sin I have never seen. Get some men down there, Inspector—"

"I know the place, Ma'am, and your suggestion has been noted. Once again, all your help is very much appreciated." Forth collared a passing WPC and instructed her to see the old lady out. "And make sure that cat goes with her."

Mrs Maunley finally relented, albeit reluctantly. Forth watched her depart and shook his head. The woman clearly meant well, but in his line of work that kind of zeal could hinder as well as help. Still, he supposed she was harmless enough compared to the murderess standing before him.

"Take her to interview room one," he told the constables holding Veronica. "Let's see if we can get a confession out of the merry widow before teatime."

As she was led away, he glanced back to the police station entrance. Mrs Maunley was descending the steps to the street outside and talking down to her feline companion.

"Someone needs to do something about the people in that place, don't they, Fiddlesticks? Yes, right as usual, my dear."

The door to Kayla's apartment was opened by a dumpy woman in pink jogging trousers and a leopard print singlet. Her wiry blonde hair emulated the snakes of Medusa and she looked upon her caller with an appropriately stony expression.

"Good afternoon, Mrs Jameson. My name is Thomas Locke. I am a private detective—"

"I know what you are," cut in Mrs Jameson. "What do you want?"

"I would like to ask you a few questions about your daughter."

The only sound in the interview room was the whir of the tape recorder on the table until Inspector Forth leaned forward and spoke.

"Mrs Drysdale, can you tell me when you last saw your husband?"

Veronica considered her nails. One of them had been broken during her failed assault on Mrs Maunley.

"A question like that should have a straightforward answer," she said, airily, "but it turns out my life isn't that straightforward."

Forth looked at his partner and then across at the duty solicitor by Veronica's side.

"Is that so? Maybe you'll find this question a little easier." He produced a plastic bag and set it down in front of her. Inside it was a small gun. Veronica glanced at it and then returned to studying her nails. Forth leaned forward still further and waited until Veronica finally deigned to look at him before asking: "Is this the gun you used to shoot your husband?"

"She's guilty," said Mrs Jameson. "Whatever it is you're here to accuse her of, she did it. Buggered off with our toaster only this morning. Sold it for fags is my guess. Call her a thieving little witch and you'll hear no complaints from me."

Locke stood in a flat scarred by countless unfinished attempts at re-decorating. Wallpaper clashed with paint, which fought for space with errant carpet tiles. Random drapes helped cover the worst of the chaos. The floor was littered with baby toys, while the infant itself was in the kitchen, having its nappy changed by Mrs Jameson.

"That's not why I'm here," said Locke. "I wanted to ask

you… does Kayla have any hobbies?"

Mrs Jameson stepped from the kitchen. She held a white rag soiled by baby food reconstituted into brown sludge.

"Hobbies? She lies, cheats, steals. She screws boys twice her age. Is that what you mean by hobbies?"

"Yes," said Veronica, simply.

The duty solicitor stared at her. Forth's partner failed to suppress a self-congratulatory grin. Forth himself couldn't believe it was this easy.

"You shot your husband with this gun?"

"You're recording this, I shouldn't need to repeat myself," said Veronica. "I'm a killer and I deserve to go to prison for a long time. You wanted a confession, you've got one. Everyone's happy. Now, I think it's my turn to ask you a question."

Mrs Jameson sat on the sofa and fed the baby from a bottle. Locke sat beside her, listening to her talk.

"I was fourteen when I had Kayla and she was fourteen when she had Britney here. You would have thought she might learn from my mistakes, but brains don't run in our family."

"What about Kayla's father?"

"You're the detective, you tell me. He could have been any number of men. None of them would be worth a damn."

"That's not how an interview works, Mrs Drysdale," said Forth. "We ask the questions."

"It's just your face reminds me of someone," said Veronica. "Maybe I'm wrong, maybe it's nothing, but I have a friend whose stock in trade is coincidences. I think you might just be one of them."

Forth picked up the plastic bag from the table and dangled it in front of her.

"A bullet from this gun killed a policeman. Did you pull the trigger then too?"

"It really is uncanny. The nose, the eyes… If you could just pout petulantly for a second, that would be the clincher."

The Inspector's fractious reaction was instinctive. He

wasn't even aware his lips protruded and his nostrils flared, but Veronica saw and she sat back in her chair with a smile on her face.

Forth tried to continue the questioning: "Tell me about the policeman, Mrs Drysdale."

"Why don't you tell me about the girl you screwed at Kirkfield Towers? Did you know you left her pregnant?"

Seconds later, Forth stood outside the interview room with his head resting against the cool plastic fascia of the coffee machine.

"It didn't look good, you storming out like that," said his partner.

Forth straightened up and patted his colleague on the arm.

"I've got to go somewhere," he said. "Keep an eye on that witch."

The apartment door was thrown open. It slammed against the wall and rebounded back into Kayla, who swore, kicked the door again and then stormed off into the kitchen. The noise set Britney off screaming.

"Shut that door, missy!" demanded Mrs Jameson.

"Shut it yourself," said Kayla.

"This isn't a hotel. I'm not here to clean up after you."

"I know," said Kayla, returning to the living room with a can of lager in hand, "that's why this place is such a bloody mess. What's he doing here?"

Locke tried to fade away against the dank ochre fabric of the sofa, but failed.

In the shadow of Kirkfield Towers, Mrs Maunley made slow progress across the waste ground leading from the bus stop. She was acutely aware of the youths ranged around the burnt out car. They were watching her, exchanging comments and turning laughter into a game of intimidation.

"Don't pay them any mind, Fiddlesticks," she said to her cat. "They're silly boys angling for attention they don't deserve."

The sound of hurried footsteps approached from behind. Mrs Maunley tried to walk faster, but creeping arthritis and osteoporosis limited her pace. A figure strode by. She kept her head down and avoided eye contact until Fiddlesticks meowed. A look up revealed it wasn't one of the youths.

"Ah, Inspector, you took my advice then?" she called out.

Forth turned his head, but kept walking.

"Sorry?"

"This place, Inspector," she gestured toward the tower block. "If anywhere needed the firm hand of the law—"

"I'm afraid I'm here on a private matter, Ma'am."

He bobbed his head in apology and hurried on, his walk turning into a jog before he reached the tower block's entrance.

"Pity," muttered Mrs Maunley. "Looks like it's up to us, Fiddlesticks."

The cat looked up at her and then over at the gang by the car. As soon as the policeman disappeared inside the building, they began to move. Mrs Maunley's stiff little steps were quickly over-taken by the youths' long strides.

"What you doin' here, Grandma?"

"Don't you know it ain't safe round here?"

"Here, pussy, pussy."

"You talking to the biddy or her cat?"

The laughter was all around her, but Mrs Maunley kept her gaze fixed on the ground in front of her feet. She didn't see the dog charge out of nowhere. It leapt onto one of the youths. He tried to beat it off with an arm, but its teeth found his neck. The other boys cried out in alarm and tried to help, but blood was already flowing.

They soon forgot Mrs Maunley.

She stepped inside Kirkfield Towers and located the apartment with a number one on the door. She knocked, waited and then greeted the woman who answered with a smile.

"If you want to keep living here, you'll do as I say!" shouted Mrs Jameson.

"Nathan said I can move in with him if I want," shot back Kayla.

"What? So he can hit you whenever he feels like it?"

"Mother, you know nothing!"

Kayla's baby was screaming too, but only Locke noticed. He sat quietly on the sofa, trying not to draw attention. The front door was still open, tempting him to try a cowardly retreat until a man appeared at the doorway and knocked politely. Locke cursed under his breath. The warring Jamesons agreed a momentary ceasefire so they could turn and stare at the arrival.

"You're still here then, Cerys," said Inspector Forth.

"Who the hell is this?" asked Kayla.

"Eddie," said Mrs Jameson, turning a simple exhale into meaningful punctuation. "I hope you've not come back here expecting—"

"If I'm right, Cerys, I had to come back. I am right, aren't I?"

"What's going on?" demanded Kayla.

"Kayla, this is Eddie," said Mrs Jameson. "He's your father. Probably."

Kayla scrutinised Eddie Forth long and hard with narrowed eyes and a wrinkled nose. Then she turned to Locke, her lips curled into a snarl.

"Is this your idea of a fucking joke?"

Veronica sat alone in the interview room twiddling her thumbs; first forward, then backward. Either way, it struck her as a tiresome way to pass the time. She stopped and checked her watch. She'd spent the last half hour expecting someone to come and drag her off to a cell.

A camera watched from the corner of the room as Veronica stood and walked casually to the door. She tried the handle, expecting it to be locked. It wasn't. She looked around at the fish-eye lens and waited for the inevitable response. No one came. Veronica mulled over the significance of this, then thought 'sod it' and walked out.

Police officers walked up and down the corridor like extras in the background of a TV crime drama. Inspector Forth's partner was talking with the duty solicitor by the coffee machine. They didn't notice Veronica walk past.

She reached the station lobby without anyone giving her a second glance. Veronica was beginning to believe that perhaps Locke was right about Lafarge's magic, but lingering doubts quickened her pace as she reached the main doors. Once outside, she ran down the steps and immediately flagged down a passing taxi.

* * *

Kayla face was flush with blood, her heavy make-up transforming the emotion into a gentle shade of pink with purple highlights.

"I asked you to find a man to love me! I did not ask you to find my father!"

Stress was placed on key syllables through a jab at Locke's chest. He was pinned against a wall where prancing clowns contested space with splodges of thick peach emulsion.

"Kayla, listen to me," said Inspector Forth. "I never expected that I could just turn up here and have you suddenly accept me as your father. This is going to be hard for both of us—"

Kayla turned on him.

"No, mister, it's really dead easy. You're my father, I get it. I just don't care. Why should I? I've done fine without one for fifteen years."

"Maybe you should go now, Eddie," said Mrs Jameson.

"No, Cerys. I should have been here for her from the start."

"Oh, please," said Kayla, "I don't need you to be here for me. I don't know what kind of daughter you were expecting, mister, but I ain't her."

Locke edged toward the open door. This was a family matter. Leaving them to it was only polite. He fully intended to at least consider coming back and seeing how they were doing in a year or two.

"And don't think I've finished with you," snapped Kayla, fixing him with a pointed finger. "'Cos I haven't. Not by a long shot."

The taxi pulled up alongside the waste ground in front of Kirkfield Towers. Veronica climbed out the back, removed her high heels and began running toward the tower block in her stocking feet.

"Oi! You haven't paid!" shouted the cabbie.

He struggled from his seat to shout further obscenities, but that's as far as he got in terms of taking chase. Veronica was already too far away and he was too fat to catch her in any case. He settled for shaking his fist in frustration.

Veronica skidded to a halt inside the building. She slipped

her shoes back on while crossing to the lift, then stopped short of a half-dried pool of blood gathered at the bottom of the doors. She looked around. The artificial lighting here was as bad as on the other floors, but rays of sunshine spilled into the corridor through the open doorway of the first apartment.

Veronica ventured forward. There were no sounds to alarm her, no sudden movements to catch her eye. She peered inside Number 1, Kirkfield Towers. It was a squalid flat like all the others here, with second-hand furniture, outdated décor and damp festering in the corners.

Then she heard a sound – a soft creak – and saw movement – a gentle swaying just visible through the kitchen door. It was a body, hung by electrical cord.

Further up the corridor, shadow hid another body. The lop-sided face showed signs of stroke. Veronica hurried to the stairs as a groan of masonry preceded a cloud of dust exploding into the hallway. When it cleared, Veronica saw the ceiling of the first apartment had collapsed. Another corpse lay in the rubble. The only thing she recognised about the face was the death in its eyes.

Veronica ran up the stairs with her heels back in hand. Her gaze flashed over each step in turn, alert to the risk of a discarded needle waiting to pierce her foot. She paused for breath on the fifth floor and saw distant figures moving beyond the dirt-fogged glass of the stairwell. She pushed the door open a crack.

"I don't know who you think you are, throwing accusations around like that."

The man was trying to sound confident, but a note of fear rang out behind his words. This despite the fact he stood two feet taller and wider than the little old lady standing outside his door.

A piebald cat trotted out of the flat between the man's legs. It held a DVD in its mouth.

"Now, it wouldn't surprise me in the least if this little disc contains all the horrible details of what you did to those children," said Mrs Maunley.

"I'll be gone long before the police get here."

He slammed his door in the old lady's face. She didn't seem to mind. Instead, she turned and walked on to the next apartment.

"Should I have told him I smelt gas, Fiddlesticks? You smelt gas too, didn't you?"

A few more steps and then flame blasted into the corridor, removing Mrs Maunley and Fiddlesticks from view.

Veronica arrived at the Office of Lost and Found to find Fiddlesticks waiting outside. Mrs Maunley was nowhere to be seen.

"I'm not going to let her get me like she got all those others," she told the cat.

Veronica put her shoes back on and opened the door. Fiddlesticks rushed in past her.

The gun lay on the floor where Locke had thrown it. Veronica picked it up and looked for the cat, but it was lost amidst the maze of boxes, no doubt sniffing out evidence. She exited the flat.

Fiddlesticks remained, nosing through the assembled paraphernalia and into the bedroom. There was little here in the way of creature comforts. A damp mattress lay on a rusty frame. The only blanket was riven with holes. Books were stacked beside an old oil lamp, but the spines were broken and blighted by missing pages. All of these things were examined and discounted. Fiddlesticks finally found what he was looking for hidden between the bed and the wall: a five-inch tall statuette of a slender black cat.

"Kayla, listen to me," said Inspector Forth. "I don't know who this man is, but he's got nothing to do with me coming here."

"I ain't listening to you," said Kayla. "I don't know you. And I bet he did bring you here, somehow, didn't you?"

Locke gave a little shrug.

"Okay, okay," said Forth, raising his hands in defeat. "Maybe I should go. But I do want to see you again. Can I do that?"

"Do what you want. Hell, stay if you like, 'cos I'm leaving."

But her exit was blocked by Mrs Maunley.

"My, my, deary," said the old woman, "I don't think I need Fiddlesticks to tell me what crimes you've committed."

"What? Piss off, crone. Get out my way."

"Kayla! Don't talk to people like that," said her mother.

The teenager tried to push past the old lady, but found her a curiously immovable object.

"Mrs Maunley?" said Forth. "What are you doing here?"

"I'm here for justice, Inspector. The police cannot prosecute every crime, but every crime must be punished."

"Whatever," said Kayla, trying to barge past Mrs Maunley once again. She only succeeded in prompting a few tuts and a shake of the head.

"I don't know what you think my daughter's done," said Forth, "but whatever it is, you can talk to me about it. I've... I've never been there for her and maybe if I had... Whatever she's done, I should take some of that responsibility."

Mrs Maunley looked at him and frowned.

"Perhaps you are right."

A gasp came from Forth. He raised a hand to his throat. Exhaling became a painful wheeze. When he tried to breathe in, his face turned red and the veins bulged on the side of his neck. He collapsed onto the settee.

"Eddie?" said Mrs Jameson in alarm. "Oh Lord. Kayla, he's having an asthma attack, help me find his inhaler."

She began rifling through his pockets. Kayla stood frozen by the door.

"His guilt does not absolve you of your crimes," said Mrs Maunley, smiling at the teenager's confusion. There was no reassurance in that smile. It was a patient smile born of utter certainty.

Clack.

Clack.

Clack.

The sound broke Kayla's trance. She stumbled away from Mrs Maunley and over to her mother, who was panicking at her failure to find the inhaler.

Mrs Maunley turned her head. Smoke was rising from the floors below and gathering against the hallway ceiling. Veronica's arrival sent wraithlike eddies swirling away against the walls.

"Who appointed you judge, jury and executioner?" she asked.

"That's not important," replied Mrs Maunley. "What's important is that justice is served. Justice that will see you damned, Veronica Drysdale."

"I'm damned already."

"Not to my eyes, deary. Ah, Fiddlesticks, what have you got there?"

The cat scampered past Veronica and displayed the figurine held in its mouth.

"Evidence? But this isn't her crime… This is…"

Locke approached the door. Mrs Maunley's eyes fell upon him as the blood drained from her face.

"Dear Lord, what did you do?"

He didn't answer; instead he made a grab for the model cat. Fiddlesticks danced clear and fled to a stairwell now full of thick, gray smoke. Locke took chase.

"Fiddlesticks!" cried Mrs Maunley. Her desperate gaze tracked the flight of her pet until Veronica's gun came into view.

"One chance. Leave now and don't come back."

Veronica's finger curled around the trigger. Mrs Maunley stared down the barrel and shook her head.

"Your crimes must be punished. His crimes must be punished."

"Maybe so, but not by you. Your justice serves no one. Society is set no example. No one serves their time. There's no chance of redemption."

"You can't be allowed to kill again."

"You think you can stop me? I told you I'm damned. If I die, I'll come back, again and again, and I will kill again if I have to. Do I have to do that, old woman? Or are you going to accept your justice is good for nothing except satisfying your own vindictive sense of righteousness?"

Her words were bold, but Veronica's hand was beginning to tremble. When would Maunley's curse strike? Would she even have time to pull the trigger? She saw herself dying there and then, finally punished for what she had done to her husband. Except what punishment was death when it didn't last? And how could it compare to the purgatory she suffered now?

Her hand steadied. If she was judged today, then so be it. However dire the consequences, she couldn't regret pulling the trigger on her marriage.

"There's just no reasoning with some people," said Mrs Maunley.

"Quite right," agreed Veronica.

The bullet knocked the old lady clean off her feet. She landed with a dull thud on the floor. Veronica fired another shot into Mrs Maunley's head, then threw off her shoes once more and ran for the stairs.

Fiddlesticks sat at the edge of the rooftop with the figurine in his mouth.

"Here, kitty, kitty," said Locke. He approached the cat slowly, making no sudden moves. The statuette was almost in reach.

Veronica threw open the access door. Fiddlesticks bolted. The fake cat fell from his mouth. It bounced against a railing, teetered for a moment on the metal, then toppled over the side. Locke dived after it.

Veronica watched in silent horror as he disappeared from sight.

Locke didn't notice the rush of air against his face or the waste ground rising up to claim him. His only focus was on reaching out and wrapping desperate fingers around the falling figurine.

Then he had it. He gripped the statuette to his chest. Locke's smile lasted for the briefest of seconds. It vanished not on impact, but on seeing the black figure waiting below.

A legion of fire engines, police cars and ambulances crowded around the base of Kirkfield Towers. Hoses snaked inside the building and up ladders, fighting the fire with torrents of water. Police officers took statements from those left standing, while paramedics tended to the injured.

Inspector Forth lay on stretcher. His skin was white and an oxygen mask was strapped over his mouth. When he was loaded into one of the ambulances, Kayla climbed in alongside him and held his hand.

No one accompanied the corpse of Mrs Maunley as it was ferried from the scene. Fiddlesticks was too busy licking his hind legs clean atop a panda car. Past his anus, he could see two people sat apart from the rescue efforts on the bonnet of the burnt out car.

"Did you know he'd be there to catch you?" asked Veronica.

Locke shrugged. "You know, my earliest memory was waking up in the Office. Lafarge was in front of me and this cat was beside me." He gave the statuette a little wave. "That was two years ago."

"Nothing before that?"

Locke shook his head.

"I can't remember much before my wedding," said Veronica. "It's like my life only started when I said 'I do'. Then it ended when I shot him."

The ambulance bearing Inspector Forth and his daughter sped off toward the hospital, siren wailing. Veronica watched it go and then went back to staring at the smoke rising from the burning tower block.

"If there's anything left of the Office when they're done..."

"There's always an Office of Lost and Found," said Locke.

"... then I'd like you to find my parents. If you can. Please."

She didn't look at him while waiting for his answer. In turn, his gaze remained fixed on the ebony figurine until a piece of burning debris landed on the dry grass in front of them. It fluttered in the wind, turning over and over on the ground until the fire was out, and then it lay still, a piece of lined paper with familiar words written in thick black marker.

Veronica bent down to pick it up, but another gust of wind carried it out of reach, up around their heads and away across the waste ground.

Locke hauled himself stiffly off the car's bonnet and traipsed off in the erratic wake of the piece of paper. Veronica looked back at Kirkfield Towers for one last time and then followed.

Interlude II

"The idea of just... ceasing to exist, it's always stirred a sickening hollow in the pit of my stomach."

Veronica clutched her middle as she sat on the bare floor next to Locke's ragged mattress. He had been sleeping until Veronica told him she couldn't.

"If it's true there's nothing else afterwards," he said, "how is dying different to sleeping? As far as we know, we cease to exist for those hours before we wake. Isn't that why the French call it la petite mort?"

"I thought that's what they called orgasms?"

"Oh, well, they're French, so maybe. Still, the little death of sleep makes more sense to me."

"But after sleeping you wake up. When you die, that's it. Well, unless you're us. Seems we don't get that particular terror. We get to survive, live on and that... that seems almost worse. Wouldn't eternity make every experience insignificant? What's the point of anything if there's no end?"

Locke shrugged.

"I think the only way I could bear coming back is if I remembered nothing from before," said Veronica.

Locke turned away and pulled his moth-eaten blanket up over his shoulders.

"I think that's enough for talk for one night."

Souled

"My mother's dead and my father's in a lunatic asylum, that's what he told me."

It was the first time Veronica had spoken since they'd left the graveyard. The desk lamp on the floor painted her kneeling form in stark lines of light and shade. She stared down at a piece of paper held taut by her gloved hands.

"You always thought he was lying," said Locke. He stood at the office window, holding vigil over the street outside.

"No, not always," said Veronica, softly. "And I never suspected he could have done this."

Locke left the window and crouched down beside her.

"Someone's coming. We need to go."

Veronica hastily returned the sheet of paper to a filing cabinet and slid the drawer shut. Locke switched off the desk lamp and took Veronica's hand. When the door opened moments later, the two intruders were gone.

Sunlight floods through impressive bay windows, painting the empty room's bare floorboards a warm amber.

"But this is not an empty room, it is a blank canvas. Paint a picture with your imagination."

Picture this room with a plush red carpet running wall to wall. Drape matching curtains from a golden rail running above the windows. That wall; line it with wardrobes – fitted, white, mirrors covering the doors. Picture a bed, silver-framed and opulent and throw onto it a couple, whispering words of love and exchanging kisses…

But now the room is empty and that couple are descending the stairs. She looks up at him with keen eyes. He tells her to watch the next step; she's eight months pregnant, she has to be careful.

"Look past the bricks and mortar, see the kind of future your family might have here."

A future where grinning clowns tumble across nursery wallpaper and a baby stares up from its cot at plastic farmyard animals dangling from wires. Where gurgling curiosity gives way to confused silence and a mother stands over an empty cot, wondering where her baby has gone.

The mother and father argue on the stairs. They shout recriminations in the hallway. His rage kicks a hole through the wall. She hangs herself in the dining room.

In the kitchen, before this future comes to pass, there is an awkward pause in the conversation. Peter Scott stands with arm around his wife, Lorraine.

"I can see you two being very happy here," says the estate agent. "Now, I'm afraid we've already had a number of offers that meet the asking price…"

"But you said we might be able to get the house for less," says Lorraine.

"I did," admits the estate agent. "I'm sorry."

"Then I'm afraid we're wasting your time," says Peter.

"But Pete—"

"There's no way we can afford it, Lorraine. No way. We'll just have to find somewhere else."

The estate agent watches them trail disconsolately into the hallway before he speaks again.

"There… may be a way."

Lorraine turns her head. Peter does not. His reluctance to jump at the opportunity stills her enthusiasm.

"We haven't got the money, Mr Drysdale," she says with regret.

The estate agent smiles.

"This way doesn't require money, dear. It requires your soul."

The dream house was an unprepossessing detached property with a modest front lawn and a driveway paved with zig-zagged bricks. Locke studied it from a neighbouring kitchen window. Veronica sat at the table behind him, her stylish black attire a stark contrast to the pastel blue tank top and floral pink shirt of the man opposite her. He was called Mr Murray and she was supposed to be interviewing him, but Mr Murray didn't need the excuse of a question to provide long, rambling answers.

"They looked so happy and hopeful when they arrived to look at the house," he recalled. "She was pretty as a picture in this sunflower yellow summer dress and he almost made brown chinos work. Made me hopeful for them, it did, but they left arguing."

He ended the sentence with a scowl that fell away into a frown. Everything he said was accompanied by an exaggerated emote: a big smile when recounting good times, sniffs and a handkerchief when relating something sad. Locke turned from the window, baulked at the overt theatricality and decided to examine a cupboard more closely.

"But my parents came back," said Veronica.

"They did," said Mr Murray, before lowering his voice to a whisper and raising his hand conspiratorially. "I heard something about an inheritance. They could never have afforded the place otherwise."

"And after they moved in…?"

"Kept themselves to themselves. Had their hands full with the new baby, I think. But you want to know when it all went wrong, don't you?"

"Did they give you this waffle-iron?" asked Locke, holding up the item in question.

"He did, yes," said the neighbour. "Said he wanted rid of everything after she… you know. Gave away all the things he couldn't sell." He looked sadly at Veronica. "Even you, dear. Mad house was the best place for him after that."

"Do you mind if I borrow this?" asked Locke, waving the waffle-iron.

The neighbour's sidelong glance made clear he suspected Locke was another bound for the asylum. He shrugged. "Sure, I don't waffle much anyway."

"I don't suppose you know what might have caused things to go wrong for my parents?" asked Veronica.

"Sorry, dear. Years passed and they seemed happy enough, but one night everything changed. The whole neighbourhood could hear the shouting…"

"You lied to me!" Peter shouts at her before stalking over to one of the mirrored wardrobes and pulling out a suitcase.

"I was right!" Lorraine shouts back.

"There's nothing right about what you did," insists Peter, slashing the air with his hand. "You sold your soul—"

"And nothing's changed! Except we have a house. A home.

A family. So what if there was no inheritance. We got what we wanted. What does it matter?"

"You don't understand..."

"No, I don't. A soul's nothing. It's... it's a myth; an outdated theological concept. Hell, I should have sold him my appendix too, because I don't use that either."

"We have to leave this place." Peter grabs her clothes from the wardrobe and throws them into the suitcase.

"This place is our home!"

"Not any more." He snaps the case shut and forces it into Lorraine's arms. She stares into his eyes and shakes her head.

"I'm not leaving Peter."

The contest of wills holds them fast for long seconds, neither looking away, neither blinking. Peter caves first. He grabs a second suitcase from the wardrobe. This one is already packed.

"Fine," he says, leaving the bedroom and hurrying down the stairs.

"Peter!" Lorraine doesn't follow straight away. She still thinks the sound of her voice can bring him back. "Peter!"

His footsteps reach the hall. Maybe her voice isn't enough. She hurries down the stairs, but freezes halfway. Peter walks from living room with their baby held in the crook of one arm.

"Peter, no."

"I'm not leaving her here."

"Peter, you can't."

He sets down the briefcase in order to open the front door. Lorraine stumbles down the remaining steps and makes a grab for his arm. Peter shrugs her off and picks up the suitcase. He doesn't look at her.

"I'll be back for Veronica's things."

The door slams shut behind him.

Drizzle pattered on the railway platform where children played. Their game was seeing how many windows they could smash in the old station house. They were up to three when a shadowy face appeared in the darkness, bisected by the edges of a broken pane.

"Shit!"

"Crap!"
"Run!"
Seconds later, the kids were running up the overgrown tracks and back toward the new housing estate half a mile up the abandoned line.
Veronica watched them go. It felt like she'd spent her whole life watching other children play. The waiting room seemed to share her unease. It was full of boxes and teetering piles of pots, pans, clothes, gadgets, items big and items small, here one moment, gone the next and everything imbued with a sense that it shouldn't be here, but had nowhere else to go. A paper sign taped to the door called this 'The Office of Lost and Found'.
The door swung open. Thomas Locke leaned back against it as he manoeuvred a dirty white dishwasher inside. Walking the appliance to the centre of the room by pivoting it from one corner to the next, he left it in a circle of household appliances.
"Not bad, eh?" he said to Veronica, nodding at his handiwork. "Forty-eight percent of your mother found and I reckon I'll have the rest by the end of the week."
Veronica blinked at him.
"Are you saying my mother is trying to reincarnate as the contents of a homeware catalogue?"
Locke pulled off his woollen hat and scratched his balding head. He considered the objects he'd collected.
"Saying that would suggest I know what's going on and I wouldn't ever claim that. Now, don't you think it odd all of this stuff has the same brand name? Have you even heard of Daex before?"
Before Veronica could respond, a knocking came at the open door. A straw boater dipped in greeting before revealing a face bearing a trim black beard and rose-tinted sunglasses with oval frames. The arrival wore a loose-fitting suit of dark green velvet. His shirt was purple, his bow tie red. The chain of a pocket watch hung across a waistcoat struggling to contain a burgeoning pot belly.
"Salutations, greetings and other pleasantries," said the stranger. "My name is Colfish Hasmek and I am here to extend a most gracious invitation to the widow Drysdale

requesting her attendance at an auction of her late husband's possessions as conducted by my venerable employers, Tootings of Harper Street, auctioneers of the unconventional since 1683."

He bowed again, briefly, and smiled.

"I'm not interested," said Veronica, flatly.

"A shame," said Hasmek, "but these formalities must be observed. Alas, despite your rejection, we still require your attendance. Our staff will pick you up at six o'clock this evening."

"Mr Hasmek, save your staff the trouble. I am not going to your auction."

"Apologies, condolences and excuses, but I'm afraid you are," stated Hasmek. "Lot 17, Veronica Drysdale, goes on sale at 8pm sharp. You will be there, Mrs Drysdale. Tootings of Harper Street has a reputation to maintain."

"You're saying she's on sale?" asked Locke, incredulous.

"Along with all of her husband's earthly possessions. Please don't look at me like that, Mrs Drysdale, I am merely a messenger and one whose message has been delivered and who must now be on his way. Good day to you both."

Colfish Hasmek withdrew from the room. Locke hurriedly closed the door after him. He turned expecting to face Veronica's wrath, but instead she just shrugged.

"I'm not for sale, whatever Tootings of Harper Street might think. Now, we still have my father and fifty-two percent of my mother to find."

Baby Veronica cries. She cries and wails.

"I want Mummy! I want Mummy!"

The room is dark. Damp creeps across walls rife with cracks. The stink of tobacco from the previous resident still lingers in the air. The single bed harbours springs that sag and prod in equal measure, but no one lies there and no one sits in the worn armchair. The old portable television on the chest of drawers by the sink is on, but the grim voices of the newsreaders do not calm Veronica. Her cheeks are ruddy and damp with tears, but no one answers her cries.

The room is darker still when Peter returns. The suit he wears and briefcase he carries weigh him down. With relief he tosses the briefcase aside before switching on the light and hurrying over to his baby's cot.

"Hush, dear. Hush now."

"I want Mummy!"

"I'm late, I know. Reg needed something doing and I'm sorry, but I'm here now."

"I want Mummy!"

"I know, I know."

He picks up the child and holds her before crossing to the bedside table and an answering machine. He presses a button.

"No new messages," it tells him.

He closes his eyes and grits his teeth. He hits another button.

"First saved message."

Lorraine's voice, tinny and removed, repeats the words Peter has listened to countless times before.

"It's me. Laura gave me your number. I've rehearsed this, but… what can I say? Please, can't we talk? I want to see you. I want to see Veronica. I can't… I can't talk to a machine."

On hearing her mother's voice, Baby Veronica's distress begins to subside.

"Next saved message."

"Peter, you were right. Take away someone's soul and all that's left is pain and hurt. But it's not a signature on a piece of paper that does that. You do that by making someone love you more than anything and then walking out the door with her baby, you fucking bastard! I won't let you keep her, Peter! I won't! I'm going to— Hey, what are you doing here?"

"Next saved message."

"Hello, Peter, this is Lorraine. I have come to terms with our separation and see that it is for the best. I hope you have come to the same happy conclusion, but I've changed all the locks, just in case. Good-bye, Peter."

"No more messages."

Veronica is quiet now, exhausted by her earlier efforts and reassured by the recorded words she doesn't understand. Peter strokes her head and brushes a tear away from his own cheek.

A knocking comes at the door. It didn't close properly after Peter's hasty entrance and now it swings open with a groan. His landlady's head pokes into the room.

"You finally got her to quieten down then? Been crying for hours she has."

"I'm sure my sister did her best to stop her crying."

"I ain't seen your sister today, Mr Scott."

"She left just before I got in."

"I ain't seen anyone else here today, 'cept yourself. Ain't right, I said to myself. A little one like her, left all alone. Crying out for her mother, she was."

"I'm sorry, it won't happen again." Peter begins to close the door, forcing the landlady back out into the corridor.

"'Course, it's not my business. Not saying it is. I'm just saying a little one like that, needs her mother she does."

Peter smiles grimly, nods and closes the door with a final shove. He waits until the landlady's footsteps walk away and then looks down at the baby in his arms.

"We both need her, don't we?"

"If you need a new dishwasher, you've come to wrong place," declared the salesman. "If you want *more* than a new dishwasher, if you want your dishes to sparkle and your cutlery to shine, if you want the answer to all your dishwashing prayers, then you're not only in the right place, you're in the only place for people with discerning taste like yourselves."

That place was a cavernous showroom with wares raised on plinths and illuminated by movie star spotlights. The same brand name twinkled on every one and hung from the ceiling in glowing electric blue in case you missed it: Daex.

"Did I mention our lifetime guarantee?" asked the salesman. Veronica and Locke shook their heads. "Our products never break and never fail or your payment is immediately refunded in full."

Veronica and Locke nodded, impressed.

"We're interested in re-fitting our whole kitchen," said Veronica, hugging Locke's arm in a wifely manner. "You don't have a catalogue, do you?"

"I have one here," replied the salesman, taking them to a desk behind a ten foot tall fridge freezer. "They say the answer to all life's questions can be found in here, but that's just our marketing department getting a little carried away." He hesitated before handing it over. "You did say you had a referral, didn't you? I'm afraid we only do business from referrals."

"Mr and Mrs Scott," said Locke.

"They recommended you most highly," added Veronica.

"I'm sure they did," said the salesman, leaving them with the catalogue and edging backwards into the darkness. "Can I leave you for two minutes? I'll be right back."

Once he'd gone, Locke began studying the catalogue.

"And does it contain all life's answers?" asked Veronica.

"No, just a few about your mother."

Lorraine tries to slam the door shut, but Peter's foot is in the way. He's a weary figure in a crumpled shirt, with bloodshot eyes and a baby in his arms - a wreck compared to her. She stands tall and straight, a slinky black dress showing no signs of her recent pregnancy. The silver choker around her neck sparkles like her eyes. The only flaw is the sneer on her face.

"Go away, Peter, or I'll call the police."

"I'll go, I will go, but your daughter needs you."

Lorraine looks at the bundle in his arms, then down at the foot blocking the door. She tries kicking it away, but it won't budge. She walks back along the hall and Peter pushes his way in behind her. His victory is short lived. She picks up the phone and dials 999. He rushes up to her and holds up Baby Veronica.

"Take her. Isn't that what you wanted? Your daughter back?"

Veronica gazes into the mirror above the telephone table and checks her immaculate hair.

"Hello? The police, please. I wish to report a domestic disturbance in progress."

Peter spins away from her, trying to fathom what has caused his wife to change like this. A guilty conscience mutters words he can't make out, before he realises the words aren't inside his head, they're coming from the living room. He enters to find three suited businessmen sitting stiffly on the settee. Peter stares at them. They try to pretend he's not there. When that doesn't work, one of them smiles weakly and lifts a hand in greeting.

Peter storms back into the hallway.

"Are they why you didn't want us here? Who are those

men? Are they… My God, that's why you're dressed up like this. You've become a high-class prostitute, haven't you?"

Lorraine smiles a stiff-lipped smile. She slams down the phone and marches into the living room.

"Gentlemen," she says to the businessmen, "I think it would be best if you left now. I can only apologise for this unfortunate interruption. I hope we can conclude our deal at some other time."

The businessmen rise from their seats and shuffle uncomfortably from the room. Once Lorraine has seen them out the door, she turns on Peter.

"I was selling them photocopiers, Peter. That's what I do now. It is part of the happy life I lead without you."

"And without Veronica," he says. "Or have you been so happy lately you've forgotten your old life includes a daughter?"

"You took my old life away from me, so I found a better one."

"Shagging stiffs in suits?" He spits the words out, hoping they hurt.

Lorraine doesn't flinch. She just turns away and sashays into the living room.

"He found me broken and lost," she explains, "and he showed me the way." She smiles back at Peter over her shoulder. "This dress was the first thing I bought." Her hands caress the fabric as it flows over her curves. "I was a mess, a pitiful mess until I got this dress. I put it on and I felt…" Her grin tells of the rapture. "Then came the shoes and the jewellery and the new kitchen… I bought the television only yesterday."

Lorraine giggles and picks up a foot long remote from the coffee table. A button press brings the sixty inch set to life. The remote tumbles from her hand. She collapses back onto the sofa and stares wide-eyed at the screen.

"How could you afford all this?" asks Peter.

She doesn't reply. Her attention is fixed on the television.

Peter sets baby Veronica down on the plush carpet, steps over to Lorraine and challenges her with folded arms.

"Lorraine! How did you pay for all this?"

"Huh? What?"

She treats him to a confused glance, then dismisses him

with a hand and goes back to watching two soap actors arguing in high definition 3D.

Peter snatches up the remote control, intent on silencing the television, but something else on the coffee table catches his eye – a catalogue. He picks it up and flicks through the pages. He finds the television set on page seventy-three. Below the extensive list of features and easy payment options is the price. It is expressed in words instead of numbers and says simply: 'Attention Span'.

Peter scans more pages, his horrified gaze flicking between price tags and objects dotted around the room.

The mini-bar by the window: 'self-restraint'.

The clock on the mantelpiece: 'punctuality'.

The mirror over the fireplace: 'humility'.

Peter staggers backward; overwhelmed by the sight of things his wife has lost. Everything here is tagged with a price, even Lorraine - her dress costing 'modesty', her shoes 'virtue', her earrings 'discretion'...

He jabs his finger down on the remote control. The television goes black. Lorraine's eyes swivel around to look at him.

"He made you do this, didn't he?" accuses Peter.

She smiles wistfully and toys with the silver choker about her neck.

"I bought myself happiness."

Peter thrusts the open catalogue in front of her.

"At what cost? What kind of a person exchanges bowel control for a bidet?"

Lorraine meets his gaze, her face blank. Then she farts quite loudly.

Peter shakes his head and closes his eyes. When he opens them the nightmare remains. Breathing hard, he seeks back through the pages of the catalogue for something glimpsed and disregarded earlier. Once found, he looks upon Lorraine, touches her cheek and then rushes from the room.

Lorraine finds him in the kitchen. He's staring at the tumble dryer. The 'Daex' name twinkles back at them. The catalogue lies face down on the kitchen floor. Lorraine picks it up. Turning it over, she's presented with a picture of the tumble dryer, a list of features and a price expressed in words instead of numbers: 'free will'.

Peter turns and cups her face in his hands.

"I'll get back what you've lost, somehow, I promise."

"He said he would be waiting."

Peter's face darkens. He marches to the front door and throws it open. A glance back shows Lorraine standing dumbly in the hallway.

"Watch our daughter while I'm gone."

He leaves and the door bangs shut. Lorraine turns her head and looks into the living room. Baby Veronica gazes up at her. When Lorraine approaches, the child smiles and reaches out. Lorraine crouches down and frowns at the stubby fingers extended toward her. It's been so long it takes her a while to figure out what to do next. Understanding comes with a smile. She unclasps her silver choker and hands it to baby Veronica, who looks at it in bemusement.

"Now you can be happy too."

Veronica stood in front of a tumble dryer raised on a spot-lit plinth. The Daex catalogue was gripped in one hand. Locke tried pulling at her arm, but she wouldn't move. He cast nervous glances into the empty darkness around them.

"That's why his hold over me ended," she said. "My free will for a tumble dryer that broke. Their guarantee gave me back the right to choose."

She dropped the catalogue to the floor and pulled a gun from her handbag. Locke scooped up the catalogue and put a hand on Veronica's shoulder before she could shoot the appliance dead. A nod drew her attention to the lights winking out across the showroom, faster and faster, a diminishing spiral centred on them that eventually left the tumble dryer's spotlight as the only illumination.

"I could sell you a better gun," said the salesman's voice from the darkness. "A more powerful gun. One that could kill more efficiently and effectively than any other gun ever made. And all that it would cost you is your peace of mind."

Veronica swung her gun round, trying to locate the salesman. Locke stared at the tumble dryer's Daex logo and shoved the catalogue up under his jumper.

"Is this where you make us disappear?" he asked. "Like Mr and Mrs Scott?"

"Disappear, yes. Like Mr and Mrs Scott… no."
The last light went out.

Peter is breathing hard. He's run a dozen red lights and chanced his luck a dozen times more to get here, but he doubts anything could have stopped him, not when the receptionist had him booked in for an appointment that coincided with the very minute he stepped through the estate agent's door.

But now Mr Drysdale is making Peter wait while he finishes off some paperwork. Peter stands over his desk with fists clenched tight. Mr Drysdale corrects a few spelling mistakes, checks the document a second time, then carefully sets down his pen, steeples his fingers and smiles up at his visitor.

"Oh, hello, Peter. This is a surprise."

Peter surges forward, throwing himself across the desk to grab the estate agent by the collar.

"Give her back to me!"

Mr Drysdale raises his eyebrows and then sets about straightening Peter's tie.

"She's not mine to give."

Peter slaps away the estate agent's hands and steps back, loosening his tie again.

"But you made those deals. The house. The dress."

"Her choices, Peter."

"No! She didn't choose this. She didn't know what she was doing. I told her, but she wouldn't listen." He stumbles backwards and then collapses on the floor, tears welling in his eyes. "It's my fault. I shouldn't have done it, but I loved her. I still love her."

"It's really not your fault, Peter. Have a tissue." The estate agent offers him one from the box on his desk.

"It is my fault and it's why your contracts aren't worth the paper they're written on."

Their wrists and ankles were chained and they were locked in the back of a van transporting them to a watery grave. Despite this causing Veronica genuine concern, she found herself more bothered by the fact that Locke had slipped his gag, whereas she was still struggling with hers.

"But I don't understand why your parents had to disappear," he said. "Him, maybe, but she gave her soul to buy the house. I found a piece of her in all those appliances. By all accounts, she was a very good customer."

Veronica's obscene reply didn't make it past the cloth bound tightly around her mouth.

"You're right," agreed Locke, "it might not be important, but I disagree about the river. You won't be dying there."

"Mmf?" queried Veronica.

"Because it's just gone six o'clock."

The van stopped abruptly, throwing them across the bare floor and into the partition separating them from the driver. The engine's rumble ceased. The approach of heavy footsteps outside preceded the back doors flexing, buckling and then flying open.

Colfish Hasmek stood there with hands on hips, flanked by two associates who bore more than a passing resemblance to Panzer tanks.

"Looks like someone has done half our job for us," remarked Hasmek. "Take her."

His associates stepped into the van and hauled Veronica out. She struggled, squirmed and swore, but done of it did any good. Locke tried to follow, but by the time he fell awkwardly from the back of the van onto unyielding tarmac, Veronica was in the boot of Hasmek's car and three streets away.

Locke tried to stand and hit his head on one of the van doors. He tried again and fell over – the chains were tight and unforgiving. When he finally got himself on his feet and balanced, his only option for locomotion was hopping.

He didn't hop that way, in pursuit of Hasmek's car. He hopped this way, which seemed as good a way as any, given he didn't know where he was. He took heart from the knowledge that directions don't matter when you know you'll always end up where you need to be.

Locke hopped until he found a discarded skateboard, after which he rolled along on his belly instead. He rolled along until reached a driveway. This driveway was home to a car. Locke struggled upright and saw a 'For Sale' sign propped up behind the windscreen.

"You interested, buddy?" asked its owner, emerging from the garage and wiping his hands on an oily rag. His cheerful greeting gave way to suspicion on seeing Locke's bondage accessories.

"Certainly," replied Locke, brightly. "This looks like a car with personality."

"Err, yeah, that she is. Lovely ride, but bit of a temper. You know, I was never one for naming a car, but this one… oh yes, this one's different."

"You called her Lorraine, didn't you?"

Speechless, the owner could only nod.

"I did it because I loved her and I was afraid."

The estate agent looks at Peter with pity. He leaves his desk and moves to the drinks dispenser on top of the filing cabinet.

"Can I get you a cup of tea? Coffee?"

"I was afraid I'd lose her," continues Peter. "At first I knew we'd always be together, then… she told me she was pregnant. I got scared. I asked her to marry me, but even after she said yes… I mean, I was happier than I'd ever been before, but at the same time I'd never been more scared that I'd lose her. It was eating me up inside."

"Custard cream? Bourbon?" The estate agent proffers a tin of biscuits. Peter doesn't notice.

"I don't know if I believed it, but I wanted to. The fear made me believe, that and the wine. We'd been drinking and she found the contract."

The estate agent sits down and nods for him to go on while dunking a custard cream in his packet-fresh cup of tea.

"I told myself that if she signed she'd never be able to leave me. All along she thought it was a joke. She laughed as I pricked her finger. The blood should have made me stop, but it didn't. Her hand was unsteady. I held it for her. Come morning, she'd forgotten all about it. But I couldn't. That night changed everything."

The estate agent leans forward from behind his desk.

"Peter, what exactly did you do?"

"It was only afterwards I realised what it was worth. People looked at me differently. They knew, I could tell. Some turned away, but others… they approved. I made friends. I got promotions. And the things I could buy…"

"Peter, what did you do?"

The estranged husband looks up at the estate agent.

"Lorraine couldn't buy your house, because she signed her soul away to me when she was twenty-three. It paid for my car. It cost us our marriage."

The estate agent stares at Peter until a clump of his sodden custard cream drops off and falls into his tea with a plop. He considers the ripples bouncing around inside his mug.

"Oh dear."

The owner of the car bought with Lorraine Scott's soul removed Locke's chains with a heavy duty wire cutter.

"He said him and his wife were going away," explained the man. "That's why they were getting rid of all their stuff. Said he wouldn't need it where they were going. He said he was really looking forward to it. Can't say I blame him. I mean, cruising around the world, can't be bad, can it?"

"Peter Scott said he was going on a cruise?" asked Locke.

The man nodded as the last of the chains fell away.

Locke whipped the Daex catalogue out from under his jumper and threw it open on the bonnet of the car. He rifled feverishly through the pages until he found a double-page spread showing a gleaming cruise ship – 'The Regent's Wake'.

Night mist wreathed the docks as the prow of the cruise-liner slid silently into port. A gangway was lowered and two people disembarked. They crossed cold stone to reach a waiting horse-drawn carriage. The driver held the door open for them before returning to his seat and spurring the horses forward with a flick of the reins.

Inside the carriage, the couple from the Regent's Wake stared at the unexpected man sat opposite them.

"Good evening, Mr and Mrs Scott," he said. "My name is Thomas Locke. I am a private detective and what I'm about to say might sound strange, but it is absolutely true."

Veronica Drysdale was no longer bound by chains. Instead, the bars of a golden cage held her captive. The light here was dim, but bright enough to show that she was surrounded by a life she thought she'd left behind.

"Good evening, ladies and gentlemen." The voice came from an adjoining room. Despite travelling through a wall, the words remained clear and crisp. "We are gathered here for the auction of the property and earthly possessions of Mr Vincent Drysdale, bequeathed to the late Mrs Elizabeth Rose and offered for sale here by her husband, Gavin."

There was the dining table punctured by the bullet that missed her husband's head. There were the earrings he gave her for their fifth wedding anniversary. Even their toaster was here, ready to be sold.

"I would like to say that it is my privilege and pleasure to preside over the auction of so many fascinating and valuable items…"

Everything was tagged with a number. Searching around the top of her cage, Veronica found her own tag – lot seventeen. She tried to pull it free, but the cord that held it on would not break.

"… and I wish each and every one of you the best of luck with your bidding tonight."

Veronica sat back in her cage and promised herself that she would kill whoever came for her. Then her gaze fell upon another lot seventeen. It was trapped behind the glass of a cabinet and took the form of a printed piece of paper.

"Now, without further ado, let us begin."

"You don't understand anything, do you?" said Peter Scott with a mocking sneer.

"Enough to find you," replied Locke. "And you are going to the auction, aren't you?"

"Yes, but not to buy back our daughter," said Lorraine.

"We are dead to her," said Peter.

"That was the way he wanted it."

"So you see she's not our daughter any more."

Veronica's parents looked at each other and began laughing.

"She's our fortune."

Baby Veronica crawls along the floor of the hallway, clutching her mother's silver choker in one stubby hand. At the end of the hallway is the doorway to the kitchen. Inside stands her father, hanging his head, defeated. Her mother is ranting at him, while the estate agent drums his fingers thoughtfully on the worktop.

"How could you do that to me?" asks Lorraine. "I didn't know! You took my soul and did what with it? Threw it away!"

"That's a good car!"

"There is no car worth what you took from me."

The estate agent speaks. Unlike the warring couple, he speaks softly.

"Lorraine, Peter, you defrauded the agency. You are living in a house you have not paid for. Squabble later, here and now redress is required."

"Please, Mr Drysdale," pleads Peter, "I can sell the car. Lorraine can sell everything she bought."

"Why should I sell anything?" asks Lorraine. "It was your mistake. Tell him, Vincent, tell him I don't have to give anything back."

"I'm afraid the penalty interest accrued and the nature of your crime..." Vincent Drysdale shakes his head. "It is no longer a question of payment. It is a question of punishment."

This word brings silence to the room. It is a silence that tells of punishment, of the pain it will bring and the eternity it will last. The mother and the father cannot comprehend the form this punishment will take, but they can see its genesis sparkling in the estate agent's eyes and it chills them to the bone.

Oblivious to all of this, Baby Veronica crawls on. She's almost at the kitchen door.

"Yet... there may be a way." Mr Drysdale's words lift the silence and offer hope for escape. "There is one thing that would pay off your debts and serve as recompense for your crime. There may even be wealth left over." He does not look at the hope rising in the couple's eyes; instead he frowns and shakes his head. "But it is a most rare and precious thing..."

"Please, we'll find it, Vincent..."

"Yes, Mr Drysdale. We'll get it for you..."

"Then what you must give me... is a symbol of pure,

untainted love."

Their faces freeze as they try to understand the import of his words. Peter and Lorraine turn to each other and look into one another's eyes. Whatever love once existed between them has become corrupted, spoiled by enmity and an unwillingness to forgive. How could they ever hope to deliver such a symbol now?

The silver choker lands on the kitchen tiles with a dull thunk. Husband and wife look around and down at the child in the doorway. Veronica looks up at her parents and burbles happily.

"And now we come to Lot 17, Veronica Drysdale nee Scott, wife to Vincent and allegedly responsible for his death. As her free will is currently intact, I shall start the bidding at the reduced price of ten thousand. Do I have ten thousand?"

She stood at the head of the auction hall. She could not move.

"Ten thousand from the gentleman in the third row."

She stood on a plinth of her own, dressed in a purple velvet frock trimmed with white lace. Her silver choker was around her neck and she wore the diamond earrings he'd bought her on their fifth anniversary.

"Eleven thousand from the anonymous buyer on line five."

At her feet was the deed of ownership for Veronica Drysdale nee Scott, signed by her mother and her father and trapped within a glass frame.

"Twelve thousand from the gentleman in the third row."

She could only stand and stare down the length of the hall. The auctioneer orchestrated the sale from the pulpit beside her. Before him, rows of pews lined a narrow aisle leading to an archway blocked by two solid oak doors and guarded by the human tanks that brought her here. Veronica saw those sat on the pews as nothing more than vultures dressed up in human flesh. Auction house employees manned old-fashioned box phones fastened to the walls. Stained glass windows depicting saints and sinners rose above them, each criss-crossed with iron bars.

"Thirteen thousand from—"

The main doors suddenly flew open. Heads turned to

appraise the intrusion. Veronica watched with a delight she couldn't express as Peter and Lorraine Scott strode in with Locke in tow.

But he only managed a few steps. The heavies grabbed him by the arms and threw him back outside. The doors were pulled shut once again. Veronica's parents quietly found seats together on the fourth row.

"My apologies for the interruption, ladies and gentlemen," said the auctioneer. "Now, where were we? Ah yes, thirteen thousand from the anonymous buyer on line two. Do I have fourteen thousand?"

Veronica stared at her parents. She tried to move, to do something that would make them look, make them see her, but she remained utterly frozen while they shared a private joke and paid her no attention at all.

Locke rose to his feet, rain water from the street damp against his back. He faced the doors to the auction house. Another guard looked down at him and shook his head in warning.

The private detective backed away and then ran around to the side of the building. It was old; a crumbling, red brick wedge overlooking the convergence of Humberstone Road and Harper Street. Black drainpipes climbed like haphazard tendrils of steel ivy up to the roof, but all the windows were either too small to provide access or barred.

Locke hurried on to an alleyway that ran behind the auction house. He saw a door. He tried the handle. He kicked and rammed it with his shoulder, but it wouldn't open. His eyes sought upwards. More windows, too small, too secure, except… except one, high up, a precarious distance from the fire escape, but worth a try.

Locke began to climb to escape ladder.

"I wouldn't bother," advised a voice. Locke looked down to see Colfish Hasmek leant against a dumpster, lighting a thin cigar. "Tootings of Harper Street have not survived dealing in the unconventional since 1683 by freely admitting intruders, Mr Locke. If you have heard of Morgice deadbolts, the Redwatch Lattice or D'Courcey Prowlers, you will know that attempting entry would be very unwise indeed."

Locke dropped back down into the alleyway. He glanced at

Hasmek, then at the red brick wall behind which Veronica's life was being auctioned away. He began pacing, splashing back and forth through a line of puddles.

"She will be happy enough once she has a new tumble dryer," Hasmek assured him, "and as neither of you have a choice in the matter, it is best that you reconcile yourself to her fate, Mr Locke."

Locke stopped and stared down at his reflection, cast in the inky blackness of the gathered rainwater. His lips moved as if talking to himself. Hasmek studied him through drifting coils of smoke. He saw the private detective close his eyes and raise his head to the sky. Was that a tear running from the corner of his eye?

"There is always a choice, Mr Hasmek," said Locke. "You just have to be willing to accept its cost." He opened his eyes and turned them on the man from the auction house. "Now, I suggest that you move."

"Come again."

"You are in his way."

Hasmek raised his eyebrows and began to turn his head. He saw only the edge of a shadow within the shadows, but that was enough. His scream was silent, telling of fates worse than an estate agent's punishment.

"I am bid twenty-six thousand five hundred for this fine example of a murderous wife, do I hear twenty-seven? No more? I am bid twenty-six thousand five hundred..."

The auctioneer raised his hammer.

"Going once."

Veronica stared with desperation at her parents. They returned her stare with empty eyes.

"Going twice."

As he readied the hammer to strike home the sale, the auctioneer was interrupted by the urgent whisper of an underling. He replied with a sneer and a condescending tone.

"What on earth are you talking about?"

"Sir, please, just look."

The messenger pointed to the frame at Veronica's feet. The deed of ownership was gone.

Agitated whispers rippled through the room. One of the

employees manning the phones cowered at a volley of abuse shouted down the line. When the verbal violence ceased, the employee tapped the cradle experimentally, then shook his head to the auctioneer. The customer with the highest bid was gone and it didn't sound like he was coming back.

"Err, ladies and gentlemen," said the auctioneer, "as you can see, due to… unforeseen circumstances, it appears that we are now unable to offer this lot for sale. On behalf of Tootings of Harper Street, I must offer deep and profuse—"

The apology caught in his throat as Veronica stepped down from the plinth. She said nothing, but with an acid glance halved the value of the auctioneer's life. She didn't look at anyone else as she walked down the aisle, not even when her parents called out to her.

"Veronica, please, it was nothing personal," said Peter Scott.

"Do you want to see what I bought with my love for you?" asked Lorraine Scott. "I've got it here in my handbag."

"Perhaps we can do lunch sometime?"

The main doors opened and Veronica walked out past the guards, down the steps and over to the waiting Locke.

"I need a drink," she said.

Veronica twisted the cap from the bottle of whisky and gulped back a mouthful. While the kick of alcohol stung the back of her throat, she shoved a torn strip of newspaper down the neck of the bottle. A lick of flame from her lighter and she hurled the makeshift firebomb through one of the auction house's stained glass windows. The projectile conjured up shouts of alarm from within. A second bottle and then a third swiftly followed the first.

The main doors shuddered as the weight of those inside tried to break their way out. The stolen car parked on the steps blocked their escape. A guard's limp arm extended from under one of the tyres.

At the back of the auction house, the dumpster was on fire and braced against the rear exit. The dark of the higher windows began turning to a flickering orange.

"Help us!"

Veronica thought this cry might have been her mother.

She threw another bottle of whisky through the window and returned to Locke for more ammunition. His expression was blank. She knocked back more whisky, grinned at him and threw her arms out wide in mock apology.

"My past gives me no choice," she said, staggering backwards, holding his stare until she had to look away.

Another scream from the auction house. Was that her father? Bile rose in her throat. She lifted a hand to her mouth. She wanted to cover her eyes, but felt compelled to watch the ravenous flames devour her past. Veronica swallowed hard and then tore off her earrings. They were stuffed into a bottle along with her mother's choker and thrown into the inferno.

The burning glow can be seen from the broken window of the abandoned station, but it doesn't touch the shadows within, shadows that hide shifting piles of things misplaced and mislaid. Into these shadows fall two diamond earrings and a chain of silver fringed with a smouldering crimson – a colour that soon fades in the forlorn darkness of The Office of Lost and Found.

Interlude III

Locke followed Veronica out onto the over-grown train tracks.

"You don't have to go," he told her.

"It's clear you don't want me to stay."

"I didn't mean—"

"Yes, you did and you're right. I killed my parents, Thomas. No one wants to be around someone like that. Not even me."

Locke couldn't disagree. He watched Veronica walk away along the abandoned branch-line and became aware of a shadow watching from the broken window of the station.

"I couldn't do it," he said.

Lafarge said nothing.

Nightly Nonsense

His name was Billy and he was eight and a half years old. He lived in a regular terraced house on a regular urban street in a regular medium-sized town. Like many boys of his age, he enjoyed climbing trees and shooting his friends with toy guns, but right now it was late and his mother was tucking him up in bed. She pulled the sheets up to his chin, kissed him on the forehead and then retreated to the door. Her hand lifted to the light switch. The expression on her face dared Billy to say a word. He pulled the sheets up to his nose, hugged his teddy bear and said nothing.

She flicked the switch. Darkness claimed the room. Billy's mother became a featureless silhouette against the light from the landing.

"Good night, Billy."

The door swung shut.

Billy's breathing was fast and shallow. He heard his mother's footsteps descend the stairs. When they reached the bottom, another switch was flicked off and the light from the landing, which shone as a sliver beneath the door, was extinguished.

The young boy shuffled down beneath his covers and curled up in the foetal position. The air he gulped down was made fusty and warm by the bedclothes. He did not dare push his head back above the covers. Up there, complete blackness would be transformed into mere darkness by his eyes growing accustomed to the lack of light. And in that darkness he knew he would see it: unclear, uncertain, but there - a malformed shape cast against the window, or peering from the wardrobe; a thing that watched and waited.

Billy held his breath. His ears strained to pick out any sound of unwelcome company. He listened until his lungs were fit to burst and then, at the moment he was about to gasp for breath, it came: a deep, rasping breath expelled from cavernous lungs.

Very slowly, very quietly, Billy exhaled. To his ears, this noise was deafening. They would surely hear it. He hugged his teddy bear tighter.

The other breathing came from beneath Billy's bed, where blackness stretched as far and as deep as the sea. From those depths did this inhuman sound rise, chilling the air, making the young boy tremble.

The noise grows louder as you travel deeper, down where unseen things move; crawling and creeping and sliding over one another, their passing the sound of nails on a blackboard – a seething mass of jealous eyes void of intelligence, yet possessing intent. If you could see anything down here in the recesses of the abyss, your gaze might fix on the source of that cruel breath, where rancid vapours pass over rows of rusty barbed teeth. Eyeballs scarred and rheumy watch five slick tentacles counting down… five… four… three…

Billy holds his breath again.

Two…

Silence returns, but only for a moment.

One…

The beast speaks: "Tonight's headlines: Fresh fears of an influenza epidemic as two new cases are confirmed in Slovakia…"

Billy's Mother, Maureen, stood at the door to the living room.

"Tea, dear?" she asked.

The television's newsreader was the first to reply.

"… the Bank of England increases interest rates for the second month in a row and arsonists kill sixteen people in an attack on an auction house."

"Norman. Tea?" she prompted again.

Her husband grunted. It was close enough to a 'yes' to send Maureen heading back to the kitchen to boil enough water for two. She stopped in the hallway. A sliver of light shone out from under Billy's door.

She threw the bedroom door open. Billy was in bed, sheets held up to his nose. They were scant protection from his mother's baleful stare.

"Billy! Lights off! I'll have no more of this nightly nonsense."

She flicked the switch by the door. Once again, the bedroom fell dark. Billy whimpered.

"But I heard scary noises and voices."

Maureen's sharp rebuke faltered as unwelcome sounds intruded on the room: a muffled, rhythmic, thud-thud-thud, followed by a high-pitched wail.

Her slipper-shod feet hurried down the stairs. She grabbed a coat from the hooks in the hallway and headed outside. A moan came from the bedroom window of the house next door. This very same door was soon under assault from Maureen's fist.

The bedroom window opened above her. The head of a dark-skinned man popped out to stare down at her.

"What the—?"

"I have a young boy trying to sleep next door," said Maureen, "and your lewd and inappropriate behaviour—"

"What? What are you on about?"

Veronica Drysdale lay naked on the bed and watched her equally naked host try to reason with his irate neighbour from the window.

"He could hear you through the wall!" accused that neighbour, her voice a grating whine.

Danvil began to laugh. Veronica thought this an ill-advised response. She glanced over at the empty half of the bed beside her. A condom had been discarded in the middle of a dark, damp patch of sheet. Veronica attempted to flick the thing away with a red-painted fingernail.

"He's eight years old!" ranted the neighbour, her voice rising an octave. "He is my son and I will not have him exposed to… Oh my Lord!"

The condom flew off of the bed, but the neighbour was vexed by something else: Danvil gyrating his hips above the window sill in an impromptu display of bouncing genitals.

"Is this what you're scared of, lady?" he asked. "Or is this what you're really round here for? What? You're not staying for a bit of this?"

He laughed again. The neighbour's indignant footsteps hurried back next door. Danvil closed the window. Veronica scooped the duvet up from the floor and wrapped herself up in it.

"Budge up, love," said Danvil, returning to the bed. He

pulled himself under the duvet and pushed her over toward the stain. She managed to avoid it, but not the sloppy, inaccurate kiss planted on the side of her nose.

"Sleep tight," said Danvil. He lay down with his back to her. Moments later he was asleep.

Mindful of the damp patch, Veronica tried to find a restful position, but tiredness eluded her. She stared at the bedroom door until her eyes began to sting and she had to blink.

The bed springs creaked behind her. She did not look around, but she knew he was looking at her. She also knew that it was not the dark, jovial face of Danvil that regarded her, but the pale face of a man from her past, chilling the back of her skull with his gaze.

A hand slipped across her leg, raising gooseflesh, touching her hips before venturing on in search of a cold intimacy.

Veronica's eyes went wide. She spun around in the bed. Danvil was sleeping soundly, back to her. That unwelcome touch - the insidious feel of the pale man's flesh touching hers - was gone.

She sat upright on the edge of the bed and abruptly recoiled on finding the condom stuck to her toe. She flicked at it again. This time it landed out of sight beneath a chest of drawers. She shivered; a reaction to the befouled rubber and the cool of the bedroom. Her dress was draped over the back of a chair. She began pulling it on only to stop with it half over her head. The bed was vibrating. A few more seconds and then she heard the cause: a low, ominous rumble growing louder and louder, its bass frequency resonating deep within her stomach.

It was hard to tell where the sound was coming from. Veronica turned her head this way and that to try and locate it. Another sound, higher pitched, prompted her to lean over to the wall behind the bed and press her ear up against its surface.

"No! No! Go away!" pleaded a voice from the other side. The rumble became a roar and the wall juddered. Veronica drew back.

Silence returned.

She frowned before listening at the wall again. All was quiet for a while, then came footsteps, a click and eventually the sound of a door opening.

"Billy! I've told you! Lights out!"

"It took Mr Teddy!"

"I don't want to hear it!"

"But Mr Teddy's gone!"

"Enough, Billy! This light is going off and staying off and you will go to sleep."

"But Mummy…!"

A click, a slam of the door and then all Veronica could hear was gentle sobbing.

Bacon and eggs hissed and spat in the frying pan. Judging they were done, Veronica, now fully-dressed, ladled them onto a slice of bread.

A bleary-eyed Danvil arrived in the doorway. He grinned.

"That's what I like to see – a girl who knows how to make breakfast."

Veronica sandwiched the bacon and eggs with another slice of bread and then wrapped everything up in tin foil.

"I made me breakfast," she said, "you'll have to fend for yourself."

She flashed a mercenary smile before pushing past him into the hallway.

"Hey! What did I do wrong?"

Veronica's handbag waited on a table in the hallway. She slipped the sandwich into it.

"Nothing. I just needed a bed and breakfast. Tonight it'll be someone else's bed, tomorrow someone else's breakfast. It's nothing personal."

"I think you should go. Now."

"Already going. Thanks for the sex."

Danvil slammed the front door shut behind her. His reaction didn't bother her, he would forget their brief affair soon enough. It was nothing personal, everyone else did the same.

No, thought Veronica, correcting herself, not everyone else.

"I don't want to hear it, Billy," said the whiny voice from the night before.

Veronica saw it belonged to a middle-aged woman standing in a threadbare, pink dressing gown. She stood on the step of the neighbouring terrace and waved a warning finger at a young boy before stepping back inside and closing the door.

Billy hung his head. He was dressed for school in blazer, shirt and tie, with a satchel slung over his shoulder. The school bus stop was just up the road, but he wasn't in any hurry. He stopped on the pavement and stared down into the gutter, where oily puddles painted rainbow pictures of monsters.

A pair of sleek black stilettos stepped up beside him. His gaze ranged up slender legs in dark stockings, past the hem of a tight black dress and over a coat opened enough to reveal cleavage that would have impressed him had he been only a few years older. The face atop the body was finely-featured, but serious.

"Have you got a pen?" asked Veronica.

Billy was caught off-guard. Strangers usually offered sweets and visiting rights to puppies; they rarely asked for a stationary. He reached into his satchel and produced a ballpoint. Veronica took the pen from him, took his hand and wrote a number down on his palm.

"It's the phone number of a… someone I know. He can find Mr Teddy for you."

With that, Veronica turned and walked away.

Billy watched her go, bemused. His father exited their front gate and walked past him to climb into a parked car.

"Stand there all day and you'll miss your bus, boy."

Billy nodded and looked again at the number on his hand. He clenched his fingers into fist as if to stop the number taking flight, then turned his back on Veronica and hurried away to the bus stop.

At midday, the sun looked down on Billy's father as he led three of his colleagues past the slim shadows of the chemical plant silos to the site cafeteria.

"If the flu doesn't get us the banks will," Norman was saying. "Do you know how much I'm paying on the house now? I'm telling you the government don't know what it's like for guys like us."

His companions nodded before removing their hard hats and entering the refectory.

* * *

Maureen's afternoon involved slipping clothes onto hangers and hooking the hangars onto display racks at the charity shop where she worked. One garment lifted from the pile of neatly folded donations was a floral dress that had been expensive not so long ago.

"Oh, this is nice," she told her friend at the till. "I might be having this myself. Of course, something new would be nicer, but Norman won't buy anything new. I've told him it's not like Billy's smart enough for University and we should spend the money now, but he always says when interest rates go up and the stock market crashes we'll regret it. I say there are worse things to regret. What do you think, Linda?"

"And Linda said only the other week her Joe bought her this lovely dress," recounted Maureen, her voice loud enough to carry through from the kitchen where she was cooking dinner to the living room where Norman was watching television. "She said she was so surprised, because it wasn't her birthday or their anniversary or anything..."

"Hey, Maureen, listen to this," Norman called back. "The news is saying we've had two hundred and fifty thousand migrants since October. Quarter of a million! And that's just what the government's saying, so you can bet it's probably double that. You believe that? Quarter of a million."

The conversation continued; words drifting back and forth in the hallway with scant regard for those that had gone before. Billy subconsciously ducked their passage en route to the telephone table by the front door. He checked the number on his palm and began to dial.

The setting sun drew a line of orange across the horizon and set its rays glittering across the edges of a broken window in an abandoned train station. Inside, a phone was ringing. It sat on a table surrounded by stacks of junk. It rang and rang until the sun was lost beneath the horizon, when it fell silent.

A postman whistled as he worked his way up the street, pulling a trolley of mail along behind him. Veronica watched his progress from a bedroom window. She'd been watching since he turned onto the street ten minutes ago. In that time, long shadows had formed out of darkness as the rising sun cut bright lines between the houses.

Behind her, an Asian man lay asleep on another foreign bed. She didn't spare him a glance as she turned from the window, picked up her handbag and left.

Billy stood outside his front gate and yawned. His night was spent cowering under his duvet clutching a torch and staring at its beam to catch the moment when its light would begin to flicker. That was when he was exposed - facing desperate seconds of darkness while he fumbled a new set of batteries into place. The experience left him looking older than his eight years of age. Bags hung under his eyes and his complexion was sallow. When he set off unsteadily toward the bus stop, he made only a few steps before his father reached the gate and offered some words of advice: "Other way, boy."

The sun wheeled across the sky, the passing hours dragging shadows from West to North to East. No sign of life was visited upon the abandoned station during that time. It was sunset before the outside world intruded on the derelict building. The phone began to ring. And ring. And still no one answered.

Veronica waited at the nightclub bar. She did not have to wait long.

"Want to dance?"

The guy was tall and broad-shouldered with an unnatural tan. He was wearing a suit, but the shirt was unbuttoned and the tie shoved in a pocket.

"No, but buy me a drink and you can take me back to your place."

"Cool. What's your poison?"

"Anything toxic works for me."

Norman sat in front of the television. Its screen provided the only light in the room; an unreliable, flickering light that danced shadows across the walls. Billy had his head in his father's lap. He was dressed in pyjamas and sleeping soundly. Maureen appeared at the door and thoughtfully rubbed her chin.

The taxi drew to a halt on a deserted suburban street. Veronica and the guy she'd picked up climbed out.

"My place is just up this way," said the guy.

Veronica hesitated as the taxi drove away and then followed the lead of her one-night stand.

Norman carried Billy up to his bedroom. He laid him down on the bed and Maureen pulled up the covers. She kissed her son on the forehead and retreated with her husband to the door.

Billy groggily opened his eyes just in time to see the lights go out and the door swing shut.

The man slammed Veronica up against the wire fencing of a dimly lit cutting. His breath was an alcoholic stench under her nose. His darting tongue kept threatening to touch her lips.

"The wife wouldn't appreciate me bringing a slut like you home," he said, groping at her breasts, "so we'll do it here and now..."

He tried to force his hand between her legs.

She head-butted him in the face and kneed him in the groin. He dropped to his knees. Veronica kicked him in the crotch again. The fury was still pumping through her veins when she pulled the gun from her handbag and pressed it hard up against his forehead.

He whimpered as her frantic breathing began to subside.

"You're just lucky I can't afford to waste bullets," she said, before clubbing him around the head with the butt of her pistol and storming away.

Billy panicked on discovering the torch wasn't under his pillow. His mother had changed the bedclothes and it was now lying useless on the dresser. He should have run for the door straightaway, but his moment of panic gave them their chance. While he hid under the sheets he could hear them; their rasping breath, their pendulous weight creaking the floorboards, their furtive whispers.

Billy whispered his own lament: "She said he'd find you, Mr Teddy, but no one's there. No one's out there. No one except them."

On this night, Veronica's bed was a concrete step and her pillow the damp wood of a door jamb. She pulled her knees up to her chest and hugged them in an effort to keep warm. The chill air bit through her stockings and sapped the warmth provided by her coat. She rested her head against the side of the doorway and tried to get some sleep.

A shrill alarm wailed down the school corridor. It prompted streams of children to burst forth from classrooms, marshalled by short-tempered teachers. The flow pushed out through double doors into the playground, but in the confusion a child was lost.

Billy slipped into the secretary's office with the alarm still sounding its warning. He could hear the other children chattering outside while the teachers ran through their registers. He picked up the phone and dialled the number washed from his hand, but stuck in his memory.

After each ring he prayed that a voice would cut in before the next ring began. Disappointment followed disappointment, but he persevered. Maybe after the next ring. Or the next one. Or the next one.

When the headmaster's heavy hand fell on his shoulder, Billy's cheeks were wet with tears.

Veronica blew her nose on a ragged piece of tissue. The night had not treated her well. A bottle of medicine and packet of tablets sat on the chemist's counter, promising minor relief from her burgeoning cold. She coughed as she sought through her purse for the necessary change.

The man in the queue behind her shifted weight impatiently from one foot to the other.

"Come on," he urged, "some of us need to… hey, do I know you?"

Veronica looked around. It was Danvil.

"Sorry," he said, "I know that sounds corny, but your face is so familiar."

He'd watched that face come to orgasm only two nights ago. The same face had been splashed across newspapers and recycled for countless television reports. But since her husband had been lost, no one remembered Veronica Drysdale. Well, no one who mattered. Vague recognition was the best she could hope for.

"Err, were you at that… conference…?" asked Veronica.

"Leipzig?"

Veronica nodded. Danvil smiled.

"Look, I've got cash, I'll get this. Are you in town on business?"

Veronica lied, Danvil paid and they left the chemist deep in conversation. He bought her lunch and then they walked back to his office.

"And this is it," he declared. "Yeah, it's my house too. You probably guessed I don't get out much. The fringe benefits of the networked economy."

Veronica blew her nose again into the ragged tissue.

"Have you been to see a doctor?" asked Danvil.

"It's just a chill," she replied.

Returning the tissue to her purse, Veronica turned to thank Danvil for lunch, but froze on seeing who approached.

"Do you know how embarrassing that was for me?" asked Maureen, loudly. "Getting called out of work like that? Your father isn't going to like this, not one bit."

She tried to drag Billy through the front gate before all the neighbours could see what a scene her son was forcing her to make, but he dug his heels in. His mother tugged at his arm, but he wouldn't move.

"No one answered," Billy told Veronica. "I called and called, but no one answered."

She tried to say something, but couldn't find an answer to the little boy's forsaken stare. Maureen finally dragged him away along the path to their front door, reprimanding him with every step.

"What was all that about?" asked Danvil.

"I don't know," said Veronica. "Look, I have to go. Give me your number, I'll call you."

The phone in the abandoned station was ringing. It continued to ring as the door opened. A handwritten sign stuck to the outside of the door proclaimed this 'The Office of Lost and Found'. Veronica stepped inside. She lowered a mobile phone from her ear and cancelled the call. The phone on the table fell silent.

Veronica surveyed the room, looking for signs of life amidst the piles of bric-a-brac. One of those piles crashed to the floor as Veronica stormed over to a door hidden by shadow.

The room beyond the door was also filled with junk, but a rancid bed stood with its head up against the far wall. An empty milk carton lay beside it. The use by date came and went a week ago.

Veronica glanced around the room again and then returned to the entrance. She was about to close the door on the Office of Lost and Found when a sound from the bedroom stayed her hand.

She approached the shadowed doorway with fresh caution. Peering around its frame, she saw a man lying on the bed, naked and shivering.

"Thomas?" she asked softly.

No reply.

"I've got a case for you," she said, slightly louder.

The figure on the bed moved. With great effort and stuttering twinges of pain, it rolled upright so its feet could touch the floor. Its back remained crooked and turned so Veronica could not see a face.

"I tried calling," she said.

"I've been away," replied Locke.

"It's a kid. He's lost his teddy bear."

Billy stood at the top of the stairs. The buzz of the front doorbell reverberated around the house and made the hairs on the back of his neck tingle. Something was about to happen, he knew it.

"I said go to bed, Billy," called his mother, "I'll tuck you up in a minute."

Flustered by the noise of the bell, it took Maureen a moment to unlock and unbolt the door. She opened it to find a young woman on the doorstep.

Veronica kept her finger pressed on the doorbell just long enough to be especially annoying, then stopped and smiled. She glanced briefly at Billy. His little hands clasped the top of the banister rail.

"Yes?" prompted Maureen.

"Hi," said Veronica, "I thought I should come round and apologise for the other night."

"The other night?"

Behind Maureen, the cupboard under the stairs opened. Thomas Locke stepped out, now fully dressed in worn grey trousers, a thick green jumper and a puffy blue coat.

"I was next door," explained Veronica. "I think your son may have heard myself and your neighbour… how can I put this? Going at it like rabbits?"

Locke quietly climbed the stairs and stopped a few steps shy of Billy's position on the landing.

"Hello, my name is Thomas Locke," he whispered. "I am a private detective. I believe you have a bear that needs finding."

Billy's instinctive caution gave way to an eager nod. He led the way to his bedroom.

"I'd tell you to be ashamed of yourself," Maureen told Veronica, "but just by looking at the way you dress I can tell shame isn't something you're familiar with."

"Okay, Billy," said Locke, "we have to be quick and we have to be quiet, but most of all, we have to do it with the lights out." Billy's enthusiasm suddenly vanished. Locke put a hand on his shoulder. "They came and took him in the dark and that's the only place we'll find him. I know you're scared and so am I, but when I'm scared, I find this helps." Locke produced a cricket bat from inside his coat and handed it to Billy. "Are you ready?"

Billy took a deep breath, gripped the bat tightly and nodded his head.

Veronica watched them step into the bedroom. The light went out and the bedroom door closed behind them.

"I would thank-you for your apology, Miss," said Maureen, "but in my book a sinner who repents is just a sinner with a guilty conscience. Good day!"

She slammed the door shut in Veronica's face. Each lock

and bolt was re-fastened with particular vigour. Maureen returned to the kitchen; a mottled shadow visible through the square of marbled glass set into the door. Veronica watched her go and then turned to face the street. No one else was about. She looked over to next door. The bedroom window was dark, but downstairs light shone from behind drawn curtains.

Veronica stepped out onto the pavement and then across to Danvil's gate. She touched the latch, but an easy feeling made her pause. Something was coming.

Windows shattered at its touch. The earth trembled. Yet, as it raced on through houses, people and cars, its power began to fade. Glass merely shook, men and women no longer fell to the ground and its only power was sound; a wave that left in its wake a cacophony of car alarms and carried to Veronica's ears a mighty, percussive roar.

She looked out over the rooftops. An ominous black mushroom cloud was rising up against the crimson sunset.

"Maureen, was that you?" shouted Billy's father.

"Of course not, dear."

Their voices sent Veronica running back to their front door. The marbled glass revealed movement within: Locke and Billy were hurrying down the stairs as Maureen emerged from the kitchen.

"It sounded to me like… Who are you?" Each subsequent word ascended the motherly scale of alarm. "What are you doing with my son? What are you doing in my house?"

The sound of the explosion drew curious householders out onto the street. Fingers pointed and camera phones took pictures of the demonic cloud, its summit now a circle of darkness expanding out over the town.

"I called him, Mum—" said Billy, trying to explain.

"Norman! Come out here! There's a strange man in our house!"

Billy's father trudged out of the living room.

"Dad, I called him," said Billy. He held up a stuffed bear. "He helped me get Mr Teddy back."

"I'm sure he did," replied Norman, eyeing Locke. "Is that how your sort do it? Steal kids' toys so they have to come begging to you for help?"

"Oh, Norman, you don't think he's…?" Maureen placed a shocked hand over her mouth.

"Unless I hear a very good explanation to the contrary."

Maureen wasn't interested in hearing explanations.

"I'm calling the police."

She bustled over to the telephone table.

"Your son is telling the truth," said Locke. "My name is Thomas Locke, I am a private detective. I helped return your son's teddy bear. Now he has to leave."

"You're not taking my Billy anywhere," snapped Maureen.

"Listen," said Locke, "they are coming for him. I can take him somewhere they won't find him."

"They? Who are they?" sneered Norman, sceptically.

"I can't get through, Norman," said Maureen. "Too many callers, they're just leaving me on hold…"

An inhuman whine abruptly silenced the chatter of those gathered in the street and the hostilities inside the house. It sounded like an air raid warning from a World War Two film.

"That's the chemical plant siren!" said Norman. "Something's happened at work!"

He rushed back into the living room. Outside, Veronica moved to the window. Through a crack in the curtains she saw Norman in front of the television, stabbing at the remote control with his thumb.

"Norman!" called Maureen from the hallway.

"Ssh, woman! Maybe there's something on the news."

"But this man…! He's trying to leave!"

Veronica turned her head. The door handle turned and rattled, but the door remained closed. The handle sprang back straight and the letterbox squeaked open. Something furry began emerging from the slot. Veronica jumped over and helped pull Mr Teddy through to safety.

"Don't let them get him again," Billy told her, his wide eyes pleading through the letterbox.

"Who's coming after you?" she asked.

"Nightmares," replied Locke. "Some of them are already here."

"Get away from that door!" shouted Norman, back in the hallway. "And get away from my son!"

The letterbox snapped shut. Beyond the marbled glass, Locke faced Norman. Maureen held the phone to her ear with one hand and was beckoning urgently to her son with the other.

"Come here, Billy, come on. I've got the keys, Norman. He can't get out."

"Have you got through to the police yet?"

"I'm still trying. I said come here, Billy."

"Something's happened at the plant. If that was an explosion we heard… I told Arnold something like this would happen, I told him! But the stupid cretin wouldn't listen—"

"Norman—"

"I'll call Reg. He'll know what's going on."

He went to take the phone from his wife.

"Norman, no! I'm trying to call the police."

"Fine. I'll get my mobile then."

He sloped back off into the living room. Locke and Billy took their chance, making a break for the kitchen and the back door.

"Norman!"

Arched passageways running between every other house gave access to the back yards of the terrace. Veronica raced down the nearest. She barged through a rickety gate into a paved enclosure containing a shed, a rusting tricycle and little else.

Ahead lay a door and a window looking into Billy's kitchen. Veronica ran up to peer through the glass and saw her husband's dead face staring back her.

Her stomach lurched; she reeled backwards. Mr Teddy fell from her hand. Veronica reached into her handbag and tightened fingers around the handle of her gun, but the face at the window was gone, lingering only in her mind's eye.

She took a few deep breaths before venturing forward again.

This time she saw Locke backed up against the kitchen sink and Maureen menacing him with a knife. Maureen shouted at Billy until he left the detective's side. As soon as her son was close enough, she grabbed his hand, squeezing tight and making Billy wince.

Locke didn't seem to notice. His gaze flitted about the

room, seeing more danger in empty corners than the blade in front of him. When he glanced at the window, Maureen did likewise and gave a yelp of alarm on seeing Veronica. She jabbed the knife toward Locke before backing away, dragging Billy along with her.

Once they were back in the hallway, the kitchen door was thrown shut.

Locke rushed over and threw his weight against it, but couldn't budge the sideboard hastily pressed into service as a barricade on the far side.

Veronica fired two bullets at the lock securing the back door. They buckled the metal and ensured the door would remain shut until a trained locksmith repaired the damage.

"Find another way in!" Locke shouted to her. "Get Billy to the Office, he'll be safe there."

Veronica thought about trying to shoot out the double-glazing, then thrust the gun back into her bag, snatched up Mr Teddy and hurried back along the passage to the front garden. Disconcerting words echoed off the brickwork around her.

"This is a public health warning," announced a voice distorted by loudspeaker. "There has been an explosion at the chemical plant. Everyone must go inside. Close all windows and doors."

Veronica reached the front gate to see a small white van driving slowly up the road.

"Remain inside until an official announcement gives the all clear," continued the warning. "This is a public health warning. There has been an explosion at the chemical plant."

A wall of dark grey smoke rolled along the street behind the van. Streetlights swallowed by its passing became glowing orbs that quickly faded away to nothing.

"Everyone must go inside. Close all windows and doors."

The van was caught. It accelerated in an attempt to stay ahead of the smoke, but the voluminous cloud was relentless. The van became a shadow in its midst, before it too faded from view. The amplified voice reminded everyone to "remain inside until—" A crackle of static halted its message.

The chemical plant siren continued to wail its warning: the smoke was coming and it would swallow everything in its path.

Veronica threw herself over the fence and ran up to Danvil's door. She hammered at the wood and stabbed at the doorbell.

The hall light came on.

Smoke consumed the neighbouring house.

Danvil opened the door.

Smoke flowed over the fence and surged across the garden.

Danvil showed no sign he recognised Veronica, but he did recognise her fear. He quickly let her in and then secured the door.

They both stepped back. The glass in the door turned grey. A wisp of smoke curled through the key hole, but it soon dispersed once inside.

"Thank-you," said Veronica.

"No problem," replied Danvil. "I… we've met, haven't we?"

"Yes, a conference I think… I'm sorry, I need to get next door. There's a young boy—"

"Leipzig, right? How's that for a coincidence? You passing by when—"

"I need to get next door," persisted Veronica. She held up Mr Teddy. "I need to return this. Please?"

"You're talking about Billy? Listen, I'm sure his parents are in…"

Raised voices came through the wall on cue.

"Norman! What are we going to do about that man?"

"What can we do? The police can't come, he's trapped in the kitchen, Billy's fine."

A frown formed on Danvil's face.

"But think what he could have done," said Maureen, her high voice clear and distinct despite the dividing wall.

"I don't care what he could have done!" shouted Norman. "I care about what's going to happen to us. Don't you realise what happened tonight? What it means?"

Danvil shook his head and spoke firmly: "We shouldn't be listening to this."

He led Veronica into the kitchen to escape his neighbours' quarrel, but the argument followed.

"So I shouldn't care if terrible things happen to my son?"

asked Maureen.

"You should!" replied Norman. "And that's what I'm trying to say! They'll close the plant after this, Maureen. I'll lose my job. We'll lose this house. What'll happen to Billy then?"

Veronica touched Danvil lightly on the arm.

"Can I get next door?" she asked.

"We'll get by," said Maureen. "We've got my job and you can get another and…"

"These old terraces share loft space," said Danvil, "but come on, Billy can survive without that bear for now. Just wait here till we get the all clear and give it to him after, when everything's safe."

Veronica stared at him and wondered how many times he'd heard unnatural noises breach the wall between his and Billy's bedroom.

She made for the hallway. He tried to grab her arm, but caught only the strap of her handbag. She shrugged it off and hurried up the stairs.

"You think it's easy to lose everything and start over?" asked Norman, his voice almost manic. "Think again, woman. Think of your precious son rooting through bins and sleeping in the gutter, because that's what this night means. That's what's going to happen to us."

"Not if they get us first," said Billy, his voice light, airy, matter-of-fact.

"Billy, this is no time for—"

Maureen's rebuke was interrupted by a sudden boom that coincided with the lights going out. She cried out in alarm. Danvil, who'd been climbing the stairs in pursuit of Veronica, yelped as he missed a step and tumbled back down to the bottom.

"That was him!" screamed Maureen. "He's got free! He's cut the power!"

"This is what it'll be like, Maureen," said Norman. "No money, no lights, no food."

Veronica looked down into the darkness at the bottom of the stairs. She couldn't see Danvil, but she could hear him whimpering in pain.

"Stay close, Billy!" said Maureen. "Mummy's got a knife! She'll keep you safe!"

"Safe from the bailiffs?" asked Norman. "Safe from social services? You should run, Billy, there's no future for you here!"

"No! Billy! Come back!"

The drama next door passed from earshot. Veronica looked up to the landing and a bare ceiling. There had to be a hatch to the loft up there somewhere.

"Veronica, I could use your assistance," called Danvil from the shadows.

Reflexively, Veronica gripped the arm of Mr Teddy slightly tighter. She began a cautious ascent of the remaining steps.

"Veronica, I'm hurt. Don't leave me."

She arrived on the landing. There was no sign of a hatch here. She walked on toward the open door of the bedroom.

"Veronica, are you still punishing me?"

She stopped in the bedroom doorway. The curtains inside were drawn back, but there was nothing to be seen beyond the window, just a blank grey mass.

"Veronica, wasn't shooting me enough?"

A gunshot rang out downstairs. Veronica flinched.

"Veronica, I'm bleeding."

She walked on, scanning the ceiling, finding her peripheral vision better at picking out details. She reached the window without finding a hatch. A second gunshot echoed through the house. She felt the sound as a punch to her gut.

"Veronica, I'm dying."

She tried to ignore his words. Find the hatch, focus on finding the hatch. She turned back to the door. A shadow rose up from the far side of the bed. It did not rise far. A pale shaft of moonlight cut through the smoke and revealed the shadow had the face of a young boy.

"Billy?"

The boy shook his head.

"Don't play games, Mummy. You know my name."

He smiled at her affectionately. A young girl climbed out from under the bed and stood next to him.

"Veronica," called Danvil's voice, "think of the future we could have had."

"I don't recognise this place," said the young girl.

"This is Mummy and Daddy's room," the young boy told her.

A tug came at Veronica's sleeve.

"Will you bake me cookies, Mummy?" asked another young girl, this one wearing a ribbon in her blonde hair.

Veronica pulled her arm free, but struggled to prize her gaze from the wide eyes staring up at her. When she did, she found herself in a changed room. Fresh wallpaper hung on the walls. A different duvet lay on the bed and two more children were bouncing up and down upon it. Another boy in shorts came rushing up to her.

"Look at my picture, Mummy!"

A crudely painted picture was thrust into her hand. It showed a man and a woman smiling and holding hands with a space occupied by a flickering blur of different children that might have been.

"Did I get the eyes right?" asked the boy. "Everyone says I have Daddy's eyes."

The only patch of the blur that remained the same was a pair of dark, unblinking eyes.

"I have Daddy's eyes too!" cried the girl with the ribbon in her hair.

"And me!"

"And me!"

The children filling the room joined a chorus of "me too" and every one stared up at Veronica with the eyes of her dead husband. She forced her way out onto the landing, but the children swarmed after her.

"Oh Veronica, the future we could have had," lamented Danvil, hauling himself to the top of the stairs. "The happiness you threw away. How many times did you shoot me, Veronica? I forget."

He held her gun in his hand. He put it to his temple and pulled the trigger. The front of his skull exploded across the wall.

The children screamed, huddling together, allowing Veronica to kick open the door to the bathroom. No hatch. On to the spare room – there!

Danvil's form stirred. He spoke, but the words came out slurred and warped by his shattered jaw.

"But even death wasn't enough, was it, Veronica? You wanted me lost too."

A wind blew across the landing. She had known such a wind before. It came and changed everything. The hatch was too high, so she began a desperation search of the spare room for something to stand on.

The children appeared at the door. Together they carried a chair.

"Not high enough!" called one and they scampered off again.

"But tell me, Veronica, how can I be truly lost if you still remember me?"

The children returned with a footstool. They placed it onto the seat of the chair. When Veronica stood on it she was able to push the hatch open. She reached up and, with the assistance of the children, climbed into the loft.

"Don't forget Mr Teddy," said the girl with the ribbon in her hair.

Veronica had left him on the floor while she made her ascent. Standing on tiptoe, the girl held the bear aloft with both hands. Veronica reached down and took his furry paw.

"Promise you'll come back, Mummy," said the girl.

All Veronica saw when she looked down were the eyes of her dead husband staring back at her. She withdrew into the pitch black of the roof-space and pointed herself in the direction of Billy's house. Timber beams full of splinters were the only safe path between squares of insulating foam. She could not see the way ahead, yet did look back to the faint light from the hatch. The nervous voices of the children were lost to the rising whistle of the wind. Veronica gripped Mr Teddy's arm between her teeth and focussed on what she could feel beneath her hands and knees. She thought of nothing else.

"Billy? Billy?" called Maureen's tremulous voice from below.

"You always said he was good for nothing," came Norman's faint reply, "now that's all he's going to get."

Veronica stopped moving. Floorboards creaked directly beneath her.

"Are you hiding, Billy?" asked Maureen. "You're right to hide. That man's still here, Billy. Don't let him find you. Stay hidden. Mummy's coming. She's got her knife. She'll keep you safe."

"He's not hiding, woman, he's gone. Run away."

"Is that you, Norman? It is, isn't it? I know it's you and you can just shut up! He is here! Billy? Billy!"

Veronica edged along the beam, away from the cries of Billy's parents. The rough wood made her hands raw and tore holes in her stockings. The smell of an infrequently washed teddy bear filled her nostrils with each anxious breath.

She crawled on another few metres before stopping. There she listened until she was sure the room below was empty. Then she sat up on the beam and kicked a heel down through the insulating foam. The thin plaster below flexed. A second kick broke it open.

Balancing her ribs on the beam and transferring Mr Teddy to a hand, Veronica peered down into a bathroom. A light flashed up into her eyes. She pulled back and the beam swung away. When the retina burn faded, Veronica ventured a second look. Billy sat on the closed lid of the toilet with a drawing pad on his knees. In one hand he held a pencil, in the other his torch.

Veronica kicked away more plaster and then dropped her shoes down onto the tiled floor. She followed after them, falling awkwardly on landing.

"Maureen!" shouted Norman's voice from somewhere beyond the bolted door. "He's down here! Come quick!"

Footsteps passed by the door and hurried down the stairs.

Veronica picked herself up to sit on the edge of the bath. She slipped her shoes back on and then fingered the holes in her stockings. The torchlight illuminated her again. It moved from her face to the teddy bear in her hand, then back to the drawing pad. Shadow prevented Veronica from seeing the expression on Billy's face.

"You bastard!" cried Maureen. "You lying bastard!"

"I told you he's gone!" said Norman. "Face the facts, woman! We've lost everything, including the boy!"

Veronica leant over to Billy and studied his drawing.

"What is it?" she asked.

"The monster from under my bed," he replied.

"It looks scary."

"There are lots of them actually, but this one's the worst. He tells the others what to do."

Veronica nodded.

"I'd never seen it," continued Billy, "so Thomas said I

should draw it. He said it wouldn't stop me being scared, but least I'd be able to see what I was scared of."

Veronica looked at the crudely-rendered demon from Billy's imagination and wondered how real it could be.

"He'd be scarier with more spikes on his face and chain-saws for fingernails," she said.

Billy's pencil stopped moving. Lines creased his forehead as he considered the sketch's face and fingers. Then the lines vanished, replaced by a smile.

"Are you scared of anything?" he asked, his pencil scratching at the paper once more.

Veronica thought for a moment and then retrieved a cigarette packet from her coat pocket. It was empty save for a photograph.

"But that's just a man," said Billy.

Veronica nodded. She returned the photograph to its box and the box to her pocket. Billy frowned at the monster he'd drawn.

"Don't you threaten me, woman!" warned Norman's voice from downstairs.

"I want my son back!" shouted Maureen in reply. "Where is he?"

"I told you! Gone! Turned his back on you and your suffocating ways!"

A scream rang out from below, followed by a cry of pain. Footsteps raced back up the stairs. Veronica stood and faced the bathroom door.

"It's time I faced them," said Billy.

For a moment she thought he meant his parents, but his gaze was fixed on the finished picture in his hands.

"Are they still under the bed?" she asked.

"They're everywhere now," replied Billy. He took the pencil and reinforced the black marks that were the beast's eyes. "But this one's in the airing cupboard."

The airing cupboard stood at the far end of the room. Its unremarkable white door was closed. Billy handed Veronica the torch.

The running footsteps outside halted and the bathroom door juddered. The handle rattled.

"Billy? Are you in there? Unlock the door!" insisted his mother.

Slow, heavy footfalls ascended the stairs.
"You cut me, woman. You cut me."
Billy looked back at Veronica. She did not say anything. Mr Teddy hung limply from her hand, his button eyes black and lifeless. Billy looked back to the airing cupboard.
"He's in there! Billy's in there!"
"Give me the knife, Maureen."
"No! You open that door. You get our son."
A grunt and the bathroom door juddered again. Billy did not turn. He reached out and flipped up the latch on the airing cupboard.
The bathroom door crashed open. Norman stumbled into the glare of the torch and recoiled from its brightness. Veronica turned the spotlight onto Maureen; pale and wide-eyed, bloodied knife in her hand. Then she sent the beam sweeping across the wall and onto the boy climbing into the airing cupboard. The light did not touch the blackness contained within, but it did pick out coiled shadows that glistened and writhed and curled about Billy before a blast of fetid breath sent them lashing out into the room. The adults cowered and covered their heads, but the tentacles did not touch them. Instead, they withdrew just as quickly, rushing back into the dark and slamming the airing cupboard shut with Billy inside.

Thomas Locke and Veronica Drysdale walked up the path to Billy's front gate. The air was clear and fresh and a full moon shone down from the sky. A distant voice announced through a loudhailer that "it is now safe to leave your homes. This is an official public health announcement. I repeat: it is now safe to leave your homes..."
Locke opened the gate for the Veronica.
"I need a new handbag," she said, stepping onto the pavement. "And a new gun."
"Didn't Billy teach you that sometimes problems can be resolved peacefully?"
They turned back to the front door. Billy waved at them cheerily. Locke waved back and nudged Veronica into doing the same. She even made Mr Teddy wave a little wave of his own. Maureen kept her hands firmly by her side. Judging

that Billy had bid a sufficient farewell, she ushered him back inside and closed the door.

The private detective and the murderous widow began walking away up the street. Veronica studied the stuffed bear Billy had given her.

"So what monster did you face?" she asked.

Locke didn't reply until the force of Veronica's stare pressing at the side of his head made him relent.

"Lafarge isn't great company at the best of times," he sighed. "Less so when he's stuck in a kitchen without adequate coffee-making facilities."

She frowned. Locke changed the subject.

"Where are you sleeping tonight?"

Veronica shrugged stiffly.

"Wherever."

They walked on in silence for a while.

"I guess there are worse places."

Maureen switched on her bedside light, switched off the room light and climbed into bed next to her husband.

"I don't understand it," she said. "After all the fuss with that gas cloud and the hallucinations and everything, there's been none of Billy's usual nonsense tonight. I just checked and he's sleeping soundly with the light off."

A loud rumbling snore came in reply. Maureen nudged her husband hard in the ribs.

"I was saying he's asleep, Norman. No mention of monsters or anything."

"I heard," he replied, opening one eye a fraction to cast a contemptuous glance.

"Even over your snoring?"

"I don't snore, woman."

Another rumbling snore shook their mattress beneath them. Maureen looked at her husband and then, slowly, leaned down to stare into the darkness under the bed.

INTERLUDE IV

Locke threw his weight against the door. It flexed, but Billy's mother had clearly barricaded the far side. Two dull cracks described Veronica's attempt to shoot out the lock on the back door. The handle turning ineffectually told of her failure.

"Find another way in!" shouted Locke. "Get Billy to the Office. He'll be safe there."

Veronica hesitated before thrusting the gun back into her bag, snatching up Mr Teddy and hurrying from sight. He looked around the empty kitchen. The strip light fixed to the ceiling hummed softly. Glowing blue digits on the front of the cooker told the time. A vague scent of rotting leftovers came from the bin. The still air pricked painfully at his skin and his ears popped at a mounting pressure bearing down upon this house and the surrounding land.

A scrap of paper emerged from a crack in the skirting board caused. Palpations gripped Locke's heart. Surely Lafarge would not send him away again?

The paper reached his foot and crawled up his leg and into his hand. He straightened out the irregular folds and read the message. He took an unsteady breath.

"Yes," he told the waiting Lafarge. "May the fifth at twenty-two minutes past five."

Keepsake Garden

The note read 'The Office of Lost and Found'. Veronica Drysdale tore it from the door and threw the door open. She expected to see blood inside. There was none. But there was bone; exposed, splintered, jutting out from dry meat wrapped in pale flesh. There was a foot. There a rib. The head was thankfully hidden somewhere behind the stacks of junk that otherwise filled the room.

Speeding lights cut jagged lines through the darkness. Warning cries cleared a path. Small ones led, larger ones chased behind. The stench of death drew them on.

"Thomas!" shouted Veronica. "Thomas! Are you here?"

His face appeared at a doorway across the room.

"Is something wrong?" he asked.

"You have a dismembered corpse on your floor," she replied, "and the police are on their way."

Thomas Locke blinked slowly at her and then noticed for the first time the body parts littered about his feet.

Sirens fell silent as the convoy drew close to the abandoned train station. Authorised firearms officers checked their rifles one last time.

"The police don't come here," said Locke. "When I was back in the tower block they raided every other flat, but never The Office."

Veronica had stopped trying to convince him. She was stuffing bits of sawn up femur into a dusty carpet-bag she'd extracted from one of the junk piles.

A sniper took up position on the opposite platform. Two of his colleagues ran along the overgrown tracks, keeping low until they were out of sight of the station windows. He checked his sights and took aim at a man moving beyond one of the broken panes.

* * *

"Did I miss anything?" asked Veronica. The carpet-bag was full, as was a Tesco carrier bag and a heavily-taped cardboard box that once housed a Henry vacuum cleaner.

"What are you going to do with all that?" asked Locke.

"Get it out of here."

"You can't just take things from The Office."

"If the police turn up and find bits of dead body…"

"I told you. The police don't come here."

The bellow of a loudhailer begged to differ.

"This is the police. Armed units have the building surrounded. Come out with your hands up."

Black boots advanced into the station's entrance hall and took up tactical positions around the waiting room door. Two more officers followed carrying a battering ram.

"They shouldn't have come," said Locke.

"But they did. We need to leave. Now."

Locke nodded.

"Right after I've got a few things."

The sniper cursed as his target moved from view. An officer positioned outside the window risked a glance inside. A frenzy of radio chatter followed.

The battering ram smashed the door from its hinges. Guns swarmed through the breach into the waiting room.

"Armed police! Do not move!"

The figure standing by the window did not move. About his feet were scraps of paper. Despite the light of the bare bulb shining from the ceiling, his hat and flowing coat were cast as silhouette.

Two officers hurried forward to cuff him.

The signal box stood two hundred metres from the disused station. Veronica emerged from its rotted door dragging the carpet-bag with one hand and carrying the Tesco bag with the other. Locke followed behind. Awkwardly cradled in his arms was the cardboard box, a toiletries bag and a small, black cat figurine.

"Across the tracks and through that gap in the trees," said Locke.

The carpet-bag got snagged on one of the sleepers. Locke spilled a pectoral muscle and a foot from the box whilst trying to set it free.

Gunfire sounded in the distance. It was eerily brief.

The spilled appendages were lost until a fleeting shaft of moonlight cut through the clouds. The foot lay a few feet away in long grass. Locke returned it to the box and noticed a tattoo beneath its severed ankle - a butterfly entwined in barbed wire. Veronica found the pectoral muscle by inadvertently stepping on it.

Progress down the wooded slope leading away from the train tracks was slow. When they reached the shallow stream at the bottom, Veronica threw down her baggage in disgust.

"Did you know it'd be like this?"

"It's usually a little deeper…"

Veronica stamped into the water. It didn't rise above the hem of her jeans.

"We can't dump the stuff here."

"No," agreed Locke. It really had been much deeper the last time he was here.

Veronica glared at him. He set down the cardboard box and pushed his chilled hands into the pockets of his blue puffer jacket.

"Thank-you for coming to warn me," he said.

"How did it get there?" she snapped.

"What?"

"The body! How did it get in the Office?"

"I don't understand." Locke was sure that Veronica knew as well as he did that things just turned up at the office. There was no how. There was no why.

"No, *I* don't understand," she said, "none of this. Just accept it, I told myself, the answers will come. But they didn't."

"No," agreed Locke.

"No? Is that all I'm going to get? What about an explanation?"

Locke hung his head. His thumbs rubbed furtively against the lining of his jacket.

"You don't need to worry about the body."

"I don't care about the body." Even as she spoke, the world about them shifted. The carpet-bag disappeared. The Tesco bag followed. She waved a hand at the cardboard box as it too vanished. "What is this? Magic? Supernatural forces?"

"I don't know," replied Locke, weakly.

"You must know something."

"I know if you try to explain it, whatever reason you come up with, it'll be wrong."

"Is it him? Is it Lafarge? Should I ask him?"

Locke looked up at Veronica, silently pleading for her questions to stop.

"There's a reward, you know?" she said.

"For what?"

"Catching the killer." There had been seven other victims. All of them cut into pieces. "Maybe if you had some money, you wouldn't need to do everything he said."

Locke's gaze fell to the mud around his feet.

"It's not that simple."

"You can find anything. You can find this killer."

"If Lafarge wants me to find something, I can. Suddenly I know where to go and what to do. The rest of the time…" His words tailed off. Locke didn't know what else he could say, but still Veronica expected more. She stepped from the stream to stand in front of him with arms folded. He could feel her breath against his face. Locke turned away. "And don't ask me why, because I don't know. That's just the way it works."

"Then we'll find another way."

Harriett Bell went to the tattoo parlour two weeks after her eighteenth birthday. Her friends had been drinking, but she was sober. The slightest lingering whiff of alcohol would allow her mother to write this off as the foolish act of a young girl under the influence. But it wasn't, it was a statement. She was grown-up now. She could make grown-up decisions. Harriett told her friends the butterfly wrapped in barbed wire was symbolic of her teenage angst, but the truth was that she simply liked that picture the best in the catalogue.

The tattooist told her it would hurt.

"My life is hurt," Harriett replied, because her mother still insisted on an eleven o'clock curfew.

Five years later, Veronica Drysdale asked that tattooist whether he remembered tattooing an ankle with a butterfly wrapped in barbed wire.

He said no.

The taxi driver knew the girl was going to throw up. Even if she paid the soiling fee, that didn't make the prospect of cleaning vomit off his back seat at two in the morning any more appealing. Fate saved him that chore by sticking a nail in his front tyre.

"Fifteen minutes and I'll have it changed," he told his passenger.

She sat on the backseat with the door open and her bare legs swung out so her stilettos could rest on the curb. Her head was between her knees. She waved a hand dismissively.

"Is okay," she said, before the inevitable regurgitation of dinner landed in the gutter. Some of it splattered her ankles. The driver watched mucus dribble down past a butterfly and barbed wire tattoo.

She coughed and pulled herself out of the car. The cabbie made a cursory offer of support; extending a hand that would be whipped away if she tried to take it. Despite the short skirt, bared flesh and pretty face, the smell of vomit laced with alcohol meant he wanted to avoid physical contact.

"Is okay," said Harriett Bell again, "I'm almost home. I can walk the rest of the way."

She wiped her mouth with the back of her hand. This removed the last traces of vomit, but smeared her lipstick.

"Are you sure?" he asked.

She nodded, handed over a five pound note and tottered off down the street. The taxi driver sighed and got back to changing his flat tyre.

Five days later, he saw a picture taped to a lamppost. It showed a butterfly wrapped in barbed wire above the following text: 'Have you seen a girl with this tattoo on her ankle? If so, please call the following number: 07700 318 008'.

He did not.

* * *

Thomas Locke yawned and then sipped at his tea again. It was still too hot. He waved across the internet café at the girl behind the counter.

"Could I have a smidgeon more milk in this?" he asked.

"Sure you can, love. No, don't get up. I'll bring it over."

She dispensed the milk and then peered over his shoulder.

"Who are you looking for again?" she asked.

The computer screen he was using displayed a series of passport photographs, holiday snaps and graduation pictures. Some faces were smiling, some were sullen, all of them were lent a curious melancholy by the text running alongside: Melinda Hughes, last seen by her friends in a Bingo parlour car park, 16th, April, 2006; Temuri Hadji called into work sick on 3rd, February, 2007 and not heard from since; Freddy Tait rang his brother from Cambodia on 27th, June, 1998…

"I don't know," replied Locke. "A girl, young, probably went missing in the last few weeks."

"Didn't you think you'd found her the other day?"

Locke smiled ruefully.

"I followed it up, but she didn't have the tattoo."

"I suppose they only turn up on that website if someone reports them as missing," said the waitress.

Locke nodded and she nodded too. An awkward moment followed where both tried to figure out whether that was the end of the conversation. As neither came up with anything to say, the girl returned behind the counter and resumed vengeful fantasies about her ex-boyfriend, a guitarist who documented his infidelity with a song about a butterfly bound in barbed wire.

Veronica was at home alone when a knocking came at the door. She'd been watching television in a silk negligee and a mink wrap – she wasn't expecting visitors. She kicked a rusty revolver out from under a tatty armchair and checked the chamber. Only three bullets left, plenty.

A second round of knocking commenced.

She made no move to answer it. Whoever was outside could knock until they chose to leave peacefully or else they could make the mistake of forcing entry. She was bored, so kind of hoped it would be the latter. The news on the television continued to play out its twenty-four hour warning that a killer was on the loose and we would all be murdered in our beds. And then the knocking stopped and Thomas Locke emerged from the bathroom carrying his toiletries bag and the black cat figurine.

This rather startled Veronica. So much so she fell off the sofa.

"Sorry, I knocked," he said, "but..."

"But what?" she yelled, the barrel of the gun demanding an answer.

"I didn't want to disturb you."

"So you magic yourself into my bathroom? What if I was on the toilet? How could anything possibly disturb me more than you just turning up in my flat—?"

"I told you, it's not magic."

"Whatever. What are you doing here? And when are you leaving?"

Locke looked sheepish.

"I go where The Office goes."

Veronica glared at him and then a creeping dread turned her gaze over to a newly arrived box of crockery by the bed, then onto a rotting rocking horse by the window and a stack of CDs on the sill and some faded porn magazines on the settee and odd socks draped over the breakfast bar and a partly dismantled lawnmower by that box of crockery and...

"You cannot be serious," she hissed under her breath.

A sudden bag of mouldy football boots on the carpet almost tripped her up as she stormed over to the front door. The security chain was thrown off and the key turned in the lock. White knuckles gripped the handle and yanked the door open.

Stuck on the peeling paint of its exterior was a torn piece of ruled paper. On this, black marker pen had written the words: 'The Office of Lost and Found'.

Veronica slammed the door shut and turned back to Locke. The space between them was now filled by an upturned bicycle without wheels, a teetering pile of books and twelve-string guitar minus the strings.

"I want all of this junk out of my flat."

Three hubcaps appeared by her bare feet.

"It goes where the office goes," replied Locke, stepping out from behind a recently arrived grandfather clock missing a pendulum. "Besides, it's not exactly your flat."

"It is exactly my flat," said Veronica, stressing each syllable with a jab of her revolver, "the old woman left it to me."

"Only because she thought you were her grand-daughter."

Locke put his cat figurine and toiletry bag on the breakfast bar, which was now otherwise covered in screws, washers and pen tops.

"If her grand-daughter were here or the old woman were still alive, that might be a problem, but as I see it, the only problem here is you and all this shit you've brought along with you."

Locke half-shrugged an apology.

"And you just accept it, don't you?" continued Veronica. "No defence, no explanation, that's just the way it is." She kicked over the upturned bicycle. It crashed down on top of a set of brass oil lamps. "And it's bullshit. It's all bullshit. Like the news; obsessing over all these murders and getting nowhere. All these bodies without names - is another one going to turn up here? Am I going to wake up one morning next to the head of another girl who never existed?"

"She existed," said Locke, quietly.

"So find her."

"But that's why we've got the posters. Checking missing persons, going door to door—"

"And none of it's worked, so we try another way. Your way."

"I told you, I can't."

"And I'm telling you, I'm not having dismembered corpses turning up in my flat, so you're going to try."

There were three urinals in the gents' toilet of the Dodo nightclub. Two of them were in use, the middle one left vacant by convention. The sound of pee tinkling against porcelain provided a clear treble over the relentless, stomach-quivering bass emanating through the building.

Thud. Thud. Thud.

The heavy footsteps drowned out the bass until they stopped at that middle urinal. The two men relieving bladders on either side gave wary, sidelong glances. The arrival stared first at one man's penis and then the other. Both hurriedly tried to finish their business and be on their way, but for the slightly-better endowed of the two, their effort came too late. A large hand grabbed the back of his head and slammed his face into the wall. White tiles shattered as blood exploded from his broken nose.

Veronica squeezed the nail trimmer. A toenail flew off in the direction of the partly dismantled lawnmower by the bed. She moved to retrieve it, then sunk back onto the settee after remembering the matchbox full of dried scabs she'd found in the cutlery drawer. You couldn't be clean and tidy in the Office of Lost and Found.

Locke was hunched down in a corner, biting at his fingernails. Veronica made sure her next clipping bounced off his head.

"I told you," he muttered, "if it happens, it happens when it happens and not before."

"About time, lover-boy," she shouted over the nightclub music. "I was just about to… Hey, are you trying to start a new fashion or something?"

Lover-boy did a rapid clothing audit. His white shirt was still white, his jeans unspoiled and their flies were definitely fastened after his trip to loos. He clasped a hand to his face. Nose, mouth, cheeks; all present and correct.

"What are you on about?" he shouted back at the girl he'd met twenty minutes ago and whose name he thought was Justine.

"On your head," said Justine.

Lover-boy yelped. His fingers touched two dangling *things* protruding from his over-gelled hair.

"They're only deely-boppers," said Justine. She reached out and removed a headband mounted with two six-inch long springs, each tipped with a plastic star. "I haven't seen a pair of these in ages…"

"They look cuter on you," said Lover-boy, sliding the headband over the girl's blonde curls. He took the opportunity to kiss her.

"Did you get them then?" asked Justine once they'd come up for air.

"What?"

"You know what. What you went to the bogs for. Don't tell me you forgot."

"Of course not. I… didn't I just go in to pee then?"

She leaned close and whispered in his ear.

"Condoms."

"Oh, right," said Lover-boy, a smile creeping across his face as her tongue flicked his earlobe. "I'll definitely remember this time."

"I don't think so," replied Justine, taking his hand. "We'll get some on the way back to my place."

She led the way through the bodies thronging the Dodo nightclub. By the time they reached the exit, Lover-boy had counted another five guys wearing deely-boppers and still hadn't remembered where his had come from.

Veronica emerged from the toilet to see Locke halfway out of the window to her flat.

"I've got a lead!" he cried. "I'll meet you outside."

He threw himself over to a drainpipe and disappeared from view. She crossed to the window – a journey complicated by the flat's spontaneous accumulation of random junk over the last few hours – and peered outside. Locke was clinging to the exterior plumbing while staring intently at a spider weaving a web.

"Where is this lead going to lead us?" she asked.

"Who knows?" replied Locke.

Veronica nodded, then slid the window shut and locked it. Her negligee and wrap had been exchanged for a black dress, stockings and high-heeled ankle boots; remnants of the limited wardrobe permitted by her ex-husband. She added a long coat to the ensemble, switched off the lights and headed out.

Justine and Lover-boy headed back to her place. While he skipped eagerly along, she had her arms folded and a sour expression on her face. Only the merry bouncing of the deely-boppers atop her head matched her companion's mood.

"Are you okay?" asked Lover-boy.

"Buying condoms, good. Buying a kebab, not so much."

Lover-boy paused in mid-bite.

"But it's traditional. You telling me you don't like them?"

Justine shook her head. Lover-boy frowned and tried to weigh up the merits of sliced meat against their burgeoning relationship. Fearing she might lose out come the final judgement, Justine stepped close and rubbed her hand against the crotch of his jeans.

"You know, maybe if you got rid of the kebab, we wouldn't need to wait to get back to my place to use those condoms."

Veronica arrived in the alleyway behind her flat where wheelie bins fraternised. She craned her head back. Locke was no longer clinging to the drainpipe. He was now perched at the edge of the slate roof, three floors up, the pale skin of his face almost luminous against the night sky.

"... but the fly managed to get free," explained Locke, "and I managed to follow it this far and then... I think it went off in that direction." He pointed in that direction. Veronica didn't bother to look. "What's that building over there?"

Veronica turned her head.

"From down here, I can't see anything past the chippy," she replied.

"It's tall and pointy. Like a church."

"Then I think it's a church."

"Then that's where we need to go."

Justine was backed up against the door of the Episcopalian church. Lover-boy kissed her hard while failing to unzip his flies.

"Let me," suggested Justine.

While she unfastened his jeans, he kissed her neck and ran one hand roughly through her hair. The deely-boppers were knocked to the ground. His other hand reached down to her crotch. About five seconds later he screamed.

Veronica and Locke were fifty yards away down a nearby street. The sound set them running.

"For Christ's sake, how drunk were you?" shouted a distraught voice up ahead. "I told you my name was Justin! I told you!"

When they reached the church, nobody was to be seen.

"Whatever happened here, I think it's probably best we missed it," said Veronica.

Locke handed her a pair of deely-boppers. She dumbly accepted them. A few steps later, he handed her a half-eaten kebab.

"And what are these?" she asked.

"Clues. Where's the nearest kebab shop?"

"A bunch of folks came out the Dodo nightclub wearing 'em," said the proprietor of the nearest kebab shop, nodding at the deely-boppers. "Reckon they must have been handing them out or somethin'."

"I dunno where they got them," said a bouncer at the Dodo nightclub. "We got no promotions or anything like that on, right, Reg? Nah, hen night probably."

"You're probably right," agreed Locke. "And you say you've had no trouble tonight?"

"Nope, except with me haemorrhoids. Play up they do in this cold weather."

Veronica emerged from the ladies toilet at the Dodo nightclub.

"Nothing in there," she shouted to Locke over the music. "Anything in the gents?"

He leant against a wall with the front of his shirt collar gripped in a fist. His nostrils flared with each rapid breath. His eyes danced frantic saccades.

"Thomas, did you find anything?"

He muttered a reply she couldn't hear.

"Forget it. I'll go look myself."

Veronica stormed into the men's toilet. Shouts of protest were quickly followed by an assortment of smutty remarks. She ignored them.

Water covered the floor. Packets of condoms floated beneath a vending machine that had been beaten out of shape. The source of the flooding was the left-most urinal, the basin of which lay in two pieces on the floor. A section of tiles above were either missing or veined with cracks. Blood splattered the area.

She returned to Locke, bristling with questions. What happened here? Who did this? Why didn't the bouncers mention this kind of trouble?

His vacant eyes revealed that he didn't have any answers, only more questions. Why could no one tell them who the dismembered girl was? How could eight murders leave no clues and no trace of a killer?

It was then Veronica understood why Locke gripped his own collar so tightly the flesh around his knuckles turned white. She understood why his eyes desperately sought out an alternative explanation and she shared his fear, because they both knew who could lose things so completely they would never be found again.

The large man barged the door open. An alarm began wailing. For him it was a cry from a distant world; unimportant, ignored. He carried an awkward mass in a blue rubble sack, but barely registered its dead weight. The smell of food was pungent in his nostrils, but it did not stir hunger in his stomach.

Traces of sodium light stole in through the open door and glinted off shining metal units. The large man lumbered between them, the sack dragged by one hand while the other ran across the worktops, brushing against pots and pans. He stopped on finding a large, angular knife that drew blood when he pressed a finger hard against its cutting blade. He did not feel the pain.

Gripping the handle of the knife, the large man began untying the sack. It had been silent and still until then, but now a pained whimper came from inside.

"Ssh," said the large man. "Almost done, almost over. Then he'll come and it'll be like this never happened."

Veronica and Locke walked the street in silence while around them the night's revellers sang songs, shouted insults and fought drunkenly under streetlights.

Locke was following a girl. She was tied to a couple of friends with a feather boa and they were all wearing purple wigs. When they turned a corner, he turned to follow them, but a crisp packet skipped across the road, blown by the gusting wind. He decided to follow that instead.

The crisp packet snagged against the foot of a homeless person propped up against the metal shutters of a shop. A bottle had fallen from his hand, spilling a trail of cheap whisky that Locke tracked along a gutter. The drain that swallowed up the alcohol lay opposite an alleyway where a shrill alarm vacillated at the whim of a breeze blowing open and closed the back door of an Italian restaurant.

Veronica checked her gun as they crossed the road.

Trade waste containers lined the alleyway. The noise of the alarm reverberated around them, the screeching pulses turning into a constant onslaught of noise. It drowned out everything else; the music from the nightclubs, the exuberant voices of their patrons and the banging of that door as it swung open and closed, open and closed.

"Wait," said Locke, stopping suddenly. "Kiss me."

Veronica blinked at him.

He pushed her up against the wall and pressed his lips against hers. This burst of passion was mitigated by Locke keeping his hands in his pockets and his body a respectful distance apart. Veronica had to grab his butt and pull him close as a man rounded the corner at the far end of the alleyway. When the arrival drew level with the restaurant door, he took a moment to appraise the couple fumbling with each other in the darkness.

Veronica pulled Locke's hand from his pocket and forced it around her waist. His kiss was dry and rigid, his face screwed up in concentration. She broke off and switched to kissing his neck. This allowed her to steal a glance at the shadowy figure as he disappeared inside the restaurant and shut the door behind him. The alarm ceased moments later.

"Have you never kissed someone before?" she asked, pushing Locke away and using the back of a hand to remove his taste from her lips.

"Not that I recall," he replied.

"How did you know someone was coming?"

"I didn't," replied Locke, heaving aside the waste container next to them. "I was trying not to disturb this guy."

Hunched down in shadows previously hidden by the bin

was a spindly youth clad in a ragged cagoule. He appeared to be extracting a traffic cone from the ear of another lad passed out on the ground.

Veronica's mouth dropped open.

Discovered, the youth panicked. He gave a quick tug on the cone, which came free with a pop, then scrambled to his feet and ran off down the alleyway.

Locke took chase. Veronica hurried after them, but did not risk breaking into a run in her high-heeled boots. She turned one corner to see Locke rounding a second. When she reached that corner, he was gone.

She walked to the T-junction at the end of the passageway. There was nothing to her left, but to her right was Locke and a dead end piled high with rubbish.

"Where did he go?" asked Veronica.

Locke didn't need to answer, for it was then she saw the black, broad-brimmed hat and a long, flowing coat. A fresh breeze whipped up vortices of dust and the surrounding trash began to tremble.

Lafarge stepped forward and conjured a gale that drove paper into the air and sent shadows racing across the brick-work walls. Veronica threw her arms up in front of her face as the dead end's detritus swirled about her head, the noise a roaring in her ears. She closed her eyes tight and in the featureless blackness behind them she found him waiting.

The wind subsided.

The paper rustled gently as it drifted back down to the ground.

Veronica opened her eyes. Locke picked up a scrap of paper from the mass that lay at their feet. It was not from the rubbish pile. It was torn notepaper, wide-ruled, but void of words. Instead it was smeared with a slick and bloody red.

"He doesn't want us looking any further."

Veronica was shaking. She didn't know if it was from fright or rage, but she decided on the latter.

"Fuck him! I don't care what he wants. We're finding this girl. We're finding out what he's done. Come on!"

She set off back the way they'd come.

"Where are you going?" called out Locke after her.

"The guy who had the traffic cone in his head, he must

know something."

"What did you see?" asked his benefactor.

"Everything," said the large man. "I didn't want to look, but—"

"You did. You had to. That was the agreement. Now what did you feel?"

"Nothing. It was like someone else doing those things. Part of me wanted it to stop, but part of me..."

"Yes?"

"Part of me wanted to see the moment when the life went from his eyes."

"Good. Then it is time I fulfilled my part of the deal."

"I asked for a rose, didn't I? It's for my garden, you see? I love my garden. I love all my pretty flowers. That's why I asked for a rose. Did you bring it?"

The large man looked up with child-like eyes at the figure standing over him. He thought not of the blood covering his hands, nor of the slick pool of blood in which he knelt. His only thoughts were of the promised rose.

"Yes," said his benefactor, "but first I bring oblivion."

Niall Dovey's journey back to wakefulness ended with a jarring headache and stomach cramps. His bed felt as it was vibrating in time with the blood pulsing around the back of his head. He rolled over and buried his face in a pillow, wishing sleep would come and banish the world once more, but the sound of his housemates making breakfast in the kitchen below cut up through the floor and the smell of frying bacon reached his nose.

He grunted and roused himself. Even if his belly was in no mood to keep food down, he wasn't about to pass up the chance to crib a free sarnie off Ella.

Niall's head swam as he threw back the sheets and hauled himself into a sitting position. Stretching hurt, so he didn't, opting instead for the slightly less taxing feat of opening his eyes. His first sight of the day was a traffic cone sitting on his bedside table. His second sight of the day was Veronica and Locke sitting on the end of his bed, smiling back at him.

Niall screamed.

"I don't remember anything," insisted Niall.

He found himself unable to take another bite of his bacon sandwich; his appetite was gone, stolen away by the hangover and cold questioning from the woman sat on the other side of the kitchen table.

"I'm sure it'll come back to you," said Veronica, leaving unsaid what she might do to him if it didn't.

He flinched and held a hand to his pained forehead. Niall's housemates were also in the kitchen and just as perturbed by the presence of this charmless woman and her companion, who was eating Rice Krispies straight from the packet.

"So you two met up with him last night?" asked Ella.

Veronica nodded.

"We found him in an alleyway having an intimate moment with a guy in a cagoule."

"Like Hell you did!" snapped Niall.

"So you remember now?"

Niall scowled and dropped the sarnie back onto his plate.

"I don't suppose these look familiar?" asked Locke, pointing to the salvaged deely-boppers he wore.

Niall shook his head.

"Just three of you live here then?" asked Veronica, enjoying the unease she was causing.

"Yes," said Ella. "Me, Niall and Brian."

Brian was in the living room watching the television news.

"They've found another body down at the tip," he called out. "Reporter says they're bagging and tagging the pieces now."

Veronica glanced at Locke. He raised an eyebrow. The deely-bopper's stars bobbed.

"And you're all renting, right?" asked Veronica.

Ella nodded.

"So how long has that fourth bedroom been empty?"

The two housemates in the kitchen looked at each other. Both began to answer, but stopped with a frown before words reached their lips.

"Do you mind if I use your toilet?" asked Locke, interrupting their confusion.

"Err, no," said Ella, shaking her head, "not at all. Out the door and on your right. Hey, Brian! When… when did Lizzie move out?"

"I dunno," he called back. "Six months ago? Maybe seven?"

"But old Teddington wouldn't leave a room vacant," said Niall. "He keeps moaning we don't pay him enough rent as it is."

"Maybe your amnesia is catching?" suggested Veronica.

Ella treated her to a tight-lipped smile before conferring in whispers with Niall.

"Where did you get these?" asked Locke, returning to the kitchen with three pewter toads.

Ella and Niall jumped from their seats to challenge him.

"Where did you get them?" asked Ella. "Have you been in my room?"

"What's up?" asked Brian, arriving from the lounge.

"He's been going through our rooms!" said Niall.

"That's my toad!" said Brian.

"And you don't know where it came from, do you?" said Locke.

The three housemates exchanged anxious glances.

"That's not the point!" insisted Ella.

"Yeah," agreed Brian. "Just put them down on the table and leave, now!"

Veronica stretched languorously and rose from her chair.

"There are few things in this world that irritate me more than wilful ignorance," she said. "Thomas, we should end this now."

"What do you mean…?" began Ella.

Veronica drew her gun.

"Oh shit," said Brian.

"Yeah," said Locke, sympathetically. "You know she shot me twice when I first met her?"

"Look, I don't remember anything," said Niall. "I wish I did! I wish I could tell you what you want to know, but there's just… nothing. Everything from last night is gone and… and I know someone else must have been living here, but that's gone too…" He turned to Ella. "You know what I'm talking about, don't you?" She nodded mutely. "And it's the worst thing; like having this hole in your head and you know something fills it, some part of your life, but it's just gone and no matter how hard you try, you can't get it back."

Niall fell silent. He stared down the barrel of Veronica's revolver and tears formed in his eyes.

"Have you ever heard of Capella Mementos?" asked Locke.

The housemates didn't dare look away from the gun, but managed tentative shakes of the head. Locke held up a pewter toad and showed Veronica the charioteer logo on its base. After a cursory glance, she returned her attention to the housemates.

"If you can bring me a copy of the Yellow Pages in the next thirty seconds," she told them, "maybe I won't have to start shooting."

Capella Mementos lay at the end of a short lane of mud and stones. Broad leafed trees surrounded the cottage, along with wild hedgerow and tall grass. A short wooden fence afforded entrance through a neat gate. A carved wooden sign hanging from rusting chains reproduced the charioteer logo.

Pink paving stones ran up to a front door made from blackened wood inset with an elliptical window of darkly-stained glass. Locke put the deely-boppers in his pocket and pressed the brass doorbell. It played a short piece by Gershwin.

A man in his forties answered the door. He suffered the double ignominy of being both big-boned and fat. His face was pock-marked by acne scars and bore a nose that was a little too big and eyes that were a little too small. On his feet were moccasins, his trousers were corduroy and his shirt bore orange and brown zigzags in some South American design.

"Now is not a good time," he said.

"Five minutes," said Locke. "We have some urgent business to discuss with you and I'm afraid any other time would be rather bad for us."

"You realise admission of such things only ups my price?" said the man.

"But it's still a price worth paying, I'm sure," replied Locke.

The big-boned man was called Rastuftary Nort.

"But you can call me Tary."

He explained that his brusque manner at the door was due to the presence of another guest. He showed them into a fine, rustic kitchen.

"If you could wait here, I shall just ask my friend to entertain herself for a few minutes."

Their host departed. Locke took a seat. Veronica took to pacing up and down the flagstone floor. Tary returned moments later.

"My friend has recently lost someone dear to her," he told them. "I am doing what I can to help her through this trying time. I would offer you tea, but you did say this would be quick."

"Can I just be clear on what it is that you do?" asked Locke.

Tary raised an eyebrow.

"If you don't know what I do, why are you here?"

"To find out the difference between a traffic cone and one of these."

Locke placed the three pewter toads on the table. Tary picked one up and examined it briefly before smiling.

"My friend, the difference between this and a traffic cone is the difference between da Vinci and the man who paints lines on the road. That you are here instead of consorting with one of those low-lifes that sully the memeker trade speaks volumes about your judgement, Mr…?"

"Smith," replied Locke.

"Of course, it usually is. Right, if we're keeping this short, no use dilly-dallying further. The two questions I ask now form the crux of our dealings, everything that follows mere details. What do you want forgetting? And who do you want to forget it?"

The ragged mass of meat had once been a person with a name. The forensic dissection of the rubbish dump was intent on finding out that name. While reporters watched from behind chain-link fencing, constables combed the mounds of trash for the smallest clue to the victim's identity.

One of those recording this activity was neither policeman nor journalist. He wore a grey suit and had no fingernails. His bright red fountain pen scratched neat words across notebook pages. Not once did his eyes look down to check what was written, so instinctive was this behaviour. Isthmus Kane knew better than anyone that memories could not be relied upon. Everything he did, everything he saw, was documented in this little black book. It described the police search. It described Kane's subsequent walk from the rubbish dump to the canal. It described the anglers he passed on the tow-path and the ducks he saw swimming between the patches of froth on the water. But it did not describe his arrival at a wall of stone, where creeping ivy almost hid an old wooden door. Isthmus Kane put away his notebook and produced a key. The ivy shrank back to let him pass.

Beyond the door was a narrow passage that led to an empty square. No sound intruded on this place; not birdsong, not traffic, not the whistling of the breeze. On the far side of the square was a letterbox. Isthmus Kane retrieved an envelope from his pocket, posted it through the slot and then returned the way he had come.

Veronica fumed in the kitchen while Locke enjoyed an amicable discussion about the weather with Tary's woman friend in the living room.

"There are some digestives in that cupboard," said Tary as he prepared the tea that he had suddenly decided they should stay for. "Be a dear and get them, please, Trixie?"

Trixie. It had been bad enough kissing Locke last night, but now she was reduced to playing his mistress and pretending her name was Trixie. She fetched the digestives and plotted revenge.

"I don't presume to tell you your business, Trixie," said Tary, filling a teapot, "but you do realise that a girl like you has alternatives?"

"Really? A girl like me? Flouncy, air-headed bimbo that I am?"

Tary looked at her over his shoulder and grinned.

"I think we both know your problem. If I remove his wife's memory of catching the two of you in flagrante, she'll be happy, because she'll be back thinking her husband is decent and faithful. And of course he'll be happy because his dirty little secret is a secret once more, but I don't see what you're getting out of this."

"Why? What do you think I should be getting out of this?"

"More than the occasional tacky necklace in exchange for a weekend of illicit sex, I'm sure. Trixie, I am not merely a craftsman, I am a facilitator of mutually beneficial exchanges."

"Which means what exactly?"

"There are people who buy memories. If you can provide me with a memory worth selling, you might not have to rely on cheating husbands to buy you your pretty baubles."

The woman on the mortuary slab possessed an artificial tan several shades darker than her fair hair. Isthmus Kane made a note of this in his little black book. He also noted that the body parts recovered from the rubbish dump were laid out on a table, ready for examination.

Fifteen minutes later, the detective inspector leading the murder investigation arrived with the police pathologist. The body parts were gone and the mortuary assistant on duty could explain neither their absence nor the presence of deely-boppers on her head.

"What kind of memory are you talking about?" asked Veronica. "Would I have to sleep with someone? Kill someone...?"

The memory was still crystal clear: taking aim as her husband fled across the garden, pulling the trigger and seeing his body lurch unnaturally as the bullet struck him in the back.

"No murder, please. I prefer not to involve myself in such morbid transactions, but certainly there are others who do."

"What then?"

"You should understand that most of my clients are not human beings like you or I. They exist somewhere far away, on the brink of... a void. They resist its pull only by remaining unique and different. Memories provide such points of distinction."

"I remember having a shit this morning, would they buy that?"

"Charming, but alas, mundane. The void eats mundane, it consumes the commonplace. No, my clients want memories that are rare and blessed with emotion. That may mean love, it may mean death, it may even mean standing on a station platform experiencing the thrill of a spotting a new train number for the first time."

Veronica nodded. Tary picked up the tea tray.

"If I did have an emotion like that," she said, "how exactly would you remove it?"

Framed photographs lined the mantelpiece: Naveen and Holly on the beach; Naveen and Holly on the ski slope; Naveen and Holly exiting the church as man and wife. Too many photographs, thought Isthmus Kane.

Holly returned from her kitchen carrying two mugs of coffee. Her baggy sweater did little to hide the fact she was seven months pregnant.

"You can tell me I'm silly if you like," said Holly, "but when I saw you standing there on the doorstep with your notebook, my heart skipped a beat. I thought you must be a policeman and you were here to tell me Naveen's been in some sort of horrible accident."

She shook her head and handed him his coffee.

"You're not being silly," Kane assured her, "and I'm quite certain Naveen hasn't been involved in any accident."

"Thank-you. I do keep telling myself that. I mean, I'm sure he just ended up at a friends' house after their night out, but it's nice to hear someone else say it."

She turned around and waddled over to the sofa. Kane pulled a steel hook from his pocket and stepped up behind her.

"This is what we use to tease out the memories," explained Tary, holding up a length of metal curved wickedly at the end.

"And you do what with that?" asked Veronica.

"Traditionally it goes up the nose, but in truth any orifice will do; ear, mouth… I have one friend whose modus operandi involves a boat hook up the rectum. He has a peculiar brand of clientele, politicians mostly." Tary laughed at Veronica's reaction. "Really, it's not as gruesome as it sounds. When I was starting out, I was told that as soon as the hook transforms into a metaphor as it enters the body and metaphors can't cause physical damage. In fact, when I was at school, I used to follow this kid around and every time he ate something, I'd be there with my hook and I'd whip out the memory without him even noticing. Of course, he ended up thinking he was bulimic despite weighing eighteen stone, but that only tickled my juvenile sense of humour."

Isthmus Kane pressed his hand down on Holly's mouth. His knees kept her shoulders pinned to the floor and however much she struggled, she could not break free. He deftly inserted the hook up her nose until it met resistance. Next came the delicate part: cutting into the subconscious and finding the memories of her husband amidst trillions of synaptic connections. But no memory existed in isolation; it joined to countless others. Isthmus Kane's art lay in deciding whether the links could be severed or whether the associated memories had to be excised too. He erred on the side of caution. Holly and Naveen first met when they were four years old. If that meant she would lose most of her past, then so be it.

He thrust the hook upwards, twisted sharply and Holly screamed.

The teapot cooled gently on its tray, momentarily forgotten, while Tary explained to Veronica the significance of the pewter toad in his hand.

"A stolen memory knows where it belongs, so we must leave behind a memento such as this. It keeps the memory displaced. The more complex the memory, the greater the craft required to create its counterweight. See the etching around the eyes, how they look almost alive? This represents a complex memory indeed."

Veronica nodded understanding. She swallowed hard, licked her lips and then spoke slowly.

"I have a memory for you, Tary. Once upon a time I was married. I had a perfect husband, a perfect home and I was absolutely happy. That's all gone now, but however much I try to stop myself, sometimes I can't help wishing that…" Her voice faltered. "I… I don't want to be wishing for things that are best left dead and buried. I want to forget, Tary. I want to forget it all. Can you do that?"

The memeker looked at her seriously.

"I can, but consider carefully what you are asking. Memories shape who we are. What kind of person would you be if that happy life you once lived was replaced by an empty hole?"

"I would be a person who didn't spend every second fearing that her perfect husband might come back."

Holly was no longer married. She never met a man called Naveen. His parents never had a son, his friends forgot him. Every trace recorded in bytes or on paper was wiped, except for the words in Isthmus Kane's little black book.

Kane was clearing the photographs from the couple's mantelpiece. At the memeker's feet was a black bin bag that already contained Naveen's clothes. A van would arrive soon to take the rubbish away.

Holly lay on the sofa, sleeping soundly. A bronze bonsai tree sat on the coffee table. Kane's mark was engraved into the base.

The wedding photograph was the last physical reminder of Naveen's existence. Isthmus Kane made a note of this before dropping it into the bag. He then turned to Holly and considered the bump under her sweater. How much would a foetus remember of its father? Kane drew out his memeker hook once more. Better safe than sorry.

Thomas Locke wondered why it was taking Veronica and Tary so long to deliver the promised tea while listening to his companion recount the effect a late spring had wrought on her garden. Mrs Bell was a pleasant enough woman. She wore a plain grey skirt and puce cardigan and illustrated her incessant chatter with effusive hand gestures rendered peculiar by the fact that she kept her wrists held firmly against her knees.

"If I still had fish in my pond, they wouldn't know what to make of this weather, of that I am quite sure. Summer one moment, winter the next. They do say fish have terrible memories though, don't they? Perhaps they don't remember. Not that I can imagine how they find out such things. How do you test a fish, Mr Smith, I ask you?"

Locke shrugged. Mrs Bell certainly didn't show any sign of the grievous loss Tary had mentioned. He cast another glance at the door. Still no sign of the tea arriving any time soon.

"Ah, but they're long gone now in any case," continued Mrs Bell. "My husband insisted on paving the whole thing over. He said it was too dangerous, what with having a young child in the house. Quite right too. Do you know how many children drown in ponds and swimming pools every year? No? Neither do I, but I'm sure it's a staggering number. Ah, such a shame Gerry passed away before we could have children. He would have made a fine father."

"I'm sorry to hear that. Did Gerry pass away recently? Tary said you'd lost someone…"

"Goodness, no. Gerry's been gone over twenty years now. My, they are taking their time fetching that tea, aren't they?"

"How long have you known Tary, Mrs Bell?"

"Ooh, it can't be more than three weeks now. Would you believe he was going to door to door selling these remarkable necklaces?"

She slipped a finger under the chain of sparkling beads she wore about her neck. Locke tried to get a better look at the picture etched into the clasp, but Mrs Bell glancing across the room prompted him to turn his head.

"No more questions, Mr Locke," said Tary from the doorway. "In fact, I think it's best that you forget you ever came here."

Through the ivy-covered door, at the end of the narrow passage, lay the empty square. On the far side of the empty square stood the letterbox and from its black slot came Isthmus Kane's envelope. Once ejected, it floated down to the ground, twitching as it fell. When it hit the smooth paving stones, the envelope's flap came unstuck. The folded paper burst open and then stiffened, darkened, returning to the brown and brittle texture of wood. Green shoots darted forth and then dissolved into drops of water and sunlight. The sliver of bark crumbled away to dust. Yet something lingered. Something that was, that had been, but no longer had any right to be. It lingered and it remembered.

"I want all of this junk out of my flat," insisted Veronica, kicking at the hubcaps lying by her feet.

"It goes where the office goes," replied Locke, stepping out from behind a grandfather clock missing a pendulum. "Besides, it's not exactly your flat."

"It is exactly my flat," said Veronica, stressing each syllable with a jab of her revolver, "the old woman left it to me."

"Only because she thought you were her grand-daughter."

Locke put his cat figurine and toiletry bag on the breakfast bar. They joined two squat china dogs amidst assorted screws, washers and pens.

"If her grand-daughter were here or the old woman were still alive, that might be a problem—"

"Stop," said Locke.

"What?"

"This has happened before."

"You mean this isn't the first time you've waltzed into my flat?"

Locke touched the head of the black cat figurine.

"Two years ago, I woke up in The Office of Lost and Found. Lafarge was in front of me, this cat was beside me. I remembered nothing."

"You told me, but I don't see how this relates."

He picked up a china dog.

"These dogs weren't here when I stepped out of the bathroom. It was a different newsreader on the television. The sky was grey, but it wasn't raining."

Her instinctive reaction was to tell Locke he was wrong, but reality was proving less reliable since she'd met him.

"Was it Lafarge?"

"I don't know…"

"This is what he does, isn't it? Loses things. You said that when he takes things, he has to give something in return. It explains the dogs. It would also explain why no one has been able to catch this killer. What if it's him, Thomas? What if Lafarge is behind it all?"

Locke shook his head slowly.

"Who is he, Thomas?"

"I don't know."

"*What* is he?"

"I… don't know."

Her questions sent him reeling into the corner, where he cowered with eyes averted. Veronica glared down at him, then banished the contemptible sight by turning to the window. Rain-water streamed down the glass and distorted the world outside. She remembered dancing on a balcony with her husband in the rain, when the warm press of his body and the cool drops against her skin made her feel more alive than any moment before or since. This rain made her feel dead; a ghost divorced from the mundane world below, where cars waited at traffic lights and people hurried along with umbrellas raised against the downpour.

She thought the sudden bleeping came from the pedestrian crossing before realising it was Locke, hunched over his mobile, dialling a number with a shaking thumb. He looked up at Veronica as he raised the phone to his ear. She imagined it ringing… once… twice…

The window shook in its frame. Rain hammered harder at the glass.

Three rings… four…

Locke's gaze did not waver, pinning her to the spot, daring her to look away. She closed her eyes and found the nightmare was already there, the black within the blackness doffing his hat in greeting.

"Veronica," whispered Locke.

"Did he come?" she asked.

Silence forced her to open her eyes. She saw Locke and the breakfast bar and the grandfather clock, but couldn't see Lafarge. She didn't need to; she knew he was standing behind her. The gun in her hand felt leaden and useless.

"He wants us to follow him," said Locke.

Veronica nodded stiffly. He attempted a reassuring smile that barely curved his mouth, before depositing the china dogs in his coat pockets and walking past her. She turned to see him step through a man-sized, matte black stain on the wallpaper.

She took several steadying breaths. Outside, pedestrians continued to hurry through the rain. Cars waited impatiently for traffic lights to turn green. Pigeons sheltered under eaves as water sluiced off the rooftops above. Out there, everything remained normal. Veronica looked back at the stain on the wall. Another deep breath and then she switched off the television, turned out the lights and departed for elsewhere.

Bin bags containing personal effects and mementos of people otherwise forgotten filled the warehouse. They had been brought here to burn and burn they did, flames melting away black plastic and feasting on the clothes, books and photographs inside.

Veronica found herself in the middle of the blaze, but she did not feel the heat. Furious tendrils of orange wrapped about her legs, but they did not burn her. Carbon filled the air, but it did not blacken her lungs. Nevertheless, it was still a distressing situation to be in.

"Thomas!"

If he replied, the roaring around her drowned out his words. She tried to move, but the combustible mass beneath her shifted suddenly and she fell into a cradle of fire.

I should be burning, Veronica told herself and the thought brought a warmth to her skin that steadily grew until sweat began to bleed through her pores. She scrambled across the pyre, slipped again and came face to face with a hand jutting up through the refuse. It was bereft of fingernails and clutched a little black book. Before her stinging eyes the pages steadily turned to ash and its owner's flesh blistered away, revealing boiling blood and charred bone.

She imagined herself suffering the same fate and a searing pain engulfed her body. The world raged red and yellow and orange and then... faded away to a flickering grey. Veronica checked her hand; the skin remained unblemished, even as the flames around her flared higher and spurred the smoke to ignite, sending a furious wave of destruction across the ceiling.

Why am I not dead? Veronica asked herself, before a shadow at the heart of the inferno appeared over her and held out a hand.

Locke defended the warehouse office with a fire extinguisher. At his feet were items rescued from the fire; charred photographs and video tapes, optical discs and official forms.

Lafarge let go of Veronica the moment they were through the office door.

"Thanks," she muttered, rubbing at fingers tingling with pins and needles.

The fire extinguisher spluttered out the last of its contents and Locke retreated, slamming the door shut against the fire.

He crouched down and touched the frame of a photograph he'd saved with a tentative finger. It proved cool enough to pick up. The glass of the frame was cracked and the picture's emulsion blistered in one corner, but the face of a woman was still visible. She wore a fake smile and stood next to a grey, featureless shape.

"That's not fire damage," remarked Veronica.

"Someone's missing," said Locke.

"So what's new?"

He tapped the face that remained.

"We've found someone who's missing them."

Lafarge vanished into another stain against the wall. The others followed. Veronica experienced another terrifying spell of utter blackness before Locke's voice once again indicated the way.

She arrived into a quaint hallway. Sunlight streamed through a stained glass oval set in a front door and across a thick pile carpet of purple swirls, red circles and white lines. An anguished moan drew her into the living room where she joined Locke and Lafarge. A heavy-set man knelt on a Persian rug and cradled a plain-looking woman in his arms. Veronica did not remember him, but she did recognise the woman.

"She was the one in the photograph."

Locke nodded.

Rastuftary Nort stroked Mrs Bell's forehead with one hand while sand trickled through the fingers of the other. Veronica noted with alarm that the woman was still breathing, even though her eyes were utterly dead.

"I know you can find it," he said, directing teary eyes first at Locke, then at Lafarge, "but can you stop it? Can he?"

Lafarge walked away through another wall, staining it with his silhouette and opening a third phantom doorway through which Locke followed.

"It wasn't my fault!" protested the grieving Tary. "I didn't know. None of us knew. I was just doing him a favour!"

He jumped to his feet and grabbed for Veronica as she entered the portal.

At the end of a pleasant suburban close, removals men ferried boxes from their van into a nearby house. Veronica appeared on the road with Tary holding her wrist. She pushed him away.

"Please, you have to understand," he said, holding up a hand and letting more sand fall through his fingers. "These are her memories, perfectly crystallised in silicon. I can't break them. I can't bring them back. It left her as nothing more than an empty shell and it won't stop there. It will do this to *everyone*."

Veronica folded her arms.

"And what do you expect me to do?"

Tary held his breath, waiting for an answer to move his lips, then sighed and watched the last grain of Mrs Bell's past tumble to the ground. Veronica turned away. Locke and Lafarge entered the house and she hurried after them. No one seemed to notice their passing. When Veronica reached the door, a bald, heavily-muscled man jogged out to intercept one of the movers and almost collided with her, but even then he didn't spare her a glance.

"I'll take that, thanks, fella," he said.

"Err, sure, Mr Moffat," said the removals man, handing over a cardboard box well-wrapped with masking tape.

"What's that?" asked a female voice.

"Nothing, love," replied Mr Moffat as he headed back inside and up the stairs.

"Paul, I thought I told you dump them before we moved," his wife called after him.

"Yes, dear."

Veronica couldn't find Locke downstairs, so followed the husband to a bedroom bare of furniture. Mr Moffat ripped tape from cardboard box and was about to delve with eager fingers into the contents when his wife called again. He muttered under his breath and left the room.

Curiosity led Veronica over to the box. She peered inside. Laid out carefully on layers of foam were hundreds of two-inch-high plastic army men. Her curiosity was disappointed. She was about to resume her search for Locke when a scrap of notepaper drifted past her ear and landed on the military toys. Words in thick black ink told her to 'break them'.

She checked over her shoulder and jumped. Tary stood there, an over-grown little boy lost.

"Watch for anyone coming," she told him and picked up one of the plastic soldiers.

"What is that?" he asked.

"It might be a clue."

She dropped it on the floor and stamped on it with her boot.

"Why did you do that?" asked Tary, nervously.

Downstairs, Paul called out to his wife.

"Rachel!"

Veronica crushed a second soldier beneath her heel. Tary stepped toward her, trembling hands clasped together.

"Why are you doing that?"

She ignored him and reached into the box again.

"Rachel!"

"What is it, Paul?"

"It's… it's the strangest thing."

"Oh, for Heaven's sake, what is?"

Veronica snapped the head off a third soldier with her fingers.

"And again," said Paul. "Why would I suddenly remember…?"

A heavy hand fell on Veronica's shoulder.

"I think you should stop," said Tary, firmly.

"Remove your hand," she replied.

"Weren't you listening outside? This isn't going to help. You need to—"

This time it was Tary's foot on the receiving end of Veronica's spiked heel. He cried out and hopped backwards. She drew her revolver and pistol-whipped him across the temple, knocking him to the floor.

"You need to show a little respect," suggested Veronica.

Tary glared back at her.

"I was at school," recounted Paul's voice from below. "It was lunchtime. I'd just finished my packed lunch when this other kid – what was his name? – he comes up to me, this mad grin on his face. Out of his pocket he suddenly whips this evil little hook and… and the bastard shoves it up my nose. Christ! How do you forget something like that? And it wasn't just the once. Other lunchtimes he did it, in the playground too. And every time I just let him walk away afterwards. It all just suddenly came back to me."

Locke appeared at the bedroom door. He took in the sight of Veronica threatening someone else with her gun and rubbed his face wearily.

"I've searched the house, but I haven't found anything," he said.

"Have you got those dogs from the flat?" asked Veronica.

Locke nodded.

"Smash them."

He pulled them from his pockets without asking why.

"Paul, where are you going?" called Rachel.

"And every time he did it to me, he left behind one of those toy soldiers," replied her husband, starting up the stairs.

Locke threw one of the dogs to the ground. It bounced. He picked it up and hurled it at the wall. The dog ricocheted off and rolled to halt on the bare carpet.

"You don't break craftsmanship like that so easily," sneered Tary.

Veronica swung her gun around and put a bullet into the china hound, which duly exploded into jagged shards.

She remembered.

She was back in Tary's kitchen. The tea was cooling on its tray and Locke was talking to Mrs Bell in the living room. Tary stood before her with a pair of curious spectacles perched on his nose. The lenses were multifaceted like a diamond, the effect an eerie kaleidoscopic of blinking eyes.

"Now, hold still," instructed Tary. "I must see this memory of yours before I can extract it."

He squinted and adjusted rotating bezels on his glasses. Veronica felt an itch behind her eyes that began to move, triggering recollections from her past until it brought up the face of her husband.

Tary's eyes opened wide with shock.

"You belonged to him."

Before she could react, Tary had thrust his hook up her nose and she was screaming.

Veronica swung her gun back toward Tary as Paul burst into the room and rushed over to the box of soldiers, forcing her to jump aside.

Tary took his chance. He ran for the door only to collide with Rachel.

"Who on earth are you?" she asked.

Paul looked round.

"Where did he come from?"

Tary grabbed Rachel and ducked behind her. When she struggled, he whipped out his memeker hook. It flashed an inch from her eye and she became very still.

"Don't hurt her!" pleaded Paul.

"Drop the gun," ordered Tary.

Paul stared at him with a terrified confusion. He was aware of only three people in the room. He couldn't see Locke or the gun or Veronica shaking her head.

"But you need me!" insisted the memeker. "I know what Kane was up to. I know how to send that thing back!"

And then his eyes went wide. A faint shadow against the wall opposite grew darker and sharper, coalescing into a shape that reached out with a black hand and stole something from inside Paul's head. Once it was gone, his rediscovered memories connected with the present – the hook wielded by the man in front of him was the same as the one carried by the kid in the playground.

The blood slowly drained from Mr Moffat's face and into muscles filling with adrenaline.

"Thirty years," he muttered, advancing. "Thirty years to lose that weight. Thirty years to convince myself I wasn't mad. And now I'm finally happy, you appear out of nowhere to threaten my wife?"

"Paul, I… I'm sorry," stuttered Tary. "I was just a boy. I didn't realise. Listen to me. Try and understand—"

But there was no reasoning with Paul. He had lost his temper. He grabbed the hook, cast it aside and drove a fist into Tary's face.

"We should have stopped him," said Veronica. She was back in her flat along with Locke and Lafarge. "He may have been a shit, but Tary knew what was going on. We needed to make him talk."

"We'll find our answers another way," said Locke. He

crossed to the breakfast bar and smashed the second china dog with a nearby dumbbell. It took a moment to process the memories recently stolen from him. "The woman at Tary's house, he told us she'd lost someone, but when I asked—"

"She didn't remember," guessed Veronica, giving a wry smile. "He made her forget someone who was murdered and didn't he say it was a favour—?"

"For whoever was burning all that stuff in the warehouse," concluded Locke. "But I don't understand that photograph. It was going to burn anyway, so why bother erasing that other face?"

Lafarge remained motionless while Veronica and Locke tossed their ideas back and forth, but the Office around him did not. Where items normally appeared and disappeared only out the corner of an eye, those close to him shifted and altered in a blur of lost and found.

"You might as well as ask why anyone would bother killing all those people in the first place," said Veronica. "Thomas, we're clearly dealing with a bunch of crazy people who are out playing by the rules of your crazy world and I'm beginning to realise that I'm actually quite happy not understanding all the finer points of this craziness." She spun the chamber of her pistol. "I just want to catch this killer and get our reward. So get Blacky here to open up another magical doorway and lead on, Sherlock."

"But it's not that sim—"

He didn't finish his oft-repeated protest. Instead, he followed his fixed gaze over to the grandfather clock and removed the deely-boppers from their place hooked around the minute hand. He stroked the headband, then strode over to the flat door, squeezed one of the stars into the keyhole and then turned it in the lock.

Locke opened the door and stepped through into a living room. A starched middle-aged couple sat on a settee and regarded two youngsters standing in front of them.

"Mom, Dad," said one of the youngsters, "I've got something very important to tell you." He took a deep breath, shuffled his feet and dabbed sweat from his brow with a finger. "Mom, Dad... this is Justin and... we're in love."

"Justin?" exclaimed Dad, leaning forward and scrutinising

his son's companion. "I thought that was a girl."

"Kevin, are you telling us you're gay?" queried Mom, tremulously.

"Of course he's not," snapped Dad, "gays like guys and this Justin looks like a girl. You can't be gay if you're going out with someone who looks like a girl."

"But surely… surely the sex," stuttered Mom, "it works differently."

"They can't do anything a girl and a boy couldn't do in a happily consenting relationship. Kevin, you tell me you get turned on by willies and moustaches and I'll believe you're gay, but until then I'll maintain my son likes tits and ass like the best of them."

Veronica joined Locke and leaned close.

"Why are we here?" she whispered.

Locke held up the deely-boppers and snapped the head-band in half.

The blood drained from Kevin's face. He doubled over and threw up on the carpet.

"Kevin!" said Justin in alarm.

"Gracious dear, are you all right?" asked Mom.

Kevin fell to his knees, shaking his head. Locke walked over to him.

"What did you see?" he asked in a firm voice.

Kevin looked up at him, his eyes wide, his lips trembling.

"He smashed his face into the wall. Blood… shouts… guys tried to stop him, but… he kept hitting him."

"Can you give me a description?"

An email arrived in the inbox of Dr Reginald Sharp, chief psychiatrist at the Hopewell secure unit. He read the message with a phone cradled to his ear and then opened the attached picture file.

"I'm sorry, Inspector, but I don't recognise this man and I really don't know why you expected it might be otherwise, I've already told you there's nothing on file—"

He listened to the reply of the policeman on the other end of the line, oblivious to the man and woman searching the office around him and the shadow standing by the window.

"I wouldn't presume to tell you your job, Inspector, but I

hardly think you can call a witness credible when it's a boy who only realises he's seen this man after breaking – what did you call them? Oh yes, *deely-boppers.*"

Veronica smashed open the framed qualification certificates hanging behind Sharp's desk and then pulled apart a stethoscope. Locke stamped on a Parisian snow globe, a Captain America coffee mug and a long arm stapler. The doctor just sniffed and shifted the phone to his other ear.

"Calm down, Inspector. So you now have five witnesses with broken deely-boppers giving this man's description, that doesn't mean I can help you."

Behind him, Veronica turned to Locke with hands raised.

"We've broken everything. Are you sure—?"

"Yes," he said. "We must have missed something."

Every pen on the Doctor's desk had been snapped in half. His papers had been torn to shreds and the photo of his wife and two daughters was impaled on a mangled darts trophy.

"That's a very fancy chair he's got there," remarked Veronica.

"A very fancy, well-crafted chair," agreed Locke.

The doctor leant forward to pinch at his forehead with his fingers and Veronica attacked the back-rest with a silver letter opener. The blade duly snapped.

"Wait!" said the Doctor. "That man, it's Howard Briggs! Yes! He was convicted for a string of murders fifteen years ago. I can't believe I didn't remember. He became quite a celebrity in my field. He swore he had no memory of his crimes and every test we ran said he believed it too. What was that, Inspector? Oh, yes, he was released three months ago." The Doctor smiled. "Glad to be of assistance."

He put the phone down and leant back in his ergonomic chair. The smile faded from his face as he gradually became aware of the carnage wrought upon his office.

"We've finally got a suspect, lads," announced the detective inspector. "We know he's killed before, so we go in armed and we don't take any chances."

The police officers in the briefing room listened intently as their superior pointed to a map and explained the plan of attack. Thomas Locke wrote down Howard Briggs' address and rejoined Veronica and Lafarge in the corridor.

"We should leave this to the police," he said. "We're not going to get any reward now."

"We might if we can get to Briggs first," said Veronica.

Locke looked at Lafarge. His partner took the address from his hand and opened a portal before them. Veronica went first this time, leaving Locke to linger behind.

"It took four of us to hold him down," said one nearby constable to another. "I can't guess what the other guy must have done. Our perp kept saying something about thirty years ago, but who holds a grudge that long?"

"Yeah," replied his colleague, "forgive and forget, I say."

Locke hung his head and then stepped through the stain on the wall.

The houses stood terraced and uniform. Their doors opened onto cracked and uneven pavements. 'For Sale' signs shaded the few windows that weren't already boarded up. No cars parked here and no litter lay in the gutters. Even the graffiti had gone unfinished, as if the artist had been drawn away from this forsaken place by the siren call of urban congress; eager to engage in the virtues and vices promised by the executive apartment blocks that lay beyond the rumble of the town's inner ring-road.

The evening sun cast Veronica's shadow long down the road, while Lafarge's darkened the sky. Locke walked past them to Howard Briggs' house, a crumbling end-terrace with lines of timber showing through holes in the tile roof.

The front door was ajar. He pushed it open and peered inside. The short hallway within housed a staircase of broken steps with a banister rail that terminated in jagged splinters halfway up. Dank green fungus clung to wallpaper peeling from disintegrating plaster. Several dead mice rotted upon bare floorboards.

Veronica entered; her revolver drawn and ready. The first door on her left was the kitchen. Raw potatoes, carrots and celery lay by the sink. All looked fresh. The knife beside them looked rusty.

She moved on, watchful of the stairs, mindful of the sound her boots made on the floor. The next door was closed. She drew back against the wall for cover and prepared to push it open.

"Better leaving it to him," suggested Locke.

Lafarge surged past, ignoring the door beside her and continuing on to the one that lay at the end of the hallway. It dissolved before him, revealing a large conservatory. The light of the sunset outside became strained and sickly as it passed through a wall of slanting glass, casting rays thick with swirling dust motes onto a large man sat quietly upon a chair, his head bowed low, his hands resting upon his knees. Around him, potted plants lined shelves bolted haphazardly to the walls. Boxes arranged on the floor were fit to bursting with gaily coloured flowers.

Veronica aimed her gun at the man and took a step forward.

"Howard Briggs?" she asked.

The seated man did not stir.

"The police are coming," called Locke from the front door.

"We have to get him out of here," said Veronica.

"What?"

"They get him, no reward!"

"He's killed people!"

"Easily done."

She advanced on the doorway, but as she drew closer to Lafarge, the more her aim wavered. Shadow began to impinge on her vision, crowding her senses like a black migraine. When she tried to blink the affliction away, a hat and a coat danced with flickering stars behind her eyelids.

"Too late," said Locke, grabbing her around the waist and hauling her through the closed door into a dank living room.

He didn't expect her to laugh.

"Your partner really doesn't want you to catch a break, does he?"

"I can live without the money. Now keep quiet and keep still. Even when lost in Lafarge's shadow, a keen eye can still—"

"Ssh, they're here."

Their boots hammered on the bare floorboards like thunder. Shouts of warning echoed around the house. A snub-nosed rifle appeared at the door and swept the dark of the living room. Other armed police rushed on down the hallway, reaching the conservatory.

"Armed police! Do not move!"

"Kitchen clear!"

"Living room clear!"

"I said armed police! Do not move!"

"Upstairs clear!"

"What the Hell is that?"

"If you do not stop, I will shoot!"

"This ain't right, Sarge!"

"Final warning…"

"Sarge, it can't be real, you can't—"

Veronica stared up at Locke as three staccato shots sounded in the hallway.

"Fuck."

"Sarge?"

"Fuck."

Someone screamed.

"Clear out! Everyone out!"

"It's him! He's here!"

Gunfire rang out again. Plaster exploded into the living room as stray shots punctured the wall.

"It's the train station all over again…"

"I said out!"

The police fled. There was no order or discipline in their flight. They fought each other to reach the exit and two men fell. One cried out, briefly. The other scrambled on without looking back, his rifle forgotten. As his footsteps faded away to nothing, voices whispered through the fetid gloom, all speaking the same words in a chorus of discordant malice.

"They may be scared of you, but The Company knows better."

Veronica edged from their living room hiding place to the hallway door. Locke beckoned frantically for her to come back. She ignored him, so he felt compelled to follow.

"The Company knows you can't lose a memory that's already lost," continued the voices, "and that's all I am here."

Locke and Veronica peered around the doorframe and saw Lafarge's familiar shape standing at the end of the hallway.

"Over there is another matter. Over there I am something

more. Whereas you… you are exposed."

And suddenly, Lafarge was gone. Locke's breath caught in his throat.

The voices sang out from the conservatory. A policeman lay in the doorway. The rise and fall of his chest showed he was alive, but the pile of sand by his head said he was as good as dead. Inside, Howard Briggs still sat motionless in his chair, but around him moved…

Harriett Bell; head and shoulders rendered in glossy colour, the rest of her a warped, translucent negative.

Naveen Jupta: the handsome groom, missing an arm where Holly once stood in her wedding dress.

Koji Uematsu; fixed with a smile caught on camera in front of the bandstand in Grenadine Park.

Geraldine Beckett-Howe: mother, grandmother, confined to an armchair that slid around the room, eyes reflecting a television screen frozen at the moment of her death.

Isthmus Kane, grey and insubstantial, watching it all; pen scratching observations in his little black book.

Harriett Bell again: a haphazard image with screaming lips painted a vivid red and slit eyes drawn with heavy blacks.

There were others. Dozens of them, repeated like reflections of reflections, with sizes ranging from passport photographs to larger than life. They were real and yet not; memories of flesh and blood that scuttled around each other and through each other and vacillated between crystal clarity and the incoherence of a familiar face dreamt up in the mind's eye.

"We need to go," whispered Locke, pulling Veronica back into the living room.

"That's what Tary was talking about," she whispered in reply.

"We need to go."

"He knew how to send it back…"

"Lafarge is gone," said Locke, his voice almost breaking.

Veronica stared into his eyes and finally understood. However much Locke feared his partner, he had been there from the first moment Locke woke up without a past; an ever-present nightmare that banished all others, until now.

She touched his arm and smiled faintly.

"Nightmares never really go away."

She slipped her gun into a pocket and stepped back, out into the hallway. Locke shook his head in dismay. Susurrus attention drifted from the conservatory as she turned to face the grotesque multitude.

"I think it's time we met. My name's Veronica, who are you?"

"Henceforth known as The Company," replied the chorus of dead memories.

"That's a bit of a mouthful. How about I call you Bob?"

Locke staggered back in the living room and his legs gave out beneath him. He collapsed to the floor and sank his head into his hands.

"The Company has had many names. Many more now – Harriett, Naveen, Isthmus, Koji, too many to mention – but the first came in a place far, far away."

"I guessed you weren't from around here," replied Veronica, unsure of where to look. Voices came from all of the warped pictures and each had eyes that regarded her hungrily.

"First was The Port Royale Trading Partnership," they said.

"Henceforth known as The Company."

"Yes."

"But that must have been a long time ago," she said, walking forward. "And old memories fade, don't they? You've had to find new ones. That's why you stole all their pictures."

"The pictures are nothing; weak memories that merely cling to the strong. The Company is strong and Howard Briggs shall make The Company stronger still. He shall kill for The Company and The Company shall remember his terror and his thrill and The Company shall endure."

Locke raised his head.

"Will you have him kill me?" asked Veronica.

"Yes," replied The Company.

She laughed. "But what of my memories, Bob? What if they put poor Howard here to shame?"

The Company delivered its answer as a torrent of squeals, howls and legal jargon. Locke reached the door to see Veronica fall beneath The Company's host of forgotten victims. He watched in horror as they pinned her to the ground and seethed across her chest, fighting with each other as gleaming hooks appeared about her head.

She stared up at an invisible point on the ceiling above. The Company's ghosts were everywhere, but she did not look at them. Dead faces leered and snarled around the periphery, but she refused to let terror overwhelm her. Tary's words about metaphors rang hollow as the hooks bit into the flesh of her face, tearing the holes from which they would pull her memories. There was no itching this time, just a lancing pain as her life was wrenched into view; a placid tableau documenting her non-existence as a happy housewife hanging on the arm of her perfect husband.

Locke stepped over her without looking down. He ignored those of The Company that grabbed at his legs and then at his hands as he picked up the abandoned rifle.

Veronica could feel the blackness beyond. Once her memories were gone there would be nothing. The void would claim her, leaving this body nothing more than an empty shell. Veronica resisted, but the hooks dug deep. They pulled hard. However much she held on, she could feel shards of her past begin to slip away.

Locke advanced into the conservatory where Howard Briggs sat. The Company was upon him, trying to drag him down with its hooks, but he managed to level the barrel of the gun and open fire at the potted plants lining the walls.

Howard Briggs' head jerked upright and his eyes sprung open.

Veronica's memories did not go. The hooks broke. The Company screamed in frustration and came again. More barbs bit into her memories and the pain was not just now, it was also then, a pain that filled every waking moment she could remember; constant, unrelenting, intent on delivering her to that void, but the pain was not alone. Wherever it went, her perfect husband followed. They tried to tear him out, but he just smiled and their metal would snap.

The Company faded a little each time a flower exploded at the passing of a bullet. The boxes broke into splinters. Pots shattered. Locke kept firing until every petal lay curled up and smoking on the floor. Then he released the trigger.

The Company was gone.

He dropped the gun and hurried over to Veronica. The

hooks left no visible marks, but her face was deathly white and tears were welling in her eyes.

"He wouldn't let me go," she whispered, barely finding the strength to speak.

Locke just nodded and reached down to help her up, but Howard Briggs' chair slammed into his back and sent him sprawling. A heavy boot stamped down on Veronica's hip, before a second landed on her shoulder. One more stride and then Howard Briggs lifted the chair again.

Veronica heard the wood strike flesh. Thomas cried out. She barely had the strength to wince, but as one dull thud followed another, she willed herself to move. She rolled onto her side, drew her gun and fired blindly down the hallway.

Blood spurted from Briggs' arm. He turned. She fired again, but his mighty hand gripped hers and the shot buried itself in the ceiling. A last pull of the trigger produced nothing more than an impotent click. The chamber was empty. Briggs snapped her hand back and tossed the gun aside.

"You destroyed my flowers and made me remember. Now they're all I can see. When I close my eyes, their dead faces are all I can see."

His groan of anguish rumbled in the pit of her stomach.

Veronica fell onto her back and stared again at the invisible point on the ceiling. From her memories, Vincent had saved her. Her perfect husband had come to the rescue. She managed a small laugh. She'd been right: nightmares never really go away.

A shadow passed over her.

"Please," said Howard Briggs, "when I close my eyes, they're all I can see. Lose those memories. You can do that, can't you? Lose things?"

Veronica saw a shadow standing over her. It wore a broad-brimmed hat and a long coat and it lifted a hand to Howard Briggs' forehead.

A piece of paper fluttered down the hallway, skimming past Veronica's nose. She glimpsed the writing before it was whipped into the air, showing Howard Briggs the last words he would ever see: 'You chose to kill before you chose to forget.'

And then Howard Briggs' sight was burned from his eyes,

condemning him to share darkness with his victims forever more.

Though the sun shone down and a blue sky crested the rooftops, rain still whipped across the street from grey clouds above. It sent Veronica hurrying across the zebra crossing while cars waited impatiently. She passed a woman struggling to keep an umbrella from blowing inside out and smiled. When Veronica saw dark clouds gathering outside the hospital, she considered catching the bus home, but chose instead to walk and savour the chill drops of rain hitting her face.

Climbing the stairs to her flat, she held the day's mail between the finger and thumb of her right hand, which was otherwise bound up in plaster. Every letter was addressed to the old lady who no longer lived there. They went in her mouth while her unfavoured hand struggled to turn the key in the lock of her flat's door. She spat them onto the settee once she was inside.

Locke sat at the breakfast bar, his head wrapped in her inexpert bandages. He hadn't moved since last night.

Veronica made herself some tea and drank it while watching television. With Howard Briggs in custody, the police were slowly locating the rest of his victims. Even the morbid delight of the news was beginning to wane, fatigued by too many reports of dismembered corpses.

The rain cleared over the course of the afternoon. After dinner, Veronica went out and got drunk on the meagre reward they'd received for confirming Briggs was in the house an armed response unit had run away from.

She came home shortly after two in the morning. She staggered through the dark of the flat and when she reached out to steady herself on the breakfast bar, gentle hands caught her and guided her through to the bedroom. Once her head was on a pillow and she was sleeping soundly, Thomas Locke returned to the kitchen and went back to staring at the black cat figurine he'd woken up with two years ago.

Interlude V

"Thomas, if I wanted to forget something, could Lafarge lose those memories?"

"Don't ask that, Veronica. Even the worst memories are worth holding on to."

"But that's what *he's* doing, holding on to them. Ever since the business with The Company, he's become like an infection in my head. Anything I remember, he's there, even when I know he wasn't. And it's getting worse. I… I go to the toilet and I come out and I know, *I know* he wasn't in there, I know I didn't see him, but I still remember glimpsing him in the mirror."

"But without your memories—"

"I know and I don't care. If I have to become someone else, so be it."

"But what if the person you become glimpses your husband in the mirror? She won't know who he is. She won't know what he did. She might reach out to him."

"If I don't do something, he'll drive me insane."

"Then think of something else. Block him out. Whistle some catchy advertising jingle over and over."

"So I have to end up mad whatever I choose? Thanks, this little talk has been very uplifting."

Afore Saint Zu's Festival of the Muse

When the gentleman sat next to him on the train asked his name, his reply was Darren Wynne. This was the latest in a series of questions that had interrupted Darren's reading of the well-worn book in his hands.

"And I suppose you're here for the festival," said the gentleman, nodding at the violin case by Darren's feet.

"That I am," he replied, accepting defeat by closing the book, "though this town and me go way back. Alas we parted in acrimonious circumstances. Hopefully me and my music can make amends."

Darren Wynne's train sped into the heart of the old town. Its wheels ran along rails laid across a series of brickwork arches; a passing that sounded as a thunderous roar beneath those arches, drowning out the report of a gun and desperate cries to "shoot the thing, shoot it!"

The thing moved fast. Frantic torchlight caught it for no more than a moment before it was gone again. The underside of the arch was sealed off by a wooden wall, but narrow shafts of daylight fell through gaps in the planks and the thing cut through them as a flickering blur.

The final carriage passed overhead, leaving behind rumbling echoes.

"It's over there, over there!" shouted Thomas Locke.

Veronica Drysdale lazily fired off another shot. A shrill cry signalled another hit.

"Bullets aren't going to kill it," she said.

"What do you suggest then?"

"Your coat," said Veronica. "Next time it comes near—"

"Ah! It's got my leg!"

"That makes things easier."

Locke had just about shrugged off his jacket when Veronica reached him. She tore a stubborn sleeve free of his arm and threw the coat over the creature before diving on top.

"Now what?" gasped Locke, dragging his bloody leg clear of whatever it was they'd captured.

"We beat it to death, obviously," said Veronica, driving an elbow down hard onto the writhing mass.

Locke hesitantly joined in, stamping down on twitching cuffs and pockets until his coat finally lay still. He exchanged a look with Veronica. She drew back and exposed the thing beneath to the glare of torchlight.

"What is it?" she asked, repulsed.

The skeleton was rusted iron; lengths of metal loosely bolted together onto which animals clung. The muscles and sinew of this creation were rats and cats, pigeons and voles, tied to the articulated frame and each other by what looked like piano wire.

"One day you'll give up asking such questions," said Locke. "Now, you know what we're looking for, it must be around here somewhere."

He began searching across the floor and walls. Veronica remained still. How had this thing at her feet been able to move like that, behaving as if it were a single creature? How had it come into being in the first place?

Another train passed overhead. Once again the archway shook and filled with noise – the rhythmic beat of the wheels, a melodic groan of steel flexing under the weight and finally a rush of air through tiny cracks that whistled a tune Veronica fancied she'd heard somewhere before.

"It might be hidden behind a loose brick," said Locke, picking at a seam of mortar with a pen knife.

Veronica sniffed and noticed for the first time that the sewn together carcasses smelt as foul as they looked.

"I need some fresh air," she said and left.

Veronica returned to the archway three hours later. The setting sun left behind a ruddy sky crying raindrop tears onto the street outside its wooden door.

"It's not here," said Locke, limping back and forth across the dusty stone floor.

"You should get that bite looked at," said Veronica, "that thing probably carried all sorts of infections."

"Lafarge won't be happy."

"Shame, I'd like to see him do happy. I have this picture in my head of him turning pink if he's happy."

"But finding things is what I do and it was here, I know it was—"

"Thomas, I'm sure you'll find this key sooner or later, but Lafarge is going to have to wait until later, because it's your turn to cook dinner."

Darren Wynne dined at a fast food restaurant in town. He ate his bespoke sandwich and looked out the window. The buildings outside were the same, but every shop had a new name and every shopper was a stranger. He'd been away a long time.

It was dark when he arrived at the Jubilee Guest House. The sign by the door was the only point of difference from the other houses lining this terrace and the dozens of others that stretched as far as the eye could see.

"You'll be here for the festival then," said an old woman who showed him to a room barely big enough to lie down in.

"That and catching up with some old friends," said Darren, laying his violin case and sole suitcase down on the bed.

"That wouldn't be one of those euphemisms, would it?" asked the old woman. "You haven't got a gun in that there musical case, have you? Because I won't have that sort of thing in my house, not unless you pay extra."

Darren opened his violin case to reveal an ageing violin inside.

"I am but a humble musician, ma'am, nothing more."

The following morning, Veronica completed her morning ablutions, left the bathroom and whistled a tune to herself. She didn't know what the tune was or where she'd heard it, but for some reason she knew there was more to it than the few bars she could remember.

Breakfast was going to be reheated chilli con carne left over from the night before until she found an array of semi-dissected pigeons and rats strewn across the worktop alongside the articulated frame and piano wire found beneath the railway arch. Locke's creepy cat figurine stood over the mess wearing its usual supercilious expression. The detective had clearly spent the night searching through the creatures' foul little innards for Lafarge's key. A note apologised for the mess and explained that a new case had come up at short notice. A second glance at the dead vermin convinced Veronica she could skip breakfast.

She dressed and whistled as she did so, stopping when her skirt's zip proved uncooperative. She grunted and tugged at it, then froze as the tune she'd been whistling continued as a series of glassy chimes. She hurried to the window in time to see a cat disappear from sight. A line of rainwater-filled milk bottles still wobbled from its passing.

The bell over the bookshop door bid a shrill farewell to Thomas Locke. As soon as he was out of sight, the store's owner, one Arturo Blank, hurried over back the counter. His finger jabbed at the keys of a phone and then he was speaking into the handset.

"He was here. It went just like you said."

"Of course it did. Signs and portents, my friend, signs and portents."

Locke stopped on a street corner twenty-four paces from the bookshop. He sniffed the air, asked a passer-by what the capital of Peru was and then caught a lift on the back of a passing rubbish truck.

A man watched from behind the wheel of an expensive green saloon. His name was Tobias Gretch-Featherly. He owned an antique shop and his favourite colour was purple. He put the car into gear and pulled out from the kerb. Arturo Blank's voice issued from a hands-free speaker on the dashboard.

"Where's he going now?"

"Down Broughton Avenue," replied Gretch-Featherly. "The district library is this way... No, wait, now we're headed North."

"Trunkstone lives in that direction. Do you think—?"

"He's stopping, he's getting off at the traffic lights. There's some bum trying to clean people's windscreens and... he's looking at something in the bum's suds bucket. The bum doesn't like it. There's some pushing and shoving—"

A horn sounded behind Gretch-Featherly. The lights had

gone green. He waved an irritated hand at the car behind and then drove on past the escalating conflict on the pavement. By the time he had found a safe place to stop and turnaround, Locke had fled the potential fight, wandered into the garden of a posh house, climbed up to the top of a monkey puzzle tree and then climbed back down again.

Gretch-Featherly watched Locke exit through the house's gold-painted gates.

"I think our man might be mad," he said.

Locke spent the next forty-eight minutes sitting on a park bench watching council workers string up bunting and lights for the first of night of Saint Zu's Festival. Gretch-Featherly was forced to take a comfort break around minute forty-six and emerged from the public toilets in time to see Locke up and running.

Back in his car, Gretch-Featherly sped along the road circling the park. He glimpsed Locke entering a narrow alleyway. Unable to follow, the antique dealer was forced to turn onto the next street. He slowed and tried to glimpse his quarry through the gaps in the houses.

Then Locke darted across the road in front of him, into a garden and over a fence into a backyard.

"Gods be damned!" exclaimed Gretch-Featherly, accelerating hard up to the next junction and taking the next right. Another right turn and Locke was ahead, regaining his breath on the sidewalk. Gretch-Featherly parked a safe distance away and watched his mark enter a church hall. The notice board outside declared that today was the day of a Bring-and-Buy sale in aid of Africa's poor. Gretch-Featherly locked his car and hurried inside.

There were a dozen or more stalls ranged around the interior. Crowds of people clustered around each, examining chipped ornaments, handmade jewellery and assorted junk retrieved from the back of someone's garage. Locke stood before a table covered in battered toys. He had a book in his hands and was haggling over price with a thirteen year old boy.

"Two pounds," said Locke.

"Five pounds," replied the boy. "That's what it says on the sticker, that's what you're paying."

"That's clearly a two."

"Only if you hold it upside down."

"So how come the pound sign is the right way up this way round?"

"Because the pound sign is upside down, obviously."

"I'll pay five pounds for the book," said Gretch-Featherly, appearing beside Locke and pulling out his wallet.

"It's only worth two," said Locke.

"Five pounds, here you are," said Gretch-Featherly, holding out a fresh banknote to the boy.

"I suppose I could stretch to five pounds ten," said Locke, fishing around for change in his pocket.

"I thought you said it was only worth two," said Gretch-Featherly.

"I was trying to haggle," replied Locke.

"A skin-flint, eh? Well I'm feeling generous. How about I give you ten pounds for this book, boy? What do you say to that?"

The boy looked at his two customers. "I say the price is now fifteen, that's what I say to that."

"Okay, fifteen, done," said Gretch-Featherly.

"Hang on," said Locke, "I think I've got… sixteen pounds… thirty pence… no, forty… forty-six—"

"Twenty pounds," countered the antiques dealer.

"If you can hang on a moment, I can nip to the cash-point—"

"Fifty pounds!" said Gretch-Featherly. "Fifty pounds, here and now. Come on, boy, have we got a deal?"

The boy grinned. "Fifty quid for this shitty book? Nah, mate, if you're willing to pay that much, I'm guessing I can make a shed-load more selling it some place else. No deal."

"Don't be stupid, boy, fifty pounds – it's far more than the book's worth. Take the money, go on, take the money and give me the book."

"Gav!" shouted the young boy. His call brought over a shaven-headed bulldog of a man. "Bruv, this 'ere gent's trying to make me sell this book to him. Getting all unfriendly about it too."

"Is he now?" The brother called Gav glared at Gretch-Featherly. "Happens I know a thing or two about being unfriendly."

"Fine," spluttered the antique dealer, "I'll find myself another copy."

He shot a sideways glance at Locke and then hurried away.

"Hear that, Gav?" said the boy. "Another copy. He was willing to pay fifty smackers for this one, so them others must be worth a bit too."

"Good thinking, Chips," said his brother, before noticing Locke was still there. "What you looking at, pal?"

"Nothing," said Locke. "I'll buy that transforming robot dinosaur, please."

Veronica had been working as a barmaid at The Drum and Cockle for several days now and while the regulars didn't remember her from one day to the next, the job did at least allow her to pretend she was once again part of the real world.

"I think I'll have a pint of Best and a bit of how's your father," said Albert Button.

He usually followed his order with a grope of the attending barmaid. Whether she giggled coyly in reply or slapped him around the face, he would always laugh uproariously. This tradition ended several days ago, shortly before a trip to the hospital immobilised his groping hand in plaster cast.

Veronica served Albert Button his pint of Best and went back to filing her nails.

There were few people in the pub at this time of the morning. Aside from Albert Button, three students skipping lectures were playing pool, a writer with a laptop was humming to himself as he typed, while an old man's battle with a crossword puzzle in a corner was adding fresh lines to an already heavily wrinkled face. Veronica idly wondered if his wrinkles would soon reach a critical mass and turn his face smooth as glass, then jumped as the old man banged his palms against the table.

"Would you stop with that bloody humming!" he shouted at the writer.

"Oh, err, was I humming?" said the writer.

"Bloody too right you were!"

"Sorry, I didn't realise. I—"

"You bloody youngsters, no bloody consideration!"

"Really, I didn't mean to—"

"Exactly. Didn't mean to. What kind of excuse is that? Doesn't matter whether you meant it, sonny, you bloody well did it."

"Hey, hey now, it… it wasn't my fault. It must have been her with her whistling," said the writer, waving a hand at Veronica. "She must have put that damn tune in my head."

"I've been meaning to ask about that," said Albert. "What is that tune? I'm sure I know it from somewhere."

"What's it matter?" asked the old man. "As long as he stops bloody humming it."

"I've stopped, okay?" said the writer. "Can't we just leave it at that?"

The old man grunted assent and returned to his crossword. The writer resumed writing and Albert asked Veronica in hushed tones what the tune was. She shrugged.

Two minutes later, Darren Wynne entered the pub with his violin case under an arm. He looked around with a wistful grin on his face and then wandered over to the bar.

"Hi there," he said.

Veronica looked up briefly and then went back to filing nails that were already comprehensively filed.

"Not much of a talker that one," Albert told the arrival.

"So I see," replied Darren. "I don't suppose you know how long this place has been the Drum and Cockle?"

Veronica stopped filing. She knew that voice belonged to the stranger who had just arrived, but her memory now swore blind that it was ex-husband who had walked up to the bar and said, hi there. She looked up in panic. Seeing Darren Wynne's unfamiliar face helped calm the sudden cold sweat that sucked her blouse to her flesh.

"Three years, give or take," said Albert. "Was the Fiddle and Jug before that and the Piano and Pedestal before that."

"That's it! That's what it was called when I was last here. Piano and Pedestal. Had some fine times here."

"Drinking or playing?" asked Albert, nodding at the violin case.

"Bit of both," said Darren. "Had me a band back then. Played all over town, but… there was something special about this place. Had an atmosphere all of its own." He noticed Veronica was staring at him. "You know, I wouldn't mind a drink, Miss, if it wasn't too much trouble."

"What'll you have?" she asked, trying to keep her voice steady.

"Guinness, please, and may I say you've got some mighty finely manicured nails there?"

Veronica sniffed and set about fulfilling his order. The glass shook beneath the pump as she fought the inexorable sense that her ex-husband stood right in front of her.

"So, you and your band going to be playing at the festival?" asked Albert.

"Not sure about the chances of that," said Darren. "A lot's changed since them days. Doubt I'd be able to find any of my old crowd. Crying shame too, because we did use to make some beautiful music." Veronica's attention once again distracted him. "Err, Miss, are you all right there? Looked like you were going a bit cross-eyed for a moment."

She had to look at him; had to keep proving to herself that it wasn't her ex-husband, but how could she keep staring so desperately at this complete stranger? She wanted to put a gun to her head and pull the trigger there and then, but knew even that was no guarantee of oblivion. She served him his drink and fixed her gaze on the reflection he cast in the drip tray.

A burst of noise came from the jukebox – a brief series of lilting chords before a high-pitched squeal silenced the machine.

"That was it!" cried Albert. "That's the song everyone's been singing. What was it? What song did you pick?"

The student standing by the jukebox shrugged. "None of them, I'd only just put my money in."

"Means it's got to be on there though," said Albert, hurrying over to jukebox.

"I'm sure I know it too," said Darren Wynne. "The name of it's on the tip of my tongue, but I can't quite…"

He shook his head and then hefted his violin case onto the bar. He took out the instrument, rested it against his neck, closed his eyes and started to play.

Everyone turned to watch and listen. He stroked the bow expertly across the strings and the notes conjured into the air wheeled about the room like playful children. Veronica let her eyes close. No longer did she see her ex-husband in the darkness, there was only the music.

When Darren finished there was an appreciative pause.

"That's the song all right," said Albert Button. "What is it, lad?"

The violin-player laughed. "I don't know. I know how it goes, but its name still escapes me."

"What's your name?" asked Veronica.

"Darren Wynne, Miss."

"Call me Veronica," she said. "If you want to find your old band-mates, I have a friend who might be able to help."

Thomas Locke stood before the open door of a house with maroon curtains.

"Yes, I used to have a copy of that book," the householder told him, "but I sold it to someone else twenty minutes ago."

Tobias Gretch-Featherly drove back to his shop with his recently purchased prize sat on the passenger seat next to him.

"No problems with this one, my friend," said Gretch-Featherly into his hands-free phone, "like taking candy from a baby."

The traffic lights ahead turned red. He stopped behind a white van. His self-satisfaction vanished as his car jerked forward, crashing into the van and exploding an airbag in his face.

It took a moment for the shaken Gretch-Featherly to regain his senses. Figures ran along either side of his car. The passenger side window was smashed. He turned his traumatised neck to see the young boy from the bring-and-buy sale snatch the book from the seat.

"You little thief, stop!" he cried.

A tapping came from the window beside him. He awkwardly looked round. The brother called Gav scraped a knife across the glass.

"All these books are ours," he said, "you got that?"

Veronica spent her lunch-break in the park with Darren Wynne. They walked together past groundskeepers who'd moved on from stringing up bunting to hanging paper lanterns from tree branches. A string quartet was practising at the bandstand. Darren kept an ear turned toward their music. Veronica could tell he was itching to join them.

"It's like when I was boy," he said. "The promise of things to come was everywhere. I could taste it, smell it, feel it in the air. That anticipation was half the fun, getting all excited for something that came and went in the blink of an eye. After being away all this time, I can see I ended up taking it for granted. I started to think I'd seen it all before, so the magic faded. The excitement faded. And then, with a word, it became something else entirely and I forgot what all this was really about."

"Maybe you didn't forget," said Veronica. "Maybe there never was any magic. You simply opened your eyes and realised all this was just a cheap show."

"Oh, but listen to that music. That's what it's all about. Close your eyes. Breathe it in. Tell me that's not magic."

Veronica closed her eyes, but only for a moment. If she saw magic there, it was magic of a dark and sinister kind.

"Locke said he'd meet us here," she said as they arrived by the duck pond. "He's not usually late."

She took out her phone and dialled his number. Thomas Locke could not answer his phone at that moment because he was desperately hanging onto the roof of a mobile library travelling at speed down Baskerville Road. He guessed it was Veronica reminding him about their meeting, but then thought it could be Lafarge with a more urgent request. Ignoring Lafarge would be foolish.

His right hand gripped the front of the roof more tightly as his left dared slip down to his pocket. Every muscle tensed in anticipation of being thrown off at any moment.

His fingers curled around the phone. The van made a sharp left turn. Locke's momentum carried him over the edge. Nails tore across fibreglass before finding a scrap of purchase. He slammed against the side of the mobile library and his phone dropped from his hand. It skittered away along a road skimming past his shoes at fifty miles an hour.

Locke sighed as the uncaring wind buffeted his face. Tiring

fingers threatened to let go, a pained shoulder considered dislocating, while the younger brother known as Chips looked back at him from the driver side wing mirror in disbelief.

"Typical," muttered Veronica, opting not to leave a message. She turned to Darren. "I'm sorry, he's obviously… What are you staring at?"

"No doubt about it, definitely jazz," he said, nodding.

Veronica narrowed her eyes and listened for music. The string quartet was taking a break, leaving the birds in the trees to chirrup a fragmented melody.

"I don't hear—"

"Only because you've heard it for so long you've tuned it out. It's like the sound of blood rushing round your head - always there and yet you hardly ever notice."

"I'd notice jazz."

Darren smiled. "I've long thought that everyone has their own song. Yours is played in a smoky bar by a drummer pounding out a beat as if the devil was on his back, a bassist plucking strings until his fingers bleed and a trumpet that sings the sorrows of the world one minute, then punches you in the gut the next. The notes they play are the moves you make and the words you say and in your case they all come together in a sort of grim fandango."

"I don't like jazz."

"Yeah, I guessed that too. So why do you keep playing the same song?"

"I know you musical types are prone to having funny ideas, but I'm not playing any song and especially not jazz."

"Then give me a smile, dance across this pond to an Irish jig."

Veronica raised an eyebrow.

"Ha!" said Darren. "That eyebrow – classic jazz trumpet."

Veronica sighed. "Listen, I don't hear this music of yours, I can't—"

"And that's the thing! We can't hear our own music, so we never think to change it, but you know what? I think you deserve better than that."

He set down his case on the path and took out his violin.

"What are you doing?" asked Veronica.

"I'm going to play you an Irish jig."

"If you think I'm going to dance across that pond—"

"Shush. Don't say anything yet, because anything you do say will be that infernal jazz speaking."

"I suppose I can't even raise an eyebrow, can I?"

"Like I said, classic jazz trumpet. Okay, I'm going to start playing on a count of four and if you're not smiling on a count of ten, I shall renounce music and all its charms for a whole twenty minutes. Now, a-one, a-two, a-one, two, three, four—"

Darren Wynne started playing and despite herself, Veronica was smiling before the count of ten.

Chips cried out in alarm as water rushed into the foot-well of the mobile library. The door wouldn't open. He wound down the window and climbed out as more of the canal sluiced past him. He climbed out onto the roof of the van as it slowly began to sink.

Locke didn't stay to watch. He walked off along the tow path with a plastic-covered volume under his arm.

"We'll get that book sooner or later," Chips shouted after him. "We'll get you too! You and that friend of yours, me and Gav will get you both!"

Veronica returned to the Drum and Cockle with water still dripping from the damp hem of her dress. Albert Button watched her return behind the bar.

"You know, girl, you've got a right pretty smile there," he said. "You should show it off more often."

"Maybe I will," she replied, before gesturing toward the jukebox. "Did you find out what that song was?"

He shook his head.

"Went through every title on the damned thing, but I'd bet my last penny it's not on there. One of them students even tried whistling it into his mobile phone. Apparently you can ring up these places and they tell you the name of whatever song you got playing. But not this one. It's got everyone snookered."

"Somehow that doesn't surprise me," said Veronica. "You want another?"

Albert finished off the last of his pint with a grin and

pushed it across the bar. While Veronica refilled the glass, a bony man with grey bristles covering his chin and a long coat covering almost everything else sidled up to Albert.

"I don't suppose you'd be interested in buying a book?"

"A book you say?" queried Albert. "Not a TV? Or DVD player? Or a perfectly legit coffee maker just off the back of a lorry?"

"Nah, nah, nah. What do you take me for? I'm a serious businessman. Besides, books are the thing nowadays. Especially this particular book. Very much in demand it is. I'm telling you, everybody wants a copy and I happen to be able to get hold of one."

"Do I look like a man who reads? On your bike, sunshine."

Darren Wynne arrived back at his temporary lodgings with a spring in his step and a smile on his face. The string quartet at the park had said he could join them for a festival performance at Uther's Beer Garden that evening, while the exceptionally pretty barmaid from the Drum and Cockle had agreed to come and watch him play. It was almost enough to make him forget his old band, but the echo of those times couldn't be drowned out quite so easily.

He opened the door of his tiny room and stepped inside to find the old woman who owned the bed and breakfast rifling through his suitcase.

She stopped the moment he entered and her hands tried out various poses in the hope of finding one that would express an innocent explanation for her actions. After a few seconds she accepted it was futile.

"You could do with some new underpants," she told him.

"It's usually only me who gets to see how worn out they are," said Darren.

"Take from it a woman who knows, it pays to have a quality pair in your wardrobe just in case you get lucky." And with that, the old lady went back to blithely searching through his possessions until she found the book he'd been reading on the train. "Well, well, what do we have here, Mr Wynne? I happen to know a fair few people who are rather desperate to get their hands on a copy of this."

"I had it, bruv! I had it in the back of this van and I was bringing it here and then he was suddenly there, hanging from the side and I'm thinking, how the Hell? And then I start spinning the wheel this way and that and trying to knock him off with lampposts and walls and I'm sure I did, I'm sure I saw him fall three times or more, but he kept coming back. The last time I hear him land on the roof, so I slam my foot on the brakes and he goes flying off onto the road ahead and I think I've got him. I stick it in gear, hit the gas and then there's suddenly this other guy standing in front of me and he's got this whole black hat and coat deal going on and I think, screw it, I'll run him over too, but something goes funny with the steering and suddenly I'm heading toward the canal and I can't stop and—"

"You lost the book," said Gav. The older, balder brother was standing opposite Chips in a commercial garage. A Ferrari awaited its M.O.T. while mechanics drank tea by stacks of tyres.

"I'm telling you, Gav, there's something seriously freaky about that guy."

"It's not a problem. We'll find him. We'll get the book. I've already found a buyer for the other two and just got word of a third."

"Oh, where would that be?" asked Thomas Locke from the door to the manager's office.

Everyone turned to stare at him. He gave a little wave. The brothers' copies of the book were in his hand.

"How the Hell did he get in here?" roared Gav.

"Transforming robot dinosaur," explained Locke, withdrawing into the manager's office and closing the door behind him.

The mechanics charged the door and smashed it off its hinges. The room beyond was empty.

"He was there one minute and gone the next," said Arturo Blank. He sat in his bookshop's storeroom with Tobias Gretch-Featherly, who held a bag of peas against his neck. "Was it really a man or just a trick of the light? While I ponder this question, the boy somehow ditches the mobile library into the canal and this Locke fellow manages to retrieve the book from the back. It was all very… odd. I'd venture to say it might have looked rather like magic to the credulous of mind."

"As it would to anyone well versed in the occult!" declared a great bear of a man suddenly at the door. He had a bushy beard and wore a rich velvet overcoat.

"What are you doing here, Trunkstone?" demanded Arturo Blank.

"Proposing a truce," replied the bearded man, pulling up a chair. "Our individual efforts have clearly fallen short of success, so combining our resources would appear to be a most sensible course of action."

"Or we just quit," said Gretch-Featherly. "These books can't be worth what people are paying for them."

"Have you boys not done even the most cursory of research? Do you even know who the author is?"

"Of course we know," snapped Gretch-Featherly.

"The book was written by John Monroe," said Blank. "He worked as an investment banker."

"He self-published the book and barely sold a dozen copies," added Gretch-Featherly.

"John Monroe wasn't *just* an investment banker," said Trunkstone. "He was a brilliant aberration in the field. When he gambled, he always won, but he never bet too big. He never got greedy. Some say he was blessed, some say he did a deal with the Devil."

"And others put it down to insider dealing."

"They would be the same people who'd have it that Arturo saw a trick of the light. The wise know better. There are things in this world that cannot be explained by science and reason. One does not need faith to know that God sits in his Heaven and Satan in his Hell; one only needs to look upon this world with sufficient scrutiny. I submit to you, my friends, that what Arturo saw earlier today was a demonic manifestation. This adds credence to my firm belief that the books of John Monroe contain the secret of his otherworldly pact. That is why every man Jack and his dog are after them and why we must not delay in obtaining one of these books, for the first to perform the necessary rite will lay claim to a power beyond their wildest dreams."

* * *

The house was grand without being ostentatious. Its greatest extravagance lay in the security that subjected Locke to numerous checks before allowing him to proceed. Multiple cameras watched him walk up the driveway to the front door It was opened by an old lady in a simple t-shirt and beige trousers.

"Three more," said Locke, handing over a bulging carrier bag.

She accepted them grimly before forcing a smile.

"Only one to go, Thomas."

He nodded and left.

Darren Wynne's copy of the book was back in his suitcase. He carried it away from the Jubilee Guest House.

The landlady said his decision to leave was a gross overreaction and besides, she added, it was entirely within her rights to search through her guests' things on security grounds, what with terrorists being everywhere nowadays. But Darren was not to be swayed from his chosen course of action. The landlady insisted he pay for the repair of a giant crack running down one wall of his room that definitely hadn't been there when he checked in. He said it was, she said it wasn't, he sighed and headed for the door. She threatened to call the police. He turned the handle. She apologised and offered to make him a nice cup of tea before he went. He stepped outside. She called him the feeble-minded son of a disease-ridden whore. He walked away. He managed thirty nine steps before two battered Citroens pulled up outside the Jubilee Guest House. The cars ejected half a dozen men, who hurried straight to the front door.

Darren quickened his pace and turned right at the next corner, heading on past another terrace. Maybe the men were friends of the landlady, but he knew all too well that some people had long memories. When the Citroens rounded the corner moments later, he started running.

One of the cars sped past, hit the brakes and mounted the kerb in front of him.

He skidded to a halt. The other car was stopped behind him. Men were climbing out. Fear twisted at Darren's guts. He didn't recognise any of these people.

A man with a bony face and bristles on his chin stepped forward.

"Give me the book," he demanded.

Darren just stared at him, trying to work out what the book had to do with what happened here all those years ago.

Then metal crashed into metal; a van swatting aside the Citroen parked on the pavement. Shards of bodywork tumbled across tarmac as the doors to the van flew open and a second group of men jumped out. Without pause or warning, they attacked the first gang with spanners and wrenches.

Fracas raging round him, Darren shrank back against the wall of the nearest house. A door opened beside him.

"Quickly, come inside. You'll be safe in here."

Darren took the advice and stepped into a hallway wallpapered with a repeating motif of ducks in flight. The owner of the house closed the door and slid home three bolts, fastened two chains and turned a key in each of five locks. When he turned to Darren, Darren saw that his saviour wore a starched shirt and tie beneath an unseasonal Christmas jumper. He also had rheumy eyes that squinted at Darren above a less than reassuring smile.

"So, you have a copy of that book, do you?"

Veronica returned home after her shift at the pub. She opened the front door to reveal a strange man searching through the ever-changing menagerie of lost objects filling her flat. He had a pleasant enough face and his clothes were all produced by respectable brands, but on seeing Veronica he pulled out a flick knife and ordered her to come inside and close the door behind her, otherwise he'd chase her down and cut up her vagina.

She mutely did as instructed.

"I was told there were some books here," said the intruder. "Where are they?"

Veronica said nothing. Instead she picked up a remote control from the breakfast bar and switched on the television.

"I asked you a question, bitch!"

A repeat of an American police procedural drama was on. Veronica turned up the volume until it was uncomfortably loud.

"Are you deaf or something? Do I need to spell things out to you with this?"

He pointed the knife at her face and began an awkward advance through the mass of bric-a-brac filling the room. Unperturbed, Veronica took her gun out of her handbag, took careful aim at the intruder and then shot him in the genitals.

His screams of pain could barely be heard over the television. He fell into the junk, hands clutching at the blood flowing from between his legs. Veronica realised this was the music Darren had told her about – the incidental music of a woman who could pull a trigger without thinking; a woman who remembered taking aim while her ex-husband whispered in her ear. "Shoot him, he deserves it."

Veronica stared at the pistol in her hand, then looked up and searched the room until she found a pearl-encrusted jewellery box sitting atop a pile of components for a high capacity communications satellite. She opened the lid and placed the gun inside.

Irritated thumping came from the flat above. Veronica turned down the volume on the television. The intruder's screams had died to pitiful whimpers, but his mobile phone was demanding attention, the ring-tone eerily familiar. Veronica beat off minor resistance to take the phone from his pocket, but rather than answering the call, she stood hypnotised by the tune that had been following her all day.

Locke opened the door to the flat. His coat and trousers were scored with scratches and streaks of dirt.

"Answer it," he said.

She reluctantly did so. Locke appraised the injured stranger while Veronica listened to the caller's message.

"Apparently one of his friends is chasing down some guy with a book," she reported.

"We need to get that book," said Locke.

"And I need to talk to you about helping out a friend," said Veronica.

"You can tell me on the way."

"And what about…?" She nodded toward the intruder.

"He'll be gone by the time we get back, but hang on to that phone. I lost mine and need a new one. Now, come on, time is short."

He headed out again. Veronica hesitated in the doorway and looked back at the jewellery box, but it was already gone.

Darren Wynne ran along the train tracks above the railway arches, the book clutched in one hand while the other held the violin case to his chest. His suitcase had been left behind in the house of a madman wearing a starched shirt and a Christmas jumper.

A helicopter hovering overhead tracked his progress. Men pursued him along the railway line. He wanted to give them the book, but as he escaped the melee outside the madman's house on the Number 45 bus, he remembered shouts from all sides promising to kill him if he gave the book to anyone else. They'd probably kill him if he dared throw the book away too. There had to be a way out of this mess, but he was too tired and afraid to think clearly.

The horn of an approaching train caught him by surprise. He threw himself against a metal gantry at the side of the track. The train sped past, catching his flailing arm and knocking the violin case from his grasp. Darren watched his livelihood tumble down onto the street some thirty feet below.

He closed his eyes and tears swelled. The rushing air from the passing train pulled at his body, urging him to let go and succumb to a quick death beneath the morbid beat of the clattering wheels. It was the same beat that lay behind the unknown song he'd played in the Drum and Cockle. He suddenly thought of Veronica. She was expecting to hear him play that night. He couldn't let her down, not like he had the others.

The train removed his pursuers from view. Darren stuffed the book down inside his shirt and judged the distance to a streetlamp flickering into life over the road below. He jumped.

The head of the lamppost struck him in the stomach. Stunned, he barely managed to wrap his arms around the pole before he started slipping earthward. He slowed his descent with the soles of his shoes and then collapsed onto the pavement.

The sight of his violin case spurred him to his feet again, but the approach of whining engine sent him back into the shadows of the arches.

A moped puttered into view and then drew to a halt by the violin case. The rider considered it for a moment then looked around. Darren pressed his back harder against the crumbling brickwork providing his cover and felt it tremble to the beat of rotor blades passing overhead. Dust whipped into the air as a searchlight shone down from the helicopter.

The rider hastily reached down, picked up the violin case and rode off. Darren glimpsed a Christmas jumper beneath the leather jacket as the moped passed by and groaned despair.

The helicopter moved on; its ominous form disappearing over the façade of a railway workers' pub that had long since been abandoned. Darren left his hiding place in a futile pursuit of the moped. He followed the road through an open arch running underneath the railway line and emerged into a maze of garages, industrial units and workshops. Every wall was topped with barbed wire, ripped polythene bags sat in the gutter and company signage competed for space with 'To Let' notices and crude graffiti.

He listened for the distinctive noise of the moped, but instead heard men shouting and the helicopter drawing near once again. The door to a parked car opened. A bearded man dressed in a velvet overcoat leaned out.

"Good evening, Mr Wynne. My name is Olaf Trunkstone. I am here to offer you a way out of this sorry mess."

"Darren used to live here, years ago," Veronica told Locke as they walked alongside the railway line. "He was in a band with some friends. He came back to try and find them."

They passed workmen in orange jackets preparing for a night spent repairing signals. One whistled a tune to himself. The others talked in hushed tones.

"I heard if you die if you read it," said one.

"I heard one of them has a bookmark with the number to a Swiss bank account worth, like, fifty million."

"I heard—"

"Thomas, pay attention," snapped Veronica.

"Sorry," said Locke.

"It's that bloody tune again, isn't it?" she said, glancing back at the whistling workman. "Everybody seems to be singing it or whistling it or humming it – I'm getting sick of it."

"What tune?"

"Forget the tune, I was telling you about Darren. I thought you could help him."

Locke frowned.

"I'm sure Lafarge wouldn't mind," added Veronica. "You'd just be doing me a favour."

"It's not that," said Locke.

"Which means you won't."

"I can't."

"Why not?"

"Because… I can't find them."

"This isn't a confidence thing, is it? Just because you didn't find that key, you think you can't—"

"Darren Wynne's old friends don't exist any more. Take a left here."

Veronica led the way down a short embankment and through a ragged hole in a chain-link fence. They started across an empty car-park of scarred concrete slabs and burgeoning weeds.

"What do you mean they don't exist?"

"Friendship isn't something you can count on to last forever. My guess is Darren burned some bridges before he left, others probably got washed away in the years he was gone."

"So there's no one left for him here?"

A rueful smile flickered across Locke's face.

"I wouldn't say that."

They climbed over a rusted metal barrier as an expensive saloon pulled up at the roadside. Darren Wynne climbed out of the back with a violin in hand. He thanked whoever sat inside and gave Veronica and Locke a sheepish grin as the car drove away.

"I've had the craziest evening," he said.

"Do you have the book?" asked Locke.

Darren glanced at Veronica.

"Is your friend always this to the point?"

"No, usually he's much more obtuse," she replied.

"Well, in answer to the question, no, I do not. Those fine gentlemen in that there car offered me a deal whereby they would get all the mad folk who've been chasing me off my back and in return I'd give them this tatty old book my Nana gave me. Not only that, but to sweeten the deal they offered me this here violin too. Course, doesn't have the sentimental value of the one I lost, but it is a Stradivarius. Probably worth a fortune."

Locke sighed and began tramping off after Trunkstone's car.

"What's his problem?" asked Darren.

"He hates his job," said Veronica. She produced her phone and began dialling for a taxi. "Now, don't we need to get you to a gig?"

The three merchants of antiquity sat in a circle atop Ester's Tor, a modest hill to the south of the town centre. It was the centre-piece of a small park ignored by the festival. Though lacking in bunting and lanterns, it did provide a fine view of the setting sun.

Olaf Trunkstone was reading aloud from John Monroe's book. Occasionally he would reverse the words, clang a set of miniature cymbals or light another of the black candles arranged at the points of two bisecting pentacles.

To begin with, neither Arturo Blank nor Tobias Gretch-Featherly were convinced by this ritualistic pantomime. They played their parts in begrudging silence until the air began to press against their skin and a tingling sensation rose in their fingertips. They looked at one another as Trunkstone's monotone voice echoed unnaturally off the trees and houses surrounding them. Whatever energy surrounded them grew in intensity as the sun sank below the horizon.

"Psst, Tobias," hissed Blank. "Does that look like...?"

Gretch-Featherly looked over his friend's shoulder.

"You might want to speed things up, Trunkstone," he said, "that Locke fellow is here."

The bearded man acknowledged the warning only by raising his voice louder and louder until he was shouting the last of the twisted words at the sky. Then he lit the final candle, slammed the book shut and jumped to his feet.

Locke arrived at the top of the hill, puffing and panting.

"You are too late, sorcerer!" declared Trunkstone. "The ritual is complete!"

The detective swallowed a few more breaths before asking: "What ritual?"

"The ritual hidden in the pages of this book! The ritual that will allow us to command the power of the fates!"

"Which book?"

"This book!"

"That book?"

"You know as well as I the power it contains."

"I thought it contained the story of a middle-aged investment banker who fantasises about having an affair with his secretary."

"The superficial only hides its deeper meaning."

"Really?"

"Yes."

"Well, you seem very sure, so I won't try to argue. I will ask whether you still need the book now you have the power of the fates. You see, I got paid by the author's wife to find and return to her all the copies, so…"

Trunkstone's conviction faltered.

"I… I'm afraid not. If we need to conduct the ritual again—"

"In case it didn't work this time, you mean?" asked Locke. "How exactly does this power over the fates manifest itself anyway?"

"Well…" Trunkstone looked around at his two companions. Both were singularly unable to provide any support.

"Look, forget I said that," said Locke. "I'm sure your ritual worked and you don't need the book, so—"

He was interrupted by the ringing of a mobile phone. Eyes turned upon Arturo Blank, who muttered an apology as he fished the device from his pocket.

"What's that ringtone?" asked Locke.

"Oh, err, I don't know," said Blank, "I've just been hearing it all day and then someone sent it to me and I thought it was quite a nice tune—"

"That's not a tune," said Locke.

"What? Of course it is. Can't you hear—?"

The bells of a nearby church began ringing out the same melody. The men atop the tor looked out across the town as the chimes of the first church were joined in concert by other churches further afield. The mobile phone kept ringing. Trunkstone began whistling. Gretch-Featherly started humming to himself.

"That's not a tune," whispered Locke to himself, "it's a key."

"Today I met a beautiful girl and discovered a new song that I'd like to dedicate to her," said Darren Wynne, standing with the string quartet in the corner of Uther's Beer Garden. "Veronica, I hope this song can change your tune and keep that beautiful smile on your face forever more. As for the rest of you… feel free to clap along."

Veronica blushed embarrassment, but the attention of the crowd around her was soon lost to clapping and cheering as Darren's new violin led the performance of a piece now echoed at every one of the hundred festival venues dotted throughout the town. The music did not just come from the instruments playing live to enthusiastic audiences, it also came from phones and radios and televisions and the sirens of emergency vehicles and the wail of car alarms and empty cans rolling down streets and bottles blown by the wind and dogs barking and cats meowing and doors slamming and shoes walking out to see what all this noise was about; a noise that came from everywhere and made the air feel alive with an intoxicated buzz that made you want to laugh and dance with whoever's hand would take your own and lead you down the road to where the lights shone brightest and gay colours were strewn from pillar to post in celebration of this most joyous of nights.

Thomas Locke ran through the crowds of whirling dancers until he reached the Grenadine Park, where the portal stood. It reached hundreds of feet into the night air, clouds wreathed about its summit, trails of vapour drifting into the black void now open beneath its arch.

The revellers did not drift across its threshold, they waltzed and jived and skipped and sung and if any one of them was aware of the great door through which they passed, the knowledge did not slow their step or slacken the smile stretched across their face.

Locke looked about in panic. He tried grabbing at a passer-by, but they shrugged off his attempt to hold them. An old woman took his hand and swept him along for a few steps, before passing him off to a grinning man in a Christmas jumper. The macabre square dance led Locke closer to the looming maw until he tore his hand free from the grip of a man in a long coat and punched him across a bony jaw.

Even free of the dance, Locke was buffeted forward, carried on a tide intent on passing through the unholy arch. He dropped to ground and clutched his hands about his head, suffering inadvertent kicks and stamps rather than let himself be taken any further.

The music was not music to Thomas Locke. Instead he heard words he did not understand, whispered by dissonant voices. When the sound of a violin reached his ears, it was not playing a harmonious melody, but scratching across strings that howled in pain.

He risked a look up and saw Darren Wynne and Veronica drawing near. Their eyes were locked upon one another, lost in a fantasy headed for a place beyond this world.

"Veronica!" shouted Locke.

She did not hear. Darren stopped playing for a moment and she embraced him. They spun around together, holding each other close, feet tracing interwoven steps across the beaten grass.

Locke forced himself to his feet. Passing bodies tried to knock him back, but he barged them out of the way and fought toward the couple ahead.

"Veronica!" he shouted again.

When Darren kissed her, it caught her by surprise. Her eyes opened wide, then closed as she lost herself in the moment. She held onto him until Locke pulled them apart.

"Thomas! Why aren't you dancing?" she asked.

"Can't you see it?" he asked in reply, waving a hand at the gargantuan arch looming over them.

"I can't see anything except the music," she said, smiling at him with glazed eyes. "It's a sparkling waterfall casting rainbows in the air. Dance with me, Thomas."

She tried to take his hands, but he grasped hers instead and held them together at the wrist.

"I can't let you go," he said.

"We can go together."

He glanced over his shoulder at the darkness. Once they passed over the threshold, it took only a few steps before the dancers vanished from sight.

"We need to stay here," he told her.

"Veronica!" shouted Darren. He was doing a tango with Albert Button. "Come on! Keep up or you'll miss all the fun."

"I'm coming!" she called back and pulled against Locke's grasp.

He shook his head.

She laughed and pulled again.

"Come on, Veronica!" called Darren Wynne.

Over Locke's shoulder, Veronica watched Darren dance through the doorway and disappear into darkness.

"The music's fading, Thomas, we have to go."

The number of people passing by was growing less. She fought to free herself more vigorously. She bit at his arm. She tried to knee him in the groin. His grip faltered.

She tore herself away, but she could not run for the door. She had to skip and prance and twirl in a desperate pursuit of Darren Wynne. Locke shunned such frivolity. He charged after her and threw himself at her legs.

She collapsed into the dirt as the doors began to close. They moved inexorably slowly, swinging inwards to seal shut the great arch. Veronica tried to drag herself on toward the diminishing column of darkness, but Locke bound his arms about her legs and pressed his full weight against them.

Dancers passed them still, laughing and singing the song that could no longer be heard.

The doors finally shut at midnight. Veronica lay sobbing in the dirt inches from where walls of stone came together one moment and then vanished away to nothing the next, returning the park to how it was before, save for a mass of muddy footprints leading up to a line of pristine grass.

John Monroe's wife stood with Locke and Veronica in the back garden of her house. A small bonfire slowly turned the last of her husband's books to ash.

"He died wishing his legacy would not be a god-awful book written by a man plumbing the depths of a mid-life crisis. Thank-you, Thomas, for allowing me to give him that."

Veronica hung her head and walked away. Mrs Monroe looked at Locke questioningly. He sighed and stared into the fire.

"If only all our sins could be erased so easily."

Interlude VI

The memekers were busy with their hooks that night. Come morning, those who woke in the town would wake with strange new ornaments on their mantelpieces. Lafarge watched the day break from atop an ageing cooling tower.

"Did you know?" shouted Locke from the stairs below.

Lafarge said nothing.

"All those people, Lafarge! Where did they go? Why did you have me find that key?"

Lafarge said nothing.

"Would you believe that sometimes I let myself think you might be something approaching human, but that's… that's what humans do, we fool ourselves. Now, I don't pretend to understand what you are or why you do what you do, but if… if you're capable of it, there's something you have to understand: I can't do this any more."

Constance

Veronica entered the dark of her kitchen at 3am wearing only a cotton t-shirt. A restless night had prompted a craving for nicotine and she was hoping to find a spare patch lying around. Crossing to the worktop, she trod on something sharp that caused her to yelp in pain.

Blood welled around her fingernails as she pulled a black shard free of her sole. Veronica tossed the injurious object into the sink and limped on, only for her good foot to land on a whole mass of sharp things.

Minutes later, the lights were on and Veronica was sitting on the floor with torn strips of her cotton t-shirt serving as makeshift bandages for her cut feet. In front of her, hundreds of glassy black fragments lay on the floor where Locke's black cat figurine had been smashed to pieces.

Thomas Locke's thoughts kept him from paying attention to where he was going. He walked where instinct took him; down to the river, where the water was so still the moon cast an unbroken reflection upon its surface. He continued over Argent Bridge, where a girl gazed up at the stars. The first time she called out to him, Locke lowered his head and kept walking.

"Excuse me," she said again.

This time he turned. Her pale face, framed by a halo of golden hair, could not decide on an expression. Thin eyebrows rose in surprise, then dropped low over a suspicious stare. A flicker of a smile. Teeth bit nervously at her lip. She looked away and then looked back.

"Yes?" said Locke.

"What's your name?" she asked.

He hesitated before answering.

"Thomas."

"Do you have somewhere to go, Thomas?"

The path ahead of him was empty; an orange-lit road running between silent apartment blocks.

"I should be getting home," he said, but made no move to continue his journey.

"Do you want to hear a joke?" asked the girl.

"Err, okay."

"Then you'll have to tell me one first, because I don't know any."

"Oh. I'm afraid I'm not very good at remembering jokes. I'm even worse at telling them."

"That's… a pity."

"I'm sure… I'm sure someone will come by with a joke eventually, though at this time of night—"

"I wanted to make someone laugh. When I saw you walking past, you looked as if you needed a laugh."

"Right now, I don't think I could."

"Then what about tomorrow night?"

"Tomorrow night?"

"Come back here tomorrow night with a joke and I'll tell it to you. Maybe you'll be able to laugh then."

Veronica returned home from work. She closed the door and listened. From outside came the sound of passing traffic. A toilet flush upstairs sent water rushing through the plumbing. The refrigerator buzzed quietly. Over on the worktop, the remains of the cat figurine were still wrapped up in a polythene bag. Everything was just as she'd left it.

There was nothing appetising in the refrigerator, so Veronica called out for pizza.

The girl waited on Argent Bridge, gazing at the stars, just as he'd left her the night before.

"What's your name?" asked Locke.

"Have you brought a joke?"

"Yes."

"My name's Constance."

She smiled briefly, unsure of whether that revelation deserved a smile. Locke took a piece of paper from his pocket.

"I got someone to write it down for me. I haven't seen it. I thought that way, maybe…"

He shrugged and offered her the joke.

"That's a good idea," said Constance, taking the paper, studying the words and then frowning. "Umm, I don't get it."

"Can I have a look?"

"I'm sure it's a very good joke," she said, handing it back. "It's probably me. Funny people know jokes, don't they? Maybe that's why I can't remember them. Maybe that's why I don't get this. Maybe I'm just not funny."

"That makes two of us because… oh, hang on… I see. You really need to read it aloud. If you're American when you go into the bathroom and American when you come out of the bathroom, what are you while you're in the bathroom?"

"I don't know. Well, I know because I read it, but—"

"You're a pee'in.'"

"Peeing. Yes. Or rather no. I still don't get it."

"You're a pee'in… European."

"Ah. Hmm."

"Jokes never work as well when you have to explain them."

"I'm sure it's me."

"No, it just doesn't make much sense written down and I told you I can't tell jokes. I bet you can tell it better than I can."

"Thomas, I really—"

He pushed the joke back into her hand and nodded encouragement. Constance sighed and then read aloud.

"If you're American when you go into the bathroom and American when you come out of the bathroom, what are you while you're in the bathroom? You're a pee'in."

"Ha! Ha ha! Ha ha ha!" said Locke, holding his sides, before falling to the ground with mirth.

"You're just humouring me," said Constance.

"Is it working?"

"A little."

"Should I keep going? I can jab myself in the eye to simulate tears of laughter if that would help."

"Would you do that?"

"If I say 'yes', would you expect me to really do it?"

"Of course."

Locke gave her a hang-dog look, raised a finger and then poked himself in the eye. And the girl on the bridge laughed for the very first time.

Veronica was looking for her fourth job in three days. She blamed this on Lafarge. If it wasn't for him, people would remember her from one day to the next. That they didn't made holding down a regular job difficult. It was also his fault that the Drum and Cockle closed down after all the regulars danced off into oblivion along with the one man who'd been able to change her tune.

She circled possible opportunities in the local newspaper while eating a Chinese takeout from a foil tray on her lap. These two purchases had left her with only eight pounds forty-three from the fifty she'd made selling objects from The Office of Lost and Found at the nearest pawn shop. That trick wasn't likely to work again, given all those objects were now back in the flat, lying in the shade of a large golfing umbrella.

Lafarge arrived without a sound. He waited by the window until Veronica caught sight of him out the corner of her eye.

"If you want Thomas, I don't know where he is," she said, without sparing him a direct glance.

Veronica found it hard to tell if the shadow across the room was looking at her or staring out at the rain running down the window pane. This ambiguity persisted for the rest of Veronica's meal and through two episodes of an American sitcom before Lafarge disappeared.

When Veronica turned in for the night, she found him waiting in the bedroom.

"You're the bloody magic man," she said, "and he's your bloody partner. If you want him, you find him."

She went to bed with Lafarge still standing there.

Locke went to sleep with his head on Constance's shoulder. He woke alone and looked around the bus station in confusion until he remembered the events of the night before. They had broken into the central library in search of joke books and a definitive answer to how many things could be black and white and red all over. They found instead that reading passages from Tolstoy could be just as funny as 'knock, knock' jokes, provided you enunciated in a suitably comic voice and your partner in crime was as drunk on the fumes of criminal trespass as you were. Once the hysterics had passed, Constance was keen to explore the library's wealth of knowledge further and this led them to a shelf of atlases that in turn prompted a sudden desire to go see the sea.

The bus that would have taken them there pulled into its bay. Locke watched a few passengers disembark. No one climbed aboard. It was still early; the morning rush had yet to begin. The bus driver spread a newspaper out over his steering wheel and began reading.

Locke couldn't believe that Constance would have gone to the seaside without him, but also couldn't understand why she would have left him without leaving at least a note behind.

He left the bus depot in a daze. The only thing he could think about was the number of hours until nightfall and whether Constance would be waiting at the bridge when it came.

During the day his mobile phone rang several times, but he ignored it, certain that if he let anything from his regular life intrude on this dream, the dream would surely end and he'd arrive at the bridge to find it empty.

He killed time. It died slowly. The morning lasted days, the afternoon months and the minutes before sunset stretched themselves out over many years.

And then suddenly the day was gone and he was hurrying through the night to the Argent Bridge, hoping, praying and finally grateful that she was there, smiling, waiting for him.

"Have you seen this man?" asked Veronica.

She showing the driver of the street sweeper a magnolia picture of Thomas Locke printed on a printer running low on yellow toner.

"Why? What's he done?" asked the driver.

"Nothing that would make a difference to whether you'd seen him or not."

"Well, that's not a great picture. It's hard to say."

"The fifty people I asked before you found it very easy to say they hadn't."

Veronica returned the picture to her purse and began walking away.

"Well, that's probably because they hadn't seen a guy who looked kinda like the guy in that picture walking into an off-licence back up that way about five minutes ago."

Veronica couldn't manage more than a canter on her high

heels. When she got a new job and received her first pay cheque, she resolved to buy herself a pair of decent running shoes.

She reached the off-licence as Thomas Locke walked out onto the pavement and over to a people carrier parked by the roadside. When he drove away, Veronica was in a taxi and telling the driver to follow that car.

"Would you believe it?" said the cab driver. "Fifth time today someone's said that to me. Eighth time this week. Common misconception it only happens in movies. In my experience, everybody's chasing somebody—"

"He's gone left! You're losing him!"

"No, I'm not. There are temporary traffic lights down there. They'll hold him up. We take the next left, double-back, catch him on the ring road. Less chance of him realising he's being followed. Like I said, you're dealing with an expert here."

When Thomas Locke ended his journey in a driveway on a quiet suburban cul-de-sac, Veronica was at the end of the street paying the taxi driver the last of her money. She hurried up the short road. Her quarry walked up to the nearest house with a bottle of wine in hand.

"Excuse me," she called out.

"Yes?" he said, turning.

"Thomas?"

"Err, yes."

"Thomas Locke?"

"Yes, can I help you?"

Veronica stared at him a moment.

"You don't know me," she said, voicing a fact evident on his face.

"No, I can't say I do."

The more she looked at this man, the more Veronica found herself sure this was Thomas Locke, but also certain there was some ineffable difference separating him from the Thomas Locke she last saw almost a week ago.

"I'm sorry," she said, "I think there's been a mistake. You're not the Thomas Locke I'm looking for. Please, don't let me keep you."

She raised an apologetic hand and walked away. It was a

few seconds before she heard Locke continue on to the house, open the front door and step inside. She glanced back in time to see the door close.

"Stupid girl," she whispered to herself, "I started looking in the wrong place."

While the rest of the world lay sleeping, Thomas and Constance played. They explored museums and galleries, parks and playgrounds, sharing jokes and pretending that they had the Earth all to themselves.

More and more messages accumulated on his voicemail until those who called finally got the message and gave up. He chose not to go home. He bought fresh clothes from thrift stores and dined in discount diners and cheap cafes. He took lodgings at a seedy motel on the south side of town and slept during the day so he could see her at night. Each night she would thank him for his company and depart before morning.

It was a childish existence and both knew it couldn't last, even though this truth was never spoken. They lived in the moment and did not let themselves worry about the time when that moment would pass.

Seven nights after they first met, Locke arrived at the Argent Bridge. Constance wasn't there. He looked for her. He waited. He called out. He searched up and down the river bank, fearing the worst while trying to convince himself there was a mundane, rationale explanation.

Eight nights after they first met, Locke was already sitting with his back against the bridge wall when the sun set. Aside from short trips for food and toilet breaks in an alleyway that ran behind an adult book store, he had stayed there all day. He stayed there all of the following night, but Constance did not show.

On the tenth night, he sat on the bridge with his head bowed when her hand touched his face.

"I missed you," she said.

He looked up into her smile, his hunched body instantly transforming into something vital and alive.

"I missed you too," he said. "I almost went out of my mind with worry while you were gone—"

"Thomas—"

"It's okay, you don't need to tell me where you were or why. It doesn't matter. I don't care. I just care that you're back."

She smiled.

"I care, Thomas. It's right that you should know, but not yet. We have the whole of the night to enjoy first."

And enjoy it they did; first attending a midnight screening of a French film neither of them understood and then breaking onto the roof of a town centre office block with a collection of water balloons they dropped on unsuspecting drunks passing between the local nightclubs and bars. They hid in a dumpster to watch a fox search for food amidst restaurant rubbish. They played Pooh-sticks on the Argent Bridge using empty crisp packets instead of sticks. Finally, they sat on the bridge wall, dangled their legs over the water and watched the shining sliver of the waning crescent moon begin to fade from view as the sun cast its first rays over the horizon.

"This is what you should know about me, Thomas," said Constance, touching his cheek and turning his head so she could look into his eyes.

He frowned, unsure of what she meant, until he began to see shapes beyond those eyes; the harsh edges of the buildings beyond.

"Connie..."

"Ssh."

She kissed him, but the brush of her lips was no more substantial than an autumn breeze.

"I don't understand," said Locke, as the girl before him slowly vanished away.

"You will," she promised, now nothing more than an ethereal voice. "Tomorrow I'll explain everything."

Southerly Rare owned an impressive four-storey town house over-looking Grenadine Park. As a man, he was less impressive. Standing barely five foot tall, he wore stacked wooden clogs to compensate for his lack of height and suffered from a virulent rash of freckles that left many wondering if his skin was brown traced with white or white dotted with brown.

Veronica wondered neither of those things as she stood on

his doorstep. She wondered only if he would be able to provide some answers.

Southerly Rare studied the shining black fragment she had handed him and tapped the white mark etched into its surface.

"Yes, this is my mark, but I don't remember ever crafting a cat..."

The significance of his words drained the colour from his face. Veronica knocked him aside and strode into his house. Ornate tapestries hung from the walls of a dimly lit hallway. She considered them briefly before storming into a living room where a mantelpiece full of delicate vases, crystal animals and matchstick ships lined the top of a large fireplace.

Veronica smashed them all.

Southerly Rare knelt down amidst the aftermath and wailed his grief.

"Do you remember now?" asked Veronica.

"Get out!" Rare cried. "I'll call the police! I'll call the Vandenark!"

"Do you remember?" asked Veronica again, grabbing the man by his chin and staring into his teary eyes.

"No," he spat.

Veronica let him go and glanced around the room. Intuition told her that the object she was looking for wouldn't be on public display. It would be hidden away. She made for the stairs.

On the fourth floor, in a small room locked by a key that was in turn locked away in the secret drawer of a dusty old armoire, a jade hummingbird was sealed inside a mahogany box. It was a tiny thing and Veronica felt even her lightest tough would snap the wings. She lifted it from the red silk cushion on which it lay.

Southerly Rare's distress gave way to an anger fomented and concentrated by this strange woman's cavalier defilement of his home. His breathing was steady and deep as he stepped past the broken door. His hand did not shake as he drew out his memeker's hook. Never before had he torn a person's entire life from their skull, but such was his rage that whatever moral code he possessed was cast aside for the punishment of Veronica Drysdale.

"I've had a thousand of those hooks all trying at once to pry my memories free," she said, turning slowly, "and yet every single one remains. So, please, be my guest, slice that hook into my head and do your worst, but be aware that when you are done, I will still remember *everything*."

Southerly Rare hesitated.

"In the meantime," said Veronica, "let us see what you can remember."

And she crushed the hummingbird in her hand.

A group of work colleagues left their office together, laughing and joking en route to a few drinks and dinner in town. One of their number slipped away to catch their boss, who had to forego the revelry to attend a parents' evening.

"Mr Rachman, can I have a word?"

Mr Rachman stopped in the midst of opening his car door and checked his watch.

"You have twenty seconds, Miss Mulligan."

"Thank-you. I just wanted to talk to you about Miss Dent. I… I have a concern about her work on the Hargreaves project. I heard her expressing misgivings about our proposed solution."

"Are these misgivings well founded?"

"That's not my area, sir. My issue is that she mentioned these misgivings to the client. Now, I'm sure she did this with the best of intentions, but if Rachel is putting the interests of a customer before those of our company…"

"I see. Thank-you for bringing this to my attention, Miss Mulligan."

"Just doing my duty, sir. Enjoy your evening."

Miss Mulligan hurried back to her colleagues. She was soon joining in with the jokes and laughter and took a moment to compliment Katie Dent on the gorgeous shoes she had chosen for their evening out.

They were followed by Locke and Constance. He wanted to ask questions, but she just pressed a finger to his lips and told him to keep watching.

They watched Miss Mulligan's party continue on to a bar where a few rounds of drinks were drunk, before proceedings switched to a Spanish restaurant overlooking the canal. Locke and Constance shared a simple starter in the corner while the office workers dined at three tables by the window. Locke couldn't follow their conversation, so turned his gaze to Constance, scared she might fade away again without warning. He took hold of her hand. It was warm; her soft flesh as real to the touch as his own. Could he have dreamed her disappearance at sunrise or, despite the evidence of his senses, was this the dream?

After the main course was finished, Miss Mulligan went to the toilet. On the way back she bumped into some friends at the bar.

"We're going to see this band at the Peacock Lounge," one of them told her. "Liz dropped out, so we've got a spare ticket if you want to come."

After quietly gathering her coat from the back of her chair, Miss Mulligan slipped out with her friends, leaving her work colleagues to foot the bill. When an irritated call came through on her mobile phone twenty minutes later, she answered it smoothly.

"I'm so sorry, Rachel, I got a call that my Mum had another fall. It sounded serious and I'm afraid everything else just went quite out of my head. Please apologise to the others for me and I'll pay you back later, I promise."

Constance and Locke couldn't get into the Peacock Lounge without tickets and had to wait outside until Miss Mulligan came stumbling out drunk several hours later. She declined her friends' offer to share a taxi and tottered off toward the river. She crossed the nearby Argent Bridge at 2:16am and entered an apartment block on the far side. Her insistent knocking at flat number eighteen brought to the door a blond-haired man wearing only pyjama bottoms.

"Oh, thank God, Mark. I was scared you wouldn't be in."

"What? Why…? For Christ's sake, it's almost half two in the morning."

"I know and I'm sorry, but I was working late and I missed the last bus home. I thought I could just walk, but then I heard someone following me and I saw this man and I got scared, Mark. I know it was probably stupid and probably nothing, but I really don't want to be out there on my own."

"Err, you want me to call a taxi?"

"Would you? Though I'm not sure I'd feel safe even in a taxi. I mean, you never know, do you? Could I… could I stay here tonight? I won't be any trouble. I'll just sleep on the sofa."

It took another few minutes for her to persuade him. Once she was inside, Locke and Constance listened at the door and heard whispered voices.

"You should have said no."

"I couldn't do that. She was afraid—"

"Mark, you know what she's like."

"Yes, I know she's not as bad as you make out."

"You just can't see what's right in front of your nose when it comes to her, can you? That's what I don't get. I'm your girlfriend now, but you always notice when I do something wrong."

"Don't be like this."

"She leaves before breakfast. That's my final word."

When flat number eighteen fell silent, Constance and Locke returned to the Argent Bridge. Clouds hid the stars and moon and left the river an undulating carpet of dark and darker shades.

"Why does she look exactly like you, Connie?" asked Locke.

Constance stroked at a curl of hair hanging down against her cheek.

"We are… sisters. She's why I can only come here when the sun is gone and the moon is shining in the sky."

"But how—?"

"She's not a good person, Thomas."

"I can see that."

"If I was in her shoes, I wouldn't be like that. I'd try to be nice and considerate to everyone."

"I know you would."

"Then would you give me that chance?"

"What do you mean?"

"She was born to a life that could have been mine, all because of a mistake made long ago, but there's still a chance we can put things right. We can put things right and be together, Thomas, always."

She smiled at him and the thought that he would never

again have to see her vanish before his eyes made him hold her close and whisper in her ear.

"I'll do anything for you."

"Then come with me to see the Umivatoré."

Southerly Rare sat in his living room and turned the marked fragment of Locke's black cat figurine over and over in his hands.

"It was the finest artefact I ever created. Five days spent tracing every line of its fur, every curve of the muscles, but it was the eyes that took the longest. They always do. In art, eyes are as much the windows to the soul as in life. Get them wrong and the memories won't hold."

"Why did you take them?" asked Veronica.

"Listen, it was just a job. One of those very well-paid jobs where it pays not to ask questions."

"But you must have seen something in his memories to explain what it was they wanted him to forget."

Southerly Rare snorted derision.

"I was extracting decades of experience; untangling the personal from the practical across a whole lifetime. From all that you expect me to recognise the significance of a detail that may have amounted to no more than a few fleeting seconds? Ha! Your friend may not even have been aware of what he did to suffer this punishment."

"Then who hired you?"

"Like I said, I didn't ask questions."

"Does that mean you're going to make me ask twice?"

Southerly Rare considered her look.

"The deal was done through a broker. I don't know who the client was, but I can give you the broker's number."

"Thank-you."

"No need to thank me," said Southerly Rare, smirking. "You won't get any answers out the Umivatoré."

Constance took Locke to a stretch of waste ground next to a chemical plant. In a corner formed by a pile of rubble and forest of nettles was a caravan. Constance knocked on the door. A small boy answered. He wore a purple and white tracksuit and a heavily stained apron.

"We are here to see the Umivatoré," said Constance.

"Have you brought a suitable offering?" asked the boy.

Locke and Constance looked anxiously at each other.

"Banjo-Pelota," said Constance.

"It's like regular pelota," explained Locke, "except played with banjos."

"And you get bonus points for getting the ball to hit the banjo strings to the tune of the Basque national anthem," added Constance.

"And after playing the ball, you have to play a tune that the other player has to try and repeat after returning the shot."

"Though we thought that could prove quite difficult, so we decided to shrink the pitch and play with a balloon rather than a ball."

The boy stroked his chin.

"It sounds novel," he said. "I'll run it by the Umivatoré. Wait here."

The door closed.

"What if he won't see us?" asked Locke.

Constance shrugged, took his hand and held it tight.

The door opened again.

"The Umivatoré hadn't heard of such an idea before," said the boy. "You may enter."

The interior of the caravan was filled with a stale green light and pungent smell. Constance and Locke both had to stoop as they were led to the cramped dining area, because a net slung from the ceiling held an elderly man above their heads. He was listening to music via a pair of earphones and the beat could be seen as pulsing light travelling along a vine whose roots reached in through his eyes and nose and entered the liver spots on the top of his head through scabrous holes. Others in the caravan were similarly afflicted. A young woman sitting in the sink stared at a handheld television with bloodshot eyes. The tendril burrowed in her head carried away impressions of faces and places along its length. A creature that at first glance was human, at second glance looked like some peculiar hybrid of gnome and fish, was squished beneath the dining table. It read a stolen library book, the words sucked up along another vine and up to a tangle of vegetative matter that lay on the table. Protuberances from this amorphous shape squirted liquids of various colours into an arrangement of flasks.

"The Umivatoré," announced the boy.

He placed a china tea-cup on the table. The Umivatoré promptly filled it with a stream of viscous yellow liquid. The boy drank the contents, let the fluids settle, then spoke.

"The Umivatoré knows why you are here, Miss Constance Mulligan, and it wishes you to know that it is obliged to report your transgression to the appropriate authorities."

"I just want to ask it one question," said Constance.

"You may ask your question," replied the boy, "but then you must run, for that is the way of things."

Locke squeezed Constance's arm. "I'm not sure about this."

"Your companion is wise," said the boy, "though also, the Umivatoré suspects, ignorant of what has been asked of him."

"The only thing I need to know is that she needs my help," said Locke.

The boy smiled and then raised his eyebrows at Constance, prompting her to make her request.

"I wish to know how I can get the chance I never had."

Another cup was filled, this time with green slime. After drinking it, the boy opened up a cupboard. From within he took four test tubes. He placed them in a rack in front of the Umivatoré. From a second cupboard he removed a jar of what Constance and Locke hoped were not brains. Whatever the wrinkled contents were, they were fed to the young girl in the sink without complaint.

Moments later, the Umivatoré was carefully dosing liquid into the test tubes. One was half-filled with brown, another a third filled with turquoise. The remaining two barely contained the pink fluid pumped into them.

"I shall hand them to you in the order you must drink," the boy told Constance.

Locke watched fretfully as she downed each in turn, a disgusted expression preceding each desperate gulp. When she was done, she held a hand to her mouth, then her stomach, then closed her eyes until the moment of nausea passed.

When she opened her eyes, they were wide and aflame with excitement.

"I know what to do," said Constance. "Come on, Thomas,

we haven't much time."

Veronica left Southerly Rare's townhouse with her mobile phone held to an ear. She listened to it ring a dozen times before she cancelled the call and dialled a new number.

"Hello," she said when a voice replied, "I need an address for a phone number..."

Constance and Locke ran along a street of shops closed for the night. The lights within and those shining from the lampposts were strobing on and off in a slowing rhythm that ultimately ended in darkness.

Constance stopped by a manhole cover.

"Help me shift it."

Locke joined her in heaving aside the iron cover. The sound of it scraping across the road set his teeth on edge.

"We haven't got a light," he said, staring down into the open hole.

"It'll be okay. I'll find the way," said Constance, taking his hand and attempting a smile.

Whatever reassurance Locke might have drawn from this was undone when her eyes slipped from his to stare in dread at the sky. He quickly looked round and up and barely had time to register what he saw before his hand was tugged toward the hole.

"Constance, why are the stars falling?"

Veronica walked for forty-five minutes to reach the warehouse. It took her another five minutes to find the locked door and a further three to locate a window she could smash and climb through.

The cavernous space within was filled with a hundred or more shapes hanging in rows from the ceiling. Veronica didn't pay them much attention at first. She was more concerned by the brown sludge that covered the floor and dirtied her shoes. Then she inadvertently brushed against one and recoiled instinctively.

It had feet.

There was barely enough light to make out any details, let alone faces, but the shapes were undoubtedly people.

Veronica made sure to avoid touching any more as she headed toward a lit doorway on the far side of the warehouse. She hoped that the brown sludge wasn't the cumulative effect of dozens of people being strung up like fresh meat.

Drawing closer to the light, Veronica was able to see that steel hooks held the bodies aloft, but those hooks were suspended from chains wrapped in some sort of vine. This vegetation spread across the ceiling of the warehouse and reached down to insinuate its tendrils into the heads of the unfortunate souls housed here. Veronica noted that whatever this plant was, it was not in the best of condition. The vines were flaccid and a sickly yellow in colour. The brown slurry came from cracks and pustules spread across their length.

The room beyond the doorway offered a refuge from the unsettling contents of the main warehouse. It was here Veronica found the boy. He was huddled in a corner, muttering to himself.

Locke could see nothing in the darkness of the sewer. He felt Constance's hand holding his and heard their feet splashing through water that reached up to his ankles, but the lack of visual reference left him expecting the ground to drop away with each new step.

Despite this anxiety, he didn't once question whether he should be here, blindly following this girl wherever it was she needed to go.

Booming noises from the world above grew closer. Constance ran faster. Locke stumbled as he tried to keep up, then a sudden blast of noise coincided with him being slammed face-first into the water.

An instinctive gasp drew foul liquid into his mouth and he jerked to his knees, coughing. He could hear nothing except shrill ringing in his ears, but he saw Constance ahead, groggily recovering from the shockwave. He realised light must have entered the tunnel.

The source was a large dagger-like object that had broken through the roof of the sewer behind him. It glowed white and emitted a regular pulse that rippled the water and brushed across his skin.

Constance grabbed his arm. She shouted words he could

not make out over the persistent ringing. But he got the message; they needed to keep moving.

Veronica guessed the boy was no more than twelve years of age. He wore an expensive suit marred by stains and creases that suggested he had worn little else for a week or more.

"I'm looking for the Umivatoré," she said.

The boy ceased his muttering to stare up at her.

"Bad idea, bad idea," he said, shaking his head. "That's what it does, churns out these bad ideas. It started getting ideas about me. That's why I had to make it sick."

"Well, as long as it's not dead, you can point me in the right direction and I'll go ask it my questions."

"It was easy in the end. I just needed the right kind of brain. Lucky for me the world's full of pessimists. Feed long enough on their ideas, anyone gets sick."

"Kid, I just need to know—"

"But what if it gets better? I need to know, don't I? I need to know if it's going to send its roots after me. So I can't go. I have to stay and make sure it stays sick."

"Sure you do," agreed Veronica and walked back to the door. She looked up at the diseased vegetation. "So if that's the Umivatoré, I guess this mean I need to play plant doctor."

Another dagger-like shard crashed through the roof. The ringing in Locke's ears was subsiding, but he still couldn't tell if it fell nearby or far away. He could feel the strange vibrations reaching toward them from all directions. How many of those things were there? Were they the stars he had seen falling from the sky? In his dazed state, he could see stars reflected in the sewer water as he chased after Constance.

"… two hundred and fifty-eight… two hundred and fifty-nine! This is it!" she declared, stopping and pointing at an unremarkable brick halfway up the wall.

She bent down, scooped up some fetid water in cupped hands and lifted it to shoulder height before letting it flow out.

Locke watched in amazement as the liquid began tracing shapes in the air as if drawn along a series of invisible tubes. Constance lost no time in grabbing at the shapes as they formed and re-arranging them into a new configuration – a symbol that when formed set the ground beneath their feet trembling.

"It's okay," she told him, "where we are going, not even the Vandenark will be able to find us."

Veronica found a step ladder and fire axe. She set the ladder up at the end of an incomplete line of bodies. She hoped this meant the people suspended here were the latest to be added to the Umivatoré's collection.

Climbing the ladder brought her face to face with a corpulent woman whose penchant for excessive make-up was still evident despite both the poor lighting and the unnatural vegetation swathing her skull.

Veronica swung the axe at the vines twisted about the chain above the woman's head.

This provoked an agonised scream.

The boy ran across the warehouse floor, shouting.

"Stop! You can't! You mustn't!"

Veronica swung the axe again. Black liquid began spurting from the lower-half of the partially-severed vine. Before she could cut it completely, the boy barged into the ladder and sent it toppling over.

She landed heavily, brown sludge splashing up around her. The boy attacked before she could recover, beating at her with his fists. She wrapped her arms about her head and lamented the fact she no longer had a gun to hand.

The pain felt curiously welcome; a brutal reality easily understood, unlike so much else in this world she now found herself in. She prayed that rescue would come from a passing policeman, but instead vengeful tendrils hauled the boy back. They were no longer yellow and flaccid, but green and vibrant. Veronica watched in numb horror as they spewed a torrent of purple effluent into the boy's mouth.

Then he was released.

He convulsed, choked and coughed in a vain attempt to purge his body of the Umivatoré's seed, but nothing came up.

Veronica pulled herself to her knees and reached for the reassurance of the fire axe.

"No need for that, Mrs Drysdale," said the boy, taking a

deep breath and then wiping traces of purple from around his mouth. "I have come round to the notion that my purpose is to serve the Umivatoré and am therefore once again able to speak on its behalf."

This only served to make her grip the fire axe more firmly.

"I'm here about Thomas Locke," she said. "I want to know what you made him forget."

The boy smiled a queer little smile.

"Only a life that never happened and a girl that never was..."

A flight of spiral stairs took Constance and Locke down past sights that made no sense. The sewer was replaced by verdant grassland. A few more steps and they were surrounded by high street pharmacist's aisle of laxative products. They continued their descent; Locke's unease growing with every new sight, both alien and familiar.

"Where are we going?" he asked, trying to keep the anxiety from his voice.

"In search of Atlantis!" cried Constance. "And Lord Lucan! And the crew of the Mary Celeste—"

Locke stopped. Constance continued on until his hand slipped from her grasp. She took one more step and then turned to look up at him, a frown on her face. They were surrounded by an ocean of swarming fish.

"Connie, I... I'll go anywhere with you," he said, "I'll do anything you ask, but all this... I can't even tell if it's real. I mean, it can't be real, but I... I can feel this and I see you and—"

"I'm real, Thomas," she said, stepping close and wrapping him in her arms. "I am real, but this is a dream and it's one I've been dreaming too long. We have to find the end of it before we can wake up and be together."

"I'm scared if I wake up, I'll lose you."

"You won't, I promise. When everything changes, I'll still find you. We're meant to be together, Thomas. Nothing and no one can stop that happening."

He held her beautiful face in his hands and smiled at the determination in her eyes that sparkled like stars. His smile faded when he realised her skin was sparkling too; points of light pulsing from her cheeks, her arms and the hands that still held him tight. Constance noticed too and stepped away, staring as the dots began to draw glittering lines across her flesh.

"You have to go, Thomas."

"*We* have to go—"

"No!" she cried. "They'll get you too and one of us has to do this."

"Connie—!"

"Seven hundred and seven more steps, Thomas and then look for a pen and paper."

Locke couldn't say anything. The lights were darting off into space and tearing strips of Constance with them. Even the blood that fell glistened before it hit the staircase and then joined the other stars in heading off to who knew where.

Constance spoke her final words to him and then disappeared before his eyes for a second time. When she was gone, Locke hoped beyond hope that they could still be together at the end.

"Why did you have Thomas Locke's memories taken from him?" asked Veronica.

"Mercy," replied the Umivatoré's boy.

"Mercy?"

"How can a man live with the knowledge that because of his actions a billion people ceased to exist?"

After descending another seven hundred and seven steps, Locke found himself in a cavernous hall whose heights were lost in darkness. There were houses here, but also mountains and rivers and piles of keys and stacks of books and a ship beached on the roof of a golden temple.

He tentatively left the staircase to explore.

There were other creatures here. Locke saw glimpses of them at the end of streets formed by abandoned cars and ancient statues; fat, flightless birds chased by bipedal lizards. A posse of rats watched him from the mouth of a golden monkey. More unsettling; the distant sound of music warning Locke humans might also live here.

He travelled for hours, unsure of where to go or if he

would ever get back home. He passed under a great bridge and walked along avenues of mismatched socks. Occasionally he would hear a mobile phone ringing, but dared not investigate the scenery too closely.

A tingling sensation on the back of his hand drew his attention to a pin-prick of light pulsing beneath the skin. He panicked at the thought of suffering Constance's fate and began running. He didn't know where he was going, but with no pen and paper in sight, so all he could do was strive to get to some place else it might be as quickly as possible.

Locke reached his destination three minutes later. A clearing circled by towering bookcases contained a simple wooden table. On the table lay a marker pen and a notepad of lined paper. Breathing hard, sweating from every pore and sparkling as if he'd been dusted with glitter, Locke staggered over to the table and picked up the pen.

"Once upon a time," the boy explained to Veronica, "a man and a woman had sex. He ejaculated three hundred and fifty-nine million sperm inside her and each one of those sperm set off on a long and dangerous journey to fertilise a solitary egg. Few of them came close to reaching their goal. Two entered the final stretch neck and neck, but there could only be one winner. The girl that resulted from this happy union was called Constance Mulligan and she was, by all accounts, a manipulative cow. The girl that almost resulted from this happy union, the girl whose progenitor sperm came second, was also called Constance and it was she who Thomas Locke met on the Argent Bridge two years ago."

When Locke finished writing his request on the notepad, a gust of wind tore the page free and sent it dancing off into the hand of a pitch black man in a pitch black coat. The freshly revealed page on the pad slowly darkened with ink, crude lines scribing a single word: 'Deal.'

Locke never got the chance to read it. His eyes were already stolen by the Vandenark, their lights diligently shredding the rest of his body. Splinters of bone burst out through what was left of his skin, but it didn't matter. The dream was ended. Soon he would be with Constance again.

"So where is Thomas now?" asked Veronica.

"That I do not know," said the boy. "Attempting to atone for his sins perhaps? A whole branch of reality was snapped off and replaced with another by that simple change of history; one sperm losing out to another. Still, I'm sure the Umivatoré would be able to concoct a few ideas for you."

Veronica looked up at the vegetation spread across the ceiling. It wasn't leaking brown sludge any more, but the memory of the boy being force fed purple plant puke still came readily to mind.

"No thanks, I'll see what I can come up with on my own."

Thomas Locke remembered everything the moment his black cat figurine smashed on the floor. He fell to his knees under the weight of a life forgotten and wept at what he had done.

Eventually, he went home. A married couple with a collie dog lived there now. They'd built a new porch at the front and a conservatory at the back.

He travelled to visit his parents, but couldn't bring himself to knock on the door. Instead he stood outside, listening to them watching a game-show on television until a paperboy gave him a funny look, at which point he got embarrassed and hurried away.

The old friends he found didn't recognise him. One of them now had blue eyes instead of brown. Another was picking up guys in a gay bar when he'd been happily married before.

The Argent Bridge was still the same. Locke stood alone in the moonlight, watching the stars reflected in the ripples of the water below.

It took him a week to summon the courage to go and see her. When he arrived, Veronica was waiting for him. Together they watched the other Thomas Locke loading cool-boxes into the back of his people carrier. Two children ran back and forth on the driveway, shooting each other with imaginary laser guns. Constance locked the front door and joined her husband by the car. Locke averted his eyes when his other self kissed the girl of his dreams.

The family finally departed for their day out at the seaside. The car passed Veronica and Locke with those inside singing about the wheels on a bus going round and round.

"She was right," he said. "We did live happily ever after."

She touched his arm. "But you—"

"Thomas Locke got to be with her," he insisted, before lowering his head and turning away. "I'm just a man who no longer exists."

Interlude VII

"I am not having you moping around my flat all day complaining about how you don't exist," Veronica told Locke. "If you really didn't exist, you wouldn't keep eating all my biscuits."

"You're out of nicotine patches again, aren't you?"

"What? Hell, yes, I'm out of nicotine patches! And I'm out of biscuits! And I have no money to buy more of either and that's your fault!"

Locke shrank back on the sofa and muttered to himself: "it's really not—"

"Don't you dare! Don't you dare try and say this isn't your fault. As I understand it, this branch of reality only exists because of you and that means you are responsible for everything, from the spot I found inside my ear this morning to the latest civil war being fought in the arse end of nowhere and you will just nod and accept it, because if you don't, I will take that standard lamp in the corner and shove it so far up your ass when you blow your nose your eyes will light up."

Instead of nodding, Locke shrugged and sighed. This only served to aggravate Veronica further, but before she could carry out her threat, a knocking came at the door.

May in January Square

"I bring a message from beyond," said the woman at the door.

She wore traditional gypsy attire, but her features were typically Scandinavian and the floral scarf around her neck was obviously Marks and Spencer.

"From who?" asked Veronica.

"Not who, from beyond."

"Beyond where?"

"Beyond the veil."

"What veil?"

"The veil that separates our mortal plane from the one that lies beyond."

"I see."

Veronica slammed the door shut in the woman's face.

Two hours later a white-haired gentleman arrived claiming to have news from the other side. He was followed by a young girl wearing prescription spectacles bearing urgent tidings. After lunch, eight more mediums turned up, a Wiccan healer and three outwardly normal callers who then proceeded to explain how they were instructed to deliver a very important message by, in order, a glowing angel, a spindly grey alien and a peculiar set of burn marks on the short-crust of a Cornish pasty.

"I am beginning to get pissed off with these people," said Veronica after turning away the prophet of the pasty with a stream of invective.

"Beginning?" queried Locke under his breath.

"Shut it! Where's that standard lamp?"

It was safely hidden in the airing cupboard. Locke put it there while Veronica was kicking the Wiccan healer in the shins and challenging them to 'heal that!'

While she searched, Locke roused himself from the sofa to examine the Cornish pasty scattered on the landing outside the flat door. It didn't take long to piece together the fragments of crust. The burn marks did indeed instruct the bearer to travel to this address. They also spelled out a simple message:

'He is coming for the child.'

When Veronica finally found the standard lamp and returned to the living room brandishing it purposefully, Locke had gone. He rang her three hours later to say he needed her help with a new job worth fifty thousand pounds.

Derek and Irene Wilson lived in an expensive, four bedroom house. The interior was decorated and furnished to the exacting specification of a professional designer, including the double-garage, which currently contained a Range Rover, a Mercedes and a quad bike. A cleaner called on Monday, a gardener on Tuesday and, up until two months ago, a nanny slept in the fourth bedroom. They'd kept the nanny on for as long as they could, but as days turned into weeks and the weeks became months without the police making any progress, they were forced to accept the brutal reality that they did not a need nanny when their daughter was gone.

Veronica sat across from the couple in their sun lounge. Irene tried to recount the fateful day Emily disappeared, but soon broke down in tears. Derek apologised on behalf of his wife and continued the story, but Veronica already knew all the details – they'd been recycled endlessly by the news at the time. So, instead of listening to Mr Wilson, she listened to some music instead. The earphones hidden by her dark hair had become an almost permanent accessory since she discovered music was the one thing that banished memories of her ex-husband.

The meeting concluded with Veronica promising to find the missing girl. The couple thanked her profusely and gave her a photograph that she reluctantly accepted. Emily was four years old when it was taken. She would now be five.

Veronica wanted to feel nothing. She didn't care about these people or their loss; she was only here because of the reward money. But her own future had been stolen away when she was only a child. The thought that the wide-eyed, smiling girl in the photograph might grow up to face what she saw in the mirror every day made Veronica feel something despite herself.

She felt angry.

* * *

Veronica sat with Locke at a table outside a café. Despite the warm spring air, he was hunched up in his coat and staring across the road at a small park protected from the surrounding square of houses by carefully-tended trees and pristine black railings.

"You should have talked to them yourself, you didn't need me," she said.

He gave a vague shake of his head.

She threw a teaspoon at him. He flinched as it bounced off his skull.

"How long are you going to keep acting like this?" she asked.

Locke shrugged.

She emptied her cup of tea and then threw that at him too. This time he ducked and it struck a chair behind him.

"Hey!" cried the man sitting in that chair.

He twisted around to voice indignation at the perpetrator. He didn't expect to find Veronica glaring back at him.

"What?" she asked. "You want a fight? Come on then, I'm in the mood for one right now and if we don't start in the next thirty seconds, you're going to forget this ever happened."

The man shook his head and dismissed her with a hand. He turned back to his companion and thirty seconds later had forgotten all about Veronica, Locke and the tea cup.

"Thomas," said Veronica. "Thomas!" Locke reluctantly looked up as Veronica leaned forward across the table and pointed a finger at his face. "You are the only person apart from Lafarge who remembers me from day to day and he's not even a person, so I need you to crawl out from up your own ass and start being someone I can—"

The next word caught in her throat. Rather than force it out, she retreated back into her chair and folded her arms.

"I'm going to the toilet," said Locke.

"Fine," said Veronica, retrieving her earphones from her handbag. "How much longer have we got to wait?"

"Three hours."

He walked inside the café, leaving Veronica hoping the strains of Irish folk music would relax her. Halfway through the second song, the music began to fade away. It was replaced by a voice.

"I know you, don't I? I'm sure I do. I never forget a face and especially not when it belongs to the beautiful wife of a colleague of mine."

Veronica opened her eyes. A strange man had taken Locke's seat.

"My name's Christian Weeks." His deep, smooth voice sounded clearly in Veronica's ears. When she removed the headphones, the incidental noise of the square grew louder, but his voice remained just as clear. "I suspect from the look on your face that you don't remember me."

"I suspect that means you're an eminently forgettable person," said Veronica.

Despite her words, his perfectly proportioned face and sparkling eyes challenged her natural cynicism.

"Oh, really?" said Weeks, smiling broadly. He had a most alluring smile. "This troubles me, it truly does. I am not a man used to being forgotten. Speaking of which, how is your husband nowadays?"

Veronica tensed. "Vincent is no longer any concern of mine."

"Really?" Weeks raised an eyebrow. "You know we used to work together quite closely, Vincent and I. Then I got transferred to a different office and while I'd been meaning to get in touch, with one thing and another, I never got around to it. I thought you might be able to give me his number."

"Sorry, no."

"Does that mean you two are…?"

Veronica didn't respond to that. She just folded her arms and glared at him.

"You know what I'm thinking, don't you?" he said.

"You're a man, you're all pretty transparent."

"You're being very defensive."

"You're being very presumptive."

"Did Vincent hurt you that badly?"

"It's okay, I got better."

"Did you?"

"Don't you have somewhere else to be?"

He leaned forward.

"I can see your scars. I can see the wounds that still lie

open. Without someone to treat them, they will only get worse. I can help."

"No, thank-you."

"Look at me, Veronica." He really was very good-looking. "Look at these fingers. It would only take a touch. The faintest of touches, stroking this flesh across yours and I could take away the pain. Stop you worrying. Stop you blaming yourself. One touch, Veronica, and then, if you turn me away, I will go without another word."

He reached his hand across the table toward hers and then stopped a fraction short of her fingers. Veronica stared at the space in between. She knew he was staring at her. She knew if she looked up into those eyes, the primal desire in the pit of her stomach would sweep aside her better judgement.

She wanted Locke to come back.

He didn't.

Veronica was left caught in that moment, alone, frozen, barely able to breathe. Then Weeks' hands were brushing across her neck, running through her hair, provoking tingles of unwanted excitement that coursed across every inch of her skin.

"Come with me now," he whispered into her ear.

And she nearly did, until she remembered Emily.

"I… can't. We're… we're waiting for someone."

"Is that what he told you?"

Veronica pulled away from his touch. He didn't seem to mind. He walked leisurely back to the chair on the opposite side of the table and sat down.

"What do you mean?" asked Veronica.

"Ask your friend."

"Ask him what?"

"Ask him what he's not telling you."

Veronica stormed into the gents toilets. There was a man washing his hands. He took one look at Veronica and made a hasty exit.

The doors on three of the stalls were closed. She thought about kicking them in, but decided not to risk it in heels; another good reason for buying a pair of decent running shoes when she had the money.

"Thomas?"

If he was hiding in here, he wasn't about to give himself away that easily.

A minute later she returned to the toilet with a fire extinguisher that she proceeded to discharge under each stall door. The first two stalls ejected startled gentlemen aggrieved by her attack. Further blasts of pressurised foam curtailed their complaints and persuaded them to leave. Veronica emptied the rest of the fire extinguisher's contents into the final stall, then dropped the canister and leaned against the door.

"I know you're in there, Thomas."

"Obviously," he replied.

"Do you want to tell me something?"

"No."

"You think I'm going to take no for an answer?"

"Why can't you just leave me alone?"

"Because I don't like you that much."

"The feeling's mutual."

"Someone's just told me you can't find Emily."

"Who?"

"A friend."

"You don't have any friends."

"An acquaintance then. Is he right?"

Silence from the stall.

"Is he right, Thomas?"

"He might be."

"Then why are we here?"

"Because… because Lafarge asked me to find him an opportunity. It's going to present itself on May the fifth at twenty-two minutes past five."

"Today?"

"In three hours."

"And what has this got to with Emily Wilson?"

There was a long pause and then the stall door opened. Locke shuffled out and over to the sinks, foam dripping off his trousers. He ran some water and splashed it over his face.

"Thomas?"

"He's coming for her, Veronica."

She didn't understand what Locke meant at first, then she thought back to the procession of nutcases that had plagued their doorway the day before, each one saying the same thing: 'He's coming for the child.'

Veronica raised a hand to her forehead and paced away and back across the tiled floor. Locke leaned against the sink, his head sunk low, his back crooked.

"I promised her parents, Thomas. I promised we'd bring her back. You need to find her."

"I can't," he said. "I've tried. It's like..." He snorted amusement. "It's like she no longer exists."

"Then maybe he's already—"

"No, somebody hid her away from him. That's why I can't find her. And maybe... maybe that's for the best. If she's hidden, she's safe. If I find her..."

"And us waiting around here is better? What did you expect to happen? Lafarge would get his opportunity and what? You'd try to reason with him?"

Locke shrugged.

"I'm not letting him take her, Thomas."

A wry smile tugged at a corner of Locke's mouth. He looked up at Veronica and saw an expression born of icy resolve.

"I don't care what he is," she said, "and I don't care what he can do, I am not letting him take her."

Locke's usual grim frown returned.

"What do you propose?"

Christian Weeks sat down on a bench beneath the trees of January Square. He reached into his pocket and found his wallet gone. He smiled and withdrew a packet of chewing gum instead.

The iron railings surrounding the small park made it feel like a private world unto itself, detached from the business of the square beyond; the chatter at the café, the shoppers passing in and out of the shops and the young solicitors sharing a cigarette outside the law firm that took up two doors of Georgian terrace.

A young couple lounged on the grass across from Weeks, books open for study ignored in favour of longing looks into each other's eyes. For them, even the world of the park was distant from the one they found themselves in.

Then, for the merest of instants, all of these worlds altered. The laws of perspective flexed before snapping back into place.

Weeks frowned and patted the park bench.

"I know, my friend. I know."

When Locke removed the key, it reformed itself into Christian Weeks' wallet. Veronica was still counting the money she'd found inside as he led the way through the unlocked door into an office.

"Enough for a new gun?" asked Locke.

"I told you, I'm done with guns," replied Veronica, "but I do need new shoes."

Locke sniffed. "I'm not sure if that's better."

Posters of palm trees and city vistas hung on the walls, each one inviting the viewer to escape to the exotic with the 'Unbound Travel Company'. Christian Weeks had done exactly that, as evidenced by the photographs pinned to a corkboard opposite the door. Veronica idly perused these while Locke tried to get some information out of the travel agent's computer. In each picture, Mr Weeks was smiling broadly, often with a sun-tanned beauty on his arm.

Then Veronica saw him. Vincent Drysdale. Her ex-husband.

The sight of him alive and well alongside Christian Weeks made her feel sick. The nausea grew worse when her memory changed. No longer did she remember standing alone in front of the photographs while Locke searched the computer keyboard for the 'K' key. Instead, Vincent had insinuated himself into her recollection to stand by her shoulder, whispering mint-scented breath onto her neck.

"That was taken on a business trip in Rome four years ago," he told her. *"We'd both been drinking, of course, and we persuaded a pair of pretty young locals to take our picture. We started showing off for the camera and ended up frolicking in that fountain."* He laughed softly. *"And then the girls joined us and tops were removed and I think we ran out of film shortly after that. Fortunately, Christian had a video camera back in his hotel room."*

Veronica tore the corkboard from the wall and threw it to the floor.

"Good idea," said Locke, "checking for hidden wall safes. You might want to rip down those posters too."

She did so, venting fury in the hope that it would erase her manipulated memories.

"Hmm, no wall safes then," observed Locke. "No matter, I found your friend's password and got into his email. Take a look at this."

Veronica glared at the screen. It showed a message from one Theodore Genuflect Broadsheet complaining about the shoddy service he'd received at the hands of the Unbound Travel Company. Specifically, how their ineptitude prevented him from returning home as scheduled.

"Missing your point," said Veronica.

"That's because I haven't made it yet. Mr Broadsheet sent quite a few emails over the course of about two months, most of them just as snotty as that one. However, the first one is different. The first one says what a wonderful time he's having. And it comes with a picture."

Locke opened the attachment. It showed Mr Theodore Genuflect Broadsheet standing in front of the local town-hall. He wore sunglasses and a broad-brimmed hat and was giving two thumbs up to the camera.

Veronica leaned forward to study the picture more closely.

"But he's—"

"Yes, a spindly grey alien. Or something that looks very much like one."

"Didn't one of those lunatics who turned up at the flat say they got their message from a spindly grey alien?"

"Indeed. I think we should go and find this Mr Genuflect Broadsheet."

A diminutive figure stood in the alleyway behind a betting shop, sucking on a rueful cigarette after losing fifty quid on a sure thing running in the 3:15 at Chepstow. He wore ill-fitting motorcycle leathers and a helmet to disguise his alien features, but the visor was open to accommodate his smoking habit – two cigarettes stuck in a pair of slit-like nostrils. Huge, glassy black eyes looked up at the sky when the light in the alleyway dimmed. Clouds raced overhead with unnatural speed, bringing a brief, frantic deluge of rain, hail and then snow.

The spate of abnormal weather ceased as abruptly as it began. The alien blinked with three sets of eyelids and muttered to himself.

"Bad juju. Bad, bad juju."

"There he is!"

A man and woman hurried down the alleyway toward him. Theodore Genuflect Broadsheet casually discarded the cigarette, flicked down his visor and then bounded away as if he had springs on his feet.

Thomas Locke hauled himself over a wall the alien had cleared without breaking stride. Behind him, Veronica staggered to a halt in her high heels and waved a dismissive hand.

"Sod that. Call me when you catch him."

Her words reached Locke just as he toppled over the wall's snow-dusted summit and fell onto a collection of sodden cardboard boxes. Mr Genuflect Broadsheet disappeared around a corner. Locke scrambled to his feet and ran on, but by the time he reached that corner, there was no sign of the spindly alien.

He took a few moments to catch his breath. He checked his watch, looked around, looked down. There was an empty milk bottle lying in the gutter. He moved it onto the pavement and set it spinning. When it stopped, it pointed thataway. That was the way Locke duly went.

The shop assistant bobbed a smiley face into Veronica's peripheral vision and asked if she needed any help. Veronica turned her head, glared at the assistant for a moment and then removed her headphones.

"What?"

"Err, is there any kind of shoes you're looking for in particular?"

Before Veronica could answer, her memories shifted again. Without music to block him out, Vincent insinuated himself into the moment before. He'd been standing behind the assistant, holding up a tempting pair of black and gold stilettos.

"I'm after trainers," said Veronica. "Ones good for running."

* * *

When Theodore Genuflect Broadsheet was sure his pursuer was lost far behind him, he scampered up a drainpipe and onto the roof of a house. From his new perch, he surveyed the street below.

"He's wasting time, wasting time," muttered the alien.

A skylight opened behind him. Locke poked his head out.

"Then the sooner you and I have a chat, the better."

Veronica paid for her new shoes with the money from Christian Weeks' wallet and wore them out of the shop. They were remarkably soft and springy compared to her trademark high heels, but they also made everyone else appear several inches taller. This would take some getting used to.

She passed a litter bin and considered throwing her old shoes away. He made her wear them, just like he made her smoke those cigarettes. She decided to dump the heels and move on. But… Vincent had always said how sexy she looked in them.

While she was stuffing them into her handbag, her phone rang. It was Locke.

"How far are you from Grenadine Park?"

At the centre of Grenadine Park was a large boating lake. On a summery bank holiday it would be full of hapless landlubbers taking to the water and attempting to row around the small island in the centre of the lake while those landlubbers who knew their place promenaded around the lakeside or picnicked on the grass. But today was a normal working day. The water was left to flotillas of ducks and swans.

A large white pavilion overlooked the lake. Once it had been an up-market restaurant, now the windows were boarded up and signs warned that the premises were guarded by a security firm instructed to prosecute all trespassers. By Veronica's reckoning, there were at least fifty trespassers currently in the main hall and if they were ever taken to court, she wouldn't be the only one questioning her grip on reality.

A man sat at an abandoned restaurant table reading 'Paradise Regained'. His hair was golden, his bare torso bronzed and giant, feathered wings sprouted from his back. Aliens sat around another table playing Gin Rummy. A translucent human couple dressed in early Victorian attire argued about the refereeing decisions in last night's football match and drifted through decayed fixtures and fittings. Juvenile troglodytes ran around with arms outstretched pretending they were Daleks, while their parents watched on wearily from alongside a stack of suitcases.

"So this is what a fantasy convention looks like," remarked Veronica.

Theodore Genuflect Broadsheet just grunted in reply and led her over to a set of glass doors whose view of the promenade was blocked by planks of wood. Locke was there arguing with a potted plant.

"And how do you suggest I stop him?" asked Locke.

"Find a way!" said the potted plant. "That's what you do, isn't it? Find things."

"He wouldn't let me find that."

"Then find the girl. Find her and then find some place safe to take her."

"I've already told you that she's—"

"Hidden, yes, you keep saying that," said the plant, shaking its leaves irritably, "but have you considered finding out *how* she's been hidden away?"

Veronica interjected.

"Why do you lot care about Emily Wilson?"

"We don't," said Broadsheet. "We care about getting home."

"The slipstream only flows when they bring her here," explained the potted plant. "Since they hid her away, no one has been able to travel from nowthen to whichwhen."

"And if Lafarge loses her for good, we'll never get home," added Broadsheet. "That's why we need you to stop him."

Veronica and Locke walked around the edge of the lake.

"He must be doing this for a reason," said Locke.

"There is nothing reasonable about Lafarge," said Veronica. "Have you forgotten we're talking about a five year old girl?"

"I didn't understand why he took my memories until I smashed the figurine, but I do now. He was trying to save me from remembering the truth."

"Remember the dancers' gate, Thomas? All those

people…" She hesitated, thinking of Darren Wynne. "You didn't think Lafarge was the spirit of benevolence after that."

"I'm just saying we shouldn't jump to conclusions. Why should we trust what a potted plant tells us? Or a travel agent? Seems wiser to assume nothing until we understand more about what's going on."

"Ha! That's rich coming from the guy who keeps telling me how we can understand nothing and that's the spiteful way of the world. We don't have time to figure out who's telling the truth, Thomas. We need to act and I'd rather put my trust in a shrubbery than have faith in your partner."

"Then your trust would be misplaced, Mrs Drysdale," said a park warden planting flowers by the path.

"Excuse me?"

The warden stood up and dusted soil off his hands.

"There are things of the edge and beyond that are far worse than Mr Lafarge. On behalf of The Ministry of Checks and Balances, I do respectfully ask that on this occasion, you let him do his job."

And then all the birds became mice and fell from the sky in a chorus of alarmed squeaking.

"Another aberration," said the fat man, looking out the second floor window of an exclusive gentleman's club.

On the roof of a car in the street below, a pair of stunned rodents tried to work out where their wings had gone.

"Yes, sir," said Christian Weeks, "it's consistent with a disruption on plane thirteen."

The fat man shook his head and returned to a red leather armchair and a glass of brandy. His most trusted employees stood to attention around him.

"I suppose that means Carstairs is…"

"Yes, sir."

"How soon before—?"

His question was cut short by the tessellated pattern running across the wallpaper twisting into a map of Chipping Sodbury. The carpet – previously a thick pile of burgundy and cream – undulated and rippled until it became a morass of upmarket ice cream. The men in the room were too professional to voice their shock, but they felt the gravity of the situation in their bowels. Christian Weeks consulted a mole-skin gyroscope.

"Plane twelve, sir," he reported. "At this rate we have an hour at most."

His boss rubbed a finger between his eyebrows and then raised a hand. It was supposed to be a calming gesture, but it lasted only a moment before falling flat against the padded arm of the chair.

"Gentlemen, I advise you all to put your affairs in order. Weeks, please notify the families of Carstairs and whoever we had on plane twelve that… well, you know."

"Yes, sir. Sir, are we still—?"

"We must, Weeks. The future of the business is at stake." The fat man hung his head. "And without the business we have nothing."

"What is wrong with this picture?"

A question from two seconds ago. A question that had never been asked. A question Vincent Drysdale posed to his wife while gesturing at the park warden.

Veronica couldn't see anything wrong with this picture. The man before her appeared quite normal. True, his rigidly placid expression suggested he was unaware his face could communicate anything other than smugness, but that was more irritating than wrong. His uniform was muddied about the knees, his shoes unremarkable. What was she missing?

"There are some things that are meant to be lost," said the warden.

"But why this girl?" asked Locke. "What has she done?"

"It's not what she's done," replied the warden, "it's what she is. I can explain further, if you wish. I have a shed over there. It has tea-making facilities."

"He's holding us up," said Veronica, "trying to make us waste time."

"I am trying to stop you from making a mistake."

"Look at his shadow."

The afternoon sun was still high in the sky. Most of the shadows falling across the park were short, but the warden's stretched long, too long for the man stood before them.

"Saving Emily won't be a mistake," said Veronica. "Come

on, Thomas."

"He saved you both, once," the Warden said as they walked away. "Do not think he will be as generous if you cross him."

"What if he's right?" hissed Locke to Veronica. "And even if he's lying, how exactly are we supposed to stop Lafarge?"

As soon as he finished his question, Veronica remembered hearing Vincent speaking at the same time.

"The warden can show you the way."

"Veronica, are you all right?" asked Locke.

"You should do what the shrubbery suggested," she replied. "Try and find out how they're keeping Emily hidden. Call me if you make any progress."

"And what are you going to do? Buy a tracksuit to go with the new shoes?"

"Maybe I will. Now get going. It's half past four. We have less than an hour."

Veronica fished out her headphones as Locke hurried off and then froze. The music had been a blessed relief from Vincent's incursions into her memories, but now, however much she hated the idea, she wanted to hear what he had to say.

She ran back to where the warden had been.

He was gone.

She looked around. The warden was walking toward a park exit. She ran after him. He stepped out onto the pavement as a mother with a pushchair passed by and then did a smart about face and began walking back again.

Veronica ducked out of sight behind a tree.

"Look at the shadow!"

The silhouette of the warden darkening the path by his feet was back to its proper dimensions. Veronica raced past him onto the street to see the mother with the pushchair now trailing an unnaturally long shadow behind her.

The office administrator looked Locke up and down, but mainly down – she was well over six foot tall, but still felt the need to wear three inch heels.

"So you're the clerk who's starting next week?" she asked.

"Yes," said Locke.

"Well, in light of your irrational keenness, I suppose I

should give you the tour. Follow me."

The giantess led Locke through an open plan office. Partitions divided up dozens of deskbound workers, each busy in front of a computer screen. Locke glanced at one monitor in passing and guessed the company's business was corporate solitaire solutions. He didn't know how this place was connected to Emily Wilson's disappearance, but he trusted his talent. Locke checked his watch. Less than half an hour to go.

The shadow became increasingly difficult to track as it led Veronica along a busy road and jumped from once person to another. The sun passed behind a cloud.

"Shit!"

"Watch the reflections."

Veronica could no longer tell if she was just remembering Vincent's words or hearing them for real. She glanced at the shop windows lining the street. For one man, they acted like a house of mirrors, warping and distorting his reflection while leaving the reflections of those around him unchanged. Then the effect jumped to a woman… a child… an old lady.

Veronica ended up following a pasty-faced youth in a blazer between the concrete grey tower-blocks of the town's technical college and into an underground car-park.

"Go carefully, my love."

She flinched at the words, but took the advice. Moving silently from a pillar to the cover of a car, she watched the youth open a door bearing a warning that danger of death by electricity lurked within. When he stepped inside, Veronica hurried over and peered around the doorframe.

The room beyond was empty save for a mirror. This mirror did not distort the youth's reflection, but rather transformed it into a much taller man wearing orange overalls. The man and boy kept walking as they reached the mirror, but instead of hitting glass, they passed straight through, each taking the other's place, the boy walking away in the mirror-world, the man heading out toward Veronica.

"You need to get through there."

"Naturally," she muttered.

She ducked out of sight and then returned to the door

when the man in orange overalls had gone. She forced it open.

The mirror stood before her. It reflected an empty room. Veronica walked over and touched a cold, unyielding surface.

"It's a sub-office of The Ministry of Checks and Balances," explained Vincent Drysdale. *"For something to go in, something must come out."*

"So how—?"

"By listening to me. You always used to be so good at that."

"Only because you sold off my free will to buy that tumble dryer."

"Is now really the time for a marital tiff?"

"Just tell me how to get through there."

"Okay, step back. Keep going. Stop there. Now, close your eyes."

She drew in an anxious breath and did as instructed.

"If you're messing with me, Vincent…"

"It's my raison d'être, Veronica dear. You may now open your eyes."

Looking again upon the mirror stole the air from her lungs. She reeled backwards, a trembling hand held to her mouth. Vincent Drysdale now served as her reflection. He smiled slightly and nodded his head.

Veronica averted her eyes, told herself he couldn't be there; this was all in her head.

But he was there, in the mirror, waiting patiently with hands clasped behind his back.

She turned her back on him and fished the headphones from her bag. When music was playing in her ears, she dared face the mirror again.

Vincent Drysdale was gone.

Veronica's racing heartbeat began to subside. She walked up to the mirror. It felt as solid to the touch as before. She took a deep breath, then retreated and rubbed her hands down her face. Those same hands began shaking when she lifted them to her ears. Deep breaths, she told herself. Think of that smiling girl in the photograph, think of Emily. Do it for her.

She removed the headphones and faced the mirror.

Vincent Drysdale pointed to his watch.

Veronica strode towards him. He matched her step for

step, drawing closer, his eyes never leaving hers. She couldn't help but think the faint smile playing on his lips was triumph at her walking willingly back into his arms.

She almost stopped, unable to bear being this close to the man who had stolen her life away and forced happiness upon her in return, but instead she kept walking and kept her eyes open as her face reached his and his touch became an open door to the Ministry of Checks and Balances.

"This is the break room and this is the coffee machine," said the office administrator. "It does tea and hot chocolate as well, but they all end up tasting like coffee, so you're kidding yourself if you press any of the other buttons."

Locke nodded, but he wasn't really paying attention. Instinct told him the answer was here. He pressed the button for coffee. Coffee was duly dispensed. He pressed the button for tea. Coffee was duly dispensed. He pressed the button for chocolate…

"Mr Harris, if you don't mind, I still have to show you the toilets."

"Would you mind giving me a hand to shift this?" asked Locke, attempting to move the vending machine from its position by the wall.

"Yes, I would. I don't know what you're playing at, Mr Harris—"

"A-ha! This is it," said Locke, locating the vending machine's plug. "Coincidence, I think not."

The plug bore a label stating when it was last checked by an electrician.

"This is the same date Emily Wilson went missing," said Locke. "I don't suppose you know if it was same date this machine arrived?"

"Why would I know that?" asked the office administrator, throwing her hands in the air. "I have to say, I am beginning to doubt you are Mr Harris."

"Doubt's a healthy thing; I wouldn't beat yourself up about it. I don't suppose you can lend me a pen?"

"No. Can I see some form of identification?"

"No, it's okay. I've found one."

Thomas Locke carefully over-wrote the year written on

the electrician's inspection label. When he was done, a curious thing happened. The vending machine slipped out of focus, its lines and details suddenly unclear, as if seen through marbled glass. Then it began to twist and change, rotating through a kaleidoscope of colours and dimensions until it finally resolved itself into the shape of a middle-aged woman in a black dress, kitten heels and gold hoop earrings.

"Now, that wasn't so bad," said the woman who was previously a vending machine. "Certainly better than being a prosthetic leg, though not, I fancy, half as good as being a canal boat."

The office administrator's jaw hung open.

"Who are you?" Locke asked the woman in the black dress.

"Who are you?" she asked in reply.

"I asked first."

"That's hardly the point. If you don't know who I am, that suggests you are not with the company, which suggests… Oh no. You brought me back early, didn't you?"

"I just got the feeling that if I changed the date—"

"Where's the photocopier?" demanded the woman.

Locke looked at the office administrator, who continued to stare, mouth agog.

The black-dressed woman's eyes went wild. She grabbed Locke by the arms, her voice rising an octave as she asked again: "Where is the photocopier?"

"I think it was back this way," he replied, leading her from the break room into the open-plan area.

Rows of desks blocked sight of the photocopier, but its location was evident from the commotion erupting on the far side of the office.

"I hope you know the way to the fire escape," said the woman, backing away from the alarmed shouts.

"Why?" asked Locke. "Who's the photocopier going to turn into?"

The black-dressed woman looked at him, her face deathly pale.

"Hurricane Betsy."

Christian Weeks once again sat on a bench in the garden of January Square. He watched an old man in a light blue tracksuit jog round and round the square in what Weeks guessed was a daily defiance of both age and the rush hour crowds.

Beyond the park railings, commuters hurried home after a day at work. They past junior solicitors celebrating the prospect of another evening of unpaid overtime with a bitter cigarette. A girl with pink hair closed up a flower shop and crossed to the café to greet a man who, his dark skin aside, was the spitting image of Humphrey Bogart.

The rustling trees were first to give voice to the rising wind, then the café awning began to flap noisily. Cups on the tables below began to rattle. The sudden gale buffeted the commuters, prompting many to lower their heads and pull up their collars. Blue sky to the east gave way to black clouds.

"Welcome back, Betsy," said Christian Weeks. He fished some more chewing gum from his pocket.

The wind grew stronger. The elderly jogger stumbled and fell into the road, forcing a car to brake suddenly. The girl from the flower shop rushed over to help him. The old man clutched at his chest. The black Bogart shouted for a doctor. A junior solicitor rang for an ambulance.

Weeks sighed and checked his watch.

"Please hurry it up, Mr Lafarge, a man get bored of waiting for his fate."

Everything was made of numbers: the worn stone blocks under Veronica's trainers; the chains that wound around gears in constant motion; even the grain of the wooden shelves formed digital sequences. Flickering lights, clocks and timers showed yet more numbers, each one counting up or down in response to some unknown calculation.

Veronica walked on into a mist where the ever-changing figures hung in the air, drawn by lasers shining from a ceiling impossibly high above. A belt of coiled number eights rose up out of a hole in the ground beside her and turned a cog that wound a pulley that pulled a bank of computer screens overhead. As Veronica watched it pass by, she half-tripped over a mass of cables leading up to a column of rotating crystals that looked to have streams of numbers running through them.

"The metrics of reality," said Vincent Drysdale, *"measured and monitored and kept in perfect check."*

"Why?"

"Oh, I don't know. Someone probably thinks it's a good idea."

"Then that someone should be paying more attention, because from my point of view, reality hasn't been living up to its name lately. What am I supposed to be doing here anyway?"

"Paying attention."

"To what?"

"The numbers of course."

Veronica huffed irritation before studying the crystal column more carefully. She could make no sense of the numbers within. They could be counting sheep for all she knew – a steady, diligent totting up of all the sheep in the universe. As she watched, the figures began changing faster and faster, accelerating until they became a frantic blur.

The chaos passed as swiftly as it arrived, the numbers around her slowing to their previous, stately progression, even as those further along the passageway began accelerating. A wave of mathematical disruption was surging through this sub-office of the Ministry of Checks and Balances.

Veronica blinked her thoughts into gear.

"That's him, isn't it?"

She didn't wait for her husband's reply before racing off in Lafarge's wake.

Locke and the woman in the black dress hunkered down in a recessed doorway. One hundred mile an hour winds blasted bins, bicycles and unfortunate pedestrians down the street in front of them.

"My name is Rossalyn Doden," she explained, shouting over the roar of the storm. "I'm a folder by trade. I take things and turn them into other things. It's a simple enough skill, provided you can get the hang of manipulating matter in fifteen dimensions simultaneously. When we're asked to hide something, it's standard practice for us to go into hiding until such a time it is deemed our knowledge can no longer harm our clients. You bringing me back earlier triggered one of the measures put in place to safeguard that knowledge."

"The hurricane."

"Precisely."

"Well, I'm afraid your good work hiding Emily Wilson was in vain. Lafarge is coming for her. If you can tell me—"

"Save yourself the trouble, young man. You can't stop him. I told the men from the company the same thing, but I think they already knew."

"Please. I'm doing this for a friend. I've got to try."

Aided by her new trainers, Veronica managed to overtake the anomaly sweeping through the metrics of reality. She didn't know where it was going, but she was still determined to get there first.

The frantic numbers chased her up a flight of stairs, across a gantry and into another maze of shifting clockwork.

Veronica skidded to a halt. Ahead, chains and axles spun gears and lifted counterweights around numbers of all shapes and sizes; numbers cast in metal and wood, light and ink and yet, together, they drew lines and shapes that Veronica vaguely recognised. She squinted and the picture became clear – these numbers measured the reality of a place she knew.

An ambulance pulled onto January Square as the squalling wind shook lampposts and toppled a rickety chimney stack from its roof. Bricks crashed against the road below, but the sound was lost to the roar of the hurricane.

The paramedics exited their vehicle and fought their way through the elements to reach the café. Moments later, the elderly jogger was on a stretcher and being lifted into the back of ambulance.

And then world went mute.

The storm did not subside, but if it gave off sound, no one could hear it. The paramedics glanced at each other warily before continuing their work. The people gathered in the café communicated their confusion with troubled faces and distraught gestures.

"We apologise for this temporary failure of service," announced a disembodied female voice, "we are doing our best to fix the problem as quickly as we can."

The surrounding trees shook first to crackling static and then to a few bars of an obscure country and western song nobody recognised.

A strong smell of creosote swept through the square.

Green became black became blue became red.

Christian Weeks tied a silver cord about his waist and fastened one end to a stake covered in abstract symbols. This stake was driven into the ground, where the point cut through dirt and dimensions and anchored itself solid. The colleagues standing by him in the garden did the same.

A ripple of static raised hairs on the back of necks. Visions of distant heavens and earthly hells swam in front of eyes. Memories of lives lived long ago danced with memories of breakfast, lunch and dinners to come.

The flow of time stuttered, re-wound, stopped. How long it remained like that, no one present could tell.

"Thank-you for bearing with us, normal service is now resumed."

Time flowed. Visions faded and colours cycled back to their original hue. The screaming assault of the hurricane began again, now louder than ever. Christian Weeks hefted a giant gun of gold loaded with iced fury and shouted louder still.

"Brace yourselves!"

Veronica smelt the burning of gears turning too fast. Digital displays flickered and flashed up blocks of corrupted pixels. Counterweights flew back and forth overhead. She took refuge beside a clattering abacus and covered her head with her handbag.

The panic lasted only a few moments. The counters returned to their regular, steady pace. No more numbers accelerated to a blur. The disturbance had ended its journey here without further incident.

Then she saw it; a single, unassuming digit, written with ink upon a scrap of paper. While all the others describing January Square kept changing, this number remained constant.

The number was zero.

"Still no pulse!" said the paramedic.

He was in the back of the ambulance, performing CPR on the elderly jogger. His partner was beside him, priming the defibrillator.

"What weight do you reckon he is?"

"Sixty-five kilos."

"One-thirty joules, charged. Clear."

The jogger bucked on his stretcher in response to the shock, then the whole ambulance rocked to the sound of mechanical wailing outside.

"Jesus, feels like world war three's kicking off out there."

The first paramedic continued his attempts to resuscitate.

"Still nothing."

"Upping the dose. Clear."

The defibrillator delivered another shock. The electrocardiogram continued to flat-line.

"Stubborn old bastard, isn't he?"

The back doors of the ambulance suddenly opened. A man climbed inside.

"Hey!" cried the first paramedic.

"What the Hell are you doing?" asked his partner.

"Trying to save her life," said Locke, pulling off the jogger's left trainer and sock.

"*Her* life? What? Just get the—"

But Locke had already snapped off the old man's big toenail and revealed Rossalyn Doden's mark – a Celtic symbol he pressed with a similarly marked ring.

The two paramedics watched dumbfounded as the old man melted away into a twisting morass of fractals, which swelled and spun and slowly reshaped themselves into the form of a five year old girl.

Veronica had never heard architecture scream before, but that was the only way she could describe the sound that filled the sub-office of the Ministry of Checks and Balances. Hydraulic rams pushed floors and walkways into new positions to accommodate the descent of the ceiling. Great chains pulled the walls closer together, but not fast enough to prevent a series of twisted minarets crashing through a section of masonry. A great dome exploded up through the floor some distance away.

The whole place was contracting around Veronica and she didn't know where to run.

* * *

"What in God's name just happened here?" asked the paramedic, backing away into the cab of his ambulance.

His partner just stared at Emily Wilson as she sat up on the stretcher and nervously surveyed her surroundings.

"It's okay, Emily," said Locke, "your parents hired me to find you."

She gave a fearful squeak and backed up into the corner, hugging her knees to her chest.

"Oh, Jesus Christ. Jesus Christ this is bad," muttered the paramedic in the cab.

"She looks more like some kind of miracle to me," said his partner.

"Not her. Take a look outside."

Thomas Locke did not look out the window. He ignored the bright flashes of colour that washed the inside of the ambulance and the terrifying noises that followed. Instead he held his hand out to the young girl and spoke softly.

"Emily, my name is Thomas Locke. I am a private detective and what I'm about to say may sound strange, but it is absolutely true. There is a man coming who wishes to wipe you from existence. Hold on to my hand and do not let go."

Christian Weeks was the only one left. Black chasms defied gravity to reach up from the ground around him into the storm-wracked sky. The dead walked as fire. Blood hung in the air. His anchoring cord felt hopelessly tenuous as the black shadow clad in hat and coat walked toward him, but the company man did not waver.

Weeks fired his gun, but the ammunition lost its way on leaving the barrel and blasted a tree into a frozen expression of rage. Scraps of paper whirled around his feet; laughter written in felt tip letters.

Christian Weeks forced a grin.

"You think this was the best we could do?" he asked.

Lafarge said nothing.

"We were merely the appetiser."

Lafarge kept coming.

"The bait for the trap."

Christian Weeks triggered another unfolding: the benches; the trees; the scarred paving stones underfoot, all warping from what they were into creatures barely constrained by physical form.

And then Christian Weeks lost his mind.

The contraction of the Ministry of Checks and Balances sub-office abruptly ceased. The once vast interior had shrunk to become a large room with shards of other buildings cutting through it.

Veronica crept out from behind cover and swept dust from her hair. She looked upon the numbers of January Square and saw they weren't numbers any more. They had become eldritch symbols the sight of which struck pain into her eyes. She covered her face as the measure of unearthly monstrosities steadily engulfed that single zero.

Locke ran with Emily into the café. The windows had shattered, leaving shards of glass littered amongst the remains of the people who had been sheltering here; collateral damage from the battle outside.

They ran behind the counter and into a back room. There was a door. It was locked. He began trying to kick it open.

Veronica dared to remove the hand that covered her face. The alien numbers were still there, but one by one they were falling, succumbing to a tide of zeroes.

Locke finally broke open the door, but stark blackness waited beyond.

His phone rang. He answered it while doubling back.

"He's still coming," Veronica told him over the phone.

"I know."

Locke pushed open the door to the gents toilets and led Emily inside.

"Where are you?"

"Not close. I… I don't know what I can do."

The windows in the toilets were all narrow and set high in the wall. They too showed darkness outside.

"Cross your fingers."

"Already crossed. Thomas… if you can't reason with him, don't…"

"Don't what?"

"Don't think that just because you don't exist, no one will care if you get lost."

Locke turned in desperation to the door, the only way out. He could feel Lafarge drawing near. He looked down at Emily. She attempted a brave smile despite her trembling bottom lip.

"Thanks Veronica," he said into the phone. "If I don't see you… well, I hope you find everything works out."

He hung up, gathered Emily in his arms and hid in the last of the toilet cubicles.

Veronica watched a sea of digits gradually flipping over to zero. She tried to stop them. Where pencils wrote numbers on scrolling paper, she tore the paper and broke the lead. Where coloured beads shuttled back and forth across metal rods, she hammered the rods out of shape with the soles of her old high heels. Where cards flipped over on spiral bindings, she tried to hold the zero back with her fingers. But the system fought against her, grinding gears and forcing more pressure through its pistons until Veronica was beaten.

She collapsed onto the floor.

"What can I do?" She looked up, raised her voice. "Vincent, talk to me! Tell me how I stop him."

Emily Wilson did not ask any questions. She remained dutifully silent in Locke's arms. He squatted on the toilet seat, staring at the bolt securing the door in front of him.

He just loses things, Locke told himself. I do the finding. He won't find us. We'll be okay.

A loud bang admitted a breeze that swept dirt and dust across the floor of the toilets. Locke looked down to the gap beneath the stall door. A scrap of paper tumbled into view, followed by another and another. They began to dance this way and that as the wind grew more capricious. Some fluttered into the cubicle. Locke could read the writing without bending down.

'Where are you, Thomas Locke?'

'Give me the girl, Thomas Locke.'

'Where are you, Thomas Locke?'

'She must be lost, Thomas Locke.'
'Give me the girl, Thomas Locke.'
'Give me the girl, Thomas Locke.'
'Give me the girl, Thomas Locke.'

Veronica ascended. As the matrices of January Square reduced to zero, balance was maintained by a counterweight rising through holes cut in the floors above. Veronica held onto the rope that hoisted the counterweight and attacked the twine with the sharpened point of a nail file.

Locke saw a shadow fall across the floor outside the cubicle and then the door was gone. Lafarge stood before him.

"This wasn't part of our deal," said Locke.

Lafarge said nothing.

The rope snapped. The weight plunged downwards, carrying Veronica with it.

She made a frantic grab for a passing ledge and reached it with desperate fingers. Her legs swung wildly beneath her, eroding her tenuous grip, but she held on and prayed Vincent's plan would work.

"Trust me. This will put things right."

Long seconds passed and then a faint crash rose from below.

In a town notable for not very much stood an unremarkable building. Inside that building was an apartment. Taped to the front door of that apartment was a scrap of notepaper with words scrawled in black marker pen.

That note now falls to the floor. The paper crumples into a ball and the ink bleeds until the words can no longer be read and its blackness stains the floor.

Up until a few minutes ago, the apartment contained all manner of things, but those things have been disappearing one by one until all that remains are furnishings bequeathed by an old woman to a grand-daughter who never came. And, lying in a dusty corner, a choker necklace and a pair of earrings.

A man who was not there a moment before picks up the

necklace and the earrings. He handles them with care, collecting the jewellery into a handkerchief. He leaves shortly after.

Locke did not move from the toilet stall. Emily Wilson had her arms wrapped around him and her head buried against his chest. She showed no signs of wanting to let go. He stroked her hair and stared blankly into space.

"It's okay, it's over. It's all over."

Interlude VIII

Emily and her parents fed the ducks at Grenadine Park until their bags of breadcrumbs were empty, then they waved goodbye to Veronica and Locke, who were idling across the lake in a rowing boat. He was exhausted from ferrying aliens, angels and other assorted tourists to the slipstream portal on the island in the middle of the lake, while she didn't like the idea of exhaustion and refused to row back to shore.

"You know, I don't see Vincent any more," she said.

"I didn't know that, but that's good. I'm happy for you."

"Do you think Lafarge is gone too?"

Locke sighed. "Sometimes I find myself dreaming of that joyous day when you finally realise I never know the answers to your questions and you stop asking them, but alas—"

She punched him on the shoulder. "Pretend they're rhetorical then!"

The boat rocked, sending ripples out across the surface of the water. Locke watched them go; each one become fainter the further it ran away.

"It feels like he's gone," he said.

"And are you happy about that?"

"I don't know. I think I've forgotten what happy feels like."

Veronica smiled ruefully.

"At least maybe now you'll have a chance to remember."

Ice Cream in the Afterlife

The moment of awkwardness arrived. Locke raised his eyebrows noncommittally. Veronica nodded, checked her shoes, glanced around the station platform and then, for a fraction of a second, met his eyes. They both managed a smile and silently agreed to shake hands instead of risking the sentimentality of a hug.

"Well, good luck," said Locke.

"Yeah, you too," replied Veronica.

He boarded his train. If he had any intention of lingering in the vestibule end to wave goodbye, the other passengers put paid to that, pushing Locke and his battered suitcase on into a crowded carriage.

The train began pulling away with Locke still trying to find a seat. Veronica raised a hand, but he didn't see her. When Locke did turn his head to look out of the window, she was already walking from the platform.

Veronica arrived back at her flat. Without the ephemera from The Office of Lost and Found, it felt larger, yet the empty space also contrived a sense of sheepishness about its newfound lack of purpose. Veronica switched on the television to fill the living room with noise and headed into the bedroom.

She pulled her most formal clothes from the wardrobe and laid them on the bed. In a box pushed to the back of the wardrobe was an old pair of black high heels. This was retrieved too, albeit without enthusiasm.

Veronica sat down on a chair and began unlacing the trainers she wore.

Locke stared out of the train window at the countryside passing by: fields, fences and distant villages. He waited for a glimpse of the horizon he knew lay beyond the confines of the town he'd left behind, but remained frustrated as embankments rose up on either side and reduced his view to a wall of grass and weeds.

And then the land abruptly fell away and Locke was overcome by the sight of a dream he'd once shared with a girl called Constance; a dream of sea and sky stretching off into the blue.

The office was a small and poorly lit. The only window looked out over a noisy shop floor where workers were busily assembling handbags. Behind the single desk sat a bushy-eyebrowed gentleman. The lettering on the door identified him as 'Mr Froggarty, Managing Director'. Sat on the opposite side of the desk was Veronica. He studied her over his spectacles.

"Oh, it's suddenly come to me!" he said. "I know where I've seen your face before. Your picture was in the paper, wasn't it? You helped find the Wilson girl."

Veronica squirmed inside.

"We weren't looking for publicity," she said.

They didn't even know a reporter had been outside the Wilsons' house until Locke picked up a discarded newspaper on the bus and began leafing through it. She expected the police to come calling as a result, but they didn't. Her crimes remained forgotten, even though Lafarge's spell had been lifted and people could remember her again. This should have come as a relief, but instead it felt as if some part of her took a perverse pleasure in being anonymous and detached from the ordinary world and resented being recognised again.

"This all rather begs an obvious question, doesn't it?" said Mr Froggarty. "Private detective to personal assistant? It's not the most obvious career progression."

"My… associate decided to take early retirement," explained Veronica, "and as I'd only fallen into the business by accident, it seemed a good opportunity to start something new."

Locke arrived at the village train station to be met by a Miss Gilling from the letting agency. They walked to her car discussing the fine weather, but on seeing a newsagent, Locke momentarily excused himself to buy a postcard.

Ten minutes later they were driving up a winding road leading away from the village. The view through the rear window perfectly matched that of the postcard – stout white houses clustered around a small bay, with fishing boats bobbing on the water.

Their destination was a cottage near the cliff-side. It was small, but fully furnished. The village could be seen from the kitchen window, rolling fields from the bedroom, while the lounge looked out toward the sea, even though the sea itself remained tantalisingly out of sight beyond the garden fence, road and cliff edge.

"I hope you'll be very happy here," said Miss Gilling as she handed Locke the keys.

"I'm sure I will," he replied.

One week later, Locke's postcard lay on Veronica's desk at Froggarty Premium Accessories Limited.

"Did he send this?" asked Sharon from accounts, picking it up.

"Depends which he you're talking about," said Veronica.

"'I think I've finally found where I belong, Thomas'," read Sharon. "Just Thomas? Not 'Love, Thomas' or 'Yours, Thomas' or—"

"He's not my Thomas and our relationship was purely professional."

"Relax, Ronnie, I was only asking." Her new colleagues had decided Veronica was a name with too many syllables. Vera was rejected as too old-fashioned and Nickie as too frivolous. Veronica didn't like being called Ronnie, but she wasn't about to admit it. "Still, I suppose it's quite sweet. I hope I find some place like that one day."

"Maybe you've already found it."

"What? Are you saying I belong in this dump? You are an evil woman, Ronnie. I won't ask if you're coming out for drinks after work now."

Veronica came along to the pub regardless. This was partly because Sharon had gone on to tell her that Martin would be miserable and depressed all evening if she didn't make an appearance, partly because she felt she should savour the company of people who could remember her from day to day.

The alcohol helped put her at ease. The jokes weren't always funny, but she laughed anyway, because everyone else was laughing and the novelty of socialising made her feel a little giddy. When it was her round, Martin came with her to collect the drinks from the bar.

"How long were you married?" he asked as they waited to be served.

"Too long," she replied.

"And now you're what? Divorced? Separated?"

"None of the above."

"I… I'm sorry, I didn't realise—"

"He's not dead either. It's complicated."

"Oh."

The barman came over. Veronica gave him their order.

"Martin, don't worry, my ex-husband is not an issue any more."

"And what about your old partner?"

"You mean my business associate."

"So you weren't—?"

"If you want to ask me out, ask me out. If I say no, it won't be because I have unresolved romantic issues; it'll be because I find you as attractive as a weasel with gout."

"A what?"

"Of course, if I say yes, it might just be the drink talking. Who's to say?" She paid the barman. "Get the drinks, Martin."

After they returned to the table, Martin was unusually subdued and Veronica found herself unable to engage with the conversation as before. She glanced around the pub. It was crowded with people drinking and talking. The last time she'd been in a place like this, the patrons had danced off into oblivion.

She excused herself and went outside for some fresh air. There was none directly outside thanks to the smokers gathered at the door. Sharon was amongst them.

"Are you off?" she asked. "It's still early. Not even eleven o'clock yet."

"Too late for me," said Veronica.

"Fine, have a good weekend then, lightweight. See you Monday."

"Yeah. You too."

Veronica started walking. On reaching the next junction she did not take the turn for home. Instead she took a road she had never walked down before. When she passed a couple walking in the opposite direction, Veronica checked the shadows they cast under the streetlights.

A cutting hidden between houses took her to a narrow park, bordered by the fences of backyards. A single path wound up a hill to a copse of trees. Unseen dogs barked as she passed. Halfway to the top, she had to step aside as a group of young lads careened down the path in a shopping trolley. One of them had a traffic cone on his head.

She reached another road of dark houses with lights out and curtains drawn. Faint music drifted on the breeze. Veronica headed toward its source and found a group of musicians playing in the car-park of a boarded up pub. While a guitarist played melody, a drummer beat rhythm on a tom-tom and a girl sang to the few people gathered around them. Plastic bags provided cans of beer, while a man with a drooping moustache dispensed category B substances in hand-made roll-ups.

Veronica walked away. She knew there was another side to this world, hidden around corners and in the depths of shadows, but now when she sought it out, it was nowhere to be seen.

Locke couldn't sleep. The still silence of the cottage unsettled him. The lack of sirens, traffic and noisy passers-by was welcome, but he had grown accustomed to the peculiar atmosphere of The Office of Lost and Found. Few others would have noticed the air inside dancing this way and that as objects appeared and disappeared, but for Locke it was the heart-beat of a universe going about its unknowable business. The feel of this silence was a pulse stopped; the universe left dead and cold outside the confines of his bed.

He got up, dressed and went outside. The sea told him to shush with each surge of water against the rocks below. The village in the bay was dark, but atop the cliffs on the far side a pair of headlights navigated the headland. Locke was reassured the universe continued to function, but he did not return to bed.

He walked beneath stars undimmed by pollution. He walked down to the sea and let the tide wash up against his shoes. He walked until the sun began to rise over the horizon, turning the inky black sea into rippling white and gold.

On a lonely beach of grey shingle he found a used signal flare covered in seaweed. He picked it up, washed it off in the surf and then placed it in his pocket.

Locke arrived in the village shortly after eight o'clock in the morning. The newsagent was just opening for the day.

"Good morning," said the owner, a lady in her sixties who looked as spry as a teenager. "You're the one who's moved in up at the old Brooker's cottage, right?"

"That's right. I'm Thomas Locke."

She shook his hand.

"Please to meet you, Thomas. I'm Agatha Joseph. Hope you've got a good deal on your rent, because I for one wouldn't want to be living up in that place."

"Why? You aren't going to tell me it's haunted are you?"

"I could if you liked, but I ain't ever heard tell of it being so. I will tell you to make sure you've got yourself some candles and a camping stove handy though, 'cause I do know the electrics up there are as flaky as my eldest nephew."

"I'm not sure if I have, to be honest."

"Get yourself over to Paul Deacon's store then. I can write you down some directions if you like."

"Thanks."

She headed inside the shop and Locke made to follow, but a notice in the window gave him pause. It was written in a shaky hand on a piece of torn card.

'Dog missing, brown and white terrier, responds to the name of Polly. Reward offered for safe return.'

There was also a phone number.

Locke read the message twice more, took a deep breath and chose to ignore it. He headed inside after Agatha Joseph.

Wednesday; Veronica bought her lunch from a pastry shop. She exited into bright sunshine and walked to the crowded town square. Children were playing in the fountains. She found space on a bench and sat down. It was easy to imagine everyone had come out to take advantage of the good weather. While she ate, Veronica watched the world go by, paying particular attention to the bare arms and legs of a group of male students circuit training up and down the town hall steps. By the time she'd finished eating, they'd worked up quite a sweat. She considered going over and offering to help them towel off.

Her phone rang. It was Sharon.

"Ronnie, you're not going to believe this," said the girl from accounts.

"Shazza, I don't believe, I just accept."

"Right. Well, there's the hottest bunch of guys up at the town hall. They've been working out on the steps and, Ronnie, I'm telling you, their vests are literally clinging to their muscles and their muscles are kind of glistening and Joan and I figure they're probably dehydrated, their mental faculties are diminished and frankly, babe, it's fresh meat there for the taking."

"I'm already there."

"Great, I've bagsied the blonde one. If you can out-run Joan you can have the brunette, otherwise I'm afraid you'll be stuck with the ginger."

"This is why I wear trainers to work."

Veronica hung up and saw Sharon and Joan climbing the town hall steps, trying to look coyly seductive while bearing cones of rapidly melting ice cream. She stood up and disposed of the paper from her lunch into a bin.

Her phone rang again, an unknown number. She answered it.

"Look to your left, Veronica, and please do not be alarmed."

But she could not turn her head. She could not bring herself to look, because she recognised that voice. Only the burning need to be sure cured her paralysis.

He walked toward her across the square. The world should have stopped to allow his passage, but it didn't. He had to stop to let people pass and was forced to walk around others, but to Veronica he might as well have walked straight toward her. He stopped a respectful distance away.

"I had to tell you myself," said Vincent Drysdale. "I couldn't let someone else do this for me. I couldn't risk you glimpsing me out the corner of your eye and wondering whether I was real or whether you were going crazy."

She felt sick, confused, betrayed, angry, scared – a delirious bedlam of thoughts and emotions that she dared not show.

"I might have preferred crazy."

"All I can say is this: I don't know why it happened, but I do know that the Vincent Drysdale you knew, your husband, he has been lost forever and is never coming back and I know… I know I wear his face and speak with his voice and that's why I am now going to leave. I promise you will never see me again."

With those words, he turned and walked away. Veronica was left in a state of shock, unsure if this moment was real or another fictitious memory.

Her phone rang again. It was Sharon.

"They were all gay. Who was the guy you were just talking to? He was cute."

Thomas Locke had the collar of his coat turned up against the chill sea breeze. He knelt on damp shingle, disentangling a prosthetic foot from a frayed fishing net. A shout rang out from across the beach.

"Ho there!"

Locke turned his head. A Dalmatian scampered up and began sniffing his nose.

"Leave the man alone, Dotty!" ordered the dog's owner, a tall man whose head appeared to be a writhing mass of grey hair.

The instruction only prompted Dotty to switch her attention from Locke's face to his protruding rear end. He stood up quickly.

"I take it that's not yours," said the dog's owner, walking up and nodding to the foot in Locke's hand. The wind briefly swept aside enough beard and fringe to confirm the man possessed a human face.

"Err, no," replied Locke, "but I thought there might be an unfortunate fisherman hopping around on a boat somewhere and he would be grateful if a passer-by saw fit to salvage this."

"Ha! Good! Good thinking! I'm Roland, Roland McCaffrey."

He held out a hand. Locke held out the foot, then caught his mistake and swapped it for a hand. The two hands shook.

"My name's Thomas Locke. I'm renting—"

"The old Brooker's cottage, I know, Agatha told me. Have the lights gone out yet?"

"No…"

"They will. Trust me. Make sure you've always got a carton of UHT milk in, that's what I'd suggest. Your fridge goes dead and you don't want your house stinking of bad milk."

"That's true, I wouldn't want that."

"Well, good meeting you, Thomas, but got to go, me and Dotty are on a mission."

"On a mission?"

"She's sniffing out a missing terrier. At least she's supposed to be. Keeps getting distracted by men crawling around on beaches. Ha! That'll be you, Thomas."

"Yes, I rather guessed it was."

"Come on, Dotty, you prefer sniffing bitches' backsides anyway."

Veronica was curled up on her settee, arms wrapped about her chest, headphones tight against her ears. The music was as loud as it would go. The bass vibrated through her skull. The tone of the melody became flatter the more she listened and her eardrums hurt, but it wasn't enough. She still couldn't stop thinking of him.

She didn't sleep that night. Restless hours in bed were abandoned for the television, for food eaten until her stomach was bloated, for pacing around the streets until the sun began to rise. It was bad when he was a ghost inside her head. Knowing he was alive, out there, somewhere – that was worse.

She called in sick.

"I've got the flu," she told Sharon.

"The hangover flu?"

"Something like that."

Veronica spent the rest of the day at the library using the free internet. The following morning she waited outside the apartments down by the Argent Bridge. Vincent Drysdale emerged at half past eight. She didn't need to tell the taxi driver to follow her ex-husband's car, he already knew the drill.

They were led to a semi-detached house with a paved front

garden and a furry white cat in the window. The top of a blue and red climbing frame peeked over the gate to the back garden.

Vincent Drysdale rang the bell. The door was answered by freckle-faced woman in a blue gingham dress. Vincent Drysdale was invited inside. He didn't leave until half past three that afternoon.

Three minutes later, Veronica rang the doorbell. The freckle-faced woman opened the door.

"Hello?"

"I'm sorry, but is he still here?" asked Veronica. "Did I catch him?"

"You're after Mr Drysdale?"

"I'm too late, aren't I?"

"I'm afraid he left not five minutes ago."

"Darn it," said Veronica. "I've tried calling him, but I keep getting his answering service. I'm sure you know what it's like. You never really get a feel for whether you can, you know, trust someone until you speak to them properly and when children are involved—"

"Oh, absolutely I know what you mean. When I heard Gina had taken her young Luke out of school for private tuition I was, I'll admit, a little concerned. Then I heard the price and I told her that you don't get anything good for that kind of money and this is your son's future we're talking about. But then I met Mr Drysdale…" The woman closed her eyes for a moment and smiled. "And, well, I'm sure it says everything that my Joshua started taking his lessons at home the very next day."

Thomas Locke stood at the newsagents' counter with a bottle of UHT milk and a newspaper.

"I can't stand the stuff personally," said Agatha Joseph, taking his change, "tastes like piss to me. Actually no, I tasted piss once, when I was in Cambodia, and UHT milk tastes worse."

"Thanks. Hopefully I won't have to drink it."

"Sorry, Mr Locke, but I fear it's only a matter of time."

"The letting agency promised me—"

"Of course they did, Mr Locke, of course they did."

"Right, thank you then."

"My pleasure."

On leaving the newsagents, Locke checked the window. The notice about the missing terrier was still there. He shook his head and set off home.

Locke spent the evening learning that the newspaper couldn't tell him anything he wanted to know. The news it reported bore no relation to life in the village and was wholly ignorant of the life he'd known back in the town. He threw the paper on the fire.

The phone in his new home rang for the very first time at two minutes past midnight.

"You should be in bed," Veronica told him by way of greeting.

"Maybe I was."

"You weren't."

"You know me too well."

"Unfortunately."

"Odd time to ring for a chat."

"Yeah, well, I thought you'd appreciate odd."

"Not really, though it does have a certain comforting familiarity."

"What are you doing?"

"Well, I was just getting ready for bed."

"God, you're not naked are you?"

"I'm going to say yes, just to distress you."

"But I know you're lying, so it won't work."

"Shame. I suppose I should ask how you are."

"I'm fine."

"Did you get the job?"

"Yes."

"Going well?"

"I suppose."

"Made lots of jolly new friends?"

"I wouldn't describe them as jolly."

"Good. You can't trust jolly."

"There's this terrible reality show thing on television right now."

"There usually is. Given I'm retired and you're the one with the job, shouldn't you be in bed?"

"Not tired."
"You can't sleep, can you?"
"If I was tired, I could sleep."
"Are you seeing him again?"
"…"
"Veronica?"
"Are you okay, Thomas?"
"I'm fine."
"Good, then we're both okay."
"Clearly."
"You should really watch this. It's really terrible."
"I'm putting it on now."
"Excellent, because I need to mock these people mercilessly and that's never as much fun when there's no one else around to listen."
"Well, it's on and I'm listening."

Vincent Drysdale arrived at the house of Joshua Dunne at nine o'clock sharp. He was always perfectly on time and always caught Joshua's mother, Mary, by surprise.
"Come through, come through," said Mary. "Luke's already here and playing with Joshua in the back garden, but there's someone I'd like you to meet first."
Mary led her son's teacher through to the kitchen, where a young woman dressed in clothes more appropriate to a ninety-forties black and white thriller was sipping at a cup of tea.
"This is Mrs Malone. She's thinking of submitting her daughter Alice for your tuition programme."
There was only the briefest of pauses before Vincent Drysdale offered his hand to shake.
"Pleased to meet you, Mrs Malone."
"Likewise, Mr Drysdale," said Veronica, declining the offered hand in favour of nodding her head and delivering a wry smile.
"Can I get you some tea, Mr Drysdale?" asked Mary.
Before he could reply, boyish shouts came from outside. Mary opened the back door.
"Luke! Joshua! Stop that!"
She ran out into the back garden. The only movement

from Vincent and Veronica was the loss of the polite smiles raised when they were pretending to be strangers.

"I tried to stay away," he said.

"You didn't go far enough," she replied.

"You didn't have to come and find me."

"After everything you've done, how could I not?"

Mary re-entered the kitchen dragging two young boys along by their earlobes. One was dressed in shorts and a t-shirt. The other was dressed in shorts and a fluorescent orange workman's jacket. When she let them go, the boys rubbed reproachfully at their ears.

"Explain yourselves then," ordered Mary.

"Tell him to go home!" insisted the one in the fluorescent jacket, staring daggers at the other.

"Joshua, I cannot tell Luke to go home," his mother replied. "He's here for his lessons and Auntie Gina's gone out to work."

"But he's a moron," said Joshua. "And a cretin."

"You're the moron," said Luke.

"You're the moron."

"What is it with you two today?" asked Mary.

"He said roadworks were rubbish," said Joshua.

"They are," said Luke. "They're rubbish. Only morons like roadworks."

"Roadworks rule. Only morons would say they don't. And only morons who are also cretins would say that direct mailing is better."

"Don't you go slagging off direct mailing!" cried Luke.

Vincent quickly stepped in to prevent another fight.

"I think we should separate them until they've both cooled off," he suggested.

"Good idea," agreed Mary, before waving a finger at her son. "You're going to your room, young man, and you're going to think carefully about what you've done here."

While Vincent took Luke into the dining room, Veronica followed Mary and Joshua upstairs.

"But mummy, I called a spade a spade. Daddy always says you should call a spade a spade and I did. Only the spade was Luke and he's a moron."

"Were they really arguing about roadworks and direct

mailing?" asked Veronica.

"You know what young boys are like," said Mary, reaching a door with a pint-sized 'Men at Work' road-sign Blu-tacked to it. "They go through phases and Joshua's is currently roadworks."

The bedroom was dark, the curtains still drawn, but in the gloom Veronica could make out various scale-model construction vehicles scattered across the floor. Books on building roads lined the shelves. A black bin bag in the corner was brim-full of stuffed animals and toys without links to road construction and maintenance. Luke jumped onto the unmade bed and hugged a traffic cone lying by the pillow.

"Don't expect Mr Coney to have any sympathy," said Mary. "You wouldn't catch him fighting anyone."

Veronica stared at the traffic cone and then excused herself, leaving the mother and son to head back downstairs.

Vincent was talking softly to Luke in the dining room.

"Have you ever seen direct mail encouraging anyone to hit anyone else around the head with a plastic spade?"

"No," sniffed Luke, "they're usually on about loans and stuff."

"Exactly, interest free loan for six months good, fighting bad."

"I suppose." Luke sniffed again. "What's she doing here?"

Vincent turned his head. Veronica stood behind him with hands on hips. She smiled sweetly at Luke.

"Why don't you go and play with the knives in the kitchen?" she suggested.

Luke's eyes lit up.

"Can I?" he asked his tutor.

Vincent sighed.

"Just for a second. And only the blunt ones."

Luke ran off. Veronica waited until he was out of earshot before speaking again.

"What are you doing here, Vincent? What are you doing with these children?"

"I am teaching them to read, to write and to perform basic arithmetic."

"And what else?"

"I've taught Luke how to juggle—"

"You traded souls. You destroyed lives. And now you expect me to believe you've become a simple teacher?"

Her ex-husband just shrugged.

"Is that the best response you've got?"

"Veronica, you've already judged me. Nothing I could say or do would convince you that you're wrong."

The Wilson family chose a good day to visit Thomas Locke. Sunshine welled in the bay and villagers pulled chairs outside to bask in the warmth. While her mother and father drank tea in a café overlooking the quayside, Emily Wilson played foreman to Locke's labourer in a project to dam a stream coursing down the beach to the retreating tide.

"Look what I've found," said Emily, running up to the squat wall of pebbles and shells that just about held a growing pool of water at bay.

"I'm not sure if a rubber glove is good dam-building material," said Locke.

"Of course not, silly. I thought you could add it to your collection."

"Ah, yes, I could at that. Thank-you, Emily."

They spent the afternoon walking along the cliff-tops until it was time for the Wilsons to head home. The four of them returned to the village and ascended the main street. Emily ran ahead, peering into each shop window she passed.

"Does she ever talk about the time she went missing?" asked Locke.

"We try not to mention it," said Emily's mother.

"I don't even know if Emily believes it really happened or not," said her father, "but there's a boy she's made friends with at school—"

"We try not to mention him either."

"They like each other, Irene."

"He's a troubled young boy. Emily can find better friends."

"Well, possibly, but they play this game—"

"It's not a game, it's an argument."

"An argument then. She says to him that one day the bogeyman came to snatch her away to the underworld. He tells her that for years monsters lived under his bed and one day they came out and the world nearly ended. So Emily says the world nearly ended worse when the bogeyman came. Then he says his monsters are worse than the bogeyman and—"

"It's all very childish," said Irene Wilson, "as you'd expect. The sooner they grow out of it the better."

"Quite," agreed Locke, making a mental note to call Veronica. "Besides, everyone knows which is worse."

Up ahead, Emily was jumping up and down and pointing to an advertising standee swinging gently in the breeze.

"Ice cream, Mummy! Can we have ice cream? Can we? Can we? Can we?"

"Are you sure you wouldn't prefer a nice bowl of Brussels sprouts?" called her father.

Emily pulled a face and stuck her tongue out.

"What do you think, Thomas?" asked Irene. "Ice creams all round?"

"Sounds good to me."

"Yay!" said Emily.

"But if you drop yours on the floor again," warned her mother, "you're not getting any of mine."

They exited the newsagents a few minutes later with two lollipops and two Cornettos.

"Have you seen this, Thomas?" asked Emily, licking her ice cream and pointing to the notice about the missing dog in the shop window.

"Oh, no, can't say I had."

"You should find it, Thomas."

"Emily, I... I don't do that any more."

"But you can find anything."

"I used to be able find anything, but now—"

"Thomas! It's a little dog! It needs finding!"

"Emily, I'm sorry..."

"Stop harassing him, Emily," said Irene. "Remember what he did for us. Be grateful for that."

Emily pouted and grumpily folded her arms across her chest. Locke looked again at the notice, but the notice was gone. Its disappearance was explained a second later when Agatha Joseph emerged from the newsagent with the scrap of paper in hand. She smiled down at Emily.

"I'm afraid your badgering of Thomas here came a day too

late, deary. A local man called Roland found our missing dog up on the moor yesterday evening. It was a bit the worse for wear and in need of some feeding up, but in a few days it'll be fine. I've been meaning to take this down."

"See, Emily?" said her mother. "Everything's worked out fine. Now stop pulling that face or the wind'll change and you'll stay that way."

Veronica arrived at the school gates as a bell rang to signal the end of lessons. She joined a handful of waiting mothers and fathers. This street was usually jam-packed with people carriers, today it was curiously quiet. The main doors opened and should have released a prepubescent stampede, but instead a sparse trickle of kids made their way outside. It was easy to spot Billy when he appeared. He grinned on seeing Veronica and trotted over.

"Hi Veronica, what are you doing here?"

"Just dropped by to see how you were doing."

"I'm good. What's with the trainers and the jeans? You look like a right scruff."

"Look who's talking. Isn't the point of a tie that it's tied, rather just draped around your neck?"

"The point of a tie is to complete a uniform and a uniform is about conformity and control. That's not how I roll."

"You've been watching too many movies, kid." Veronica glanced around. "School looks quiet today."

"It's like this every day now."

"How come?"

"Kids keep dropping out. Their parents want them taught at home instead. I've told Mum and Dad I could get taught at home too, but they won't have any of it. Say they can't afford it."

"They're probably right. I guess you've heard of this Mr Drysdale then?"

"Of course. The home-school kids won't shut up about how great he is."

"Is that why you want to get taught by him?"

"What? I don't want to get taught by that jerk."

"You have some sense then."

"Nah, the monsters under Mum and Dad's bed teach me

everything I need to know."

Veronica raised an eyebrow.

"What kind of things?"

"Black magic, forgotten history, trigonometry..."

"Billy, I'm not sure if you ought to be—"

"They also told me that the gods are coming."

"What?"

"I'll be going to stay with the monsters when they come. They promised they'd keep me safe."

"Stop, go back. Did you say *gods* are coming?"

"Yes. Can I go now? Mum complains when I'm home late and then I have to tell the monsters to stop her complaining and I really don't like having to do that."

"Okay, yeah, sure, go home, Billy."

She took out her phone to call Locke, but stopped before dialling his number. For a while she stood there, breathing hard, staring into space. Then she chose a different number and called that instead.

Locke was on the toilet when the lights went out. The curse of the Brooker's cottage had finally struck, the electrics giving up the ghost just before sunset. Fortunately, he was prepared, though it took a good fifteen minutes to light all of his contingency candles. Once done, he sank into an armchair and regarded the heap of scavenged junk piled in one corner of the living room. Emily's rubber glove lay atop a motorcycle tyre. The used flare was propped up against the prosthetic foot. Assorted plastic bottles, water-damaged toys, odd shoes and even a New Jersey license plate completed the collection. In the light of the flickering candles, the bric-a-brac appeared to shift and move under his gaze. Locke smiled, closed his eyes and for the first time in weeks, slept soundly.

Shouts outside woke him. He glanced at the clock hanging over the mantelpiece. It was almost one o'clock in the morning. Locke rose from his chair and pulled on a coat.

"Roland! Roland!"

Locke ventured out through his front gate and onto the road. A line of villagers were walking along the cliff-side shouting Roland's name. Their calls were echoed from below, where more villagers were searching amongst the rocks for signs of their neighbour.

Locke saw Agatha Joseph and hurried over.

"What's happened?" he asked.

She stared wide-eyed at him for a moment before her brain was able to respond to the question.

"It's Roland," she said. "He went out walking earlier this evening and… well, his wife knows he sometimes loses track of time, but she got concerned when it started getting dark and then Dotty came back… on her own. She was trailing her leash. They say there was blood on the handle. I came out as soon as I heard. Now everyone's out looking. If you can give us any help finding him…"

Locke said nothing. He felt numb. Agatha Joseph touched him on the arm, nodded her head and then continued on, calling out Roland's name while sweeping the way ahead with a torch.

The villagers' voices had receded into the distance when Locke slowly closed his hand into a fist. His eyes swept down from the heavens and onto the verge, where a small rabbit stood, twitching its ears.

"Show me the way," said Locke.

And the rabbit scampered off toward the village.

Veronica sat stiffly in front of a bathroom mirror while Sharon brushed her face with foundation.

"This isn't necessary," said Veronica.

"It's completely necessary," said Sharon. "The only day you came to work looking halfway decent was the day you came for your interview."

"I find that accusation vaguely insulting."

"You should take it as constructive criticism."

"I'm sticking with insulting."

A few minutes later, Veronica sat on Sharon's bed in her underwear. The girl from accounts scrutinised her figure against a selection of dresses.

"When was the last time you bought a new frock?" asked Sharon.

"I find trousers more practical nowadays," said Veronica.

"A girl does not wear trousers on a date."

"It's not a date."

"What is it then?"

Veronica sighed.

"It might just be a terrible mistake."

During the twenty hours Locke had been awake, he was seen a number of times by villagers and police officers. To them, he wandered aimlessly up and down the coastline, covering ground the search had already checked and double-checked. He was mentioned at the newsagents and discussed later at the pub. A diligent sergeant made some enquiries about this newcomer, but turned up nothing suspicious. The conversation moved on. Night fell. Bedtime prayers were offered and all hoped for Roland McCaffrey's safe return.

Thomas Locke watched a moth flutter into a gaping maw swallowing rising waves. He reluctantly followed, splashing into the cave and sending torchlight searching into cavernous darkness. A pebbled floor rose out of the water and brought a gutted fish came into view. It lay on the remnants of a frayed fishing net whose mesh was torn and trailing snake-like between the rocks.

He tracked one length of nylon twine with the beam of the torch. It wound between patches of seaweed and then stretched up a wall and across the ceiling, where it suspended the head of black-eyed seal pup.

Locke stopped. He scanned the cave again. Netting was strung around him, lacing together the remains of birds, fish and mammals like macabre carnival bunting. The pungent smell of the dead creatures ebbed and flowed with the tide lapping at the cave entrance.

A few more cautious steps brought sight of pebbles glistening red under the torchlight. Blood continued to drip onto them. Locke raised the torch and discovered what had become of Roland McCaffrey: his body and insides had been picked apart and strewn about the cavern. A leg and half an arm lay on the ground. His skull was tied against the wall, just enough skin, muscle and bedraggled gray hair remaining to be recognisable. His eyes watched Locke from atop a spike of rock in the darkness ahead; motionless, staring. But Roland's lungs moved. They hung in the air six feet in front of Locke, wreathed in wire that slowly tightened, constricting the fleshy white organs so that air flowed up a windpipe stitched together from mismatched tubes of plastic, across excised vocal chords and out between lips contorted by more wire. The noise that was produced sounded horribly like laughter.

Veronica did not smile when Vincent opened the door. He complimented her dress. He offered to take her coat. She gave it to him and entered the apartment.

"I was surprised to get your call," said Vincent.

"No you weren't."

He hung the coat in a closet in the hallway.

"You know me that well?"

"I know you better than that."

"You knew the man I was."

"You haven't changed."

"You have."

They entered a room that served as both living area and kitchen.

"That's why I won't be playing along with any of your little games," said Veronica.

"Yet you're happy to invite yourself over for dinner?" asked Vincent, raising an eyebrow.

"I'm not the least bit happy about it, but I want to know what you're up to."

"I'm afraid your logic eludes me. If you don't trust me, if you don't believe a word I say, what do you expect to learn by sampling my roast dumplings?"

Veronica finally smiled.

"Sometimes you can learn a lot from a lie."

"What are you?" asked Locke.

"The… ties… that… bind," rasped the thing in the cave.

"Why did you kill this man?"

That grotesque laugh once again.

"Because… he-wasn't-you."

"I don't think I ever cooked for you before," said Vincent, attending the pans steaming gently on the hob.

"You didn't," said Veronica, reclining on his cheap sofa and appraising the sparse furnishings. "I'm hoping you're going to reveal your grand plan before we have to eat and I find out how bad your cooking is."

"I've been forced to practice quite a bit while living on my own these past few weeks. I like to think I've got quite good."

"I asked around, Vincent. None of the memekers know what you're up to."

"The what?"

"You know what they are."

"I also know what they can do and I know they can make people forget things. Perhaps I had them tear out their own memories so they wouldn't remember my dastardly scheme?"

"I figured as much."

"But can you prove it?"

"This isn't about proof."

"Of course it's not, because otherwise you'd have to face the possibility that you might be proved wrong."

"What do you want with me?" asked Locke.

"You… find-things. You-should-have-found… the-dog."

Locke said nothing. He was struggling to suppress his gut response to the fate of Roland McCaffrey.

"You-are-here… because-I-was… betrayed."

"Admit it," said Vincent. "It's rather good, isn't it?"

Veronica ignored the expectant look coming from across the dinner table, took a few more appraising chews, then swallowed and reached for her glass of wine.

"It's not bad."

"You know what that is?" He pointed at her dinner plate with his fork.

"What?"

"It's a crack."

"I thought it was a dumpling."

"It's a dumpling and a crack."

"You're babbling."

"You came here with certain preconceived notions. Foremost among them was the idea that I was still some villainous sort up to no good. Secondary to that – and I'll admit it was a distant second – was the expectation that my cooking would be dreadful. Now you've tasted it and found my exquisitely prepared dinner to be, in your words, not bad, that cracks open the possibility that you might be wrong about other things."

"I'm not."

"Then I propose a toast."

"To what?"

"To you living your life in a world of black and white and me living in a world of possibilities."

A slithering noise prompted Locke to turn his head. The remains in the cave were moving, drawn together by the fishing wire.

"Who betrayed you?" asked Locke, edging away from the heaving lungs and trying to avoid the confluence of fish guts, human bone and seal skin assembling amidst the rocks.

"Who?" Spittle flew from Roland McCaffrey's stolen lips. "The-liar! The-cheat! Without-me… no-ties… un-bound… lost… forever."

Locke felt an unpleasant tingle on the back of his neck.

"Did you say lost?"

Veronica pouted disapprovingly.

"But you like ice cream!" protested Vincent. "Oh, unless you've changed so much you don't like ice cream any more."

"I do," she replied, "it's just a bit easy, isn't it? You could have baked a cake or made a trifle. That would have shown you put some effort in."

"Doesn't making dinner count as effort?"

"I thought you were trying to impress me."

"Whatever gave you that idea?"

"You could have just ordered a takeout and then spent the evening watching football."

"No, I couldn't have done that. That would have been the behaviour of a truly evil man."

"No, that would have been the behaviour of a typically ignorant man. A truly evil man would try to make me feel special by treating me to the best food and the finest wines before attempting to sway me to his fiendish point of view."

"Good job I fell short with the ice cream then." He dispensed three scoops into Veronica's bowl and then hesitated before sliding it across the table. "Wait, does this mean I'm only moderately malevolent? I'm not an especially proud man, but achieving only moderate success in anything feels somehow—"

"Just give me the ice cream."

"He-denied-me... this-world... but-I-shall-take-it... nevertheless. Your-partner-is... annulled. Protects-you... no-longer. You-will-find-me... my-place... amongst-the-gods."

Coils of netting tried to snare Locke's foot, but he was too quick. The jaws of ferrets and voles snapped at him as he fled for the exit, before they too became a part of the monstrous creature rising up within the cave.

"I'm going to the toilet," said Veronica.

"I'll need to go after you," said Vincent. "Don't leave a smell."

She ignored his remark and disappeared into the bathroom. Moments after she locked the door, a buzzing came from the handbag she'd left on the sofa. Vincent opened it up and pulled out a vibrating mobile phone. He noted the caller display and then pressed answer.

"Hello?" he said.

"Who's that?"

"Thomas Locke," said Vincent.

"Err, no, excuse me, I'm Thom... It's you, isn't it?"

"How's the lost and found business, Thomas?"

"Lost isn't what it used to be."

"So I've heard."

"But I have just found an old friend of yours."

"I wasn't aware I had any friends."

"The ties that bind are hard to break."

Vincent stared at the wall in front of him. From the phone came laboured breathing.

"You're already running," Vincent said at last.

"Even though you're the one that pissed it off."

"If I can send help, I will."

"Mr Drysdale, if you hurt her, it won't matter if it catches me. I will still come and find you."

"I know."

Vincent hung up, thought for a moment and then made a call of his own. When Veronica returned from the bathroom, he was lounging on the sofa, perusing the TV guide.

The thing following Locke did not run. It flowed across the beach, over fences and up the road as a tumbling mass of feet and claws.

Headlights flashed ahead of Locke. He didn't stop running. The car braked hard and swerved from side to side before coming to a halt. A second later Locke was alongside the passenger side door. He breathed relief when he tried the handle and it opened.

A man with a tiny nose and out-sized ears cowered behind the wheel.

"Jesus, please, no, don't hurt me."

"My name is Thomas Locke and I don't have time to explain," said Locke, climbing into the passenger seat. "Just drive. Now."

The man nodded with fearful enthusiasm, re-engaged first gear and pressed the accelerator. It was only then he looked out of the windscreen and saw the aberration hurtling toward him. His instinct was to hit the brakes again.

"Keep going!" ordered Locke.

The beast of wire and flesh slammed into the bumper and then careened over the roof of the car.

"What in God's name was that?" asked the driver as they sped away down the road.

"Nothing to do with gods," replied Locke. "Not if I can help it."

After Vincent entered the bathroom and locked the door behind him, Veronica found a belt in a chest of drawers and used it to tie the door handle to the frame of a radiator.

Inside the bathroom, Vincent sat on the toilet with his trousers down around his legs.

"Veronica, have you been going through my things? If you'd wanted to use my razor to shave off some unsightly underarm hair, you know you only needed to ask." He listened for a reply. "What are you doing, Veronica? I can hear you doing something out there."

He finished his business, flushed the toilet and pulled up his trousers. A crash came from elsewhere in the apartment.

"Veronica? Are you okay? Did you have an accident?"

Vincent washed his hands.

"If you did break something, that's okay. I can claim it back on the insurance. Though you should know the waffle-iron has sentimental value."

Another crash.

"That was the waffle-iron, wasn't it?"

Vincent dried his hands. He slid back the bolt on the door, turned the handle, and tried pulling it open.

"Okay, Veronica, nice practical joke. Let me out, please."

The noise of unseen activity continued.

"Veronica?"

…

"Okay, that's three minutes," said Vincent. "I would hope your amusement at this hilarious jape is now beginning to diminish."

…

"Who knew? Ten minutes and I'm already growing bored with alphabetising my toiletries."

…

"Is this supposed to be character building for me? If so, you should know that my character is already pretty well self-actualised."

…

"To allay any concerns you might have, I'm not claustrophobic, but being trapped in here like this means I have developed extraordinary empathy for the condition."

…

"I make that one hour. Can I say I am a little disappointed in how this evening has turned out? Especially because I expected to have reached second base by now…"

…

"I don't wish to alarm you, but on a scale of one to ten, my irritation with this situation has now reached six… possibly six and a half…"

…

"You know I can get out of here if I want to, but I'd much

rather you ended this little game by letting me out…"

…

"Okay, Veronica, if you want to play, here I come, ready or not."

Locke was now driving after dumping the car's owner at a farm a dozen miles back. He crested a hill and the lights of the town came into view. This only heightened his sense of urgency, which then turned to panic on seeing a stop sign in the road ahead. But it wasn't the police; it was just a man in a fluorescent orange jacket directing traffic while one lane was closed due to roadworks.

Locke brought his car to a halt and waited for the signal to go.

The man with the sign walked over. He tapped on the window, prompting Locke to wind it down.

"Could you come with me, please, sir?" asked the workman.

"Why do you want—?"

"The Ministry has passed a decree, Mr Locke. Your partner was the only reason you could stay here and now he is gone, you must leave too. Balance must be restored."

"I'm not the only one who shouldn't be here."

"We know, sir, but there was an accident in a local sub-depot and that's left us with this big back-log of—"

"I'm sympathetic, I really am, but—"

Locke floored the accelerator.

The man in orange overalls watched him go. He lifted a radio to his ear, spoke a few words and the stars in the heavens above began to fall.

The handle fell from the bathroom door, along with the restraining belt. Vincent Drysdale carefully placed the screws he'd removed into the soap tray above the bath taps and then exited the bathroom.

Clothes neatly folded and packed away in drawers an hour ago now spilled out through the bedroom doorway. He noted this and walked into the main living area.

All the kitchen cupboards were open. Much of his crockery had been smashed on the floor. Food from his fridge was strewn across the breakfast bar. Books from his bookcase lay scattered about the room.

Veronica sat on the sofa surrounded by a mess of white fibres; polyester filling gouged from the cushions by a carving knife now resting beneath her fingers. That blade, along with the tension in her jaw, betrayed her otherwise casual posture.

Vincent raised a finger, lowered it, smiled to himself, shook his head and then rubbed at his brow with a palm.

"I am confused, Veronica. With all due respect, you are not Thomas Locke. If I had something to hide, you surely know that I know ways and means of making sure you'd never find it."

Veronica's nostrils flared.

"So you're saying you wanted me to find these?" She opened a clenched fist to reveal a choker necklace and pair of earrings.

"Well…"

She threw the jewellery at her ex-husband. The pieces hit him ineffectually on the chest. He watched them fall to the floor. When he looked up, Veronica's face was two inches away from his.

"You think you're so superior, don't you?" she said. "You say one thing, but at the same time you're thinking: 'she's so stupid. She'll fall for whatever I say and she won't find her mother's damned jewellery in my bedside bloody table!' Do you remember my mother, Vincent? Yes, of course you do, because you made her sell off everything she was until the only thing she had left, the only thing my mother and father ever produced that was worth a damn, was an innocent baby girl. And you took that too, because you thought you could make me into what? The perfect wife? All the things I could have been and you turn me into that? An empty fantasy; something less than nothing. That's what you made me. And that, more than anything else, makes me *hate* every last fibre of your being, because I know – I *know* it never once occurred to you that if you'd given me the choice… I might have said yes."

Locke sped toward the Argent Bridge as stars crashed to the ground around him; blinding white shards that sent deafening pulses of sound rippling across tarmac and through buildings; cracking brick, shattering windows, chasing down Locke's flight.

Vincent met Veronica's baleful stare for a few seconds, then slowly bent down and picked up the necklace. He crossed the room and opened a pair of glass doors that opened onto a tiny balcony. He stepped out and leant against the railing.

Veronica glared at his back. Even after ransacking his apartment, her fury still demanded release. If she still had her gun, she would have pointed it at his back and pulled the trigger. The carving knife was lying on the floor by the sofa.

"Maybe you should," said Vincent.

"It wouldn't be enough," she replied. "Even if you came back and I killed you again and again, it wouldn't be enough."

"I can't apologise for what I did."

"Yes, you could, but I could never accept—"

"I'd hoped it would be a beautiful night. That we could stand out here, gaze up at the stars and maybe we would have found something romantic in that."

Veronica stepped up behind him. The knife was in her hand. She looked out at the sky and saw it perfectly black, void of stars and untroubled by even the faintest of noises from the world below.

"I can't apologise," continued Vincent, "because I'm not sorry. I saw the future you would have chosen and I know the one I gave you was better."

"Better? How could it possibly have been worse?"

"You were happy, Veronica, for a time."

"It was a lie."

"Do you know what this necklace is made of?"

"More lies?"

"Happiness. Do you know what it cost your mother?"

"I don't know, her charity?"

"It cost her nothing. It was free. Happiness is always free. It's not about money or respect or even having a roof over your head, because you can have all those things and still not be happy. No, happiness is something you choose and some people can never do that. You could never do that."

"I was never given the chance."

Vincent turned to her. He held up the necklace.

"If you want it, take it."

Locke brought the car to a juddering halt. He opened the door with a hand whose flesh had been torn away by the lights of the Vandenark.

He staggered out onto the street. An apartment block rose before him. He saw Vincent and Veronica Drysdale standing on a second floor balcony. Locke cried out, but all that came from his mouth was a cloud of sparkling dust.

He waved an arm that dissolved in glowing streaks of blood and bone, but could not tell if she saw him for he no longer had eyes to see. If she called down to him, he no longer had ears to hear.

With his last thought, he hoped she would remember him, a thought that became another sparkling light. When that too vanished away like all the others, there was nothing left of Thomas Locke.

Up on the balcony, a chill breeze prompted Vincent and Veronica Drysdale to turn their backs on the night. They retreated into the apartment and pulled the doors shut behind them.

Interlude IX

A small piebald cat watched incuriously as the Vandenark spirited Thomas Locke away to oblivion. Tail twitching purposefully from side to side, it turned its attention to the couple on the balcony. Vincent and Veronica Drysdale disappeared back inside the apartment.

Fiddlesticks displayed no signs of hurry as he crossed one road, then another, each time trusting the passing cars would brake on seeing an animal crossing the beam of their headlights. He eventually slipped into a garden, scaled a tree and then leapt onto a first floor windowsill, where he deigned to stop, sit and clean himself.

The window looked into a small living room crowded with cushions, drapes and rugs laid over one another. In a high-backed armchair, an elderly Chinese woman watched television. She didn't notice Fiddlesticks until an advert break began and she rose to make a cup of tea.

"Me oh my, what are you doing out there?" asked the old woman, opening the window and letting the cat inside. "Oh, you were waiting for me to let you in? Well, that was very presumptuous, even for a cat. I suppose you want a saucer of… What do you mean there's not much time? Oh, I see. And she has to die? Very well, wait there, I'll get my coat."

Come the Gods of Every Little Thing

"Boy, why are you sitting all the way back there?" asked the teacher standing at the head of the classroom.

"It's where I always sit," replied Billy.

"Not any more. I want you sitting at the front with everyone else."

One month ago, everyone else meant the thirty other children in Billy's class, but then Luke stopped coming to school. Three days later, Joshua was gone too. Others followed; one by one, then two, three, four or more a day. Now everyone else meant the four other children still attending Fulton Street School.

"But sir—"

"No buts, boy. I won't tolerate back-chat. Get moving."

Billy clenched his fists and fought the urge to protest further. Faint, malicious whispers swirled around him, suggesting gruesome methods for teaching this teacher respect. Billy leant down to pick up his bag and took the opportunity to surreptitiously lift the lid of his desk a fraction.

"Quiet down. It's not his fault," he whispered through the crack.

There were plenty of empty desks, but the supply teacher pointed to one right at the front. Billy set his bag down beside it and slumped into the chair. Two older girls sat to his left. They were whispering and giggling. Billy didn't know their names and he didn't care to. Beyond them was a boy called Mel, who spent every day staring out the window until the home-time bell rang. And then there was Emily. She sat off to the right, copying down the incorrect eight times table the supply teacher had written up on the board, but Billy knew whenever the teacher looked away, she went back to drawing pictures of Him.

"Now sit up straight, boy," instructed the teacher. "Slouching restricts blood flow to the brain and— what have you two got there?"

He snatched a mobile phone off the older girls. A daytime

talk show was playing on the screen; a former Fulton Street teacher onstage, complaining about the modern-day Pied Piper who had come along and stolen away her livelihood.

"Give that back!" demanded one of the girls. "It's my private property!"

"Not when you bring it into my classroom!" The supply teacher proceeded to rant about being called in with barely any notice because his peers were clearly incompetent, the local education authority ineffective and all because no one else wanted to babysit five children who clearly had no interest in learning the basic skills that would allow them to be useful members of society when they were older.

A paper aeroplane struck Billy on the side of the head and fell to the floor. The teacher was too busy raging at the world to notice. Billy picked up the projectile and unfolded it to reveal a picture of a black figure in hat and coat stamping on the head of a clumsily drawn monster.

He glanced sideways at Emily. She was looking down her nose at him. He sighed and rolled his eyes, then lifted the lid of his new desk a fraction. A shiny black tentacle whipped out, snatched the piece of paper and slunk back into the crack.

Inhuman whispering came from within the wooden desk, then a rasping, raging growl threw the desk lid open and expelled the paper as shredded fragments covered in slime.

Billy slammed the desk shut as the teacher spun to face him. The older girls were squealing and gingerly picking gooey scraps off their clothes. Mel had stopped gazing out the window to wonder what he'd missed, while Emily was once again dutifully copying down the eight times table written up on the board.

"Care to explain yourself, boy?" asked the teacher.

Billy shook his head.

"I think it'd be easier for everyone if I just went straight to the headmaster's office now."

"He so would kick their butts," said Emily, as she walked with Billy across the playground toward the school gates.

"Are you ever going to stop going on about him?"

"I'm just saying—"

"Yeah, well maybe you can just shut up now."
"I don't have to listen to you."
"I wish I didn't have to listen to you."

A group of kids were hanging around outside the school gates. Billy recognised his former classmates, Luke and Joshua, but the only thing familiar about the rest was the cocky body language that came from being in a gang.

"Look who it is," said Joshua, "the boy who pretends there are monsters under the bed and the girl who pretends her parents are real."

"Just ignore them," Billy told Emily, steering her through the taunts. "They won't be laughing once I've got home and had a word with my monsters. Maybe you could get Mr Lafarge to pay them a visit too."

"Lafarge is gone," said Emily.

"But all those times you told me—"

"The day I met him was the day he disappeared forever."

"Having met you, I can understand why."

"Why did they say I pretend my parents are real?"

"I don't know. They're just trying to upset you, that's all."

"Why would they do that?"

"I don't know. Stop asking questions. Look, there's your Mum's car, go bother her instead."

That night, Emily's father read her a bedtime story, then kissed her on the forehead and pulled the duvet up to her chin. He started for the door.

She grabbed his hand.

"Don't go."

"I've already read you two stories, Emmy, I can't—"

"Don't go."

"I'm only going downstairs."

"Don't go."

He sat down again on the side of the bed.

"What's wrong, Emmy?"

"Nothing."

"You're not scared Billy's monsters will come and get you when I switch off the light, are you?"

"No!"

"Then why don't you want me to go?"

"Because…"

"Because? Come on, you can tell me."

"Because you might disappear."

Her father laughed.

"Emmy, my knowledge of magic stretches no further than making a coin appear behind your ear. Trust me, I can't disappear."

"But how do I know? How do I know when you step into the hall and close the door and I can't see you any more, that you're still there, that you haven't just…"

She buried her face in a pillow.

"Disappeared? Well, I suppose you might hear my footsteps going downstairs. If you listen really hard you might hear the television or your Mummy and me talking, but I guess, when it comes right down to it, this is one of those things you have to take on faith."

Emily rolled her head so one eye looked up at her father.

"And what about now?" she asked.

"Now? You can see me, can't you? You feel me holding your hand? You don't need faith to know I'm here, so—"

"But you're not some sort of dream? You're real, you and Mummy; you're real and you exist, yes?"

Emily's father hesitated for the briefest of moments before letting go of her hand and hugging her tightly instead.

"Oh God, Emmy. Yes, of course we exist and I don't want you ever thinking again that we won't be here for you."

He woke up from nothing into a dark room with a single window. A cat figurine sat on the floor next to where he lay.

It was Saturday. Billy was playing on a second-hand games console in his room and eating chocolate digestives from an open pack on the floor next to him. When school friends used to visit, they made fun of how antiquated the console was. His new friends never did, though sometimes they had problems with the controller. Currently, a giant, chitinous limb reaching out from under the bed was frantically pressing buttons with its razor-sharp extremities in an attempt to stop Billy winning an eighth death-match in a row.

It failed. The anguished cry that followed sounded like

a hundred mewling kittens being fed through a mincing machine. Once all the kittens were silenced, the doorbell rang. This sounded like a bell going 'bing-bong'.

Billy's father was out working a shift at the chemical plant, so his mother answered the door. Twenty minutes later she shouted up the stairs for Billy to come down and meet someone.

"I'm in the middle of a game!"

"You can play your game later."

"But I'll lose *this* game!"

"Billy, do I have to ask you twice?"

"Do I have to refer this to our friends under the bed?"

"Oh, please don't be awkward. I'm trying to ask you nicely. Can't you just do something for your mother for once without resorting to mentioning *them*?"

On screen, Billy died. Disgusted, he tossed his controller across the floor. The chitinous limb performed an impromptu victory dance.

"You only won because I was distracted," said Billy, before stomping to the bedroom door and out onto the landing.

His mother, Maureen, waited at the bottom of the stairs. She had a man beside her. It took a moment for Billy to recognise his face. He'd seen it in a photograph shown to him by a woman called Veronica. She'd told him this man was the one thing she was scared of.

"This is Mr Drysdale," said Maureen. "He dropped by to see if we'd be interested in enrolling you in his private tutoring programme."

"You told him we weren't, right?" said Billy.

"He'd like to talk to you."

"Well I don't want to talk to him!"

Billy stormed back into his room. He slammed the door shut and leant against it, hoping his mother wouldn't call again. Then he noticed the games console was unattended and the chocolate digestives were gone. A trail of crumbs led across the carpet and underneath his bed.

"You dirty, thieving—"

Footsteps began climbing the stairs.

"I'm not coming out," called Billy.

This did not dissuade the footsteps. Billy felt his stomach

tighten like a wound spring. He whispered to the dark space under his bed.

"If she tries to make me come out, you can eat her, okay? Just for a bit. No chewing. And you spit her out before any digesting takes place, got it?"

The footsteps crossed the landing and stopped outside his room.

"I just want to talk," said Vincent Drysdale.

Billy stiffened against the door. He said nothing.

"I imagine it must be getting a bit boring at school now there's hardly anyone else there. The teacher can keep his eye on you all the time and where's the fun in that?"

"You can eat him," hissed Billy at the dark space under his bed. "You can chew him up and digest him and then poo him out all over the floor."

"Who's that you're talking to, Billy? Have you got a friend in there? Or perhaps I should be asking if you've got friends in there. It's not normal, you know, a young boy like yourself spending all his time hanging out with imaginary monsters."

"They're not imaginary!" snapped Billy.

"I'm sure you believe that, but we grown-ups are a cynical lot. Age leaves us jaded. We only believe what we can see with our own two eyes and I've never seen a monster, so while I don't want to call you a liar..."

Billy threw the door open.

"You want to see some monsters?"

Vincent Drysdale considered the proposal before nodding. Billy pointed to the bed.

"Take a look for yourself."

The unwanted guest walked over to the bed. He picked up a teddy bear from its resting place on the rumpled duvet.

"I could be mistaken, but this doesn't look like—"

"Look *underneath* the bed," said Billy. "And by the way, I told them they could eat you."

Vincent Drysdale smiled at this, returned the bear to its resting place and then dropped to his knees.

"So you tell your monsters what to do?"

"No!" said Billy. "They just... We're friends. We do things for each other."

"And what do you do for them?"

"Just… stuff. That's all."

Vincent Drysdale leaned down to get a good look under the bed.

"Should I imagine I'm seeing some many-tentacled beasties at this point, rather than a pack of chocolate digestives?"

Billy rushed over and ducked down beside him. The dark space under the bed was simply that – a shadowy gap between ageing springs and faded carpet, with wall and skirting board visible on the far side.

"Oh, help, I'm being eaten by a ferocious swarm of chocolate digestives," said Vincent Drysdale. Billy glared at him. "Are we not playing let's pretend then?"

Billy stood up, tramped over to his games console, sat down and began playing.

"And they say those things kill a child's imagination," said Mr Drysdale. "But they often say stupid things. Best not listening to them, I say."

Billy stared at the screen more intently and made a show of pressing some buttons to demonstrate how much he wasn't listening to his visitor.

"If your monsters are so real, I wonder where they could be. Might they just be asleep? I think they're fast sleep in this wardrobe. Oh, no, not there. In the chest of drawers? Behind the curtains? No and no. Ah! Could it be that they snuck up my nose while I wasn't paying attention? One moment, I shall check. Ha! Gotcha! Is that your monster?"

A finger daubed with green slime was waved in front of Billy's face. He swatted it away.

"Or perhaps they're scared and hiding away somewhere we can't find them," said Mr Drysdale, wiping the snot off his finger with a white handkerchief.

"They're monsters," snorted Billy, "they're not afraid of anything."

"But if they're not here and they're not hiding… maybe it's about time you faced the fact that they don't exist."

"They do! They just…" Billy stared at the floor, trying to think of some explanation of why his friends would not show. "They only really like coming out at night."

Vincent Drysdale stood up and placed the white handkerchief back in his pocket.

"Then maybe I should come back when it's dark."

Thomas Locke's thoughts kept him from paying attention to where he was going. He walked where instinct took him; down to the river, where the water was so still the moon cast an unbroken reflection upon its surface. He continued over Argent Bridge, where a girl gazed up at the stars. The first time she called out to him, Locke… hurried on into an alleyway that ran behind the auction house. He saw a door. He tried the handle. He kicked and rammed it with his shoulder, but it wouldn't open. His eyes sought upwards. More windows, too small, too secure, except… he was desperately hanging onto the roof of a mobile library travelling at speed down Baskerville Road. He guessed it was Veronica reminding him about their meeting, but then thought it could be Lafarge with a more urgent request.

Then something new formed amidst this jumble of memories. It came as a voice unspoken by lips; a faltering thought with a novel proposition.

"Thomas Locke… is… me?"

For the first time in his life, Billy was relieved when his father shouted, "we can't possibly afford that!"

Maureen tried to argue the case for Vincent Drysdale's private tuition, but Norman wasn't having any of it and duly enlivened breakfast by reciting last month's credit card statement. His last words as he shepherded Billy out of the door enumerated their total debt as a full stop to the conversation.

Billy arrived at school feeling upbeat and positive about compulsory education for the first time in his short life. The feeling was gone before the teacher finished taking morning registration. There were only four children in class today. With weary resignation in his voice, the teacher explained that Emily would no longer be joining them.

At lunchtime, Billy snuck out through the school gates. He caught a bus to the posh end of town using the loose change in his pocket. It was a fifteen minute walk from the stop to the long, winding driveway that led up to the white house where Emily lived.

Billy rang the bell.

Emily's father answered the door.

"Oh, hello, Billy. Shouldn't you be in school?"

"I need to see Emily."

"I'm afraid she's with her new tutor—"

"It's kind of urgent I see her now."

"I'm sure it can wait until you've both finished school for the day. Do I need to call your mother and get her to pick you up?"

"No, I'm… I'm on the bus."

"I think perhaps I should call your mother anyway."

"I'm going now. I'll see Emily later."

Billy ran off down the driveway.

"And good day to you too, young man," called Emily's father after him, before shaking his head and closing the door.

A few minutes later, Billy snuck back up the driveway and scampered around to the back of the house. He hoped he would find an open window or unlocked door, but ended up requiring neither. Emily was sitting out on the patio, a textbook open on the table before her. She was accompanied by an old Chinese woman knitting a green sweater.

"What are you doing here?" asked Emily as he walked up.

"Who's this?" asked the old woman, poking a knitting needle toward Billy.

"Who's she?" asked Billy of the old woman.

Emily beamed at the opportunity to play hostess. Billy cringed even before she used his full name.

"Mrs Hu, this is William, a person I am acquainted with through school. William this is Mrs Hu, she is my new private tutor."

"I don't think he should be here," said Mrs Hu, rising from her chair, "I should go and tell your father."

"Now, now, Mrs Hu," said Emily, motioning for her to sit back down, "I'm sure young William here wouldn't be here unless he had a good reason."

"Yeah, that's right," muttered Billy, aware that his very good reason had vanished the moment Emily's tutor turned out not to be Vincent Drysdale.

"Well, spit out then," said Emily, "I'm a busy woman." She tapped her textbook meaningfully.

"Okay, okay, I came round here…" He thought fast,

spurred by the fear of waking one night with Vincent Drysdale looming over his bed. "I need to find The Office of Lost and Found."

Mrs Hu sniffed. "That hardly sounds like a good reason to me."

"Ssh, Mrs Hu," said Emily. She turned to Billy. "I told you, the Office is gone. Lafarge is gone and Thomas told me he doesn't find things any more. Says he can't."

"But I need their help!"

Emily looked at him sympathetically.

"You could try Veronica. I know she works in town at this place called Froggarty something or other."

Billy clenched his fists in frustration and then jumped when something unexpectedly brushed against his leg. Both Emily and Mrs Hu laughed as a small piebald cat jumped onto the table and began cleaning its ears with a paw. Billy glared at the cat before making to leave.

"What's that, Fiddlesticks?" said Mrs Hu. "You want to tell Billy something?"

Billy glanced at Emily, who mouthed back: 'she thinks it can talk' and circled a finger around her temple. Mrs Hu nodded to the cat and then looked up at Billy.

"Fiddlesticks wanted to tell you that your monsters are right to be scared."

Twenty-five minutes later, Billy disembarked at the central bus station and started running. He crossed the town square, where office workers were eating their lunches and throwing scraps to the pigeons. He passed shops and pubs and fast-food restaurants and only stopping running when he reached an industrial unit on the edge of the town centre with Froggarty Premium Accessories Limited printed on a sign by the gate.

"Veronica's not here," said a woman who'd introduced herself as Sharon.

"Where is she then?" asked Billy, looking around the factory's shop-floor in case the woman was lying.

"Shouldn't you be in school?"

"No. Do you know where she is or not?"

"Yes, but I don't think I can divulge such privileged information to a rude little boy who obviously *should* be in school."

"Fine, don't tell me." Billy quickly switched his expression from petulant to wide-eyed and innocent. "Can I at least use your toilet before I go?"

"So you can try and sneak into her office instead? No, kid, you're coming with me."

Billy thought about making a run for it, but Sharon grabbed the loose ends of his tie and dragged him up a flight of metal steps. These led to a cluster of offices suspended above the shop-floor.

"This is a Fulton Street School tie, isn't it?" said Sharon. "What's say we call them up first? If they don't want you back, you'll either have to give me your parents' number or it'll be the cops and a night in the cells for you."

She took Billy into an office with 'Accounts' stencilled on the door, then told him to sit down and be quiet while she searched for the school's website. He considered making a run for it.

"Don't even think about it," warned Sharon.

She found the school's number, picked up her phone and dialled.

"Please," said Billy, shuffling his chair closer, "I only need to talk to—"

"Zip it."

He began playing with one of her pens. Sharon glared at him.

"Ah, hello," she said. "I think I have one of your inmates here…"

Billy dropped the pen and let it roll off her desk. Sharon tried to catch it, but missed. While she was distracted, Billy pulled open a drawer and began rooting through the contents. He only managed a few seconds of rooting before Sharon grabbed his hands, lifted them out of the drawer and slammed it shut.

"I'm sorry about that," she said into the phone, "I got distracted by a little—"

The dial-tone suddenly rang in Sharon's ear. Billy held down the phone's cradle with a finger. She waved the handset at him.

"You realise it's just the two of us in here? I could beat you about the head with this and if it came to trial it'd just be your word against mine."

"I've got a cousin called Nancy," said Billy. "She's only like seventeen and she's already got two kids and when we go over to visit she always goes on about how she didn't want to get pregnant and if she'd only used a condom she could still be going out and getting drunk with her friends and then she tells me when I start having sex I should always use a condom and then I won't get anyone pregnant or catch any nasty diseases."

Sharon eyed him suspiciously.

"What's your point, kid?"

"I saw the tablets in the drawer. Does Veronica know you've got thrush? How about those people downstairs? Should I go tell them?"

Veronica was out having lunch at an exclusive restaurant near the town hall. Billy could see her through the window. She was at a table with three other people: two men with their backs to him and a woman he didn't recognise who was fawning over the choker necklace Veronica wore. Billy was nervous about the thought of marching in there, but reminded himself that she'd helped before.

"Where are your parents, little boy?" asked the maitre d' manning the reception desk.

"My mummy's over there," said Billy, pointing at Veronica. "Can I go talk to her? It's about something important."

The maitre d' raised an eyebrow, then waved over a waiter and instructed him to escort Billy to table number twelve.

"It's made of pearlescent joy," said Veronica to her female companion as Billy approached.

"It's beautiful," the woman replied. "I wish we could afford—"

"Mummy, mummy!" cried Billy, running free of the waiter and up to Veronica. "I met that man you showed me a picture of and he made my monsters go away and I need to find Thomas so he can find them or Lafarge so he can..."

Veronica's peculiar smile brought Billy's torrent of words to an awkward halt.

"Calm down," she said. "Take some deep breaths. You've got yourself all over-excited, haven't you? No doubt you've been letting your imagination run away with you again."

"I haven't, I've—"

"That's enough, Billy. You're making a scene. And look, you don't need to find anybody because Thomas is already here. And this is his wife Constance and I don't know if you've met my husband, Vincent…?"

The memories kept coming. Locke had no sense of time passing, just a deepening well of personal history that began as drips splashing against his mind's eye, then grew into an ocean swirling with the currents of a life lived: his Mother and Father; growing up; going to school; passing exams; starting work and then… Constance… Lafarge… Veronica…

From the memory grew sensation. He knew he had arms and legs and he could remember how it felt to move and experience the flex of muscles and press of air against skin, but when he realised his eyes were closed and he could open them, it came as a shock. Trepidation became a function of the here and now, rather than something that he'd known once upon a time.

Locke dared to prise apart his eyelids.

At first, he wasn't sure if he had. Blackness before became blackness after. He couldn't even see himself, but that changed with a glimpse of glistening threads. They twisted and twined and drew together shining points of light. From nothing his right hand took shape before his recently formed eyes, joining up with a reconstructed arm.

He marvelled at this sight until it was abruptly pushed from his awareness. His eyes did not close and nothing obscured his view, instead a succession of memories were forced to the front of his mind in such vivid detail that his physical surroundings faded away…

Locke was in a cave. Blood washed the stones underfoot. Lips removed from a dead man's face shaped air forced out through disembodied lungs.

"You-are-here… because-I-was… betrayed."

The memory shifted to The Office of Lost and Found when it still resided at the decaying Kirkfield Towers.

"My name is Veronica Drysdale," said the woman in front of him, "and that is my husband, Vincent."

Locke examined a photograph in his hand. It showed a handsome man of middle-aged years with slick hair, parted at the side and greying at the temples. He wore a confident smile and a paisley cardigan.

"The-liar!" spat the thing in the cave. "The-cheat! Without-me… no-ties… un-bound… lost… forever."

An old lady called Mrs Maunley stood in a doorway and announced that every crime must be punished.

"Balance must be restored," said a man in orange overalls.

"You can find anything," said Emily Wilson.

Locke ran up a country road at night and said into a phone: "the ties that bind are hard to break."

Then the cave once more and the remains of Roland McCaffrey.

"You-will-find-me… my-place… amongst-the-gods."

Grotesque laughter rang out, echoing into a final memory – Locke curled up on a floor with his eyes closed tight.

A breeze touched his face, followed by a faint scratching at his nose.

He opened his eyes. A piece of paper fluttered weakly on the floor before him. A message was written upon it in thick black ink:

'Your name is Thomas Locke. You work for me now.'

Billy didn't go back to school after fleeing the restaurant. He wandered around town until his empty stomach hurt so much he was forced to head home for dinner.

"Where have you been all day?" his father asked across the dining table.

The question made Billy nervous. He knew he couldn't tell the truth, but speaking the obvious lie felt like walking into a trap.

"School," he said.

"All day?"

"Except lunchtime. I went out for lunch."

"I know you did, because that Mr Drysdale came visit me at work. Said you turned up while he was out with friends and called his wife… mummy."

Billy did not dare look up from the plate in front of him. He wanted to shrink down under the table, away from this recriminating voice.

"Did you hear that, dear?" Norman said to his wife. "Our son was calling some other woman his mummy. But don't worry, dear, Mr Drysdale said it wasn't our fault. He said it was most probably a virus or bacteria that got into our Billy's head when he was small and affected his brain. It makes him see things and say things that aren't right. Said a child suffering from such a condition can be very persuasive too, sometimes even convincing others to share in his— what did he call them? Oh yeah, delusions."

Billy had stopped trying to push his food around with his fork. He was a rabbit frozen in the headlights of his father's stare.

"But he's a stand-up guy is this Drysdale," continued Norman. "Before I met him, I thought he must be some sort of smarmy prick. Now I'll hold my hands up and say I was wrong, because do you know what he said next? He said he'd been thinking of awarding a scholarship to deprived kids who really needed his help. Said he wanted to offer it to Billy. 'Course, I wasn't just going to buy his spiel just like that. You know me, I'm no mug. Always switched on, always thinking. So I ask if he can prove he can really help our Billy and without missing a beat, Drysdale tells me he's already started. Tells me to go home and check under the bed."

Billy heard his father's chair scrape back across the floor. Norman leaned across the table and his hot breath rasped against the top of Billy's head.

"So I do as he says and do you know what I saw?"

Did he want an answer? Billy didn't know. He kept quiet.

"DO YOU KNOW WHAT I SAW?!"

Terrified, Billy shrugged and mumbled, "I don't know."

"Nothing! I saw nothing! That's when I knew I could trust this man, because he'd taken away the fear that's been hanging over me and your mother's head for all these past months."

Norman straightened up, unbuckled his belt and pulled it free of his trousers.

"Norman, no!" said Billy's mother. "We're in the middle of dinner, can't you—?"

"No, Maureen. Drysdale might be able to teach him some things, but when it comes to respect, the buck stops here. And here, my boy, is where you get the mother of all thrashings."

Thomas Locke found himself in a strange and alien place. He blinked and then ran his fingers across his face. This all felt real, even if it didn't look like a reality he was familiar with.

The sky was black. There were no stars, no clouds, nothing to mar the uniform lack of colour. Looking up gave Thomas vertigo and he banished the queasiness by scanning the alien landscape around him. The ground undulated with hills and valleys. Shifting pools of light shone up from the earth. Locke crouched down and touched what he expected to be soil. It was something else. A gentle finger passed through it as easily as candyfloss, but it turned hard as stone under pressure.

He studied an example of the local flora, which looked like a bonsai tree formed of glass. It grew even as he watched and then he had to scoot aside as another sprouted beside him – a fountain of rainbow liquid spurting upwards that rapidly crystallised into tenuous branches.

The structure quivered as Locke touched a twig, which snapped off and floated upwards. He caught it in his hand. When he opened his fingers, it tried again to escape to the void above. Locke put the fragment in his trouser pocket.

A cracking sound coincided with a nearby shrub breaking free of its roots and tumbling skyward. A second did the same thing a few minutes later. Locke came to the conclusion that it took about fifteen minutes for the glass plants to reach critical mass, at which point they succumbed to the pull of the black sky.

It took another ten minutes for Locke to reach the conclusion that these observations weren't going to help him get home. He looked around and saw nothing even vaguely resembling a hyper-space elevator, an inter-dimensional portal or a licensed taxi. Hoping some form of escape lay just over the horizon, Locke picked out a distant hill and began walking.

Two hours later, he crested the summit. A machine toiled across an expansive plain below. It was constructed of metal, wood and plastic haphazardly bolted together. Despite its no doubt immense weight, it floated along, bound to the earth by anchors that human-shaped attendants deftly inserted into and extracted from the earth. The vehicle's motion came from winches that pulled hard on the anchors once they were securely moored. At the rear of the craft, metal booms sowed the ground with a fine dust, while fine mesh nets fanned out from each side to catch the crystal shrubs.

Locke's immediate excitement was quickly tempered by caution. Figures moved around the machine. They too laboured under the gravity of the void, but prevented themselves floating skyward through use of scythes they either dug into the ground or hooked around railings criss-crossing the machine. These scythes were also used to aid the harvest by smashing the shrub's glassy roots.

As Locke approached, the blades began to worry him less than those who wielded them. They possessed a patchwork anatomy, where legs were often replaced by arms and limbs rarely matched. One could be black, another white. One muscular, another sinew and bone.

He drew close to one of the workers. Its mismatched face had multi-coloured skin framing offset brown and blue eyes. A Roman nose jutted out over pouting, supermodel lips and a square, masculine jaw. Too many teeth jostled for space in its mouth and too many of them looked like rotted fangs.

But these people might be able to help me get home, thought Locke. He wasn't convinced by the idea, but without any better options he raised a hand in greeting. On seeing him, the odd-looking farmer bounded toward him with wide swings of his scythe.

"Hello, my name is Thomas Locke."

"Ich hierbij reclamar jego voix," the farmer shouted to his colleagues, before cutting Locke down with his scythe.

Billy fidgeted in the passenger seat throughout the drive to Joshua Dunne's house. His bottom and the back of his legs were still sore from the previous night's punishment. They arrived shortly before nine in the morning.

"Well?" said his father. "Get out then."

Billy unfastened his seatbelt and opened the car door. He collected his satchel from the foot-well and stepped out onto the pavement. He felt foolish dressed up in his school uniform, but his father had insisted.

"And I don't want to hear any tales of you and that tongue of yours causing trouble. You hear me, boy?"

Billy nodded.

"Good. See you at dinner."

The car drove off, leaving Billy standing at the side of the road. To his right, red plastic barriers cordoned off a deep hole with exposed pipes at the bottom. He wanted to hide in there instead of walking up to Joshua's front door, but his father would find out and another thrashing would surely follow.

He rang the doorbell. Mrs Dunne answered.

"Ah! Billy, isn't it? Don't you look adorable in your uniform? Come inside, we've been expecting you." Mary Dunne led Billy through the house to the kitchen. "Mr Drysdale's not here yet, but most of the others are. We've got about ten of you kids running around here this morning and my guess is most of them are on a sugar high from eating those terrible cereals they keep advertising on TV. What did you have for breakfast, Billy?"

"Muesli."

"Excellent, you shouldn't be any trouble then."

"It tastes like dandruff."

"Oh. I see. Do your parents not buy proper shampoo?"

"They make me sleep in a shoebox."

"Okay, well, it's not my place to judge how others raise their children. As long as you don't give any of the others lice, that's the main thing."

A door opened from the kitchen into the back garden. The rest of Billy's new classmates were out there, running around, playing games and shouting at each other.

"Can't I stay in here?" asked Billy.

"Don't be silly," said Mrs Dunne, "I'm sure you'd much rather go out there and start making friends."

Billy looked outside a second time and then looked back at Mrs Dunne.

"Please can I stay here?"

Before she could reply, her son ran in from the hallway. He was quivering with excitement.

"Mum! Mum! There are roadworks outside! I prayed for

roadworks and they came! Take it tea and biscuits, Mum! If we keep it happy, maybe it'll stay."

"Joshy, I don't think—"

"Oh, please, Mum, pleeaasseee!"

"I'll take out some biscuits, but I'm not going to the trouble of making tea. That's all those workmen do all day anyway, drink tea."

"Thank-you! Thank-you! Thank-you!"

Mrs Dunne picked up the biscuit barrel and walked to the door.

"Why don't you introduce Billy here to the others while I'm gone?"

She left. Billy and Joshua briefly appraised each other without risking eye contact.

"Uh, hi, Billy," said Joshua.

"Hi, Josh."

"You here for Mr Drysdale's teaching?"

"I guess. Umm, so… what's the big deal about roadworks?"

"Why do people keep asking that? Isn't it obvious?"

"Err… no."

"What is it with everyone? You know, the only one who understands is Mr Drysdale. When he asked me what project I wanted to do, when I said roadworks, he told me it was a brilliant idea. A *brilliant* idea! Because you've got the machines ripping stuff up and putting it back together again and it's roads, isn't it? Everything's connected by roads. That's what makes keeping them working so important. Lifeblood of society, that's what Mr Drysdale told me."

"Mmm, okay," said Billy. "I think I should go outside and talk to someone else now."

"Uh, sure, but you know what you could do? When Mr Drysdale asks you what project you want to do, you could tell him roadworks too. We could work together. I've got loads of books upstairs and Dad's been driving me round town so I can take photographs of them. Trust me, Billy, you won't find anything better than roadworks. Anywhere. Ever."

No one noticed Billy step outside. The other children continued going about their chaotic business. A sour expression crept across his face. He recognised Luke from his old class, but all the rest were strangers – strangers sharing jokes or pulling each other's hair or fighting over whose go it was next on the plastic slide.

"Billy," said Luke, scampering over. "No, ssh, don't say anything. Follow me, come on, over here."

Billy followed Luke to a passageway running alongside the house. Once out of sight of the other children, Luke smiled and produced a bundle of envelopes from his back pocket.

"Good shit, yeah?"

Billy frowned.

"You want one?" asked Luke. "No, stupid question, of course you want one. This one's good. It's offering you a deal on home broadband. Or, wait, wait, this one's better still."

"A menu for a Chinese takeaway?"

"Yeah, it is, it is, but I didn't get it from a restaurant. No, it just appeared. Out of *nowhere*."

"Umm, didn't someone push it through your letterbox? Someone who was probably delivering a Chinese takeaway to the people next door?"

"No, no… well, maybe it came through the letterbox, but no one delivered it, because what this is, what all these represent… is the cosmic consciousness trying to talk to us."

"Is this your project?" asked Billy. "Is this the project Mr Drysdale gave you?"

"This one's my favourite," said Luke, shuffling another envelope to the top of his collection. A prominent logo spelt out the name 'Daex'. "You open this up, complete the survey inside and then you can claim a ten pound gift token, a free alarm clock or the gift of immortality."

"You are as completely mental as Josh."

Luke's eyebrows dropped sharply so he could glower at Billy. He didn't have a chance to refute the charge, because they were no longer alone.

"Hey, Luke, who's the new kid?" asked a black-skinned boy.

"Does he like cushions?" asked a girl with a cushion Sellotaped to the top of her head.

"Don't be daft," snapped another kid, flicking her around the ear. "Look at him, look at his eyes. They're the eyes of a man who's into vending machines, just like me. Exact change only."

"Do you want to see my battery collection?" said a boy with a blonde mop of hair who forced his way to the front and held out hands overflowing with watch batteries, double As, triple As and the odd nickel-cadmium rechargeable.

"Back off, all of you!" shouted Luke. "He's already said he's studying direct mailing with me."

"I never did!" protested Billy.

This prompted an avalanche of offers, threats and suggestions featuring pollen, socks, watches, chewing gum and lampposts – a cacophonic competition that only ceased when Mrs Dunne called from the house.

"Mr Drysdale's here!"

Most of the children rushed excitedly back inside. Only Luke lingered for a moment to wave a warning finger at Billy.

"Do not disrespect the direct mailing."

Then Luke too was gone and Billy was left alone. He knew he should follow and show his face to Mr Drysdale so he could look father in the eye that evening and say he'd been a good boy, but his heart was already beating too fast. He didn't know if he could face that Mr Drysdale again.

He leant against the brickwork of the passageway and listened to shrill voices telling Mr Drysdale how much they'd done on their projects since he was last here.

And then there was another voice – deeper, familiar…

"I'll be back to pick you up at four, Vincent."

Billy edged toward the rearmost end of the passageway, then heard the front door open. He ran back up the path and found the way blocked by a tall gate held shut by a padlock. Through the slats, Billy could see a mother and daughter walking up to the house.

"Hello, Mrs Drysdale," said the mother, smiling.

"Oh, Mrs Pinborough, isn't it?" said Veronica, still unseen. "How are you? How's young, err…"

"Olivia. Olivia's grand, aren't you, pet?"

The girl said nothing. She stared fixedly ahead with her lips pursed, as if attempting advanced calculus in her head. Billy decided there and then she was probably as crazy as the rest of them. He looked around and saw the hedge separating the property from next door was thin enough at the bottom for him to crawl through.

"Well, I'm sorry Mrs Pinborough, but I've got to be off to work."

"Oh, but you must stay for Olivia's big announcement. She was studying all evening and then in the middle of the night she had what you might call an epiphany."

Veronica sighed. Billy crawled along the neighbour's driveway.

"Was it a short epiphany?" she asked.

"It'll only take a moment, I promise. Ah, Mary, how are you?"

Joshua's mother greeted Mrs Pinborough on the doorstep. Billy was now at the neighbour's gatepost. He could see Vincent Drysdale in the Dunne's hallway, surrounded by the other children.

"Excuse me, everyone," said Mrs Pinborough. "Ladies, gentlemen, boys and girls, my Olivia has something to say."

Her daughter extravagantly cleared her throat and then sang out the words she'd been reciting in her head.

"Last night, a toaster came to me in a dream and from that toaster popped some toast and upon that toast writing was burnt and that writing told me the one and only true path for salvation is the worship of kitchen appliances."

The silence that followed lasted only a few seconds before Vincent Drysdale hurried over to the doorstep, clapping enthusiastically.

"That's excellent, Olivia, really excellent, but weren't you supposed to be learning how to re wire a plug?"

"Hmm," said Veronica. "Nice meeting you again, Mrs Pinborough, Mrs Dunne, assorted offspring. See you later, Vincent."

She headed back toward her husband's car, parked at the side of the road.

"I love you, Veronica," he called after her.

She stopped. Turned around. Smiled.

"I love you too."

She blew him a kiss and then clicked the key fob to the car. It beeped and flashed its lights. She walked over to the driver's side door and climbed inside. Vincent Drysdale was still watching from the doorstep as she drove away.

"I thought he was the one thing you were scared of," said

Billy from the back seat.

Veronica glanced at his reflection in the rear view mirror.

"I've lived a little since then."

"What's he done to all those other kids?" asked Billy.

"I don't know."

"Why didn't Thomas recognise me in the restaurant? Why were you with Mr Drysdale? Why are my monsters frightened of him?"

"Billy..."

He was on the verge of tears.

"I thought if there was anyone I could trust, it'd be the monsters and Thomas and you. But they're gone and he doesn't know me and you're—"

"I should take you back."

"You should help me, that's what you should do!"

"Billy..."

"Okay, fine! Take me back! See if I care!"

She drove on for some time with Billy sobbing on the back seat. He didn't raise his head until the car drew to a stop. He ventured a peek out of the window. They were parked outside a house he didn't recognise.

"Where are we?" he asked.

Veronica opened the door for him.

"The one place I know we can get an inside line on toaster psychology."

Locke returned from unconsciousness into a trembling world of agony. He was strapped to the ceiling of a brown-stained room randomly bucking up and down and from side to side. Each violent movement sent another glistening blob of his own blood falling to the floor.

Except the congealed drops never landed.

They were restrained by a shining thread that collected up the red liquid and hoisted it back up to Locke's exposed chest.

One glance showed him the gaping cuts in his torso, a second that his left arm was missing. He closed his eyes tight and clenched his teeth against the pain.

I should be dead, he thought to himself, but even now, even with Lafarge gone, I cannot rest. There's always someone who has to bring me back.

He opened his eyes again. The amputated arm was being dragged back to its socket by more gossamer threads. Locke knew then the name of his saviour. The Ties That Bind would not let him go until he'd carried out his mission.

His arm was re-attached, the incisions closed. The pain began to subside. Whole again, Locke was able to unfasten the straps, an awkward process given his own weight kept them in tension. More awkward was the falling head-first to the floor that followed his eventual success.

Locke wiped blood from his forehead and watched as lines of red stretched out from his hand and back into the fresh wound. Within a minute his fingers were clean and dry. By then, Locke had climbed out through a round hatch and into a dingy passageway. Another hatch led outside.

He was aboard the peculiar harvesting machine. The crew were gathered at the front of the vehicle and trying to net another of the crystal structures, except this one was not a knee-high shrub. This was at least one hundred feet tall and almost as many wide. What's more, it was still growing, cascading out from a pool of light that reached up into the black sky like a blinding white pillar.

Locke was thrown heavily against a railing as the craft bucked sharply, the front rising into the air. A grapple was caught on a branch that had suddenly shot up another twenty feet. One of the farmers was forced to cut the line before the machine over-turned. Shouts of derision followed his action, but they were brief. More grapples were thrown.

The roots of the gargantuan glass tree began to crack. As they did so, the light beneath faded.

It was a good time to make a run for it, thought Locke, but the only escape was into a wide-open, rolling wasteland. His flight would be visible for miles. Even if the farmers didn't see him, he might instead end up roaming this place forever. Literally, if The Ties That Bind chose to keep his heart beating.

A huge chunk of the tree snapped off from the rest and sailed into the void, prompting howls of dismay from those so desperately trying to reap its bounty.

Locke ducked back inside.

The other rooms on this deck of the craft were cramped

and perfunctorily furnished, albeit with those furnishings arranged on the ceiling. This made sense given the topsy-turvy gravity of the place. Locke didn't know why he was an exception to this law and wasn't interested in looking for explanations at the moment.

A hole led down to a lower-deck. Locke ignored the rungs and dropped into a storage area filled with crystal the farmers had collected. The wondrous shapes formed out in the open had been broken down into inch-long fragments and dumped into metal bins arranged about the ceiling. Open sacks trailed multi-coloured powder that had been dumped into a large hopper. The level of powder was falling in line with the grating rhythm of a pumping mechanism bolted to one wall. Locke guessed this was the stuff the machine sprayed across the ground from the metal booms at its rear. There was writing on the sacks, but it was gibberish… or maybe, thought Locke, it's just upside down.

The change in perspective prompted a sudden, strong desire to understand what this place was and why that name – Umivatoré - was here.

Locke resumed his search of the storage bay. He saw another door. He approached with caution. Whistling became audible over the noise of the pump. On reaching the doorway, he remembered to look up at the ceiling.

While the farmers who toiled outside retained a mostly human form, the creature in the room had decided the human form could be improved by having more of everything. More eyes, more ears, more noses. More heads. More arms, more legs, more fingers, more toes and many more genitalia. An eye on a finger on a toe on a stubby little penis was studying a fragment of crystal very closely. Satisfied with the inspection, fingers on a foot on an arm with sixteen ears took the crystal, enveloped it in a plastic bag and then moved it over to a large bubble. This bubble was almost a metre in diameter and contained what Locke could only describe as *somewhere else* – the somewhere else in question being the interior of a dingy warehouse. Stranger still, when the creature passed the crystal into the bubble, it became a shrill laugh, albeit one muffled by a plastic bag and distorted by the watery acoustics of the bubble.

The creature withdrew the plastic bag. Once outside the bubble, the crystal became a crystal once more. The creature promptly ate it. A second later the creature burped and then laughed the very same laugh the crystal contained.

A second crystal became a thermos flask inside the bubble. The creature produced an aerosol and sprayed the flask. When removed from the bubble, it did not revert to being a crystal. The flask was placed in a box marked 'Gwerthu'. Locke had no idea what that meant.

He could have continued watching this work, fascinated, had a rusty creaking not alerted him to one wall of the storage bay slowly opening. The garbled chatter of the farmers drifted in from outside.

Locke looked up at the bubble. That was his way out. Probably.

He raced over to the hopper, grabbed a sack of Umivatoré fertiliser down from the ceiling and then hurried back to the room.

"Hey!" he shouted.

The creature's many eyes looked up from its desk and down at Locke.

Locke hurled the sack upwards, striking the creature right between several eyes, square in the middle of others, with significant collateral damage to a good half dozen gonads.

The creature was stunned. Locke jumped for the bubble. His flailing hand passed straight through it.

He jumped again still too low. He needed to dive into the thing, but how?

The storage bay door was now fully open. The farmers filed in with the fragments of crystal tree they'd managed to snare. Scythes were set aside in a rack by the door and then they scuttled across the ceiling, filling the metal bins Locke had seen earlier with their harvest.

The injured creature loosed an angry cry.

The farmers turned toward Locke. Their eyes opened in shock at seeing him back in one piece.

"Waaaaarrrrggghh!" cried Locke, rushing toward them.

His manic charge provoked frowns and the exchange of puzzled glances. These seconds of confusion proved enough. Locke snatched a scythe from the rack. He backed toward the room, brandishing the blade.

The frowns turned to snarls. Patchwork hands grabbed the remaining scythes.

Locke could accept the prospect of dying, but an agonising death followed by an equally agonising rebirth held no appeal. He lunged at the encroaching crowd with his scythe and then spun around, intent on pole-vaulting into the bubble…

"Oh," said Locke, "I didn't mean… I'm sorry…"

The creature from the room had been preparing to pounce down on him from the doorway, but such thoughts had been pushed from its mind by the scythe's blade cleanly slicing into its primary head.

Shouts went up from the other farmers. They rushed forward.

Locke pushed the thing on his stick back toward the bubble and it fell through into whatever world lay beyond. The scythe was pulled in its wake along with Locke, who clung onto the handle for dear life.

"That's nonsense. You're talking nonsense," said Kathleen Muller. "Please leave."

Her front door was only open a few inches and she cowered behind it, refusing to look up at Veronica and Billy.

"We need to see your husband," said Veronica.

"Leonard's gone!" snapped Mrs Muller. "He upped and left me left months ago! No word, no warning—"

"No, your husband died two and a half years ago after he drove into a fallen tree during a storm."

"My husband—"

"Came back as a toaster."

"Don't be ridiculous!"

Kathleen Muller tried to close the door. A trainer-shod foot kept it open.

"We will leave," said Veronica, slowly, "when you've made us some toast."

Kathleen Muller stared at Veronica and then down at the boy beside her.

"I'll skip the toast," said Billy, "but if you've got any biscuits…"

Fifteen minutes later they were having tea in the kitchen.

"I thought I was going crazy," said Kathleen Muller, "but how you can be crazy when you have proof right there in your hands?" She laughed. "But who else is going to believe that a slice of toast with a burnt impression of the lakeside hotel where we spent our honeymoon is real proof? I had to stop using him, for the sake of my sanity, but… after a time… I missed him, I really did. And then I didn't care if I was crazy. I had to stick a slice of bread in there, just to see it pop out with the words 'I love you' baked on it. We actually had whole conversations, me saying one thing, then dropping in another slice and him toasting his reply. One night I got through fifteen loaves. I've kept them all, wrapped them up in plastic bags and stuck them in the freezer in the garage. That has to be crazy, right? Getting sentimental about pieces of toast?"

Veronica managed a wry smile. "I gather love's like that."

"Well, it was good for a while, almost like having him back. Then… things changed."

"How so?"

"He… he started saying funny things. He said the gods were coming, then… well, see for yourself."

She dropped a slice of bread into the toaster, pushed down the lever. They waited. One minute later, the slice popped up and burned upon it were three words:

'Pray for me.'

"And that's all he says now," explained Mrs Muller, "over and over again – pray for me."

Locke fell from the trans-dimensional bubble onto a blood-smeared conveyer belt. The scythe he clung to was still buried in the head of the anatomically mixed-up creature.

Metal crashed against metal behind him; another scythe, swung by a farmer leaping through the bubble. It missed Locke's foot by millimetres.

He rolled off the conveyer belt onto a dusty floor and scrambled toward a distant set of doors. The people here registered only as a blur of obstacles he had to avoid. He passed between towering shelves and pulled from them boxes that tumbled into the path of his pursuers.

"Atakna!"

"Cruento cehennem!"

"I'll dood te maak cette bękart!"

Locke stumbled through the doors into blinding light. He shielded his eyes and staggered on, crashing into more shelves. He wheeled away, crunching fallen detritus underfoot.

"Security to aisle 313," instructed a speaker's tinny voice. "Security to aisle 313. Also, cleaning assistant to aisle 313. Cleaning assistant to aisle 313."

Locke's vision finally adjusted to the glare of antiseptic lighting on a polished white floor. He was in the consumer electronics section of a supermarket, but his relief at returning to somewhere normal was short-lived.

He ran past a wall of televisions and then ducked down aisle 318. The sign overhead announced 'grazed knees and elbows, infant to prepubescent'. Locke slowed and cast a bewildered gaze over exactly that – shelves of grazed knees and elbows accented by subtle spotlights. There were even sections for different brands, each with their own snappy slogan.

Jauglo – Memories that last.

Imaginarium – Live the Dream.

King Ruffalo – Premium Purveyor of Memeker Commodities.

But they're just selling scabby kneecaps! Locke thought to himself. Confused and distracted, he bundled into a woman browsing two-for-one offers.

"Sorry," he said, before realising she was semi-transparent and unravelling – wisps of her person were snagged on his jacket.

"Hey, stop! You're running off with my arm!" said the woman.

Locke hastily threw off the jacket and took a left at the next intersection. This was unlike any supermarket he'd visited before.

"Welcome back, Billy," said Vincent Drysdale.

They sat opposite each other at Joshua Dunne's dining room table. Veronica stood behind Billy with her hands on his shoulders.

"I found him hiding in the back of the car," she said.

"Oh dear," said Vincent, "I don't think this was the kind of start your father had in mind."

Billy clenched his teeth and stared down at the edge of the table.

"I need to go," said Veronica. "I'm late for work."

"Yes, of course," said Vincent. "Thank-you. And I love you."

"Yeah. Ditto."

She patted Billy on the shoulder and left.

"I'm not disappointed," said Vincent Drysdale. "A boy's first day in a strange, new learning environment such as this, a little trepidation is to be expected. Who wouldn't want to run away? But I can help with that. Did the others tell you about their projects?"

Billy nodded stiffly. Vincent continued.

"Reading, writing and arithmetic have applications in every sphere of human endeavour, so why learn from stodgy old textbooks when you could instead learn about them in the light of a subject you're really passionate about? That's why I ask all of my children to choose a project. I find after a few days you're practically teaching yourselves, which definitely helps when I have to attend classes on the other side of town."

"But I don't want a project," muttered Billy.

"What was that?"

"I don't want a project."

"Oh, but you have to have a project. Everyone has a project. And it's so much better when you pick your own. I wouldn't like to have to choose one for you."

"Okay, can I do—?"

"No, you can't do monsters. It has to be something real."

Billy bit his lip. He made a show of thinking hard, even though he'd rehearsed all of this with Veronica on the drive back from Kathleen Muller's house. Think of yourself as James Bond infiltrating the enemy's ranks, she'd told him. You're our best chance of finding out what Vincent's really up to. The first step was choosing a project, but it had taken a long time to come up with something. Billy wanted to pick something harmless and innocent, not creepy and weird like

Joshua's roadworks or Luke's direct mailing.

"Well?" prompted Vincent Drysdale.

"Spoons," said Billy. "I'd really like to study spoons."

"For pity's sake, security, you've just run straight past him! He's hiding between the messy divorces on aisle 406! Get your asses back there and get him nixed before the boss has us all fired!"

Locke ducked out from under a marquee display of a child caught in a tug of love. Startled shoppers stood agog as he fled a posse of security guards and scythe-wielding farmers.

If I can still find things, thought Locke, I can find a way out of here.

He followed his instincts. He took a left turn, a right, hurdled onto the trolley of a hippopotamus wearing a fez and vaulted over the shelves into the next aisle – 'Holidays, 18-30, Costa Del Sol'.

A farmer came at him out of nowhere. Locke ducked. The scythe missed and decapitated a raffia-work donkey from Torremolinos. Locke grabbed a pair of maracas, struck his attacker in the stomach and then smashed him across the back of the head, sending splintered wood and dried beans cascading across the floor.

"There he is!"

Security guards ran toward him from the checkouts.

"Orada ta adalah!"

The other farmers appeared and raced to cut off his retreat. He managed to reach another junction. Guards were behind him, irate farmers ahead and to the left. Locke dashed right and found himself faced with a broad shard of savannah pitching up from the slick white floor and rising to the metal ceiling. Antelope grazed happily some thirty feet above. A flock of vultures feasted on the corpse of a bison by a copse of arid-looking trees that cast a faint shadow over aisle 418 – 'First kisses, ages 21 to 30'.

A prim folding sign warned: 'Danger! Reality Slip'. Locke ignored it, ducked beneath a line of security tape and then fell face first into dry mud.

He pushed himself upright. His head swam; senses trying to orientate themselves to the sudden switch in gravity. It was now the supermarket floor that stretched upwards. Above his head, security guards and farmers clashed at the intersection.

Still dazed, Locke ran toward the antelope, causing them to scatter. The nearby vultures squawked alarm. Several took flight, flapping up into the supermarket's gravity and promptly crashing down into a collection of nervously puckered lips.

Ahead of Locke was the supermarket ceiling. A gantry ran between lights and air conditioning ducts to a door set high in one wall. Locke shimmied up a hand-rail until gravity switched direction again. Up became ahead, sideways became down and Locke almost fell.

Farmers and guards had made it onto the savannah, but a pack of whooping hyenas hampered their progress.

Locke hauled himself back onto the gantry and staggered up to the door. It wasn't locked. He opened it and looked out in awe as rain splashed against his face.

The arid grassland from below cut through the concrete roof of the supermarket and curved upward into a hazy blue sky before bisecting an ocean teeming with islands and boats that hung upside down, miles above the supermarket's land of shops and offices. Black clouds drifted between the three lands, roiling and twisting and sending rain falling in three hundred and sixty degrees. A city flickered into view, like a rainbow given life by fleeting sunshine. It glittered with spires and minarets circled by fabulous winged creatures. The storm began to clear and more worlds appeared. Locke spied forests, deserts and mountains; each a sliver of land fighting for space in the heavens, impossible ribbons of reality weaving and winding their way toward a single destination – a gargantuan sphere of scaffolding that sucked in these worlds through giant pipes. Equally giant advertising hoardings plastered about the sphere announced that Daex, Jauglo, the Unbound Travel Company and countless others were proud to support this development.

Locke walked to the edge of the roof, still trying to make sense of what he was seeing. A street ran below and he hailed a man-headed dog walking along it.

"Hey, excuse me, what is that thing out there?"

"What thing?" replied the passer-by.

"The big round thing covered in scaffolding."

"Are you kidding me? That's the thing that's going to save us all! That's the Umivatoré."

Maureen sat at the kitchen table chewing a thumbnail. Her husband sat opposite, ignoring his lovingly prepared full English breakfast in favour of leafing through a pile of junk mail. He growled at each one in turn before dumping it unceremoniously into the bin.

"What's up with the world these days?" he asked no one in particular. "Who actually wants to receive any of this shit? And I'd swear each day brings more and more of it. I'm having words with our postman next time I see him."

"Your breakfast's going cold, dear," said Maureen.

Norman sniffed, dropped the remaining letters in the bin and set about a sausage with his knife and fork. Her first mission of the day accomplished, Maureen turned to her son, who was ignoring his lovingly prepared muesli in favour of staring at his spoon.

"Billy, your muesli's getting soggy," she said.

"Look, Mum," he replied, holding the spoon up in front of her face and turning it one way and then the other. "Big face, little face. Big face, little face. Aren't spoons amazing?"

"Err, yes, dear. They're even quite good for eating muesli."

But it was no good. Billy was too fascinated by his spoon to eat. Maureen turned to her husband for help. He didn't even look up from his breakfast.

"It's better than monsters, dear," he said, "better than monsters."

Thomas Locke took a taxi, a horse-helicopter hybrid and a white-water ride on the back of a purple-spotted dolphin before reaching the wide, gold-brick avenue that led up to the Umivatoré.

He wondered how he would get inside.

"Are you here for the tour, sir?" The question was asked by a smartly turned out suit. There was nobody in the suit; it was just empty fabric.

"Yes," said Locke. "Yes, I am."

"Then please join the queue over there and I will be with

you shortly."

Veronica was at work. She should have been typing up meeting minutes, but instead she was on the phone.

"Hello, Osmonby Newsagents," said a strongly-accented woman on the other end of the line.

"Hello, my name's Veronica Drysdale, I'm a friend of Thomas Locke's, I'm trying to get hold of him and I understand—"

"Love, we're all trying to get a hold of Thomas Locke."

"You mean he's gone?"

"Aye, him and another fella from around here by the name of Roland McCaffrey. Roland goes missing and your Thomas does likewise not long after. Suspicious business all round. Have the police got your number, because I expect they'll want to—"

Veronica hung up. Thomas hadn't answered his phone in over a week and now this woman was saying he was gone? She suddenly felt guilty for having dinner with his doppelganger the other day. She'd kept telling herself that the man in front of her was the fake, while the real Thomas Locke was enjoying a well-deserved retirement by the sea, but perhaps… perhaps that little act of betrayal was enough for the universe to follow through on Thomas's conviction that he was the one that didn't exist.

She felt nauseous.

"You look like you could do with a good cup of coffee," said Sharon, poking her head around the door. "Or possibly a bucket."

"And where do we get good coffee round here?" asked Veronica in reply.

"Hmm, yeah, guess we'll have to make do with piss-poor machine coffee like always then. Coming?"

Veronica nodded and left her desk, thankful for the distraction.

"Are you pretending to be the United Nations today?" she asked Sharon as they descended to the shop-floor and crossed to the canteen. The quizzical expression she got in reply prompted Veronica to point at the half dozen watches strapped to her friend's arms. "Have you suddenly got business in six different time-zones?"

"No, it's just the fashion now, isn't it?"

"Is it?"

"It is."

"If you say so."

They entered the canteen. Edmund was in there. Sharon and Veronica exchanged a weary glance. Whenever colleagues gathered around the water-cooler to play 'ain't it awful?' and bitch about work, Edmund would always take the fun out of it by pointing out how things were really far worse than they realised. He was like a newspaper headline given human form.

"Stupid thing. Stupid, stupid thing," he was saying, thumping the coffee dispenser. "It's not working. I put my money in and it's swallowed it and you know they do this on purpose? Ten percent of the profits of all vending machine manufacturers comes from stealing money like this, but I suppose on this occasion it's a good thing." Veronica and Sharon looked at each other, astounded. Edmund looking on the bright side? Surely not. "It means I won't be getting cancer from the coffee today. You do know the powder they use in these things is carcinogenic, don't you? It builds up in your bloodstream like mercury and it never goes away. You have one cup and that one cup will end up slowly killing you for the rest of your life."

"Edmund," said Sharon, "you are full of shit. Now out the way, let me have a go."

She kicked the machine. Shook it from side to side. Swore at it. Pressed the button and… nothing.

"Brilliant," said Edmund. "The power of positive thinking, plain for all to see."

"You won't get anything out of it like that," said an Indian girl on entering the canteen.

Payoja Khadri prided herself on being the factory's best machinist. This did not explain the sock pinned to her smock.

"Why are wearing a sock on your smock?" asked Sharon.

"Socks are good luck," said Payoja.

"Since when?"

"Since I won ten pounds on the lottery four weeks in a row. Now, if you all want coffee this morning, you have to do exactly what I do." The Indian girl knelt down in front of the vending machine, clasped her hands together and bowed. "Oh, great coffee dispensing deity, I do bow before thee and humbly request that you grace this poor commoner with your most delectable of liquids."

"This is patently—"

Edmund didn't get to finish his sentence. A cup of coffee was delicately filled without splatter or spillage and when Payoja removed it from the machine, it smelt like real coffee and not the instant muck they usually put up with.

"See?" she said. "All it takes is a little prayer and if you pray nicely enough, you don't even have to pay."

She left with her drink, leaving the others mystified.

"It must be broken," said Edmund, examining the machine as if he knew what he was doing.

"Since when did we have to pray to get coffee?" asked Sharon.

"Since Vincent came back," Veronica whispered under her breath.

"Behold!" exclaimed the tour guide. "Our salvation!"

An empty sleeve presented the interior of the Umivatoré with a sweeping gesture, as if Locke and the rest of the tour group had been blind to its sights beforehand. Instead, eyes widened the moment they stepped through the main entrance.

The space around them was vast and dominated by the enormous pipes that fed in through the structure's exoskeleton. These wound around each other before curling up like ammonite shells, each of which was attended by a gantry teeming with people and machines. Smaller pipes led from the shells into a central sphere. One pipe bore the colour of varnished pine, another mahogany. There were pillars of red brick, buttressed by sandstone. The handrails of the walkway above were strung together from countless radius bones, while the floor Locke stood upon was a collage of fireside rugs. And yet the Umivatoré was clearly unfinished. Workmen atop scaffolding were making rapid progress on a new pipe. Their building material came from bubbles. These contained stores of crystals. When a crystal was removed from a bubble, it became a sheet of corrugated iron.

Locke reached into his trouser pocket. Instead of touching the branch he had broken from the glass shrub, his fingertips brushed against crumpled paper. He would have taken it out to study there and then, but the tour guide was shepherding them forward.

"… no longer will our many worlds labour under the tyranny of fading memories and insubstantial dreams," declared the suit. "This formidable machine will harness the power of the Conjunction to anchor our future in a safe, reliable and renewable source of reality. For only a small investment on your part, you too can become a pioneer of this bright new frontier."

Aside from Locke, the tour party was made up of five regular-looking humans, three transparent ones, two perambulating bananas, an anthropomorphised badger and a toy robot. The toy robot raised a plastic arm.

"Can I ask a question?"

"No!" shouted the tour guide in reply. "And I shall tell you why: because words are worthless in this place. They cannot do justice to this grand undertaking. Save your questions, for I am about to show you the heart of the Umivatoré and the miracle of the Conjunction. Once you have seen them, the grand vision that brought them together will become clear and once that becomes clear… all of your questions will be answered."

"But how does a vending machine know we're praying to it?" asked Sharon, sitting on the edge of Veronica's desk and staring suspiciously at her eighth coffee of the day.

"Can't you just accept that it does?" asked Veronica, instantly realising that made her sound like Thomas.

"No. That is not how we do things in the twenty-first century. I'm going to have to conduct some science. Run some tests, do some experiments. After all, how do we know this isn't an elaborate joke?"

"If you're so rational and practical, why have you still got those six watches running up your arms?"

"I told you, I'm being fashionable. Fashion operates beyond reason."

A smart rapping at the door preceded a smiling Vincent Drysdale letting himself in.

"Afternoon, ladies," he said. "Are you ready to go, Veronica?"

"I'm just logging off," she replied from behind her computer.

"You look very dapper today, Vincent," said Sharon.

"I look very dapper every day, Sharon," replied Vincent. "And you in turn look as impeccable as ever, though, may I say, particularly á la mode on this occasion. Is one of those watches Cartier?"

"Well, it's from Hong Kong, so technically it's a cut-price Carter, but from a distance you can't see the missing 'i'."

Vincent examined the watch more closely. Sharon made sure to brush his shoulder with hers as he did so. Veronica rose from her desk and rolled her eyes.

"If you two want to skip the flirting and just get on with getting off with each other, the stationary cupboard's over there. I can work on a few emails until you're done."

Sharon's eyes lit up at the idea, but Vincent swept away to the door and held it open for his wife.

"Delightful though I'm sure that would be, I'm afraid we need to get going. I want to take a detour on the way home to see how Billy's new project's coming along."

While other children played in Joshua Dunne's garden, Billy stood in his classmate's kitchen, staring into an open cutlery drawer. He reached out toward the forks and held a still hand over them. He moved his hand over the knives. It remained steady until his fingers neared the spoons, then they began to tremble. His heart rate increased. A teasing smile pulled at the edges of his mouth.

Billy snatched his hand away and stuffed it back into a shorts pocket. This was wrong and the wrongness had started the moment he told Mr Drysdale he wanted to study spoons for his project. He only picked spoons because they were harmless and dull, so where had this fascination with their seductive curves come from?

Close the drawer, he told himself. Close the drawer, go outside and start behaving like a normal boy.

"There's no call for behaviour like this, Emily," said Mrs Hu. "We would have finished at four o'clock as normal if you hadn't decided to go and hide in the airing cupboard after lunch. But you did, so we still have half an hour of dividing numbers to do."

Emily glared at her tutor across the dining table and then resumed her tantrum.

"That's so unfair! Daddy, Daddy! Mrs Hu is oppressing me!"

"I am not oppressing you, Emily."

"You are, like those people on the news. I bet you'll be oppressing me with… with tear gas and… and water cannons any minute! Daddy!"

"Daddy is on the phone," called her father from his office across the hall. "He is taking an important business call, so could you two please sort this out amongst yourselves?"

"Mummy!"

Mrs Hu sighed. "Your mother is out at the shops and she won't be back— Emily! Emily!"

The little girl ran out of the room. Mrs Hu tapped a terse tattoo with her pen on the table before addressing the cat sitting by her foot.

"Why did I let you talk me into this, love? I'm sure your original plan would have been so much easier."

Fiddlesticks twitched his tail.

"Of course, you're right," conceded Mrs Hu. "It's not her fault, none of us can escape what we are."

The old Chinese woman stared wistfully at Emily's abandoned exercise book, left open on a doodle of a black figure dressed in a hat and coat.

Thomas Locke was the last of the tour party to step onto the platform. It rested at the base of one of the Umivatoré's many pipes.

"Is everyone on?" asked the tour guide. "Excellent. Now, I'd like to introduce you all to Mr Arbuthnot Gavenny." The animated suit put a sleeve around the shoulder of a short and balding man with a tidy moustache. Mr Gavenny looked sick; his skin an unhealthy grey-brown colour. He gave the crowd a meek wave. "Our friend here is about to embark on an extraordinary journey and we have the privilege of going along for the ride. If you would, Arbuthnot?"

A hatch opened in the pipe. At the suit's behest, Mr Gavenny gingerly climbed inside. He managed another wave before the hatch closed behind him.

"As you all know," said the tour guide, "everyone and everything here survives only by clinging onto fragments of dreams and memories. This medical report shows our new friend has collected quite a history for himself..."

The report came in the form of a snow-globe. Once shaken, it displayed a series of images, each one fainter than the last: a sepia-hued photograph of Arbuthnot Gavenny; a utilitarian library of beige brick and white window frames; a vinyl record buried in rotting vegetables and polystyrene cups; a football program for 1964's fourth round FA Cup tie between Bedford Town and Carlisle United—

The tour guide returned the snow globe to a pocket.

"Arbuthnot is a beloved husband, a lending library in Goole, three hundred copies of an album by a Belarusian blues band that ended up on a landfill near Minsk and yet, all of that, it's not enough. These memories are old. They fade more and more with each passing day. Soon they will be gone and the void will claim him."

A rising whine echoed in Locke's eardrums and the floor beneath his feet shuddered. Everyone grabbed hold of the railing running around the platform.

"But there is another way!" shouted the guide over the noise. "We need not be slave to the tyranny of fleeting memories. Arbuthnot Gavenny is one of those leading the way to a bright new future and where Arbuthnot goes, we shall follow!"

The platform rose sharply into the air and then sped along the pipe toward the heart of the Umivatoré.

Mrs Dunne hurried through her kitchen, drawn by the ringing of the doorbell. She spared a concerned glance for Billy, who was still hovering by the cutlery drawer, before continuing into the hallway. She stopped on hearing shouts coming from the downstairs toilet.

"Admit it! Admit roadworks are superior and pledge your

allegiance to Mr Coney!"

"No! Toasters are—" Olivia Pinborough's refusal became a watery scream synchronised with a flush.

"Joshua!" cried Mrs Dunne, opening the toilet door. "What on earth do you think you're doing to that poor girl?"

"Teaching this heathen to respect the majesty of road-works," her son replied.

The door-bell rang again. Mrs Dunne sighed.

"Not everyone can be as enlightened as we are, dear, but perhaps dipping her hand in hot mix asphalt would encourage her conversion? After all, that worked on your Grandpa."

Enthused by the suggestion, Joshua and two of his cronies dragged Olivia off to the back garden. His mother finally answered the door.

"Oh, Mr and Mrs Drysdale, what a pleasant surprise. We didn't expect to see you today, what with you teaching over in Winston Leys and—"

"We just dropped by to see how Billy is doing."

"Of course, of course. Follow me. He's through in the kitchen."

Emily hid in her parents' wardrobe, crouched down amidst her mother's shoes. It wasn't a very comfortable hiding place, but she was making a point and therefore prepared to suffer until it had been made. Or until her mother returned home, whichever came first.

Scratching came at the closed wardrobe door.

"I might have guessed Mrs Hu would send you to do her dirty work," muttered Emily.

The scratching stopped. She nudged the door open a fraction to see Fiddlesticks idly gazing around her parents' bedroom.

"Or is she doing *your* dirty work?"

The cat flicked his tail and sniffed at the air.

"You should know that after much thought I've decided I definitely prefer dogs."

Fiddlesticks finally looked at Emily and subjected her to a slow blink.

From outside came the sound of tyres rolling across gravel. Emily flung open the wardrobe door and raced over to the window. She looked down onto the driveway expecting to see her mother's car. Instead, she saw a van. A man climbed out. He fetched a package from the back and carried it to the front door.

"We are close to the Conjunction now," said the guide.

The tour party's platform ran alongside the pipe containing Arbuthnot Gavenny, heading toward the terminus of this and every other pipe – the Umivatoré's central sphere.

"What's it made of?" asked the toy robot.

"Looks like glass," said one of the perambulating bananas.

"No," said Locke, "bubbles. Millions and millions of bubbles."

Random memories suddenly flashed through his mind's eye: a teacher shouting; a page from a history book; a pale-faced femme fatale from a black and white film. With their words, the Ties that Bind spoke to him.

"… this is his work…"

"… an endeavour born of…"

"… his ambition."

The platform drew to a halt. The pipe continued on, feeding into a bubble just ahead. It protruded a few metres beyond the filmy surface and then gave way to a vacuous chasm between two infinite planes. Locke might have mistaken them for oceans – one above, one below; one calm, the other raging – had rolling waves crossed their surface instead of undulating spikes.

"You are looking at the skin of two realities," explained the guide, "viewed through a dimensional analogue that does indeed look quite like a bubble. That they are so close both to each other and to us is thanks to the miracle that lies at the heart of this giant sphere – the Conjunction, an entity with such gravity, realities are drawn together around it. And you see, there, where those two spikes are nearly touching, that is a phenomenon only possible in the vicinity of the Conjunction. That is the result of two realities interacting. It is why we are here."

Mrs Dunne led Vincent and Veronica Drysdale into the kitchen. Billy stood by the worktop with his back to them.

"He's spent all day like that," said Mrs Dunne. "Not that I'm complaining, he's been quiet as a lamb."

Emily ran down the stairs of her house, squealing.

"Daddy! Daddy! What is it?"

Her father stood at the front door, signing for the newly arrived package.

"I don't rightly know," he replied.

At the top of the staircase, Fiddlesticks arched his back and hissed.

A whirring drone approached the platform. Locke turned his head. A propeller-driven craft of silver and brass swept over the tour party before plunging into the bubble ahead.

"Years of research, trial and error went into perfecting this process," said the tour guide. "A moment's silence, please, for those martyred to our cause."

The craft flew between the opposing planes of reality and up to the converging spikes. Once close enough, mechanical arms extended from its body, each tipped with a fearsome hook—

Locke instantly remembered Rastuftary Nort's memeker hook, but didn't know if he'd made the connection or if the Ties that Bind prompted the recollection.

—that was used to snare each pinnacle of metaphysical fabric. Heavy panels then slid apart and revealed the centre of the craft to be an axle, about which the mechanical arms began to rotate with increasing speed.

"In technical terms, the weidforms of the Platonic and Imperfect sets have been joined," explained the tour guide, "meaning the final part of the trinity can now be introduced. In this case, our friend Mr Arbuthnot Gavenny…"

Who now flowed as sepia-coloured liquid from the pipe into the blur of spinning arms and intertwined realities. The resultant ring slowly turned a vivid gold.

"A beautiful thing is it not? No longer does Mr Arbuthnot Gavenny have to survive on second-hand recollections, instead his existence is bound to the here and now, in an ideal and a belief in that ideal."

Billy didn't notice the grown-ups standing at the kitchen door. He didn't notice Veronica put a shocked hand to her mouth. He didn't notice Vincent Drysdale's smile. He was too busy stroking the spoon he held and enjoying the electrifying tingle of its metal against his skin.

The tour guide swung a pair of lenses in front of the bubble. The view was transformed, the golden ring reduced to a mundane metal utensil.

"Or, in more practical terms," said the tour guide, "Mr Arbuthnot Gavenny has become a minor god of spoons."

And Billy could hear the spoon speaking to him. Whispering in his head. Pledging that his belief and devotion would be rewarded.

"What's going on here?" asked Irene Wilson, arriving home with shopping bags just as the delivery van drove away.

"Mummy, I've got a parcel!" cried Emily.

"What parcel?"

"This parcel," said Derek Wilson.

"And it's addressed to me!" squealed Emily. "Give it to me! I want to open it!"

"You've still got schoolwork to finish," said Mrs Hu, hobbling out from the dining room.

"It must be a mistake," said Irene. "We didn't order anything for Emily. Honestly, Derek, you should have known that and you certainly shouldn't have signed for the thing."

"I want my present!" insisted Emily.

"No, Emily. We can't open this," said her mother. "It's a mistake. We have to send it back."

"No!" cried Emily.

"It's not a mistake," said Mrs Hu.

"How do you know?" asked Mr Wilson.

"Because Fiddlesticks said it's not," explained Mrs Hu. "He also says you need put that box down right now and step away."

Locke fell against the platform railing. Memories hammered through his head - himself, Mrs Maunley, Kayla, the remains of Roland McCaffrey…

"I…"

"… must…"

"… take…"

"… my-place… amongst-the-gods."

Locke fought for control of his thoughts, but the Ties that Bind throttled his neural pathways, blocking off rebellious thought and focussing his attention on the pipe running below the platform, the bubble it penetrated and the golden ring of realities beyond.

"You must…"

"… join…"

"… the trinity…"

An urge rose within him to vault the barrier, run along the pipe and hurl himself into the theological centrifuge. Without thinking, he grabbed the sleeve of the woman beside him. In response, she threw off her coat and then punched him across the jaw.

Locke fell to the floor of the platform.

"What's going on—?" The tour guide's concern was cut short by the sight of the object now held in the woman's hand.

"Billy, it's just a spoon," said Veronica.

"Yes," agreed Billy, "this is just a spoon and yeah, there's nothing special about that, except… except that in this spoon you can see the faintest of reflections of the perfect spoon. The ideal spoon. The spoon to rule all spoons."

Veronica smiled wryly, patted Billy on his head and then turned to her husband.

"Vincent, while I truly, honestly appreciate the value of your work, this isn't right."

But he wasn't listening. He was staring off into the middle distance, a frown on his face.

"Bomb!" cried the tour guide.

He leapt at the woman. She dodged aside and produced a gun. The muzzle flared.

The bullet that hit the suit did not simply blow a hole through the fabric, it burned a hole that kept on burning, that ate through woven fibre not only in the present, but in every moment Locke remembered of the tour guide.

Sirens of screaming babies began blaring across the Umivatoré. The rest of the tour party scattered to the far sides of the platform. Locke was left on the floor beside the terrorist as she raised an arm, bomb in hand.

"Stop… her!" demanded the Ties that Bind.

But Locke did not act. He found himself willing the bomb to explode.

Wailing sentries of feather and steel suddenly descended upon them. More shots were fired. Sparks showered across the platform.

The woman tried to hurl her bomb into the nearest bubble, but the platform bucked wildly at that moment and it fell short, dropping down past more bubbles and dozens of pipes before finally exploding.

Locke remembered seeing the terrorist leap clear with bat-like wings extending from her back. He remembered crystal blue light blazing up from below and the shockwave blasting him high into the air, but the moments after that were a bit fuzzy.

Vincent Drysdale's momentary trance was ended by a scream. It came from the back garden. Mrs Dunne was the first to rush outside. She found Olivia Pinborough convulsing on the grass with Joshua and his cronies standing over her.

"But we didn't even put her hand in the hot asphalt mix!" protested Joshua before he could be blamed.

Vincent arrived and knelt down beside the stricken girl. He placed a hand on her forehead. White spittle crept out the corners of her mouth as she muttered to herself.

"… can't hear the toaster… can't hear the toaster…"

"Should I call an ambulance?" asked Mrs Dunne.

"It won't help," said Vincent, standing up and walking back to the house.

"Then what can we do?"

"Nothing."

Veronica chased after him.

"You're going to leave her like that?" she asked.

"Yes."

"But she's—"

"Not important."

"Vincent, I know I keep saying I love you, but—"

"Someone truly important will die unless we hurry."

Emily Wilson stamped her foot.

"I want my present!"

"Put the box down, Mr Wilson," repeated Mrs Hu.

"Why? Is it… is it dangerous?" he asked.

"This is so unfair!" shouted Emily.

Irene Wilson silenced her daughter with a warning finger before quizzing Mrs Hu.

"Do you know something about that box?"

"No, but Fiddlesticks does."

"How can that damned cat know anything?"

Emily tugged at her father's sleeve.

"Daddy, you can't listen to a cat."

"I can't listen to anyone with all…" Mr Wilson's words tailed off. He was staring at the parcel in his hands. It had become strangely distorted, as if seen through marbled glass.

Then it began to change.

Thomas Locke was already crawling hand over hand when awareness returned. A million silver threads stretched out behind him, drawing fragments of his being back to a torso cut off at the waist. High above, the Umivatoré's central sphere bled golden vapour from a gash in its bubbled side. Vessels of different shapes and sizes attended the damage, while wailing alarms continued to reverberate off giant pipes and pillars.

Within minutes, Locke was walking again on reconstituted legs and able to think of things other than the pain. He was lost in an Escher maze of engineering stretched around the inner-skin of the Umivatoré.

He came across a fashion magazine lying on the floor. The cover model hugged the collar of a fur coat to her cheeks. She looked strangely familiar—

Another stabbing recollection: the terrorist wore that same face.

Locke hurried on and found a discarded comic. An open

page depicted a shadowy figure with bat-like wings soaring between skyscrapers toward a patch of paper sodden with ink. It began a trail of black dots that ran off around the next corner.

Derek Wilson dropped the parcel. It fell, edges twisting and points rotating along axes that couldn't be seen, unfolding a mass of surfaces and colours beyond the capacity of conventional dimensions.

"What on earth is it doing?" asked Mr Wilson.

He backed away along the hallway to join his wife and daughter by the stairs.

"This way, hurry," urged Mrs Hu, waving hands toward the dining room.

"It's pretty," said Emily.

"It's damned peculiar," said her father.

"It's people," said her mother, mouth hanging open.

The contortions of the box resolved into three distinct people standing abreast in the hallway: a stout woman wearing a blue and white striped apron splattered with blood; a bearded man wearing a baker's hat; and finally a pale-faced man wearing leather gloves smeared with wax.

Emily pointed at each one in turn.

"Butcher, baker… err…"

"Candlestick maker," said her mother.

"Damned peculiar," repeated her father.

"And this is why our country's going to hell," Mrs Hu told Fiddlesticks, "because no one listens any more."

At the end of ink trail, Locke found a black figure slumped against a wall. For a second, he thought it was Lafarge and his heart stuttered.

The figure groaned and pulled a sign from its chest - a man at work bound in a red triangle. The sign clattered to the floor; another disguise discarded. It left behind a woman, but one unrecognisable from the magazine model. Her nose was wonky, her skin dark, her eyes sunken. A gash in her side that had been spewing black liquid now glistened red. She laughed bitterly and tried staunch the flow with a hand.

On seeing Locke, she grabbed her gun and tried to aim,

but could barely keep her arm level.

Locke raised his hands.

"If you don't shoot, I might be able to help."

"You can't help," said the woman. "I failed. Our only hope now is that balance can be restored on the far side."

"Balance must be restored," said the butcher.

He produced a weapon that looked like a crossbow with a mirrored disc fixed to the end. The baker and candlestick maker did likewise.

"Move!" cried Mrs Hu, grabbing Emily by the shoulders and throwing her into the dining room.

"Who are you people?" asked Mr Wilson.

His wife yelped as Mrs Hu yanked her clear of the hallway.

A trigger was pulled.

In the fraction of a second that followed, Mr Wilson's indecision was reflected three times over in the mirrored discs of the uninvited guests. He wanted to tell them that he was fully prepared to call the police. He wanted to know what Mrs Hu was doing to his wife. He dimly registered the warnings of his daughter's tutor and wondered if he too should vacate the hallway, but there was no time left to act upon any of these thoughts.

A bolt travelled the length of the butcher's bow and shattered the disc at the end. As the mirror splintered into pieces, so did lightning cracks rend the world caught in its reflection.

Vincent Drysdale drove without his foot leaving the accelerator. He found gaps in traffic where they should have been none. He made turns impossible at the speed they were travelling. Mysterious smoke belched up from every drain and manhole cover and eventually made it impossible to see, but still he did not slow.

Veronica sat in the passenger seat and said nothing. She had already guessed where they were going. She only hoped they could reach Emily's house before it was too late.

Paint, plaster and brickwork were sliced apart. Dust and debris fell to the floor. Cracks appeared not only in the walls, but in the very air; disorientating lines of force that warped light and briefly turned atoms of oxygen and nitrogen into fizzing particles of neon, mercury or sulphur.

At the heart of the shattered reality was Derek Wilson. His skin and bone and bloody insides were cut a thousand times, spilling down over countless fractures toward the carpet, burning, twisting, dancing as they did so, all except for a splinter of his face – an eye, a portion of cheek, one corner of his mouth – which was caught in a flickering loop of time snagged against one crack. Over and over again, that eye wavered with uncertainty and the lips twitched in anticipation of words that would never be said.

Irene Wilson opened her mouth, but could not scream, could not wail her despair, shock choking off the breath in her throat.

Locke helped the injured woman reach an access hatch. They entered a duct she was certain led outside.

"The Umivatoré I know is a strange kind of plant," said Locke as they crawled along the narrow shaft.

"It's the same thing," she replied.

"The same thing? You mean this machine—"

"The Umivatoré is a pan-dimensional entity, but few such creatures remain constant across the planes. Here it is a machine, there a plant, elsewhere a mountain or a river or a swarm of locust. Yet its nature always remains the same: it steals and seeds ideas. If my bomb had pierced one of those bubbles and fired an existential meltdown, every reality would have been freed from its menace."

"And balance would have been restored?"

The woman coughed and shook her head.

"No, not entirely. The Conjunction would still remain."

Emily had never seen her mother like this: stone-faced, but with tears running freely down her cheeks. She held her mother's hand more tightly as Mrs Hu led them into the kitchen, but was unsettled by the feeling that this was no longer her mother, just like the remains in the hallway couldn't be her father.

The baker stepped into the kitchen from the hall. He raised his mirror-bow.

Mrs Hu glared at him. The creaking house released a section of ceiling and felled the man in a cloud of dust.

"You must be strong," said Mrs Hu, turning to Emily's mother. "Fiddlesticks and I will see justice done for the crime committed here today, draw strength from that."

Through her tears, Irene Wilson laughed. "You and a cat?"

"There is no one else."

"I know someone who could help," said Emily.

"Not this time, dear," replied the nanny. "And what have I told you about leaving your toys lying around the house?"

Emily stared at her, confused and indignant.

"But I never…"

Then she remembered the small wheeled pony she'd left by the dining room sideboard. The one a murderous butcher now inadvertently stepped on. The woman in the pin-striped apron slipped, fell. Her weapon hit the ground. The impact loosed the trigger. A bolt fired. The result was a migraine sting to the eardrums of those in the kitchen.

"Go out through the conservatory," said Mrs Hu. "Get to your car and get away from here. Do you understand me?"

The baker rose up from the pile of fallen ceiling, his white hat flattened against a dust-covered head. Mrs Wilson took her daughter's hand and fled. The assassin's words chased after them.

"The Ministry must see balance restored."

"I'm sorry, Emily, I'm so sorry," said her mother as they ran around to the front of the house.

"It's okay, Mummy—"

"No, darling, it's not. We promised to keep you and protect you, but we never thought… How could we even dream of something like this?"

They staggered onto the gravel driveway as one side of their house collapsed with a crashing boom.

"Into the car, hurry!"

Emily pulled open the door and clambered onto the back seat. She was still struggling with the seatbelt when her mother told her to get out.

"But—?"

"Get out, Emily! Now!"

She scrambled back out onto the gravel. The wheels of the

car immediately started spinning. Then it shot forward, kicking up stones that bit against Emily's bare legs.

"Mummy!"

The car sped toward the house. Emily glimpsed the candlestick maker on the doorstep before he fired his bow.

Fractious lines cut through her vision. Her mother's car became the heart of a trenchant star – metal and plastic torn apart, but in thrall to inertia. There was nothing the candlestick maker could do. The shredded remains ploughed into him. Fuel lit by the burning scars of reality exploded across the driveway to where Emily stood.

She wavered as the shockwave rolled through her and blinked as heat touched her face, but remained otherwise unmoved as the explosion subsided. Emily stared at the wreckage of the car. Black smoke curled up around the residual fractures left by the candlestick maker's weapon.

Her mother couldn't be dead, just like her father couldn't be dead. Emily looked around, biting her lip and trying not to panic as she called out.

"Mummy? Daddy?"

Locke climbed out of the shaft onto a narrow ledge. His travelling companion was already there, gazing upward. The mouth of a giant pipe loomed over them. It was swallowing up a continent that stretched away as an earthen ribbon into a dome of sky criss-crossed with more slivers of worlds.

It took a moment for Locke to process the sight and then recover the thread of their conversation.

"The, err, tour guide seemed to suggest the Conjunction was some sort of reality-bending black hole. How do you destroy something like that?"

The saboteur slung a strap over a wire running from the Umivatoré to a copse of motorway signage growing on the edge of the land being devoured by the pipe.

"Alas, the Conjunction is more than that," she replied. "It was conceived of man and born of woman. It can laugh and cry and, worst of all, it can make others care. They will sacrifice their lives for it, despite every universe being at risk for as long as it exists."

Emily Wilson ventured back around the edifice of crumbling brickwork and flame that had replaced her home.

"Mummy? Daddy?"

The glass of the conservatory was shattered, the bare frame left behind cut through with those warping lines of force.

"Mrs Hu?"

The back door hung loose on its hinges. It fell to the ground when the baker barged it open with a shoulder. He was covered in bloody cuts and could barely see out of swollen eyes, but he could see enough.

"You must know what you are?" he rasped. Emily backed away across the garden. "You must know why you cannot exist?"

"Where's my Mummy?" she shouted back. "Where's my Daddy?"

"They left you long ago," said the baker, staggering after her. He awkwardly loaded another mirrored disc into his crossbow.

"They were here! They were right here!"

"No, child. Not your real parents."

Emily remembered Joshua's jibes; she was the girl who pretended her parents were real. She suddenly felt dizzy. Her legs gave out beneath her. She fell onto the grass.

The baker drew back the string of his bow. Emily's thoughts were too bound up in whirling emotion to notice.

He used both battered arms to take aim. Her reflection wavered around the centre of the disc's immaculate surface, but he hesitated. She was more than the Conjunction, she was just a little girl.

And the chance was lost. A light aircraft crash-landed in the Wilson's back garden, skidded across the turf and flattened the baker before piling through a fence into the neighbouring garden.

Mrs Hu ran down from the house, Fiddlesticks at her heels.

"Oh, Emily! Thank the heavens you're all right!"

"I don't understand," said the little girl as the old woman hugged her tight.

"You don't need to understand, Emily," Mrs Hu whispered in her ear. "You just need to do three simple things. First, you need to get yourself through that hole in the hedge at the bottom of the garden. Second, you need to run as fast as you can to somewhere safe. Third, and most important of all, every night you need to keep on doing that thing Fiddlesticks told you to do. Do you remember what that was?"

"But Mummy and Daddy—"

"Do you remember, Emily?"

"I must tell myself to… to try and dream of a pen and paper."

"That's right, Emily. Every night. It's very important. Now go."

"But where can I go?"

"You'll think of somewhere."

"Can't you come with me?"

"No, my love, I must stay here. Other people will be coming for you. I will try and stop them."

Emily stared fiercely at Mrs Hu and then hugged her again. The old woman removed Emily's arms and gently pushed her away.

"Now, Emily. Go."

Reluctantly, the little girl rose to her feet. She took a few steps back and then, pursing her lips in a determined fashion, turned and ran down to the hole in the hedge.

"We could have ended it here, Fiddlesticks," said Mrs Hu. The cat rubbed against her ankles. "Of course, you're right. We already made our choice."

Emily scrambled through the hole and then cast a glance back over her shoulder. Beyond the tangled branches, Mrs Hu faced a couple newly arrived from around the side of the house.

"Better never than late, Mr Drysdale," said Mrs Hu.

Emily started running.

Locke and the saboteur slid along the cable from the Umivatoré to the floating continent. They passed from bright daylight into late evening before reaching the copse of motorway signs. The woman dropped from the wire and fell onto her injured side.

"Damn it," she muttered through gritted teeth.

Locke was quickly by her side and helping her up.

"We need to get you to a doctor."

"No one will help me here."

"But aren't you from the Ministry of Checks and Balances? Don't you have branches or sub-offices nearby?"

"Yes, but they've all been purged. The measuring machines lie broken. The few of us who are left try to make amends..." She glanced back at the Umivatoré. "If the others had succeeded, we'd know by now. We've all failed."

"At least you're alive to fight another day."

The saboteur subjected Locke to a withering stare. He escaped it by studying their surroundings. A crowded town lay beyond the motorway signs. Haphazard buildings fought along the skyline. They were festooned with signs, hundreds of them, either painted or lit up in garish colours. Yet none of those signs bore any letters.

"The price this land paid for becoming a god," explained the woman. "There are no doors or windows in this place either. Come on, they'll find us if we linger here too long." She led the way into the eerie town. "If we're going to be travelling companions, we should make introductions. I'm Johan Helmich Roman's Flute Concerto in G-Major and you are?"

"Err, nothing quite so impressive. Thomas Locke. Just Thomas Locke."

The woman stopped ahead of him.

"Thomas Locke?"

"Yes."

"Of The Office of Lost and Found?"

He realised his mistake too late. She had already drawn her gun and was in the midst of turning.

Locke started to run.

"Balance must be restored," she said and shot him in the back.

That night, Billy thought of Thomas Locke. He remembered when they faced the darkness under the bed. The detective handed him a cricket bat to bolster his courage. He needed some of that courage now, but a cricket bat wouldn't help him fight the obsession that plagued him. And Thomas... Thomas was burning. In his memories, a hole grew in Locke's chest; cloth and flesh eaten away by ravenous flame until all

Billy remembered of Thomas Locke was ash.

He scrambled out of bed to flick the switch by the door. The light coming on banished the waking nightmare until he tried again to picture Thomas's face. It was gone. Erased.

Billy paced across his bedroom floor. What was happening? Was this Mr Drysdale's doing too?

He froze on hearing his parents moving about downstairs. Fearful of being punished for more nightly nonsense, he switched off the light. Billy returned to bed and finally allowed himself to think again of spoons. He hoped they would be burned from his thoughts like Thomas was, but instead they danced unscathed through his imagination, tapping out a seductive lullaby.

A sharp rapping came at his window.

Billy wondered why he had tried so hard not to think of spoons. They were clearly immensely cool.

Something else struck the glass. It wasn't as important as spoons, so it was ignored, but the sounds persisted. Billy finally opened his window to get a smattering of gravel chips in the face.

"Ow!" he said, dabbing at a nose that felt like it was cut, but wasn't. Below, in the dark of the backyard, Emily Wilson stood alone and silent. "What do you want?" he hissed down at her.

She puffed up her cheeks, furrowed her brow, but no words came out.

"Go home," Billy told her and closed the window.

He went back to bed. Emily was forgotten for a while. Thinking of spoons didn't leave much space in a person's head for anything else… but a faint flicker of guilt eventually found room. He threw back the bedclothes and walked over to the window to check that Emily had gone.

She hadn't.

He opened the window again.

"Go home!"

He waved in his hand in a shooing gesture. The little girl grabbed the folds of her muddied dress and squeezed them in her fists. Her feet didn't move.

"Okay, I'm coming down."

When Billy reached the back door, Emily was waiting outside. When he opened it, she rushed inside and hugged him fiercely. Billy's hands floundered at the unexpected embrace.

"Why aren't you at home?" asked Billy.

She buried her head against his chest.

"Do you want my parents to call your parents to get them to come and collect you?"

Emily managed to shake her head while keeping it pressed against him. A strand of her hair got in Billy's mouth and he had to spit it out.

"You can't stay here. We'll both get in trouble."

She just hugged him tighter.

Billy sighed. Spoons were never this troublesome.

The pain was unlike any Locke had previously experienced. He couldn't tell how long it lasted, but he did recognise the disconcerting sensation of his biology being woven back together. When he felt his eyes once again slide across the inside of their lids, he refused to open them. He didn't want to see what was out there.

"Did-you… do-that… on-purpose?"

That insidious cadence of speech was unmistakeable. It was also of the here and now, heard by freshly reconstructed ears instead of being plucked from his memories.

"You-can-speak… Thomas-Locke."

The stuttering rhythm was the same, but the voice was different. Locke could all too easily imagine the remains of the Ministry woman strung up before him, uttering these words from severed lips, fed by breath pumped from disembodied lungs.

"It was an honest mistake," said Locke, keeping his eyes closed.

"No-matter. Mistake-or-not… even-death… burned-across-time… cannot-excuse-you… from-your… obligation."

"So I gathered."

"I-will-take… my-place… amongst-the-Gods."

"Then go and take it. I found you their god factory. Isn't that what you needed? That's my job done."

"My-foolish-friend… I-am-not… a-God-yet. Your-task-now… is-to-find-us… a-way-back… inside."

Billy reluctantly shooed Emily toward the stairs, warning her to be quiet. Before closing the back door, he saw Fiddlesticks sitting on the wall of his backyard. The cat ignored him, finished cleaning a paw and then trotted off through moon-cast shadows.

On the following Monday, Veronica Drysdale paid another visit to Kathleen Muller and her reincarnated husband, Leonard.

At lunchtime, Vincent Drysdale broke up a fight between Joshua Dunne and a boy called Liam Creavins. The latter had claimed roadworks were nothing but a lowly functionary in service to the great automobile.

At dinnertime, Emily asked Billy if he had spoken to Joshua.

"Look, if I wish really hard, I can make spoons bend," replied Billy.

"But did you ask him about my parents?" asked Emily.

"Quiet down, my parents will hear you."

"And when am I going to meet your monsters?"

"Look, the spoon's bending! I'm making the spoon bend!"

Bedtime came and went. While Billy tried to sleep, the faint sound of crying came from under his bed.

At the same time, across the other side of town, Mrs Polidouris came to call.

At eight o'clock on Tuesday morning, Billy's father stepped out of his house and exclaimed: "What in the name of bloody bollocks is this?"

His car was in its usual spot at the side of the road, but the road around it and every other parked car had been dug up. Warning lights, traffic cones and striped workmen's tents stretched off as far as the eye could see.

At half past eleven, Sharon blustered into Veronica's office.

"How on earth did you get in?" she asked.

"Drove in as normal," replied Veronica. "I guess the council decided my route into work didn't need ripping up for some reason."

"Then you're the only one. I walked all the bloody way and I only did that because I'd left my mobile phone here. I need a billion cups of coffee, stat."

"You might be needing more than a simple prayer then."

"Right, you better hope Edmund gets in or you'll be the first human sacrificed to a coffee machine."

At fourteen minutes past three, Luke Goddard's eighty-six year old neighbour became the first man in history to suffocate beneath three tonnes of unsolicited direct mail.

Thomas Locke's death was quicker, a gaseous jet of frozen regret turning his head to ice and ending his attempt to regain entry to the Umivatoré.

Meanwhile, far, far away, Mrs Gunnarsson came to call.

Wednesday.

"You… you were right," said Liam Creavins over the phone.

"And?" prompted Joshua.

"I… I hereby pledge allegiance to Mr Coney."

Joshua smiled.

That night, down by the Argent Bridge, Mrs Dawkins came to call.

The town woke up on Thursday to find the roadworks gone.

"I heard the council spent all night negotiating with the unions," said Sharon in the canteen.

"Then you've been misinformed," said Payoja. "This crisis was resolved by the vigil we held at Grenadine Park—"

"Utter rubbish," snapped Edmund. "It wasn't anything to do with the unions and it certainly wasn't anything to do with happy-clappy people holding hands and singing songs. It was all because of the smoke that came out the sewers last week. The chemical plant dumped some gunk down there and caused a toxic reaction. Would've happened again too if they hadn't dug up the roads to lay down miles of absorbent foam. But I've got a mate who works in the factory where they make the foam and everyone there's saying it's never going to work."

Veronica was not part of this conversation. She was in the alley behind the factory, sliding aside a manhole cover and climbing down into the sewers with a torch. After a few minutes of walking, she found what she was looking for. The same vegetation she had once seen stretched across a warehouse ceiling now ran thick through the waterways beneath the town and much of it was charred from fire.

Burnt vines in one reality became damaged pipes and smoking machinery in another. Work crews beavered away inside the Umivatoré's mechanical incarnation to repair the damage of the saboteur's bomb. Locke was disguised as one of their number. He surreptitiously made his way toward the central sphere. This had born the brunt of the attack. A scar of burst bubbles ran down one side, leaking golden fluid onto the wreckage of the pipes that once served them.

Locke was almost at his destination when the security demons found him. He tried to fight, but their talons cut deep. He fell, a tiny figure tumbling down past the bubble-covered mass of the Conjunction.

Emily was unaware of this. She lay beneath Billy's bed and bit into the bread he'd stolen from the kitchen.

"Have you asked him yet?" she asked, crumbs spilling from her mouth.

"No," said Billy. He lay on top of the bed, staring at the ceiling.

"Why not? It's been weeks."

"Days."

"Long enough. You saw him today. And Monday."

"I forgot."

"How could you forget?"

"I was busy thinking about other stuff."

"What? Like spoons?"

"And what's wrong with spoons?"

"Nothing." Emily was still bruised from the last time she questioned spoons. "But you can think about other stuff sometimes."

"I… I try, but…"

"Do you dream about spoons?"

"I don't know. I don't remember my dreams any more."

"Mrs Hu and Fiddlesticks told me to think really hard about a pen and a piece of paper every night so I could dream about them."

"Why?"

"I don't know. And every night I try and once I think I did

dream about a pen and paper, but I haven't since and now I can't get to sleep because I'm worried that I won't be able to dream about a pen and paper and they told me it was really important, but if I can't…?"

"How can it be important?"

"I don't know. Perhaps it's like spoons."

"Yeah. Or not."

"Will you ask Joshua about my parents?"

"I'll try."

They both fell silent.

Over at the Drysdale residence, Mrs Fairfax came to call.

Billy wasn't due to go to the Dunne's house on Friday, but he went anyway. He asked Mrs Dunne if Joshua was in and she showed him into the kitchen. Her son was playing with a washing up tub full of resin-bonded aggregate.

"Now I've got laundry to put away," said Mrs Dunne. "You two play nice."

She left the two boys alone together.

"What do you know about Emily Wilson's parents?" asked Billy.

Joshua smiled.

"Only what I've been told."

"And what have you been told?"

"You know, the others think their gods are the best. I ask them to prove it, but they can't. My god proves himself every day. Do you know how he proves it?"

Billy stared at Joshua. The other boy just raised his eyebrows and waited until Billy admitted his ignorance by shaking his head.

"He proves it," said Joshua, "by telling me things no one else knows."

The land of door-less houses and word-less signs fed into the largest of the Umivatoré's many pipes. Locke crawled along this pipe toward the central sphere and a bubble of unusual shape and size. It looked as if it had swallowed up some of the neighbouring bubbles.

Locke drew close enough to make out the shapes beyond the filmy surface. Unlike Arbuthnot Gavenny's bubble, the planes of reality within did not meet at the tips of two narrow spikes bound by a golden ring. Instead, hundreds of spikes from below were tied to dozens of spikes from above by a web of red and white tape.

What kind of a god was this? Locke wondered.

"The roadworks speak to me and only to me," said Joshua, stepping toward Billy. "So why should I tell you about Emily Wilson's parents?"

Billy took a step back.

"No reason. I mean, you don't have to tell me if you don't want to. I was just asking. It's not like I care or anything."

He shuffled over to the cutlery drawer, pulled it open and began absently toying with the contents.

"Do you know why you're doing that?" asked Joshua.

"Doing what?"

"Fondling those spoons."

"I'm not." Billy hastily dropped the utensils and closed the drawer.

"It's Emily's fault," said Joshua.

"What? But how can she make me—?"

"Because if she didn't exist, there would be no gods."

Locke tried to fight against the will that compelled him, but his defiant thoughts were deftly unwoven and replaced by new ones, ones that led him to open an access hatch in the Umivatoré's great pipe and climb down into a raging torrent of stolen memories.

"Listen, Josh," said Billy, "I don't know why you keep going on about gods. I just like spoons, okay? I think they're cool. Nothing more than that."

"You think this is nothing more than cool?" asked Joshua, fetching a slice of bread from the bread bin. He dropped it in the toaster, turned around, folded his arms and smiled at Billy.

Without thinking, Billy took another spoon from the cutlery drawer and began rolling it around between his fingers.

The toaster finished its job and popped up a fresh slice of toast. Joshua held it up to show the words burnt upon it:

'Believe, Billy.'

"Yeah, so? You've got a fancy toaster."

Joshua sniffed and spread his arms out wide. A silent count of four and then he waved his hands like the conductor of an orchestra. Every car alarm within five miles suddenly began wailing to the rhythm of his swirling fingers. The kitchen light began flashing on and off in time as water fountained up from the sink's plug hole.

"My god no longer rules only over roadworks," cried Joshua, "he also rules over sewage pipes and electricity cables and the cars in the street." With a curt gesture, the noise, flashing lights and spurting water all stopped. "All because Emily Wilson exists and for that… we have Mr Drysdale to thank."

Locke found himself in a narrow alleyway. The dark buildings towering above on either side had no windows or doors. Everything around him was still. Yet… it felt as if the world was falling; plunging toward a bright light waiting in the distance.

He started walking and the light rushed toward him. He halted at a junction and the approach of the light ceased. It was close now, burning just beyond his reach.

The Ties that Bind urged him to continue, but however much it tugged at his thoughts, Locke would not move. The junction had revealed a passageway leading off to the left. This was a land without doors, but at the end of this passageway was a door. This was a land without windows, but in the top half of that door was a marbled glass pane. This was a land without words, but the glass bore words that drowned out the screaming memories of the Ties that Bind.

Locke walked up to the door, opened it and stepped through into The Office of Lost and Found.

"Emily exists because of Mr Drysdale?" queried Billy. "Are you saying he's her real dad?"

"What Mr Drysdale is," said Joshua, "is a businessman. Long, long ago he arrived in a doomed reality with a business proposition. The creation of Emily Wilson was simply a means to an end."

"The end being bringing these… gods of yours here."

"You're very slow, but you get there eventually. Have you realised yet that this world isn't big enough to hold gods of every little thing?"

"You think you're going to get me believing in your god?" asked Billy.

"Let's say I have faith. And you, unfortunately, only have a spoon. Mum! Mummy! We have another heathen down here ripe for conversion."

"I'll be down in a minute, love," replied Mrs Dunne. "I'm just putting clean towels in the airing cupboard."

Billy gripped his spoon tighter. He prayed for it to save him, but the spoon remained silent and cold. Perhaps if he had more spoons…

Without taking his eyes off Joshua, he reached back into the cutlery drawer. Common sense overruled religious fervour and made him grab the carving knife.

"I'm leaving now, Josh," said Billy, edging toward the hallway.

The other boy kept clear of the glinting blade.

"I could have a dozen cars run you down the moment you reach the street. I could have the pavement tear up beneath your feet and swallow you whole."

"Yeah, then I'll just know you were jealous of my spoons all along."

Billy made a break for the front door. He was out and gone by the time Mrs Dunne entered the kitchen.

"Oh, you let him go? But we've got a fresh batch of hot mix asphalt going in the shed."

"He believes in spoons, Mum. We don't want a loony like that turning up to carriageway resurfacing mass."

Billy's house was empty. Emily took this opportunity to sneak out from under his bed to have a shower. Once showered, she went downstairs and sought out food in the kitchen. She did not know that Billy's father would be coming home early that day and did not hear his key turning in the lock of the front door.

Locke stepped into a small office. Dust covered the floor and furniture. Next to a second door was a hat-stand holding a black hat and coat that clearly hadn't been touched in a long time. Locke took a book from the case beside him. It was an original folio of Shakespeare's 'Loves Labours Lost'. The next book he picked up was Milton's 'Paradise Lost'. The third: 'Chitty Chitty Bang Bang' by Ian Fleming.

The pictures on the walls had faded, but not enough to obscure the painted dogs playing poker. A steel filing cabinet was locked and resisted his attempts to open it. The chair at the mahogany desk was well-used, one corner of the padded seat worn to the point stuffing poked out. The desk itself was untidy. Pens were littered across a blank jotting pad. Closer inspection showed the doodles indented into the paper. Locke picked up the handset of an old, rotary dial phone. To his surprise, there was a tone. He scrubbed dirt off the plastic disc at the centre of the dial and rang the number for the operator.

"Hello, operator speaking."

"Hi," said Locke, "would it be possible to tell me where I'm calling from?"

"I'm sorry, sir, could you repeat the question?"

"I'm kind of lost and I stumbled across this place and I wondered if you could tell me where I am."

"I can tell you the number…"

"Is it in a directory? Can you give me an address?"

"Err… no, sir. But I can give you a name."

"I'll take a name."

"Your number is registered to a J H Ward."

"J H Ward?"

"Yes, sir."

"Thank-you."

"Will that be all, sir?"

"I… err… yes… no, no. Where are you?"

"I'm sorry, sir?"

"I just wondered… are you in an office? Some call centre somewhere?"

"Sir… I… all I hear is voices and… and I give them answers. I can't see anything. I can't feel… I must be lost. Do you know where I am, sir?"

"No. I'm sorry."

"Will that be all then, sir?"
"Yes."
Locke put down the phone. The Ties that Bind screamed in his head, demanding he return to the land without doors and the blinding light. Locke ignored it and opened the second door.

At Froggarty Premium Accessories Limited, Veronica buried her tear-stained face in folded arms. On the desk around her were newspaper reports of people going missing in Grenadine Park – eight people over the past month, three in the last week alone. At first they disappeared at night, now it happened during the day.

"I think they must have spontaneously combusted," said Hannah Patterson, aged eleven. When asked by a journalist why she was always the last person to see the missing people alive, she replied: "Can I help it if coincidence picks on me?"

Veronica met Hannah Patterson a few days ago at Winston Leys' Cub Scout hut. Vincent was judging a painting competition, each entry produced as part of the local children's projects. The winner was Dembe Owiti, aged seven, who had painted an eighteenth century paddle-steamer. A cutting from page six of the Evening Herald reported that Dembe was taken into care on Thursday morning after attempting to sacrifice his aunt to a pedalo down at Grenadine Park.

Tuesday's edition of the paper contained a story about an old man who'd died beneath a mountain of direct mail. The editorial claimed he deserved it, because he never gave back footballs kicked into his garden. However, a photograph of the same page told a different story – lamenting the old man's tragic fate and decrying the unsolicited mail that caused it.

The horoscopes were similarly twisted to favour direct mail:

'Sagittarius, you will receive an offer for an interest-free loan in the next twenty-four hours. You will feel the urge to accept and rightly fear that if you don't, you will be denounced by all your peers and ultimately strung up from a lamppost by your intestines.'

One article declared rubber bands to be the next big fashion craze. Another declared it to be stethoscope epaulettes.

Paparazzi had snapped a celebrity exiting a car wearing underwear made of buttons, while a politician addressed the local chamber of commerce in a tie stitched together from playing cards.

Veronica took this all as proof that the children were twisting the world around them. She was sure her husband was to blame, but didn't know how he was doing it. Maybe he had the Umivatoré pumping toxic ideas into the water supply, but surely ideas alone couldn't change the words in a newspaper or fill streets with roadworks. And what about Emily? How did she fit into all of this?

She felt like Vincent was taunting her with a riddle for which she couldn't find the answer. Every night she would arrive at his flat, smiling, hoping he would slip up and give something away, but every night he simply laughed and joked and said nothing of any importance.

"No, he won't beat me," said Veronica, choking back her tears and sitting up straight. She wiped her face dry and straightened her blouse. "I may not be able to do it like Thomas, but I will find the answer and I will stop this."

The office door opened. Edmund stepped in and looked around. He noticed the mess of papers on Veronica's desk.

"You must have lost at least one under there," he said, more to himself than to her.

He walked over and began shuffling through the newspaper clippings. He stopped when Veronica hit him across the knuckles with the long edge of her computer keyboard.

"Ow! I could sue you for that!"

"What do you want, Edmund?"

"Someone's finally nicked off with the last of the teaspoons. I decided—"

"The teaspoons are all gone?"

"Isn't that what I said?"

"Oh, shit – Billy."

"Who's Billy? What's he got to do with our spoons? Wait, where do you think you're going?"

"Your father wants a word with you," she said.

Billy's first thought was spoons, but his second was that Emily had been discovered. Panic tempted him to turn and run, but Maureen grabbed him by the arm and dragged him inside. He managed to toss the carving knife out into a flower bed without her noticing.

"You also need to explain all these," she said. Piled up against the skirting boards were thousands of teaspoons. "And those," she added, gesturing to the display shelves near the ceiling that used to show off a succession of decorative plates. Now they were lined with tablespoons standing to attention.

As Billy passed by, the spoons trembled. Their metallic chittering made Maureen pull her son closer before entering the kitchen.

Billy's father sat at the table. He had Emily on his knee.

"No, Emmy, like this."

He took from her a pair of dessert spoons. He slipped one on top of the other and then rapped them between his knee and the palm of his free hand to create a lively, syncopated beat that had Emily clapping her hands in glee.

Billy looked up at his mother.

"Don't look at me," she said, "I have no idea what's going on any more."

Veronica approached Vincent's car and was struck by the stench of rotting fish. She looked around for its source. Imposing Georgian offices overlooked the road. Rows of cars were parked on either side. A steel railing blocked access to a narrow passageway filled with loose rubbish and over-flowing bins, but the smell came from elsewhere, it came from…

Veronica lifted her head. Something moved atop one of the buildings. The brightness of the sky obscured its shape, but it didn't look human.

She hurried to the car. Twenty minutes of driving later she stopped in the road outside Billy's house. She jumped out and ran to the front gate. There she hesitated. The house next door was up for sale. Boards covered the windows. She felt responsible, guilty. Danvil Rogers had a normal, peaceful life until he met her. Now his house was empty and he was gone, just like all the other men who'd come too close to the wife of Vincent Drysdale.

Billy's mother answered the door.

"I need to see Billy," said Veronica.

"Why? Who are you? You… you look familiar."

"I'm here about Billy's project."

"Oh, then it must be important. Come in, come in. Don't forget to wipe your shoes. We're all in the living room. Before you ask, it's not a special occasion; we're just taken to little off-the-cuff celebrations like this every now and again. Or at least we are now, far as I can tell."

Veronica noted the spoons in the hallway. They were vibrating in time with a beat pounding out of the living room.

"And what are you celebrating?" she asked.

"I don't rightly know," said Maureen, waving Veronica on through the open doorway.

The sofa and armchair had been pushed back against the wall. A line of milk bottles filled with various amounts of water was arranged atop a chest of drawers. Billy beat out on a tune on them with metal spoons, his eyes closed, a look of blissful concentration on his face. His father performed an uncoordinated jig in front of the fireplace while providing percussive accompaniment with a pair of spoons. Emily danced too, skipping around in the middle of the room. She giggled at yet more spoons that spun and twirled in a lazy approximation of her moves, but on seeing Veronica, Emily abruptly stopped dancing.

"What did you do with Mrs Hu?"

Her question broke the spell. Spoons and bottles abruptly fell silent and still.

"Who's this?" asked Billy's father, waving his musical spoons at Veronica.

"It's okay, Norman," said Maureen. "Mr Drysdale sent her."

Veronica knelt down in front of Billy.

"Do you know how Vincent is doing this?"

The boy grinned and answered a completely different question.

"That was 'Cosmonauts and Astronauts' from the album 'There's no Tea in my Tea' by *Zabitych Malpaŭ*. No one's heard it in thirty years. Barely anyone heard it before that. Which is a shame, because it was the finest—"

Emily stamped a foot. "What did you do with Mrs Hu?"

Veronica ignored her.

"Billy, how did you get all the spoons to come here?"

"They wanted to come here," he said. "They wanted to hear their god."

Emily ran over and began hitting Veronica with her fists.

"What did you do with Mrs Hu?!"

"Nothing, Emily!" said Veronica, grabbing the little girl's hands. "I didn't do anything! She tried to kill us. Do you understand? She tried kill us and… what happened then couldn't be helped."

"You're just like those others, aren't you? You're like the butcher and baker and candlestick maker and you want to kill me too!"

"Josh says this is all happening because of her," said Billy, nodding at Emily.

"What has this got to do with her?" asked Veronica.

"None of your business," said Norman. "Now, I don't know who you are, but I know you're upsetting Emmy, so I think you should leave."

"I want my mummy and daddy," said the little girl, hugging Veronica's arm.

"The gods come because of her," explained Billy. "That's why Mr Drysdale created her."

"No one created me!" snapped Emily. "And I don't like Mr Drysdale. I wish Lafarge would make him go away. Why do you like him, Veronica? Why aren't you with Thomas anymore? I liked Thomas. Do you know where he is? Is he here?"

Veronica stared into Emily's wide eyes and remembered a Grenadine Park warden telling her and Locke that some things were meant to be lost. But even now she couldn't accept that. Saving Emily from Lafarge couldn't have been a mistake.

"You know what?" said Norman. "I'm not going to try and understand any of this. I'm just going to go back to playing my spoons, because that's something nice and simple I can understand. Billy, on a count of four? A-one, a-two, a-one, two, three, four…"

Billy went back to beating the bottles while his father rapped out a rhythm.

Veronica shrugged off Emily and headed back outside. The little girl raced after her.

"Stay here," she said, without looking back. "Stay with

Billy."

Emily staggered to a halt and bit her lip.

"I know you don't care," she called out, "but Thomas might. He might still want to help. So if you see him... can you ask him... can you ask him to find my real parents?"

Veronica froze in the midst of climbing into her car. Once upon a time she asked Thomas to find her parents.

"Ignorance is bliss, kid."

A chilling knot writhed in Veronica's stomach as she drove away. All of this was happening because they stopped Lafarge, but what other choice was there? The forlorn little girl receding in the rear view mirror did not deserve to die. There had to be another way. She was certain her husband knew how to undo the chaos he had wrought, but if he wouldn't talk, what else could she do?

Something fell into the road ahead.

Veronica instinctively hit the brakes. The car snaked toward... she didn't know what the hell it was. Large as a bull, it possessed no head or legs, just eyes and jaws swarming in a mass of rotted flesh and muscle strung together by glistening wire.

She released the brake and stamped hard on the accelerator.

The creature reared up. Veronica swerved into the opposing lane. It surged over to block her path. She braced for impact.

The front bumper slammed into the creature's lower half. The car bucked as the thing rolled onto the bonnet and into the windscreen. Veronica raised her arms, but the glass didn't smash. Instead, the roiling mass disintegrated into dozens of smaller creatures that swarmed over her car.

She braked again, hard. Some of the critters flew off into the road. More remained. Feral teeth bit at the rubber lining around the windows. Claws scratched at the bodywork. One landed on the bonnet and glared at Veronica; its eyes plucked from a fish and sewn into the skull of a badger. Red-raw tendons from dogs and stoats were strung to a torso of tin-cans by silver wire, just like the vile chimera Veronica and Locke once encountered beneath a railway arch.

A hiss came from the passenger-side foot-well. A rat-faced critter had gnawed an opening and was now trying to make it bigger.

Veronica yanked open the glove box. She needed a weapon. She found a chamois leather, a packet of humbugs and an A-Z of Norwich.

A crack appeared in the rear window. The scratching at the roof grew more ferocious. Scrabbling behind the dashboard suggested they'd got into the engine bay.

She set fire to the A-Z with the car's cigarette lighter and kicked the burning paper into the rat-face of the critter in the foot-well.

A shadow passed across the windscreen. Veronica looked up. The fish-eyed critter was gone.

She sat up on the passenger seat and looked in time to see a worn Persian rug sweep down and engulf the critters battering the cracked rear window. A second later, the scratching at the roof ceased.

She clambered through into the back of the car.

Outside, the rug rolled down onto the road, fabric bulging where the creatures inside fought to free themselves. It successfully held them fast until a steam-roller arrived and ground the rug flat.

Other critters attempted to flee. Several were hoovered up by vacuum cleaners. Others were crushed beneath falling pianos. An unlucky chimera of seagull, toad and inflatable water-wings fell foul of an overly-zealous pneumatic drill.

Veronica's mouth shaped an expletive-laden question, but was forestalled by the ringing of her mobile phone. It was her husband.

"What would you like for dinner, dear?" he asked.

"I want some answers!" said Veronica, storming into the flat. Her husband was in the kitchen, attending to pots and pans bubbling on the cooker. "Do you know what just happened to me? No, don't answer that, I know you do. I can tell by that look on your face. What was that thing?"

"Oh, just a thing," replied Vincent, waving a fish slice dismissively. "You know, just… one of those things."

"Those things? What things? Vincent, if you've got any kind of respect for this relationship, you will give me a straight answer."

"Very well, dear, right after I've checked the things in the oven." He checked the things in the oven. They were coming along nicely. "It calls itself the Ties that Bind. This is something of a misnomer because, except in special circumstances, it can only bind together things that are dead. I expect it was trying to kill you so it could re-animate your corpse in a vain attempt to get to me."

"I didn't realise being your wife made me a target for homicidal figures of speech."

Vincent smiled and shook his head. "You were never in any real danger. As you saw, we have friends in high places. What does concern me though is that your necklace of pearlescent joy does not appear to be working very well today. Perhaps the clasp is broken. If you let me take a look—"

"No! It's fine! It's working fine," said Veronica, covering the beads around her throat. "It's just… over-worked. No one in their right mind could stay happy after nearly being eaten by disembodied weasel teeth."

"You could be happy you're alive?"

"Okay, yes, I'm happy I'm alive and I'm sure I'll be swimming in an endorphin high as soon as I've stopped drowning in adrenaline."

"Then take this glass of wine and sit yourself down. You can relax now."

Veronica took the proffered glass and withdrew to the sofa. She didn't drink, preferring to toy with the crystal stem instead.

"How did they know I was in trouble?" she asked.

"Who?"

"Our friends in high places."

"Oh, because they're everywhere. All-seeing, all-knowing. Well, almost."

"But how can rugs and vacuum cleaners come alive like that?"

Vincent shrugged. "It's just another one of those things. Except involving less fish guts, obviously."

"Some of the children have been saying it's all because of Emily Wilson."

"They've been saying that, have they?"

"But how can that be true? She's just a little girl."

"Yes, she is. It must mean the kids are telling stories again, the little scamps."

"Did you actually just use the words 'little scamps'?"

"I'm wearing slippers and a cardigan, it seemed appropriate. Dinner is now ready. If you would care to join me at the table, I can guarantee that no one and nothing will try to kill you until well after dessert."

Three hours after dessert, Mrs Walters came to the door. Mrs Shehadeh and Mrs Nguyen took up positions by the windows. Mrs Drescher arrived in the flat above and waiting for the second hand on her watch to reach twelve before starting up the circular saw she carried.

Shortly after midnight, Vincent Drysdale stood on top of a Portakabin overlooking foundations that would eventually become a new shopping centre.

"I understand your position," he said, "and if I were in your position I expect I'd do exactly the same, so I sympathise, I really do. Whether it's luck or fate or the simple consequence of the decisions we make, it is a sad fact that once we find ourselves burdened with a role in life, we often have little choice but to play that role through until the end."

Fiddlesticks sat a cautious distance away on top of the temporary building. His ears twitched as Vincent spoke, but everything else remained still. A bulldozer in the site below pushed along a growing pile of dirt.

"That said," continued Mr Drysdale, "I can't say I entirely understand your persistence in this matter. Not only do I have protection from on high, I have life insurance. My death would be nothing more than a temporary setback. Not that I'm knocking good, honest perseverance, but there is a point at which the wise man - or in your case, cat – realises he's fighting a losing battle and sensibly decides to call it quits."

The bulldozer progressed slowly toward a dark hole sunk in the foundations marked at each corner by rods of steel.

"Do you have children? Is there a litter of little Fiddlesticks out there? If not, I can certainly recommend parenthood as a very positive alternative to visiting justice on the sinful. I personally consider it my greatest achievement."

Fiddlesticks stood up and walked away as the bulldozer

reached the hole and pushed tonnes of dirt down into the hole and over the corpses of Mrs Polidouris, Mrs Gunnarsson, Mrs Dawkins, Mrs Fairfax, Mrs Walters, Mrs Shehadeh, Mrs Nguyen, Mrs Drescher and, right down at the bottom, Emily Wilson's tutor, Mrs Hu.

Edmund Holberry was woken at one a.m. by noises coming from downstairs. At first he thought it was his estranged wife, returned to beg forgiveness, but that thought was quickly dismissed. If it was her, she was more likely to be stealing the sterling silver cutlery set they'd received on their anniversary and that was unlikely because she wasn't due back from her holiday in Greece with that Pakistani toy-boy of hers until tomorrow night.

A loud crash confirmed it wasn't just noisy plumbing. Edmund's heart raced. He hugged his pillow, hoping the intruders would be satisfied stealing his television.

But what if they came upstairs?

Edmund's mobile phone was charging on the dresser. He had to call the police.

Ever so carefully, he folded back his duvet. Sweat made his pyjama top cling to his back. Mindful of creaking floorboards, he slowly eased his weight onto his feet before standing up.

Another crash. He tried to remain calm. That meant they were still downstairs. That meant he still had time to reach the phone.

Unless there was more than one of them.

Edmund managed to reach the phone without balaclava-clad assailants bursting into the room and beating him to death with their anti-social behaviour orders. He found himself grinning as he picked up the phone and hit the first '9'.

Then floorboards did creak. Someone was marching up the stairs.

Edmund panicked and misdialled. He hastily cleared the incorrect numbers to try again.

"Edmund!" He froze. The intruder knew his name. "I know you're listening." It was a woman's voice. It might have been familiar, but he couldn't tell over the fearful pounding of his heart. "Do you want me to come in there?"

"No!" he blurted out.

"Then tell me where you've put your bloody car keys."

"They're… they're still in my jacket pocket. It's hanging in the hall."

"Of course. Why didn't I think of that?"

The intruder went back down the stairs.

Edmund finished dialling the police. While the phone rang, he ventured over to his bedroom door and opened it a crack. At the bottom of the stairs, in the gloom of the hallway, Edmund saw—

"Veronica?"

"Yes," she replied, retrieving the car keys from his jacket pocket. "Hi there, Edmund."

"What are you doing here?"

"Borrowing your car."

"But… why?"

"You don't really need to know."

"Oh? Oh, do I not? You come here in the middle of the night, try to steal my car and I don't need to know?"

His phone call received a reply.

"Emergency. Which service?"

"Hold on a moment," snapped Edmund, before turning his ire back to Veronica. "And is that my wheelbarrow sitting at the bottom of the stairs?"

"Yes it is."

"Sir, please, which service do you require?"

"I think I would like the police," said Edmund. "There is a mad woman in my house and for once it's not my wife."

"Have you got a toilet down here?" asked Veronica.

"I'm not going to—"

"It's all right, I've found it."

She disappeared through a doorway. Edmund gave his address and details of the incident to the police and then headed downstairs to confront Veronica. He waited with folded arms while the toilet flushed.

When she opened the door, he said: "I have called the police. They will be here shortly."

"That's okay, we'll be gone by then."

"What do you mean *we*?"

"You're going to help me solve a problem."

"I don't think I'm going to be doing anything with you, Veronica, except possibly sharing a day in court."

"I thought you might say that, hence the wheelbarrow."

"What's the wheelbarrow got to do with it?"

"That's to get you to the car after I knock you out with this sleeper hold I just learned off the internet."

"You really think you're going to—?"

Edmund didn't finish his sentence, because Veronica had just kicked him in the testicles. After that, it was relatively straightforward to carry through on her plan.

Veronica pushed the wheelbarrow containing Edmund Holberry into the alleyway behind Froggarty Premium Accessories Ltd. He was conscious, but knotted washing line held him still. One torn pyjama sleeve filled his mouth, while the other was wrapped about his head to keep the first in place. He did his best to shout and complain regardless.

Veronica parked the wheelbarrow by the manhole she had investigated the other day. She heaved the cover aside before returning to Edmund's car. She fetched his duvet and pillows from the trunk. They were thrown down into the sewer. Realising what she had in mind, Edmund shook his head madly.

"It's not that big a drop," said Veronica, grabbing the handles of the wheelbarrow, "but it'll probably help if you relax. Tense up on landing and you're more likely to break a leg. Not that it matters."

She tipped up the wheelbarrow. Edmund slid out feet-first, disappearing down the hole with a muffled cry.

Minutes later, Veronica dropped into the sewer beside an unbroken Edmund. She shone a metal torch into his face.

"I am now going to have to drag you," she explained. "You will behave yourself or I will do this." She struck him sharply on the forehead with the butt of the torch. "Do you understand, Edmund?"

He glared at her. She hit him again. He nodded.

The duvet served as a makeshift litter. Edmund lay on it, helpless, while Veronica hauled it along a brick tunnel, seven feet in diameter. Once it had been round, but time had deformed into a shape more akin to a swollen heart. A stream of rancid water ran along the bottom.

Veronica tried not to think too much as she walked. She didn't want to doubt her plan would work.

They reached a junction. Writhing vines clung to the brickwork and trailed down into the water. Veronica noted the Umivatoré appeared less charred than on her previous visit and even emitted a faint glow. It was recovering from whatever fire burned here. Yet now she had to kill it.

She pulled one of the vines free of the wall.

Only a few short months ago she had saved the Umivatoré – its own emissary had poisoned it with the brain of a pessimist. Veronica was now intent on doing the same.

She took the vine and pressed it against Edmund's head, much to his disgust.

Nothing happened. She had seen the bodies strung up in the Umivatoré's warehouse with tendrils clamped to their heads, sucking out their thoughts, but didn't know how the plant attached itself to its victims.

Veronica tried forcing the vine into Edmund's ear and then up his nose. Each attempt caused him to writhe about with increased panic. He slipped down beneath the water. Veronica hauled him back up and dropped her torch in the process. She pulled his gag loose. He spit out the balled up pyjama sleeve.

"What the f—?"

Veronica shoved the vine into his mouth. She clasped a hand against his forehead as he struggled against the choking vegetation.

A voice echoed along the tunnel.

"It won't work, Veronica."

"No harm in trying, Vincent," she called back.

"Your friend there might disagree."

Veronica yanked the vine out of Edmund's mouth and let it fall onto the bricks. He gasped for air and then succumbed to a fit of hacking coughs.

The torch shone out from beneath the sewage, its refracted light shifting chaotically across the walls, making Veronica's shadow dance while her husband walked up. His own torch was held steady, pointing at the floor so as not to dazzle.

"It was a good effort," he said. "I commend your

imagination."

"What you're doing to those children, what they're doing to this town, it has to stop."

"Veronica, you don't know how much it pained me to say that you could never choose happiness. I knew from the start that you'd swapped my necklace for a fake, but I hoped that given time, you'd learn the pretence could become real. Unfortunately it seems our time has run out."

He knelt down beside Edmund and began untying the washing line.

"Thank god you came along," spluttered Edmund. "She's crazy! I always knew she was mentally unstable, but I had no idea—"

"Steady, sir," said Vincent, "that's my wife you're talking about."

"Jesus Christ! Why would you marry someone like that? No, no, I understand, you never know at the time. It's only later you find out, isn't it? It just creeps up on you, getting worse and worse each day until it suddenly dawns on you how bloody mental they are. Not that it's entirely their fault. It's hormones. And the bloody media. Everyone thinks they're so bloody *entitled* nowadays—"

"You can leave now," said Vincent, unravelling the last of the washing line.

"Sorry, is that you giving me permission to leave? Because I can tell you I have no intention of staying here for another second, whether you or that insane wife of yours likes it or not."

"Okay then, safe travels."

"And now with the sarcasm. How exactly do you expect me to have safe travels when I don't have a torch? Come on, you're holding one, there's another down there, it's not like you can't spare… No! Don't give me the one that's been in the bloody sewage!"

Vincent finally handed over the torch he'd been carrying and Edmund skulked away back to the manhole outside Froggarty's factory.

Veronica sat on the curved base of the junction with her feet submerged in sewage. Vincent sat down beside her.

"You could stop all this," she said, without looking at him.

"So could you."

She hung her head. The two of them had been together in the Wilsons' garden when Mrs Hu told them of the moment she stood in Emily's bedroom, ready to will a tragic accident on the sleeping girl, only to find she couldn't do it. Emily was the victim of injustice, not the cause. She didn't ask to be born the Conjunction. If her nature was being exploited by others, then those others were the ones that deserved to pay. It was why Mrs chose to attack them. It was why Veronica chose to poison the Umivatoré. It was why none of them could kill the little girl at the heart of it all.

"I'm not sure if anyone can stop this now," said Vincent.

"Lafarge could."

Vincent reached for her hand, but she pulled it away before they touched.

"I don't want to lose you, Veronica," he said.

Veronica's eyes flashed as she turned to face him.

"Don't you get it? You never had me, Vincent! The only reason we were ever together is because you tricked my parents and even then, you didn't get me. Yes, my voice, my face, but I was just acting out a script you wrote. You didn't get what was up here," she tapped her head, "you didn't get any of that. So… so you can pull another of your tricks and turn me into your devoted puppet again, but you have to realise that's all I'll be, mindless flesh and blood and nothing more."

Veronica realised she was shaking. She stared into Vincent's eyes, unable to look away, hoping against hope that he was convinced; that he wouldn't take revenge on her betrayal by taking away her will once again.

His eyes abruptly fell away, along with the rest of him. Edmund Holberry held aloft his torch and struck down a second and third time before kicking Vincent into the water. Then he came at Veronica.

She struggled to her feet, but lost her balance on the curved floor. The torch fell heavy and blunt against the side of her head. Veronica reeled and raised her arms to block another blow.

Edmund punched her in the stomach.

Veronica stumbled backward through the sewage. Edmund kept coming. His attacks were clumsy, but driven by a violent rage that finally knocked Veronica to the ground.

He dropped down on top of her. His knees fell painfully against her stomach. Fists pounded at her head. She raised her arms to block the worst of the violence.

He grabbed her hair and thrust her head into the water. Sewage streamed up her nose. Veronica bucked and struggled, but Edmund had her pinned down.

"See?" His voice was distorted by the liquid in her ears. "See, you evil bitch? You don't like being on the receiving end, do you?"

Her starved lungs began to spasm. Edmund pulled her head clear of the water. She gasped for air and he thrust the Umivatoré vine in her mouth.

"An eye for an eye, a tooth for a tooth," said Edmund. "That's how it should be. Every ounce of pain paid back in full."

Veronica choked. She scratched at his arms, tried to force him to relent, terrified that at any moment a stream of toxic ideas would gush forth from the Umivatoré and change her mind in the same way it had the boy in the warehouse.

"My life's been full of pain thanks to people like you," sneered Edmund. "Everything I try, everything I do, there's always someone like you standing in the way, putting me down, thinking you're somehow better."

Pinpricks of light began to flash across her vision. Her ability to fight was fading. Edmund's voice lost its edge too. Even though his raging features were only inches from her own, it felt as if he was moving further and further away.

"Do you think you're better now, huh? Do you? Shall I tell you what you are? Shall I tell you just what you are?"

"She is my wife."

The weight pinning her down vanished. The vine slipped from Veronica's mouth. She collapsed against the bricks and sensation quickly returned. None of it was pleasant.

Veronica wanted to see what was happening, but that desire was weak compared to the one that made her remain still, with eyes shut tight. She heard the beginnings of a scream, but it stopped suddenly, as if it had never been uttered. Then Vincent was crouching down beside her, stroking her forehead, frowning as she blinked up at him.

She smiled at his concern, but her amusement only lasted a moment. She closed her eyes again. Her only thought now was to rest until the pain subsided.

"I'm sorry, Veronica," whispered Vincent. "I do want to make you happy. That's why I got you this."

She had to look. He held a shimmering tiara. She tried to back away, but she was still too weak. He leaned forward.

"It is called the Prism," said Vincent, gently placing it on her head.

The world became a giant kaleidoscope, the view of the tunnel and her husband reflected a thousand times. Veronica loosed a fearful cry.

"Don't be afraid," said her husband. "We all have many faces, each one showing at different times, depending on where we find ourselves, who we're with and how we're feeling. You are simply looking through the eyes of all those faces at the same time."

As Veronica's panic eased, she was able to see that it was not the same image repeated over and over again. In each shard, her husband looked subtly different. His handsome features looked menacing from a hundred points of view, contemptible to a hundred more.

"So many of those faces hate me," said Vincent, wistfully, "yet there had to be one…"

He reached forward to touch the Prism, adjusting a gemstone so that one of the shards grew larger. This vision of Vincent Drysdale was not menacing or contemptible. His features were perfect. The only thing his smile showed was care and concern. Unlike all of the other visions, this was unequivocally a good man.

As this view of her husband pushed aside all others, Veronica heard a thousand sides of herself scream out before they were silenced. Vincent stroked her cheek as a tear ran down his own.

"There had to be one who loved me."

Thomas Locke walked from the abandoned Office of Lost and Found into the cavernous nave of a church. From there he passed into a vacant operating theatre, then a mud hut, a caravan, a mausoleum, a flooded toilet in a diner halfway up a mountain and a lantern-lit alcove at the bottom of a mineshaft. In each one, Locke could see marks on the floor from where things lost once stood. As he walked, a burning pain grew in his stomach. The Ties that Bind wanted him to go back.

He finally reached a simple chamber with three blank walls and a fourth lined with large windows. Beyond was a black sky filled with stars and awash with unnatural rainbow nebulae. Locke walked up to the window and looked out upon a land unlike any he'd ever seen. Giant spires rose up out of a glistening sea shot through with shifting veins of lava. Atop these volcanic swathes moved floating islands; abstract formations of rock, covered in forest or desert or sprawling city. Roiling clouds passed above, shifting from stormy black to beatific white in seconds. As Locke watched, a cloud wrapped itself around a spire and became a misty cloak of wooden cabins built upon precarious scaffolding. An island on course to collide with another spire merely drifted through it, the land caught in the shadow of the tower turning from farmland to desert and back again as the two parted. Locke felt as if he were gazing out across one world, but glimpsing others whenever these elements combined.

Then he stepped back.

His focus shifted from the spectacular view to the window itself. Condensation from his breath revealed words once traced across the glass with a finger.

'Whosoever follows…'

The moisture quickly faded and the words disappeared. It took several more breaths for Locke to piece together the entire message.

'Whosoever follows me, know there is another way out. I found it. You too can be free of him.'

For a second Locke thought the message referred to the Ties that Bind, but then realised his path here led through past locations of the Office of Lost and Found. If the message referred to anyone, it was Lafarge and Lafarge was gone. Locke was already free of him. He'd come all this way for nothing.

A sudden, quaking pain forced him to his knees. It came again and he rolled around so he could sit up against the window and clutch at his stomach.

Silver threads started winding out between his fingers. He could feel his muscles and even bones begin to feel thinner and weaker. Red lines were scored across his skin. One of his thumbnails split in two. Another spasm in his guts and then something pushed hard against his hands. He tried to hold it in, but more threads burst out and pulled his fingers away.

Locke watched in horror as a tangled ball of wire emerged from his stomach. It sent flailing threads lashing out across the room. They scratched lines across the floor and ceiling before etching a simple message on the wall opposite.

'Go Back.'

Once the Ties that Bind was sure its message was understood, the ball of wire burrowed back inside Locke's abdomen. The pain subsided, but did not vanish; a lingering reminder of who called the shots.

Locke rose shakily to his feet. He headed back; back through the mine-shaft, the flooded toilet, the mausoleum, the caravan, the mud-hut and the operating theatre. He arrived in the cavernous nave of the church to find the door to the small office ajar. A deep, rasping breathing came from the other side. As he drew closer, other sounds reached his ears: a faint buzzing, as if from insects; a rhythmic beat so low it vibrated the stone beneath Locke's feet; harsh scraping that set his teeth on edge; and a phlegmy whispering that suggested an inhuman intelligence.

For once he took heart in the knowledge that the Ties that Bind would not let him die. Or at least not permanently. He opened the door to reveal a monstrous legion crowded into the office of J H Ward.

"Thomas Locke, we have been looking for you."

Billy did not find the living room sofa a comfortable bed. He finally got to sleep after hours of tossing and turning and a moment later he was woken by his mother calling him to breakfast. He ignored the summons and remained curled up beneath his blanket. Then his mother came in and took the blanket away.

His toes turned cold. He tried to balance a cushion on top of them to provide some warmth. It didn't help.

"Mum! Blanket!"

"Breakfast," she called back from the kitchen.

"I think I'm getting frostbite."

"That's terrible, dear. Best get up and have your breakfast sharpish so we can get you down the doctors to have your toes chopped off."

Billy groaned and buried his face in his pillow.

"It's only mild frostbite," he said.

"We still need to chop them off to stop it spreading."

"Can't you just bring the blanket back?"

"I'm sure it's too late for that."

"But *Mum*...!"

"But *Billy*... breakfast!"

He groaned again and then rolled off the sofa onto the floor. He crouched there for a time, hugging his knees, before waddling to the living room door. Peering out into the hallway, he saw his mother head upstairs.

A grin crept across his face. He raced into the kitchen, grabbed a dessert spoon from the cutlery drawer and took a standing jump over to the sink. He held the spoon just so and then flicked it against the metal taps.

"A standard quadruple beat, if you please."

The spoon struck up a ching-ching rhythm on the taps. Billy let it go and it continued playing. He jumped back over to the cutlery drawer.

Shoosh went the drawer as he pushed it closed.

Shoosh went the drawer as he pulled it open again.

Shoosh, shoosh, shoosh... sliding in and out on its own in time with the spoon's ching-ching beat.

Billy jumped over to the oven and waited for the perfect moment to make the cooking timer on the oven go bing.

Ching-ching, shoosh-shoosh, bing!

Ching-ching, shoosh-shoosh, bing!

Ching-ching, clump, shoosh-shoosh, bing!

The clump was Billy slamming shut the washing machine door. He looked around for something to contribute a melody.

Ching-ching, clump, shoosh-shoosh, bing!

Maureen appeared in the kitchen doorway.

"Billy, it's far too early in the morning for this sort of

nonsense!”

Ching-ching, clump—

“Billy, last warning.”

Shoosh-shoosh—

“Okay, everyone,” said Billy, “take a break.”

The spoon dropped into the sink. The cutlery drawer slid sheepishly closed. The oven kept its timer quiet, while the door of the washing machine wavered, half-open. Billy’s mother nodded, satisfied.

“Now get yourself away from that washing machine. I don’t want you getting snapped up and trapped inside like Kelly Wilcox’s baby. You know they couldn’t get him out until she signed an extended two-year warranty in blood? In *blood*, Billy! I don’t want to have to do that for you, not with my haemophilia. Now sit down, have your breakfast and let’s be having no more of your nonsense.”

Billy took his place at the table.

“And what about her?” he asked.

“What about her?”

“Doesn’t she have to come down for breakfast?”

“No, Billy, because you’ve been making her sleep under your bed since her parents died last week and that entitles her to special treatment.”

“They weren’t her *real* parents.”

“They were the only ones she’s ever known and that means they’re the only ones that count.”

“Sometimes I wish my parents ”

“Don’t you dare finish that sentence, young man.”

The phone rang in the hallway. Maureen went to answer it. Billy poured milk over his muesli. He heard his father’s voice shouting out from the phone.

“Can you believe this? Apparently they don’t want workers at the plant any more, they want *believers*. People who can just will the stuff to go through the pipes at the correct flow rate. I’m telling you, it’s a god-damned travesty!”

Emily walked silently into the kitchen in Billy’s dinosaur slippers. It was an unwelcome reminder that his toes were still cold. He glared at her.

“There’s no need to look at me like that,” she said. “I didn’t ask to sleep in your bed. You know it smells, don’t you? But I suppose you are a boy after all—"

Clump.

Emily stopped and looked down at the washing machine. The door was slowly opening again by her leg.

"Norman?" said Billy's mother in the hallway. "Norman, are you still there?"

"Did you make it do that?" asked Emily.

Billy shook his head.

Clump. The washing machine door slammed shut again.

Bing, went the timer on the oven. Gas started hissing out from the hobs.

"Your father was cut off," said Maureen, returning to the kitchen. "I won't say that's a crying shame, but I guarantee when he gets home we won't hear the end of it." She sniffed. "Billy, have you been playing with the cooker?"

She walked over to the oven. The ignition switch clicked. Four plumes of blue flame flared up above the hobs. She reeled backwards.

Clump.

"It's moved!" said Emily, pointing at the washing machine. "Look, it's got closer."

The appliance had indeed edged an inch forward.

"Billy, stop this right now!" said his mother.

"It's not me!" he cried.

The strip light fixed to the ceiling began flashing on and off.

Billy jumped from his chair and ran out into the hall. Emily scampered after him.

"Where do you think you're going?" called his mother.

Billy hurtled into the living room and jumped with his knees onto the windowsill. Emily arrived and hid behind him. Outside, past the front gate, they saw roadworks blocking the street. Men in orange jackets stood in a line on the pavement, looking back at Billy.

The phone rang.

Maureen answered it.

"Hello? Norman?" A pause followed. The two children looked at each other. "Billy, it's for you."

He climbed down from the windowsill and walked through to the hall. Emily peeked out at the work-men, then ran after him.

Maureen handed Billy the phone. He put the handset to his ear.

"Did you think you could hide her?" asked Joshua. "Especially from me. I have eyes everywhere. I can even see you now."

Billy looked into the kitchen. The food mixer on the work-top stared back at him.

"What do you want?"

"Did you do it because of the spoons?" asked Joshua. "I mean, spoons are a bit shit really, aren't they? You need something else if you're going to compete with the big boys."

"And who would they be? Can't be you, 'cause you're half an inch shorter than me."

"Your god broke the truce. The Conjunction belonged to all of us, so none of us could touch it."

"Yeah? What's the Conjunction?"

"No, Billy, no. You don't get to play dumb any more. It's too late for that. Good-bye, Billy."

The line went dead. Out in the street, jack-hammers thundered to life.

"I can still hear them," said Veronica.

She lay in bed beside Vincent, idly drawing circles on his bare chest with her fingernail. Her hair was tousled from the night they'd spent together, but the tiara remained in place.

"Who?" he asked.

"All the sides of me saying I should run."

"I could take the Prism off. Then you could run."

"But I don't want to."

"Only because—"

"I want to be here, Vincent, with you. All those other sides of me, they can't see what I see. They can't see this side of you. I don't want to lose that."

They made love again. The morning sunshine streaming in through the window made the sweat on their naked skin glisten. Passion sated, they lay still together once more.

"You are different, you know," said Veronica. "I wasn't sure at first, but up close like this, I've no more doubts."

"I did say the old Vincent was gone."

"So where did this new Vincent come from?"

"Your dreams."

"My dreams? Are you making fun of me?"

"Not at all. Dreams are precious things. You're my wife, so I made sure to keep yours safe."

"You make it sound like you've got them stoppered up in jars and locked away somewhere."

"Well…"

Veronica sat up and stared at him.

"You have? You've got my dreams locked up somewhere?"

"Understand that an unscrupulous sort can harvest a person's dreams and use them for all manner of nefarious purposes. And then there are things like Ties that Bind that can use them for far worse."

She laid her head on his chest.

"It won't stop, will it? Not until it's found you."

"The gods will protect us."

"And who'll protect us from them?"

"Funny you should ask that, because they've been asking how I'm going to protect them from you."

She slapped him playfully on the stomach, before frowning and biting her lip.

"What's going to happen to the children?" asked Veronica.

"I never took you for the maternal sort."

"I'm just worried about Billy. And Emily."

"Children are often more resilient than us grown-ups. They've already shown themselves better at adapting to the changes that are coming."

"But why did you have to bring the gods here in the first place?"

He sighed and stroked her hair.

"I doubt there's any answer I could give that would make sense. I can only say what's done is done and I'm afraid we all have to live with that now."

Veronica stared sightlessly into space, feeling Vincent's run his fingers through her hair and hearing a thousand echoes of her own voice telling her this was wrong.

His mobile phone started vibrating on the bedside table. He picked it up.

"What's happened?" he asked.

Veronica felt the answer beneath her ear as a quickening heart beat.

Erik Wadkin was a postman. Every morning he left the sorting office with bags full of mail and spent the next couple of hours dutifully delivering each letter to its given address. This morning was no exception. He delivered the last letter in his bag to the last house on his round, returned to his bike and prepared to cycle home. Then a whispering voice in his head told him to check his bag again.

Right at the bottom, he found another letter he could have sworn wasn't there a moment ago.

He took it out of the bag and examined it. The address was a ten minute ride away, back along his usual route. Nothing remarkable about that. Nothing remarkable about the plain white envelope either. What made Erik Wadkin's eyes open wide was the postmark. The ink circle bounded three letters: G.O.D.

Seconds later, Erik was on his bike and pedalling hard. He had heard tales – legends, even – of the G.O.D. postmark. Those who'd seen it were always friends of friends, but every postman knew what it meant when they saw the sign: they had a divine obligation to ensure the letter reached its destination safely and without delay.

A fly flew into his mouth. He swallowed it without a second thought.

His front tyre hit a pot hole. Erik managed to keep his balance and rode on.

A mother pushing a pram stepped out into the road. She was nimbly avoided.

The postman took a right turn at a crossroads and braked sharply.

The way ahead was blocked by traffic cones, red and white striped barriers and mounds of rubble dug up from the street. A sign helpfully declared 'ROAD CLOSED' and pointed out a 'DIVERSION' back the way he had come.

Erik blinked bewilderment. He had delivered mail along this street only a few minutes ago and then it had been clear.

A faint chorus of voices rose behind him. He turned his head. A crowd of people marched up the road, singing songs and holding banners. The banners bore pithy slogans like 'All-Works are His' and 'All-Work is His Work' and 'Worship the God of All-Works or die! :)'.

"Heathens," muttered Erik Wadkin under his breath.

He swung his bike around and turned right again at the crossroads. He stood up from his seat to stamp down with extra force on the pedals, but his urgent pace was thwarted at every turn by another set of roadworks blocking the way to his destination.

Erik dismounted his bike, hoisted it over a shoulder and cut through the gardens of a housing estate.

"Hey, who are you?" shouted a burly resident. His thick arms were covered in watches, his torso was bare save for bandoliers sewn together from socks and he had a cushion Sellotaped to his head. "What are you doing on my lawn? You're one of those bloody postmen, aren't you?"

He grabbed Erik's mailbag, twisting him round and causing him to fall onto his bike.

"I bet this is full of more junk you're going to dump on people," said the resident, wrenching the bag from Erik's grip. "I've had more letters about loans and special offers and charity appeals in the last month than—" He pulled out the solitary letter. "Hey, I've heard of this Emily Wil—"

The cushion Sellotaped to his head didn't stop the spade hitting him in the face.

Erik Wadkin snatched back the letter. In the distance he could hear the procession abandon their rallying songs for urgent exhortations to march faster. The resident's shed began to tremble. A hedge trimmer buzzed to life inside. A toaster threw itself at the inside of the kitchen window.

Erik picked up his bike, threw it over the back fence and scrambled after it. He landed on the other side to find a small blue paddling pool crawling menacingly toward him.

He jumped on his bike, stuffed the letter inside his shirt and accelerated down a passageway. The road printed on the letter was just ahead. Erik sped out onto the pavement. A car sped in from nowhere, mounted the kerb and crashed into a lamppost in front of him.

The postman had no time to react. His bike ran into the front wing of the car and Erik was thrown across the crumpled bonnet.

He fell onto the road, winded and shaken. Were it not for the importance of his mission, he might have lain there until help came. Instead, he dragged himself to his feet in time, then leapt clear as another car piled into the first.

Erik could see his destination: a house two hundred metres away, surrounded by more roadworks. He could hear the believers in the God of All-Works drawing near.

He started running.

More cars tried to run him down. Half-dry washing sailed over the rooftops and attempted to strangle him with chiffon sleeves and polyester trouser legs. Chewing gum stains massed on the paving stones, intent on snaring him with their stickiness.

Erik suffered vicious cuts and bruises and lost a shoe, but fought his way through.

The roadworks were just ahead. A line of workmen with deafening pneumatic drills blocked his path to the letter-box he had to reach. He slowed, unsure of how to get past them. Then he realised the drills were pounding out a beat. The nearby traffic cones were tapping out a complimentary rhythm. While whistling a barely audible melody, the workmen proceeded to back-step, side-step, twirl, in a fashion reminiscent of the simplistic dance moves of a sixties rock n' roll band.

The sight made Erik drop his guard. He didn't hear the polythene bag drift up behind him. It slipped itself over his head and tied its handles tight around his neck.

He tried to claw it off, but more bags came, covering his head, trapping his hands, cutting off every trace of oxygen that might reach his lungs.

Every time Erik tried to draw breath, taut plastic pressed against his mouth. Stressed blood vessels began bursting across his face and eyeballs.

He crawled on, barely able to see, unable to think, driven on by an unreasonable sense of duty. He didn't get far. Unconsciousness finally claimed him. Death followed soon after.

The polythene bags slowly untangled themselves and drifted away, leaving the deceased postman lying face down on the pavement.

Further up the street, the march hove into view, moving fast, chanting loudly. From neighbouring houses, people came out to witness the cause of the commotion. At first they didn't notice the body in the street at first, but when they did, a few rushed over to see if they could help.

Erik Wadkin was rolled onto his back. His pulse was checked. Grim glances were exchanged. A moment later, the letter peeking out from under his shirt was spied. Fingers carefully drew it out only for a gust of wind to steal it from their grasp.

Hands snatched for it, but it spiralled higher and higher, ducking clear of a polythene bag and avoiding entrapment in the G-cups of an airborne bra.

It dived toward an upstairs window above the dancing workmen. The frame was old and rotten and the letter managed to squeeze through a gap and into the house. The letter fluttered across carpet and down stairs until it reached those huddled in the hallway.

"I've got a letter!" exclaimed Emily.

"What? Where did you get that?" asked Billy's mother.

"Let me see," said Billy, leaning over and suspending his orchestration of spoons, saucepans and other household goods.

"No, Billy!" snapped Maureen. "You concentrate on your music. It's the only thing keeping those workmen at bay."

Billy pouted and went back to conducting his domestic symphony.

"Who's it from?" his mother asked Emily.

"Mr Drysdale," sniffed the little girl, studying the paper she'd torn from the envelope. "I don't know if I want letters from Mr Drysdale."

"That's as may be," said Maureen, "but however evil he is, you should at least be good enough to do him the courtesy of reading what he has to say."

Emily huffed dissatisfaction with this suggestion, but followed it anyway.

"Dear Emily, the gods have eyes and ears everywhere, so please do not read any more of this letter aloud."

Vincent Drysdale was at his flat, on the phone.

"I assure you this matter will be resolved."

He nodded at the reply and acknowledged Veronica as she entered the living room from the entrance hall. He gestured with his hand toward the front door. She shook her head. An errant oven and dishwasher were attacking anyone who tried to pass that way with blasts of hot air and detergent.

She stepped out onto the balcony.

"I still say we could climb down."

Vincent held up a hand – he was too busy to listen at the moment.

"Yes, I'm still here," he said into the phone, "and no, I haven't been able to get hold of Joshua. He is communicating, but only through the medium of toast." Five slices of browned bread were laid out across the kitchen worktop. "He maintains that only the God of All-Works is able to ensure the Conjunction's continued safety." The enraged response forced Vincent to hold the phone away from his ear for a few seconds. "Of course I don't agree with him, that's why I proposed the truce in the first place… No, the truce hasn't failed, we simply need… No, I don't think that would be a good idea—"

He sighed and put the phone down.

"At least that call was longer than the last one," said Veronica as her husband joined her on the balcony.

Vincent rubbed his face wearily. "The marvellous thing about children is their capacity to believe in anything, it's just unfortunate that their reasoning skills are not quite so well developed."

"I think they're being perfectly reasonable."

Vincent raised a sceptical eyebrow.

"Listen," said Veronica, "all the gods need Emily alive, but that effectively makes her a walking, talking doomsday device as far as they're concerned. She dies and they're back where they started, so whoever has Emily has their finger over the trigger. They're not going to trust anyone else with that responsibility."

"So they'll go to war instead."

"Yes, because gods don't die in wars, only people do."

Those marching for the God of All-Works broke down Billy's front door. Leading the line were the workmen with their pneumatic drills. There was no music now, just evangelical shouting.

They found the rooms downstairs empty. When they rushed up the stairs, spoons pelted them from above. This did not slow their ascent.

Stamping boots and shoes arrived on a landing littered with buttons and awash with water running out from the bathroom. The toilet within was smashed; the bowl cracked open, the lid lying snapped on the flooded floor. A mop handle jammed the airing cupboard shut, trapping irate towels inside. The ceiling bore a hole that Billy's father had been meaning to fix ever since Veronica Drysdale kicked it into existence with a high heeled shoe several months ago. It led up into loft space that connected every house on Billy's terrace. One of those houses was empty after a recent repossession. It had a fresh hole leading down onto the landing.

Billy, his mother and Emily hurried past empty bedrooms and descended the bare stairs. Maureen wore sunglasses and a fancy hat. Emily was dressed up in some of Billy's cast-offs, her hair hastily cut to a boyish length. Billy wore one of his grandmother's old dresses, his disgusted features partially hidden by a shawl draped over his head.

The gods will recognise both you and Billy, the letter told Emily, *you must disguise yourselves. But beware of the clothes. Their god is dim-witted and slow, but now Joshua has played his hand, he may finally become aware of your presence. Cut off the buttons and the clothes will not be able to see.*

They reached the front door. Zealous shouts from down the street were plain to hear. Billy hurried into the living room and peered through a gap in the boarded up windows.

The other gods will come, promised the letter. *There will be fighting and confusion. Your chance will come while their attention is elsewhere. Keep your heads down and run.*

"There are trees walking down the street!" cried Billy. "And there's a post-box fighting with a wheelchair and I don't know what that is, but—"

"Come on, Grandma Jones," ordered his mother, "we have to go!"

Never use your real names, advised the letter. *Do nothing to draw attention to yourselves. Behave the same as those around you. Get to the stop for the number forty-five bus and wait for it to arrive.*

There was already a short queue at the bus stop. No one there said a word as the three fugitives joined them. They were too busy praying that the giant construction cranes stalking over the rooftops to the east did not turn their way.

The bus drew up a few minutes later. An old man boarded first.

"Praise be to the double-decker," he said, passing the driver, "and exaltations to the line ahead of which we must not stand while the bus is in motion."

Following behind, Billy repeated this pledge in his best old woman voice while taking care to keep his face shadowed by the shawl. Emily and Maureen joined him in seats at the front of the top deck. They exchanged brief glances before the bus juddered and once more got underway.

Everything is watching. Everything is listening. From the telegraph poles passing by the windows to the chewing gum stuck under the seats. I will do my best to keep them distracted while you flee.

Flashes of light in the distance gave rise to a red glow and rising smoke. Maureen put a hand against the window. That was the chemical plant going up in flames, she was sure of it.

Billy hadn't noticed. He was too busy staring down into the street below where postmen fought bin-men, bankers fought waitresses and decorative standard lamps brought the pain to a group of unsuspecting traffic wardens.

Disembark at the Harper Street stop and turn left. Keep walking until you reach the burnt out auction house, whereupon you will see a derelict church standing on the other side of a patch of waste ground. Find a way inside. You should be safe there until I can get to you.

The three fugitives crossed an expanse of decaying concrete slabs riddled with weeds. The church lay ahead; a squat stone building with a sharp spire. Pollution stained the walls black. Slates fallen from the roof left gaping holes. Most of the stained glass had been smashed by vandals.

"Doesn't look like my idea of a sanctuary," muttered

Maureen.

A polythene bag drifted across their path. They froze. It continued on, tumbling away with the breeze.

"Let's just hope the gods haven't gone and killed Mr Drysdale while we were on the bus," said Billy.

"Ssh!" went Emily.

She pulled up her shorts – the dressing gown cord around the waist didn't work as well as the buttons they'd cut off – and strode off ahead.

"Yes, ssh, Grandma Jones," chuckled Maureen, leaving Billy to trail behind.

"No one respects the elderly any more," he sniffed.

They climbed the steps of the church and stopped before a heavy wooden door. The only noises came from far away; gods battling each other in their search for Emily.

Maureen put her shoulder against the door and pushed it open. Daylight lanced down through the holes in the ceiling, but left much of the interior shrouded in gloom. Small piles of broken plaster, dust and dirt gathered between rotting pillars. Only a couple of pews were left and they were upturned and shoved against a wall. The altar had been taken away long ago.

"Now what do we do?" asked Billy.

"Do as the letter said," replied his mother. "We wait."

Late afternoon turned to evening. The children tried to amuse themselves exploring the confines of the church, while Billy's mother fretted over her husband's fate. The letter had told them to leave phones behind, lest they be tracked, but now Maureen had no way of knowing if Norman had escaped the blast at the chemical plant. She looked across at Billy. He was shovelling dust with a spoon he'd brought along. Emily asked if she could use one of his fifteen spares, but he refused, so she tried to help with just her hands. Maureen smiled. Children were blessed with the ability to lose themselves in play, but she couldn't join them. She knew they had placed themselves into the care of Vincent Drysdale and if he was dead or his intentions were treacherous, they were all lost.

The church door creaked open. The three of them turned to see who entered.

"I've brought pizza," said Luke Goddard, sauntering up

the aisle. "I thought you might be hungry after sneaking all the way across town."

Billy narrowed his eyes at his former classmate. "You sent the letter."

"Of course I did," said Luke. "I am letters. I am mail. I am newspapers, magazines and posters. I am the printed word."

"I'll hold him," said Maureen. "You two run."

She grabbed Luke only to release him a second later. Sliced flesh sent blood streaming down her arms.

"Paper cuts," observed the boy. "Nasty."

Billy rushed over to his mother. Luke kicked one of the pews upright and put down the boxes of pizza.

"You can run if you like," he said, "but god knows what'd happen to you out there. Ha! Did you see what I did there? God knows?"

"So what happens now?" asked Maureen, getting Billy to bandage her arms with scraps torn from his grandmother's dress.

"We could eat the pizza before it goes cold?"

His levity brought only a hollow silence. Emily wandered over to where the altar once stood and church-leaders used to make offerings to a silent god.

"What if I killed myself?" she asked.

"Emily, don't say things like that," pleaded Maureen.

"But if all this is because of me, I could end it now. If I'm dead all this will stop."

"This will end when you're safe," said Luke. "Once the others realise that, they'll stop fighting."

"And how are you going to make her safe?" asked Billy.

"I'm glad you asked me that, because it was a tricky one to figure out. She needs to be hidden away from the others, but I can't just have her folded into something else because that would suspend the Conjunction and my god would leave and I can't have that. So, I used my divine powers to search high and low for an answer, until— Billy, what are you doing?"

He was drumming spoons on the floor in a beat that conjured up whirling dervishes of dust than began dancing their way toward Luke.

"Really, Billy? Really?"

Luke waved a hand. Seconds later, thousands of letters

streamed in through the door and the holes in the ceiling. They whirled around the interior, slicing apart the eddies of dust before plastering the walls and forming a carpet for the people who now marched into the church. The postal workers wore uniforms, but the journalists and copy-writers and type-setters wore no badge for their profession.

Two of Luke's followers snatched the spoons away from Billy. Another two grabbed Emily.

"How many people believe in your spoons and your music?" asked Luke, his words echoed in print across the walls. "Even your Mum here doesn't seem entirely convinced. It's believers that count, Billy. That's where the power comes from and I'm afraid far more people believe what they read in the newspapers than what they find in their cutlery drawer." Luke took a bite from a slice of pizza and walked over to Billy and his mother. "Emily will be leaving now. We've made her a fantastic new home at Cregan's Cell that I know she'll just love. As for what happens to you… that very much depends."

"You know, Luke," said Billy, "I reckon I could put up with your gloating if you weren't so dumb, but you are dumb, so I'm going to have to ask you to stop."

"I'm dumb? You say something like that in your position and you call me dumb?"

"Yeah, because I wasn't the one who just made a million letters fly through the air. You told us everything is watching. I think everything just saw what a dumbass you are."

Luke glared at Billy and scratched unconsciously at his clothes. A polythene bag drifted in through one of broken windows. A type-setter grabbed it and ripped it to shreds. Weeds pushed up between the layers of letters. A tennis ball bounced in through the doorway, hopped in place a few times and then bounced out again.

"Prepare to move out," shouted Luke.

Two empty bottles rolled up the aisle. They stopped in the middle of the church. They spun around a few times as if surveilling the room, then pointed themselves back toward the door. A postman spotted the danger and pounced. He was too slow. The bottles shattered into jagged daggers that shot across the room and glassed the two men holding Emily.

The remnants of the broken windows exploded inwards.

Letters whirled up to protect Luke from harm.

Emily ran over to Billy and Maureen, arms shielding her head, but the glass defied physics and spun away without touching her.

Roaring engines approached outside. The ground began to tremble. Dust cascaded down from the rafters.

"We need to get out of here!" shouted Maureen.

"But where can we go?" asked Billy.

"Please," said Emily, "I can stop this."

"No!" said Maureen. "Norman wouldn't forgive me if I let anything happen to you."

Together they fled for the exit.

"Stop them!" cried Luke as a hail of tennis balls fired in through the door.

Again, Emily remained untouched. Billy and his mother ducked down behind her, leaving Luke's disciples to suffer the full force of the onslaught as they tried to follow. The tennis balls were followed by golf balls, footballs, rugby balls, cricket balls, bowling balls – each hurtling into stomachs, chest and faces.

The fugitives hurried down the church steps. Letters swarmed out the door in pursuit, but polythene bags swept in to smother them.

"Mum!" cried Billy, needlessly pointing out the chaos ahead. Hundreds of religious fanatics fought amongst themselves in their attempt to reach Emily. A predatory car would occasionally scatter the crowd; stragglers knocked down and crushed beneath wheels. Above, the air was thick with possessed clothes, kites and party balloons, while the towering construction cranes they'd seen from the bus stop now stalked toward the church, clearing half a dozen streets with each stride.

The quaking of the earth grew worse. People fell to the ground. Slates crashed down from the church roof.

A deafening klaxon call blared out across the waste ground. It heralded an Iowa-class battleship smashing through the church, the towering steel hull tearing through concrete and stone. The giant vessel halted shy of the steps and turned mighty guns on the approaching cranes. A booming salvo blasted the steel girders into smithereens.

"Come on!" yelled Maureen, dragging the children across fresh rubble into the shadow of the battleship.

More letters descended upon them, but a shower of burning cigarette butts reduced them to glowing ash.

They reached the edge of the waste ground. Maureen climbed over a steel barrier, the children ducked under. Ahead was a retail park – half-a-dozen superstores serviced by a several hundred parking spaces.

"Aah!" cried Billy, suddenly under attack by empty crisp packets.

His mother began snatching them out of the air. Neither saw the pavement crack open. Emily screamed. Billy swatted away bags stinking of prawn cocktail and grabbed her hand before the sidewalk could swallow her up.

A car smashed through the barrier at the edge of the waste-ground and pitched radiator-first into the yawning fissure, which now carved a line in pursuit of Maureen and the children. It ate up paving stones and tarmac while spitting out barriers, cones and warning lights to warn passers-by of roadworks in progress.

They ran onto the retail park. Ornamental bushes outside the shops snatched at their ankles. Lampposts bent down to try and grab them. Ahead, windows shattered over the pavement and an army of white goods tumbled out into their path.

They skidded to a halt.

The roadworks surged toward them from behind, a pneumatic drill leading the charge. Fanatics spilled onto the car park, their zeal undiminished by bloody injuries. Above, paper and plastic circled against the sky like a pack of vultures eager to steal carrion from the predators on the ground.

Something shot overhead with a low whistle – a battleship shell that struck the electrical appliances and reduced them to a plume of smoke and shrapnel.

More shells rained down on the car-park, flinging hapless bodies and debris high into the air.

Emily clung to Billy, who couldn't tell if he felt terror, excitement or both. Maureen choked back her own fear and concentrated on the pneumatic drill. It drew close and lunged for her. She dodged aside, grabbed the handle and hurled it through the shop doors beside them.

"In here!" she shouted to the kids, shepherding them across more broken glass into an unlit store full of beds.

"Didn't anyone do a project on beds?" asked Emily.

"Let's hope not," said Billy.

They hurried past the pneumatic drill as it tried to regain its senses and on into a maze of affordably-priced bunks, divans, mattresses and more. At the doorway, the roadworks stopped and expressed frustration by spitting tar across the threshold.

Deep in the shadows, Maureen directed the children under a king-size bed with sheets hanging down to the floor.

"I'll try and lead them off," she said.

"But Mum!"

"Don't argue, Billy. They're coming. Quickly now."

She held up the sheet. Emily crawled under first, followed by Billy. He glanced back. His mother looked nervously toward the store entrance, then gave him a weak smile. That was the last time he saw her face. She dropped the sheet and scurried off. Billy wanted to shout for her to come back, but good sense sealed his lips and all he managed was a plaintive whimper. Emily took his hand and held it tight.

Gruff voices entered the store.

"Over there!"

"I see her."

"Where are the children?"

"The mother will know! Now get her before those damned pagans do!"

Men ran past nearby, followed by the sound of rustling paper, whining motors and clockwork mechanisms.

A bang over to the right. A crash to the left. A cry for help, then a scream.

Billy clutched a spoon, squeezed his eyes shut and prayed.

"Please let her be okay, please let her be okay."

"Where are the children?" asked a voice.

"Gone!" replied Maureen. "He came and took them!"

"Who?"

"Lafarge."

"Ha! Lafarge is gone. The children are still here. Find them. Kill her."

Billy covered his ears, but couldn't stop his mother's cry echoing through his head long after she fell silent.

Emily whispered to herself beside him.

"No, this isn't… this isn't right. Isn't right. Not right. No, no, no."

The search drew closer. Scuffles broke out between the competing factions.

Billy felt Emily brush past him. He opened tear-filled eyes to see her crawling out from under the bed.

"Where are you going?" he hissed.

"This isn't right. Isn't right."

He grabbed her ankle and began hauling her back.

"Stay here!"

"I have to go," she said, suddenly calm.

"No!"

"We can't hide forever. I don't want them to get you too."

Billy stared at her. For the first time he could believe she was more than just a five year old girl. Emily smiled and began removing his limp fingers from her ankle. But then his grip tightened again.

"Wait," he whispered.

"There's no point—"

"Ssh. Listen."

New sounds intruded upon the store. They were not human, nor were they man-made. There was a buzzing, as if from insects; a rhythmic beat so low it vibrated the floor; harsh scraping that set Billy's teeth on edge; and a phlegmy whispering that set his heart beating to an excited rhythm.

The gruff voices shouted alarm.

"My god, what is—?"

"Where did—?"

"Joey! No!"

"Dear sweet sticker album—"

"Run! Everybody get the f—!"

The shouts became strangled cries. Something brushed past the sheets and they caught a glimpse of a foot – black, slick and scaly. Another scream and liquid splashed back across the fabric.

The symphony of carnage lasted only a few seconds more and by the time it was done, Billy had a broad grin on his face. He started to scrabble out from under the bed. Emily grabbed his ankle, her earlier bravado gone.

"It's okay," he said. "Everything will be all right now."

He crawled out from under the sheet into a puddle of fresh blood. A hand reached down to help him up.

"They found you then," said Billy.

"You've got yourselves some good friends here," said Thomas Locke, lifting the boy to his feet.

They were surrounded by a monstrous bestiary of creatures. Locke looked uneasy in their company, but Billy had no such qualms. He hugged a tentacle covered in blood, was playfully tickled by a giant chitinous limb and then began high-fiving various grotesque appendages.

"Okay, you can finish with the reunions later," said Locke. "Right now we've got to find a way of dealing with Vincent Drysdale."

"This is bigger than just him," explained Billy. "The whole world's gone mental and… and did you find my Mum? Is she okay? She saved us, you know? She saved me and Emily."

The girl in question edged her way out from under the bed and eyed the monsters suspiciously.

Locke went pale.

"I shouldn't have come."

"What?"

"You have to run. Both of you."

"But—"

"NOW!"

Locke groaned and doubled over, clutching his stomach. Emily tried to help, but Billy took her arm and pulled her away.

The monsters chittered confusion.

"Kill me!" Locke told them. "Quickly!"

Razor-sharp claws rose to strike him down, but it was too late. Silver threads were already winding out from between his fingers.

Vincent and Veronica looked from the balcony of his apartment across the town. Columns of smoke rose like bars of a cage. The burgeoning sunset silhouetted rooftops, church spires and a landlocked battleship. Another volley of sixteen-inch shells arced across the sky. A series of crimson flashes appeared along the horizon.

"Do you feel bad that this is all your fault?" asked Veronica.

"I don't know if it's luck or fate or the simple consequence of the decisions we make," replied Vincent, "but once we find ourselves burdened with a role in life, we often have little choice but to play that role through till the end. I am an agent of change. For better or worse, what you see out there is the result of what I do."

They shared a silence that slowly spread across the town. The distant cannon fell quiet. The sound of fighting in the streets faded away to nothing. Only the whisper of the wind remained.

"Then what am I, Vincent?" asked Veronica. "What role do I have to play in this?"

He turned and hugged her. "You're my wife, always. Nothing more, nothing less."

A limousine pulled up in the street below. Joshua Dunne climbed out. He looked up at his teacher.

"I have to go," said Vincent.

He kissed his wife and walked to the front door. The oven and dishwasher rolled clear of the exit and let him head down the stairs. Veronica followed.

"It's about time we talked," said Vincent, arriving outside.

"The Ties that Bind has Emily," replied Joshua.

The boy climbed back into the car. He left the door open.

Veronica started to speak. "Did he say—?"

Vincent pressed a finger to her lips.

"I can't leave you like this," he whispered.

She caught his hand as he reached for the tiara.

"No..."

"Listen to me," he said. "My fate is sealed, but you can still change things and as I much as I love this side of you, this happy and hopeful you, it's not enough. If you're going to save Emily, you need to be everything you can be."

She shook her head. "I don't want to be that Veronica again."

"She wasn't so bad."

"She killed you!"

"She also destroyed the shadow within the shadow. If anyone can defeat the Ties that Bind—"

"But I only beat Lafarge with your help."

"Veronica, I will always be there for you, whatever happens, but for now, you need to think of Emily. You saved her before, you can do it again."

Veronica nodded stiffly.

"I love you," she said.

"Hold that thought."

She closed her eyes and Vincent removed the Prism. When she opened her eyes again, she saw a thousand limousines driving away – disparate points of view that slowly resolved into one before the car vanished around a bend.

Veronica threw back her head and screamed.

The scars of the brief war were vivid on the streets; pavements ripped asunder, trees up-rooted and over-turned cars burning outside half-demolished houses. Believers lay dead and dying in their own fluids.

Through this devastation trailed a man supported by a boy. They were followed by three creatures whose nightmarish character would have been more fearsome were any of them larger than a spaniel.

"Are you sure this is the way?" asked Billy. His cheeks were damp with tears.

"Yes," said Locke.

He wanted to console the boy, but was more concerned by the strands of flesh trailing from his stomach.

"Emily's mum is dead too," said Billy. His voice kept cracking into falsetto. "And her dad. They weren't her real parents, but you know, they were the ones who counted." Locke remembered enjoying ice cream at the seaside with Irene and Derek Wilson, but he no longer remembered how they'd got there. "I don't know what's happened to my dad. He's probably dead too. Just like my friends." Locke tried to forget the sight of the monsters getting torn apart by the flailing lines of silver thread. Billy choked back a sob. "Why did you bring that thing with you? Why didn't you come sooner?"

"Answers won't bring them back," muttered Locke.

"But I just want to understand!" said Billy. "Why did this

happen?"

"Because I fell in love with a girl."

"That doesn't make sense."

"No, it doesn't."

Billy shook his head, frustrated by his companion's replies.

"So what about Emily?" he asked. "What's that thing going to do with her?"

"I guess it'll try to force Drysdale into honouring their deal. He promised it a place amongst the gods."

They trudged on without words for a while. Billy was careful to avoid the bodies littering the street, while Locke did his best to ease the boy's burden by limping along, even though he could no longer feel his right foot. The three monsters that were left kept sniffing at the line of pink and grey feeding out from Locke's shoe.

Ahead lay a junction washed orange by the setting sun. A house on the corner had been reduced to a mound of bricks by shell fire. A figure climbed the rubble to stand at the summit with hands on hips.

As they drew close, Veronica's voice rang loud and clear through the evening air.

"Where the bloody hell have you been?"

"The Ties that Bind has Emily," replied Locke.

"I know." She glanced at the red-stained hand he held to his stomach. "Did you know you're—?"

"Unravelling? Yes. It's quite a thing seeing all that excess fat around your waist turn to spaghetti, not so much fun when your intestines start to follow."

"Then we shouldn't hang around here chatting. You're going to find a way to stop all this I presume?"

He chose not to dignify that question with a response. Veronica descended the bricks and put Locke's free arm around her shoulders, taking the weight from Billy.

"I'll go scout ahead," said the boy, running off with the three monsters scampering at his heels like eldritch puppies.

"Why is he wearing a dress?" asked Veronica.

"Apparently it was a disguise," replied Locke. "Though I can't say I know why he has teaspoons shoved down his socks."

"I think that might be Vincent's fault."

Locke looked over at her. She kept her eyes on the road ahead.

"When he came back," she explained, "he started doing private tutoring. Each of his pupils had to choose a project; roadworks, direct mail, toasters. Billy chose spoons—"

"And caught a bad case of religion," said Locke, nodding. "I met Billy's god not so long ago. His name was Arbuthnot Gavenny."

"Exactly where have you been, Thomas?"

"In a place where the Umivatoré is a machine and Emily is a Conjunction that pulls realities together. It's where Vincent makes his gods."

Veronica remained quiet.

"I saw you with him," said Locke, "before I died."

Still she said nothing.

"I suppose you know the Ties that Bind brought him back."

Veronica lowered her head. "I guessed as much. I think he tricked it into letting him go."

"Wish I'd thought of that."

She looked down at his wounded stomach.

"Is it still…?"

"No. I served my purpose and now…"

"You've been left to unravel."

"Yes."

"Then we'll find a way to fix that after we've fixed Vincent's mess."

Billy ran up to them.

"People ahead," he reported. "Lots of people."

"Isn't Grenadine Park just up there?" asked Veronica.

Billy nodded.

"We need a vantage point," said Locke.

Minutes later, they were climbing a fire escape running up the rear of a hotel. Locke was struggling badly now. One jacket sleeve was flapping loose and two fingers were gone from his right hand. Veronica grimly noted the trail he left; a sickly thread running down the flights of steel steps and across the delivery yard below. She also noted the piebald cat sitting motionless on one of the bins by the yard gates.

At least Locke was lighter now. Veronica hauled him onto

the roof with unnerving ease. The top of the hotel was flat and dotted with tall brick chimneys and white plastic skylights. Aerials covered a shed-like prominence harbouring a door to the interior.

Billy was already at the far side, desperately beckoning them over.

"Look! Look what it's done to them!"

As Veronica and Thomas approached, the expanse of Grenadine Park opened out before them. It was filled with people, a hundred thousand or more, their only noise an ill murmur. Veronica spotted Joshua Dunne's limousine parked by the bandstand. Joshua himself was nearby, standing with the other children at the edge of a wide clearing. Vincent Drysdale stood alone at its centre. He appeared relaxed. His hands were resting behind his back. Veronica fancied she could almost see him smiling.

Billy didn't care about any of this. He was pointing to a black mass approaching from the west. Its silhouette was a nightmare of spikes, bilious excretions and writhing tentacles that towered over the crowd frantically clearing a path.

"I thought it'd just killed them."

The surviving monsters cowered by Billy's legs, equally horrified by the fate of their brethren.

The Ties that Bind stopped before Vincent Drysdale and spoke in a chorus of buzzing, hissing, clicking voices.

"Now-is-the-time… for-restitution."

A tentacle rose high in the air. Held fast within its coils was a pale-faced Emily Wilson.

"Give-me… my-place… amongst-the-gods."

"No," said Vincent Drysdale.

Disbelieving gasps went up from the crowd. The children shouted protest – this wasn't what they'd agreed.

"She-will-die," hissed the undead leviathan. "Your-gods-will-perish."

"So be it," said Vincent.

Joshua Dunne ran forward to remonstrate with his teacher. Others followed. Vincent ignored them. He remained curiously serene.

"Your-clients… do-not-seem-happy… with-your-response."

"They have no say in the matter. You will not become a god of this world, of that I can promise you."

He folded his arms.

The laughter that followed was more foul and inhuman than Locke had experienced in the cave beneath the cliffs. It echoed across Grenadine Park and through the streets of the town beyond and chilled the hearts of all those who heard it. When the awful sound subsided, it left behind a molten rumble that shook the leaves on the trees and set glass vibrating in windows.

"Betrayer... trickster... fool. It-is-you... who-has-no-say... in-this-matter."

Silver threads lashed themselves around Vincent Drysdale. Locke felt Veronica tense beside him. Her husband struggled for a few seconds before realising there was no point. He couldn't break free.

The spiked tip of a giant, chitinous limb descended toward him.

Veronica watched without flinching as the Ties that Bind slowly cut down into Vincent's chest, piercing breastbone, heart and lungs, before breaking open his back to let blood sluice down onto the ground.

The threads then pulled taut, slicing the rest of his body apart. Only the head was left intact. This was laced with wire and lifted by a slick black tentacle to survey the terrified children ranged about the clearing.

"No-more-negotiation," said the Ties that Bind with Vincent Drysdale's voice. "Accept-my-terms... or-cease-to-be."

The tentacle coiled around Emily squeezed until her face turned purple and her eyes began to bulge in their sockets.

"Stop!" cried Luke. "Please, stop."

"We'll do it," said Joshua. "Just... stop. I'll make the call."

He pulled out a mobile phone.

The tentacle relaxed. Emily gasped for air.

"But they can't...," breathed Veronica, shaking her head in disbelief.

Billy stared up at her with wide eyes and a trembling lip.

"As long as Emily lives...," muttered Locke.

"Find another way," said Veronica.

"I… I don't know if there is another way."

"I saw that cat round here," she said, stalking back across the rooftop. "It must be able to do something. Make a space shuttle crash into that monstrosity or cause it to spontaneously combust or… or something!"

Near the bandstand was a manhole leading down to the sewer. Vines of the Umivatoré pushed the cover aside and rose up from the depths. The Ties that Bind sent silver threads snaking over to meet them.

In a parallel reality, the wired together remains of Johan Helmich Roman's Flute Concerto in G-Major climbed into one of the Umivatoré's great pipes. Ranks of dreams and memories looked on in silence.

Veronica could see no sign of Fiddlesticks in the hotel yard.

"Thomas!" she shouted. "What are we going to do?"

"I don't know…"

The tips of Umivatoré's vines split open to accept the silver threads.

Billy tugged at Locke's trousers. His cheeks were so wet with tears, Locke couldn't tell if the boy was still crying or not.

"Can I do something?" asked Billy. "If I can help you stop this, please, let me. I know I'm just a kid, but look, my monsters will help too and it can be anything… anything."

"We're almost out of time," said Veronica. "If that thing becomes a god…"

Locke stared at the distant figure of Emily, her tiny frame barely visible within the grasp of the Ties that Bind.

"She once told me that I could find anything," he whispered to himself.

The Umivatoré's great pipe fed the Ties that Bind as a stream of black liquid into a nexus between two realities. Technicians prepared to bind it to spiking thoughts and ideals, but something went wrong. The stream split into thousands of wayward strands. Panicked workers rushed to control panels in an attempt to correct the situation, but they were unable to prevent raging torrents bursting out of the target bubble and then slicing in those around them.

Billy screamed. He sank to the floor, hands clasping the

sides of his head.

"What's wrong?" said Veronica, hurrying to his side.

"I… I can feel it in my head!" screamed Billy.

Across Grenadine Park people fell, crying out and falling to their knees just as Billy had done. Veronica looked desperately at Locke.

He caught her eye for only a moment and then lowered his head.

"And you once told me that nightmares never really go away."

With the remaining fingers on his left hand, he reached into his jacket pocket.

"Thomas?"

"I think there was someone who came before me. They escaped and… maybe they're still out there. Maybe they can help if… if I've got this wrong."

From his pocket, he pulled out a pen and a scrap of notepaper that had, once upon a time, been a fragment of broken crystal – a crystal grown from a little girl's dream.

Billy convulsed violently. Veronica held him tight, trying to stifle his pain, but she doubted he even knew she was there.

"It's binding the spoons," whimpered Billy, "all of the spoons."

She glared again at Locke.

"For Christ's sake, stop gibbering and talk some sense!"

"J. H. Ward," he replied. "Remember the name."

She gritted her teeth, angry and frustrated that she could do nothing to help Billy while Locke talked in riddles. She was a heartbeat away from screaming at the detective when she saw the words he awkwardly wrote with the pen on that scrap of paper.

When he was done, their eyes met.

"J. H. Ward," she said. "Right."

Locke smiled and turned to go.

Veronica held out a hand. He hesitated.

"After everything I've done," she said, "it should be me doing this."

Locke shook his head.

"It always had to be me."

He let go of the piece of paper and began limping painfully toward the access door. The scrap danced across the rooftop in front of him, keeping just ahead of his hobbling gait. Finally, a gust of wind swept it up and affixed it to the door just as Locke reached for the handle.

He looked back at Veronica one last time.

She held Billy tighter and could only whisper Locke's name in reply.

"Thomas…"

His smile was weak. He turned away before it faltered further. Then he opened the door to The Office of Lost and Found. In the darkness that was revealed, Veronica could see something darker still – a figure in hat and coat that listened as Locke spoke.

The conversation ended with a second scrap of paper blowing across the rooftop. Veronica glimpsed the single word written upon it before it reached Locke's hand.

'Deal.'

Lafarge swept across the rooftop. In his wake lay an open door and no trace of Thomas Locke.

Veronica eased herself free of Billy and jumped to her feet. She stepped in front of Lafarge.

"I don't know what Thomas asked you to lose, but—"

Lafarge was already past her. She spun around. He crossed the park below, advancing on the Ties that Bind.

"The-underling-returns," declared the Ties that Bind, emitting another excruciating burst of laughter. "Are-you-here… to-lose-me?"

Lafarge stopped at the edge of the clearing. The god children writhing on the ground only screamed louder in his presence.

Veronica realised a piece of paper was now clenched within her white-knuckled fist.

"By-all-means… do-your-worst… but-know-that… all-these-minds… are-bound… to-me-now. If-I-am-lost… all-of-them… come-with-me."

So Lafarge did nothing.

The Ties that Bind laughed again.

Veronica uncrumpled the piece of paper in her hand.

'Remember the key,' it said.

She frowned.

Billy groaned again. The monsters were trying to comfort him, but their spindly limbs and razor-sharp mandibles were unsuited to the task.

"What fucking key?" asked Veronica.

"Get it out of my head!" pleaded Billy.

"Ssh, Billy. I'm thinking."

Vincent devised his projects to get the children obsessed by ideas – spoons, roadworks, direct mail. The Umivatoré took their obsession and bound it to desperate memories, giving rise to the gods. But now the Ties that Bind sought to infect everything—

Veronica suddenly remembered Locke's advice when she complained about Vincent invading her memories. He suggested she think of something else. "Block him out. Whistle some catchy advertising jingle over and over."

"Veronica! Help me!"

"I am, Billy, I am."

She started whistling, but the tune she whistled was not an advertising jingle. It was a tune whose name never passed the tip of a tongue, that she'd first heard whilst standing in the gloom beneath a railway arch – a tune that was also a key.

"That's not helping," spluttered Billy.

Veronica knelt down beside him.

"Hear the music, Billy." She grabbed the spoons stuffed down his socks. "Get these drumming. Work your magic."

"I can't! Everything… everything's bound in wire."

She pushed the spoons into his hand.

"Just listen, Billy."

She began whistling again and tapping a beat out against his fingers. The spoons began to chink together. Softly at first, then more loudly.

Billy sniffed back his tears and managed to hum a little. His hum was joined by a buzz from the monster beside him, then a strident beat as one of the others ripped an aerial down and began striking it against a chimney pot. The third jumped onto a skylight and began tap-dancing on the plastic canopy.

In a single bubble within the Umivatoré's god machine, a golden ring bound by toxic black lines began to crack.

The spoons were playing themselves now. Billy was humming more strongly. Veronica thought she caught traces of her whistles being sung back to her by the rising wind.

"I-hear-you," growled the Ties that Bind.

The mass of stitched together monstrosities reared up against the dying sunset.

"All… must… *believe*!"

The roar was echoed by the crowd; by the rustling leaves of trees; by car engines and radios and television sets. The chimney stacks atop the hotel howled in accord and twisted toward Veronica and Billy, smoke belching up from their depths. The aerial wielded by one of the monsters jammed itself against brickwork, bent and then snapped straight, flicking the monster off the side of the building. The other aerials detached themselves and flew like javelins at the source of the music.

Veronica picked up Billy and dived clear.

Trees shed leaves that joined a great, dark cloud of letters, litter and polythene bags that swelled against the heavens before swarming down to the hotel.

Veronica reached the access door first. The note stuck to the wood now read 'Pray for Death'. She pulled Billy inside and then pulled the door shut. Except it wouldn't close – a scuttling monster was caught in the gap.

The murderous cloud roared across rooftop.

Veronica hauled the creature through by its antennae, then yanked the door closed in time for the rush of leaves, litter and paper to hammer against the outside.

"Keep singing!" shouted Veronica as she followed Billy down a flight of stairs.

"But what good will that do?" asked Billy.

"It'll keep your mind off going insane."

He resumed his humming.

They burst onto a corridor of two-tone beige walls and numbered doors. Veronica whistled as she looked left and right. Both directions looked exactly the same and both began to warp disconcertingly. The walls twisted, the lights winked out one by one, and the carpet became a rippling tide rushing to greet them.

Vincent's muffled voice rang out from a hundred hotel televisions.

"You-cannot-escape…"

Veronica barged into the room in front of them. A mini-kettle hurled itself at her as she entered. She swatted it aside.

Billy and the remaining two monsters scurried in after her.

"You-must-believe…"

The television was on. Vincent's face was smiling out from the screen.

Billy cried out. A trouser press had his arm. The monsters leapt to his defence, attacking the press with razor-sharp teeth.

"Pray-for-me…"

Veronica continued to whistle instead. The carpet bucked up and down and tried to throw her off balance. The curtains tried to strangle her. Pots of UHT milk exploded in her face, but she continued to whistle.

Victorious over the trouser press, Billy began singing aloud. He set teaspoons rapping against the taps in the bathroom and towels intent on smothering him began to dance instead. The metal coat hangers in the wardrobe clanged together. The phone by the bed began playing out their melody with its touch-tone dial.

Vincent's face scowled on the television set.

"You-shall—"

The picture dissolved into snow. The speakers joined in with the music. Veronica turned up the volume.

"You-shall-cease!"

This command did not come from a television set. It came from a severed head held up outside the window by an oozing tentacle.

"Down, Billy!" cried Veronica.

A ten-foot spike of jagged bone lanced through the window. After it withdrew, a thick black tongue bristling with hair invaded the room, sweeping across broken glass, searching for survivors.

It found Veronica waiting with a shard of broken mirror.

She stabbed down into the writhing tongue and then jumped back as it split open and bled thousands of spiders.

"Jesus!"

"It's made of dead things," said Billy, "you can't hurt it!"

The tongue retreated, but the spiders rushed forward.

Veronica and Billy fell back to the corridor, one of the monsters remaining behind to snaffle up the swarming arachnids.

"This way," said Veronica.

It was hard to run and sing, but the music kept the twisting walls and feral carpet at bay and brought to life lights extinguished by the Ties that Bind.

A mighty crash sounded at their backs.

"Keep going!" ordered Veronica.

A giant claw had sliced through the building behind them. The far end of the corridor slipped away, creating a billowing cloud that spat out spiralling eddies of burst as letters and leaves homed in on Billy and Veronica.

She grabbed a fire extinguisher from the wall, spun round and blasted a jet of foam back down the corridor.

Billy slowed, unsure whether he should wait for her. The lights flickered on ahead. A crowd of believers rushed toward him.

"Veronica!"

The nearest lunged for him. Billy dodged clear and swung a fist that missed completely. A second hand grabbed his arm, but was promptly bitten off by the last of the boy's monsters.

"Join us," urged a woman, her face tense with pain.

"Stop your singing."

"Believe in the Ties that Bind."

"Veronica!" cried Billy.

The butt of the fire extinguisher broke the nose of one believer and then smacked another across the jaw.

"In here," instructed Veronica, holding open the hatch of a linen chute.

Billy jumped in without thinking, then found himself plummeting straight down a sixty centimetre square shaft. He kicked his shoes against the steel sides and managed to slow his descent.

A clatter from above suggested Veronica was following. He hoped she'd figured out how to brake her fall.

Voices echoed after them.

"They won't escape."

"The others will get them."

"What was that song they were singing?"

"I don't know, but I'm sure I've heard it somewhere

before…"

The chute curved at the bottom and Billy slid out into an expanse of white. Before he could make sense of the sight, it engulfed him, smothering his limbs with coarse linen.

He tried to punch and claw his way free, but he was bound too tight. The sheets pulled him clear of the chute and let him fall heavily to the ground.

A second thud came from the chute behind him.

Billy tried to sing, but fabric filled his mouth. He heard Veronica gasp alarm, then the sheets dragged him away across the floor.

I should have believed in knives, Billy told himself.

The bedclothes pulled taut and lifted him clear off the ground. Billy's confusion turned to panic – he was being pushed through a hole. The light filtering through the sheet dimmed. He kicked out and struck the inside of a steel drum.

A click sounded by his ear.

Hissing filled his ears.

He lay still for a moment, then felt damp touching his back. Hot water was sluicing in around him.

"Mmmf!" he shouted through his gag.

He strained at the sheets, but they held him fast. The water quickly rose up to his shoulders. His mouth would be covered in moments.

He imagined the water rushing into his lungs.

He imagined not being able to breathe.

He imagined sitting in a library opposite a short and balding man with a tidy moustache and a suit made of spoons. Silver threads pierced the man's skin, tying him to the books and bookcases around them.

"I'm sorry, Billy," he said. "I didn't mean for things to work out like this."

A violent juddering brought Billy back to reality. There was a bang and then the water began ebbing away.

Billy was hauled from the washing machine. His remaining monster tore away the bedclothes with its razor-sharp teeth.

"Handy little beggar," said Veronica, grudgingly tickling the creature's antennae, "shame it leaks mucus everywhere."

Billy got to his feet. The laundry room was littered with

shredded fabric. Washing machines and dryers were huddled against the far wall, beaten back by Veronica and the monster. Their electric motors growled at the humans, who hurried to the door.

On her way out, Veronica hit the fire alarm.

Water showered down from sprinklers as they ran along another corridor. The undulating wail of the alarm slowly formed itself into notes, echoing the tune coming from Veronica's lips.

"He wants you to know he's sorry," said Billy.

"Who?" asked Veronica.

"The… the god inside my head. He didn't know this would happen. He… he only wanted to live forever."

"Well, tell him from me, he's an idiot."

They reached the hotel foyer as a great roar shook the earth. Windows showed the black mass of the Ties that Bind blocking the road.

"Stop-the-music!"

It flung tentacles at the hotel façade. Cracks appeared across the ceiling. Plaster fell to the floor.

"We can't go out that way," said Veronica.

Ties that Bind lashed out again and the marble pillars lining the foyer began to crumble.

"We don't have much choice!" cried Billy.

He ran for the front doors. Veronica followed. The ceiling collapsed behind her; hundreds of tonnes of masonry crashing to the richly carpeted floor.

She made it out just as the front of the hotel disintegrated. A great cloud of choking dust swept over her. She staggered into the road, but could barely see. She could hear the squelching, rasping bulk of the Ties that Bind moving close by and this stopped her calling out to Billy. Another crash silenced the last cries of the hotel fire alarm.

But the music played on.

Hazy figures appeared ahead of Veronica. They were moving haphazardly, back and forth. Drawing closer, features became clear; happy smiles and sparkling eyes. These people were dancing and they were singing Veronica's song.

"Kill-the-music!" bellowed the Ties that Bind.

The dancers continued their merriment, oblivious to a line

of glowing orbs emerging from the fog. The lampposts swung for the revellers, clubbing some to the ground, taking others by the neck and squeezing silence from their lips.

Believers with cushions taped over their ears joined the fray. They met little resistance from those under the sway of the song. Fists bloodied smiles and blackened eyes. A man lay curled up in the gutter. He kept whistling even while a woman kicked at his head.

Veronica grabbed the woman by the arm.

"Sharon!"

She stared blankly at Veronica. Dust covered her skin and clothes; a grey ghost amongst many more. Watches still covered her arms. Rubber bands stretched around her head drew white lines across her face.

"You must believe, Veronica," said Sharon. "All must believe or it will bring us all pain."

The tentacle bearing Vincent's head rose high against a sky now black with night. His dead eyes surveyed the bodies strewn across the road before fixing on Veronica.

She wanted to shake sense into her friend, but had to run.

Monstrous hoofs pounded after her.

Veronica barged through another group of dancers, who were duly swept aside by tentacles and sliced apart by bristling talons.

The music was growing fainter.

A lamppost swung for Veronica. She ducked beneath it.

Spiked railings launched themselves toward her. She dropped to the ground and they shot overhead.

Veronica scrambled to her feet and clear of a mighty claw crashing into the road.

"Lafarge!" she cried. "Can't you do something?"

If Lafarge heard, he did not respond.

To her left, houses contorted into terrifying faces daring her to seek refuge inside. To her right, Grenadine Park bristled with grasping trees and believers eager to rip her limb from limb. Ahead, the street cracked apart in a lightning scar that rushed toward Veronica, spitting out striped barriers and traffic cones as it went.

The roadworks were upon her before she had a chance to turn.

Tarmac fell away beneath her feet. She threw out her arms, trying to grab hold of something, anything, but her fingers found only loose soil that tumbled down after her. She hit a water pipe, rolled off and continued to fall.

Veronica finally came to a rest some fifty feet down.

She did not feel at rest. She felt bruised, exhausted and afraid. Vincent's head appeared against the thin sliver of night sky high above.

"Be-silent-now," it said.

No more music could be heard.

Veronica started whistling again.

She whistled as the crack began to close; as dirt rained down on top of her; as the world above was steadily lost from view. In the moment before soil covered her mouth and face and everything became finally black, she heard distant church bells begin to chime.

Then nothing.

Nothing could be seen.

Nothing could be heard.

All Veronica could feel was the earth trying to invade her mouth, nose and ears while its weight squeezed the life from her body, yet her only thought was that the root cause of this catastrophe was a broken tumble dryer.

The dirt beneath her suddenly vanished. She fell again, briefly, landing in shallow water. She cracked her head against concrete, but remained conscious.

After brushing soil from her face, Veronica stared up at a ragged hole in the brick ceiling of a sewer main illuminated by a pale green glow from the Umivatoré's fluorescent vegetation.

She climbed to her feet and gingerly touched the back of her head. Blood matted hair stuck to her fingers.

A loud pop made her jump. She looked around in panic.

Another pop.

This time she saw the cause. A nodule on a vine had burst. White puss oozed out along with lengths of shrivelled silver thread.

More popping. All across the Umivatoré, nodules were breaking open. In a parallel reality, bubbles were bursting in accord.

Veronica splashed through the sewage to reach the nearest access shaft. She heaved aside a manhole cover and music rushed down to greet her. This was not a tune carried by a woman and boy singing to the beat of stainless steel teaspoons. This was a symphony of woodwind and brass, piano and percussion. It danced on a wind that carried it across the rooftops and set radios and television playing. Cats wailed, dogs barked and birds chirped. Litter pirouetted in the gutter. Telegraph cables plucked out a bass-line. Burglar alarms sang descant. Veronica could feel it as a tingle that ran along her skin and raised the hairs on the back of her neck.

She climbed out onto an empty street. Grenadine Park lay ahead. She lifted a hand to her mouth. Towering above the railings and the trees, challenging the dominion of the starry sky, the dancer's gate had returned and was opening once again.

Veronica moved dumbly toward it, slowly at first, then quicker, her pace progressing from a walk to a jog to a run. She passed lifeless roadworks. Disfigured lamp-posts stood motionless. Dust blanketed the scene like a fall of snow.

She raced through the park gates and past thousands of people laughing and quick-stepping through waltzes, tangos and dragon fandangos. A riotous procession streamed out from the immense doorway. Instruments of all shapes and sizes were being played. Ribbons twirled in dizzying shapes around them and coloured lanterns on sticks drew retina-burn lines through the air.

Veronica half-ran, half-skipped alongside those marching, glancing at faces, recognising none and moving on. She hurried past Sharon, now doing the jive with Albert Button from the Drum and Cockle pub. Inspector Forth tap-danced with Kayla through a pond. Joshua Dunne giddily swung a spaniel-sized monster round and round by its antennae, splattering all those nearby with mucus. No one seemed to mind.

The parade marched toward the Ties that Bind. It appeared beaten, the mass of stitched together monsters hunched unmoving in the road. The revellers kept their distance as they slowly surrounded it, their music unceasing, irresistible.

And finally, Veronica saw him.

Darren Wynne stood at the head of the crowd, playing the

violin with eyes closed and a look of furious concentration on his face.

She rushed over and then pulled up short, unsure of quite what to do next.

For a few seconds, she stood there, unable to take another step.

Darren's eyes flicked open and he looked at her. Veronica felt it an age before a wide grin spread across his face. He gave her an ostentatious wink. She started to speak, but he stopped playing and raised a finger to stop her. There was business to attend to first.

Raising his violin and bow in the air, Darren Wynne shouted to the Ties that Bind.

"There's no one left to believe in you! You're a god no longer! Be gone from here!"

A fearsome rumbling came in reply.

"Not-while-he-believes…," it said.

Veronica looked over at the beast. She ventured forward. Its tentacles and claws were shielding something from them. A nauseating certainty in the pit of her stomach told her it now held Billy as well as Emily.

"I-only-need-you," whispered the Ties that Bind.

Billy could hear nothing else. Enveloping folds of fat blocked out the music. When he tried to hum, a tentacle tightened around his throat. When he tried to recite the tune in his mind, sharpened spines dug beneath his fingernails.

"I-am-in… your-head. I-know-what… you-are-thinking. I-only-need-you… to-think-of-me."

"No," spat Billy.

He braced himself for the pain that would follow.

"I-am-in… your-head. I-can-change… your-mind."

Threads wound through his thoughts and began pulling them against his will. Billy gritted his teeth and forced out a reply while he still could.

"Arbuthnot Gavenny wants you to know something."

"Who-is… Arbuthnot-Gavenny?" Even as the question was asked, Billy felt the threads searching his memories for the answer.

"He's the last of the gods," gasped Billy. "And he doesn't want to live forever any more."

In a memory of a library from long ago, a short and balding man with a tidy moustache ripped a spoon from his suit and plunged the handle into his heart.

In a bubble holding two realities, a golden ring riddled with black lines shattered - the last trinity held within the Umivatoré was broken.

The Ties that Bind threw back its many heads, stretched claws and tentacles wide and loosed an enraged scream at the sky.

"Get the children!" shouted Veronica.

She raced forward, weaving between spikes and claws to reach the tentacle that held Emily.

Others were reluctant to follow until Darren Wynne sprinted after her. Then the crowd broke forward.

The Ties that Bind roared anger and confusion as hundreds of people pinned down its limbs.

"Cut the wires!" cried Darren Wynne.

He whipped out a pen knife. The tentacle holding Emily writhed and fought until he severed the silver thread controlling it. Veronica pulled the little girl clear as others across the way freed Billy.

They raced back to the park as musicians beat down the patchwork monster with harps, trombones and timpani drums.

But the Ties that Bind could not be restrained any longer.

A chitinous limb broke loose and sent a cellist flying through the air. It sliced apart a mariachi band and then freed a tentacle that began whipping aside others who'd dared attack.

"Watch out!" shouted Darren.

He pushed Veronica and Emily aside before a claw slashed down between them. It caught his leg. He cried out. Veronica tried to reach him, but a tentacle had already snared his foot. It flung the stricken musician clear across the park.

"God-or-not… you-shall-still… worship-me!"

Music continued to play in the distance, but it was forgotten by those in the path of the beast. They tried to flee, but few escaped. The killing appendages of the Ties that Bind sliced, flayed and crushed a path of bloody entrails that were subsequently bound up in wire and added to its grotesque collective.

The starlight illuminating Veronica's desperate steps disappeared. The shadow of the Ties that Bind loomed over her. The bandstand was just ahead. She urged Emily on, but did not follow.

Veronica turned to face the seething mass of teeth and claws. Her dead husband's head wore a mocking grin pulled taut by silver thread.

"No one believes in you any more," said Veronica.

"I-do-not… need-your-faith."

Her lip curled into a snarl.

"Wrong. Without it… you're lost."

The Ties that Bind looked up.

For all this time, the figure in the hat and coat by the bandstand had not moved an inch. But now Lafarge stepped forward and as he did so, blackness came with him.

Few words were spoken in the hours of night that followed.

When Norman found his son, he asked two simple questions.

"Why are you wearing a dress? Where's your mother?"

Billy answered and nothing more was said. Norman stared into space while his son hugged him tight.

"What's it like on the other side?" Emily asked Albert Button.

The old man gazed at the black void contained by the great gate. He thought about his answer for a long time.

"It's different," he said at last.

"Will I like it there?"

"I don't know."

"I'm not sure if I want to go."

"You saw the note Veronica's friend left," replied Albert Button. "He said you'll be safe there."

"I suppose," said Emily. She brightened. "And maybe I could find my real parents through there too."

Veronica ran across the park in reply to Sharon's shouts. She found her friend kneeling beside a doctor tending Darren Wynne's wounds.

"I thought he was a goner for a moment there," said the

medic.

"What happened?" asked Darren, blinking around at his surroundings. He caught sight of a monstrous carcass over by the bandstand. "Actually, no, don't tell me. I get the feeling I'll be quite happy enough remaining blissfully ignorant."

"Are you okay?" asked Veronica.

"Oh, you know, mustn't grumble," he said with a grin.

"His leg's a mess," said the doctor. "A few broken ribs. Contusions galore. If the hospital's still standing, I'll recommend he's put in the top half of the waiting list. Now, if you don't mind, I've got other casualties to attend to."

He headed off. Sharon studied his departing ass before patting Veronica on the shoulder and nodding at Darren.

"Don't do anything I wouldn't do," she said, then hurried off after the medic.

"I found your Stradivarius," said Veronica.

She held up a smashed violin. The remaining pieces of wood were held together by tenuous strands of catgut.

"Nothing a bit of masking tape won't fix," said Darren.

He grinned again. Veronica realised she was smiling too and looked away. He raised a hand and touched her cheek.

"I thought I'd never see you again."

"We shared one kiss."

"Sometimes that's all it takes."

"But you have to go back."

"I'm not going anywhere without you."

"Do you realise how corny you sound?"

"Do you have to be so cynical?"

"Jazz trumpet eyebrow, remember?"

"I never knew you liked jazz."

Veronica took his hand and removed it from her cheek. She stood up.

"What's the matter?" he asked.

"Did you think I wouldn't realise, Vincent? Did you think I'd forget about your life insurance?" she asked. He held her gaze without blinking. "The real Darren Wynne once tried to change the tune playing in my head, but now I realise that was never my tune. The jazz drum and bass and trumpet was never me, it was you. When we were together and when we were apart, it was always your music driving my choices."

"Veronica, I only ever wanted the best for you."

"And you were right when you said I was your wife - nothing more and nothing less."

He held out his hand. "Then come back to me."

Veronica shook her head.

"But you were wrong about always. Your jazz band has stopped playing, Vincent. Whatever you say or do, it doesn't matter to me any more."

She turned and walked away.

"Where are you going?" he called after her.

"To find my own tune."

She left his pleading behind. She reached the road and then kept walking until she found an abandoned car with keys in the ignition.

It took several hours of driving to get there. She parked outside the Brooker's cottage and checked the windows. It was dark inside. The door was locked.

Veronica walked over to the cliff-side and then sat with her legs dangling over the edge. The breeze was cold. She hugged herself to keep warm and stared out to sea, waiting for the sun to rise.

When it finally crested the horizon, she became aware of him standing a short distance away along the cliff.

"I thought you might have given him this," she said, gesturing to the view.

Lafarge said nothing, but a scrap of paper drifted up to her hand. She picked it up and read the message.

'The Office of Lost and Found needs a new partner.'

Veronica almost laughed.

Then she almost cried.

Taking a deep breath, she forced out a measured reply.

"If I was to accept, you know things would have to be different."

She glanced across at him. He remained an impassive figure, coat fluttering gently without noise.

"I couldn't be like Thomas," she said. "I'd want to know what was going on. You'd have to give me answers."

The black hat tilted a fraction.

"You could start by telling me what you gave Thomas."

The wind picked up. The grass on the cliff-side began rippling one way and then another. A sudden gust pushed at Veronica's back, prompting her to scramble away from the edge.

Lafarge walked away along the road back to the village. Veronica shouted after him.

"Then I guess that means—"

A second scrap of paper blew across from the fields. She snatched it from the air.

'I gave him what he wanted,' it read.

She looked around at the lonely cottage and then out at a wild sea painted orange by the rising sun.

"And what about me?" she called. "When I asked you to lose Vincent that time, what did you give me in return?"

The wind rose to a gale, whipping up dust from the road. Veronica had to shield her eyes with an arm. She staggered backwards before the wind finally dropped.

Lafarge was lost from view.

A third scrap of paper lay on the ground before her.

Veronica bent down and picked it up.

Two words scrawled in black marker pen revealed what he gave to her.

'A friend.'

Acknowledgements

Few books are created in a vacuum and this one in particular wouldn't have come into being if the writer had been left to his own devices, so there are some very specific people I need to thank. First of all, Sandra Ruttan, who cajoled me into submitting a story to Spinetingler magazine – a story that became the first chapter of this novel. Without further external prompting I completed another four stories before going off to write another book for a couple of years. That I went back to the Office of Lost and Found is credit to Lee Harris and that I finished it in good time is credit to the constant badgering of Adele Wearing. Finally, thanks to Al Guthrie for being an exceptionally helpful Scotsman, Andy Remic for reading the completed work and being unhinged enough to take a chance on first publishing it and then Adele Wearing again for liking it enough to re-publish under the Fox Spirit banner.

Appendix I: Bonus Short Story

Author's note: I wrote the following short story and posted it on my blog for Christmas 2010. It takes place at some point between the Prologue and 'The Office of Lost and Found'.

Jingle Bells

The small girl was blonde of hair and pink of coat and moments after she stormed into Santa's Grotto, the surrounding air turned a vivid purple.

The sound drew Herman Jeffers. He descended an escalator, pushing past rubber-necking shoppers, thinking he really didn't have time for this.

A crowd gathered around the grotto. The plywood construction was shaking. Fake snow fell from the roof. The queue of families previously waiting outside had retreated to a safe distance. The parents were muttering, the children crying.

"Stay back, everyone," said Herman, arriving on the scene and tripping over a bag stuffed full of 3 for 2 toiletries.

"Watch where you're going!" said the owner of the bag, a woman in an ostentatious fur coat. She began gathering up the scattered gifts. "If any of these are broken—"

"Then you might be causing a fire hazard as well as a health and safety violation," said Herman, climbing to his feet and dusting off his security guard's uniform. "They'd lock up people like you if I had my way."

"Herman!" cried a Christmas elf, staggering from the grotto. "Look what that little bitch did!"

Bright red fake fingernails pointed to bright red scratches running to a rouged cheek.

Herman laughed. "Britney, Britney, Britney, that kind of thing's got to be an occupational hazard when you're dealing with brats all day. Now let's see the brat in question and get this mess sorted out."

Just before Herman reached the door, the brat in question stepped out of the grotto with a good clump of Santa's beard gripped tightly in a pink-mittened hand.

"He couldn't even name three reindeer," said the little girl through pursed lips.

"Ah, you'll be our pocket Armageddon then."

"Taser her, Herman, before she tries biting your bollocks off," said Britney, cowering by a stall selling mobile phone face-plates and dabbing at her cheek with a tissue. Her language prompted a volley of 'tsk's from the assembled parents.

"You know I don't carry a Taser," replied Herman.

"I know you haven't got any bollocks either, it was just a figure of speech."

Herman ignored her and leant down before the troublemaker.

"Where's your mummy and daddy, little girl?"

"Abigail!" cried a voice from the escalators. "Abigail!"

The sound of her name being called sent the little girl scurrying off in the opposite direction. The crowd of shoppers parted to let her pass, intent on remaining curious bystanders instead of actually getting involved.

Herman caught the girl up within a handful of strides and grabbed her by the arm.

She duly bit him on the hand.

So he slapped her across the back of the head.

"What do you think you're doing to my daughter?" asked a man running up with shopping bags in each hand.

"Showing her some discipline," replied Herman. "Ow! Would you stop with the biting?"

"Yes, Abigail, stop biting the man," said the father. "And you let go of her. I can take care of things now."

Herman released the little girl and rubbed at the fresh teeth marks around his right thumb.

"I'm afraid it's not going to be quite as simple as that, sir. There are quite a few traumatised people back there. It'd set a bad precedent if we let this kind of thing go."

"But she's just a child. You know what children are like."

"I do, sir, I do. Wild, unruly, selfish - horrible things they are. I also know what parents are like. They let those stinking children run loose and then refuse to take any responsibility for all the damage that's caused. Lock up the children and shoot the parents, that's what I say."

Abigail's father stared at Herman and then made sure to put himself in between his daughter and the security guard.

"Okay, okay, this is my fault," he conceded. "If I have to pay damages, then just… tell me how much."

He fumbled a wallet from his coat pocket.

Britney the elf peered over his shoulder.

"That better be a platinum card I can see in there, because plastic surgery to fix scars like this costs a bleeding fortune."

"I really don't think money's going cut it," said Herman. "I think we're all going to have to pay a visit to the shopping centre manager."

"But—," began Abigail's father.

Herman averted his eyes from the protest and waved a hand toward a set of lifts until the father and daughter got the message and started moving.

"I still want someone to pay for that plastic surgery," said Britney as the lift doors closed. She was left behind; a mute figure in red and green beyond the glass.

"Your mother is going to be so angry with you when we get home," hissed the girl's father.

"Is she really though?" asked Abigail. "Or is that just another big fat lie like everything else?"

"Abigail, you do not say things like that!"

"But it's true!"

"It's not!" Her father glanced at Herman before continuing in a whisper. "I never lied to you."

"Then show me the real Father Christmas."

The lift doors opened two floors up and Herman led them out. There were few shops on this level, so the walkway was largely free of the festive chaos that reigned below.

"Father Christmas is a busy man," said the non-Christmassy father. "I can't just click my fingers and make him appear."

"Then I can't just click my fingers and believe you."

Herman laughed. "That one's way too smart for you, sir. You've got it right, little miss. This Christmas thing's all a big con. Brightly coloured lies tied up with a big ribbon, that's what it is."

"Don't listen to him, Abigail. I'll find you Father Christmas. I'll prove he exists."

Both Herman and Abigail snorted disbelief.

The door to the shopping centre manager's office loomed ahead, but then Herman took an abrupt right turn.

"You know what?" he said. "In the spirit of Christmas and

all that, I'm going to help you two out."

"You're going to let us go?"

"Oh, better than that. Much better than that."

The watch repair store was a tiny kiosk embedded in a wall near one of the exits to the centre's multi-storey car-park. The sign overhead was faded. The shutters were closed. It looked abandoned, but Sellotaped to the corrugated metal was a piece of torn paper with writing upon it.

"The Office of Lost and Found," read Abigail's father.

Herman banged a hand on the shutters.

"Thomas! Thomas, are you in there?"

There was no response for a few seconds, then the shutter lifted a few inches to reveal a line of darkness. A pair of bloodshot eyes appeared and blinked at them.

"Herman, I hoped you'd have forgotten about me by now," said the man within.

"I couldn't forget about you, Thomas. You're my raison d'etre. I spend all my days trying to think of how to get you out of my shopping centre when no one else believes you exist."

"Even I'm not sure I exist right now," said Thomas, blowing a red nose into a tissue. "But I am sure I'm infectious. You're no doubt all risking your lives talking to me."

"This man can find anything," Herman told the father and daughter. "Or so the stories go."

"Anything?" asked the father.

"Even Father Christmas?" asked the daughter.

"Even Father Christmas," confirmed Herman, smiling at Thomas.

The bright red coat, voluminous white beard and beaming smile were unmistakeable. When accompanied by nine prancing reindeer, a good dozen pine trees, countless glistening icicles and an example of just about festive symbol you could think of, it was hard to miss the fact that Christmas had arrived at the Redwood household. If you managed that feat regardless, the eight thousand, five hundred and six-two bulbs that made up this picture did their best to rectify the situation by flashing on and off all at the same time, then one after another and then, if you were perhaps blind and therefore unaware that Santa was waving a neon arm in warning when you ventured too close, hidden speakers would blare out "ho ho ho!" and begin a tinny rendition of 'We Wish you a Merry Christmas'.

Unlike the hypothetical blind man, Abigail could not flee at this point. Her father was dragging her up the path, while she tried both to resist his efforts and block her ears to the sound. This was straightforward with her left hand, which provided a bare index finger to block the ear canal, but her right hand was covered by a fluffy mitten and this admitted the terrifying promise that the singers wouldn't go until they got some figgy pudding.

Inside, the music was drowned out by extended family chattering in the living room. Mr Redwood and his daughter removed heavy coats and boots in the hallway without exchanging a word. Mrs Redwood's head appeared from a kitchen doorway and studied the arrivals.

"Hmm," she said. "I counted one grumpy sod leaving here earlier and I see two have returned. This must mean our last minute shopping trip did not go well."

After weeks of opening until 11pm, the mall closed on Christmas Eve at six o'clock. Herman's escape from that infernal place was done at speed. He loped across the emptying car-park and arrived at the bus stop in time for the number sixty-two to carry him away from the sickly lights and garish decorations. His job was bad at the best of times, but the month of December was a particular chore. At least it was almost over. One more chore to complete and then he could shut himself away at home and forget Christmas was even happening.

"It's completely unreasonable," muttered Thomas Locke. "Unreasonable and very probably impossible. Can't be done."

He shivered within the confines of the shuttered up watch repair kiosk and pulled his solitary blanket tighter around his shoulders.

A piece of note-paper fluttered up around his nose. Despite the darkness, he found the black writing plain to read. Thomas grabbed the paper, crumpled it up in a hand and tossed it over his shoulder.

"The finding isn't the problem." Every point of punctuation in his speech was marked by a laboured sniff. "Me dying is the problem. It's close too, I can feel it. I'm using the last of my strength to complain and when I'm done, dead. Gone. No more finding for anyone."

He coughed and cast a fleeting glance toward one corner of the darkened kiosk that was darker than the rest. Viewed out the corner of an eye, that darkness could be mistaken for the shape of a man dressed in a long coat.

An awkward silence was allowed to brood for a few moments.

"You should give that girl her mitten back," said Locke. "We don't need paying if we can't do the finding."

He expected another note to drift in front of his face. He waited, but none came. It took a long minute for Locke to muster the will to check the corner again. When he did, the man-shaped darkness was gone.

But the mitten remained.

"Okay, fine," said Locke, throwing off the blanket. "If returning this mitten is the last thing I do, then so be it. It's not like I was looking forward to seeing another Christmas anyway."

The presents under the Redwoods' Christmas tree were

stacked three and four parcels high. Two-dimensional trees, bells and holly patterned across the wrapping paper teased Abigail's young cousins, who were gathered around them, staring possessively at those with tags bearing their names and willing Christmas morning to arrive early.

"Can't we open one now?" asked Johnny Redwood.

"Yes, just one," agreed Millie Redwood.

"Or two," suggested Gavin Thremley, whose mother's maiden name was Redwood.

"Certainly you can open one now," said Grandmother Redwood, who could have been a Grimm's Fairy Tale woodcutting brought to life, albeit one decked out in Marks and Spencer's autumn/winter range.

Squeals of excitement came from the children as they reached for the most enticing of their promised gifts.

"But…" said Grandmother Redwood loudly, causing the cousins to freeze, "opening one present early means you don't get to open any more presents for another fifty-two years."

"What?!"

"No!"

"That's not fair!"

"Them's the rules, kids," said the matriarch, smiling. "But by all means, open one now if you wish."

None of the children did. Instead, they edged away from the stack of presents, glaring at them as if they had suddenly been doused in horse manure.

While the cousins sulked in the lounge, and aunts and uncles held adult conversation over wine in the dining room, Abigail was sitting at the table in the kitchen with arms folded. Her mother waved a box wrapped in metallic blue paper under her nose.

"Oh, come on, Abby, please. I promise you there's something really good inside."

"I told you, I don't want any presents."

"You know your grandmother makes up all that stuff about the rules? You'll still get presents tomorrow if you open this one now."

"You mean she lied? Like everyone lies about Christmas? What a surprise. I just want to go to bed now and you can come and get me on Boxing Day when it's all over."

"But we haven't had dinner yet! And I baked mince pies for later. You love mince pies."

"Not any more. You probably fill them with minced reindeer for all I know."

"Oh, Abigail!"

"Let her go, dear," said Mr Redwood from the kitchen doorway.

Abigail didn't need further prompting. She jumped from her chair and was racing up the stairs seconds later.

"Peter!" said Mrs Redwood.

"You know she'll just spoil it for everyone else if she stays down here being miserable." He faced his wife's glare. "Disagree with me, go on. You know what she's like. She can't sulk quietly in a corner—"

"If you hadn't tried dressing up as Father Christmas last year…," said Mrs Redwood, turning back to a worktop covered in baking materials.

Mr Redwood sniffed. "If you hadn't got some weird fetish about bearded men breaking into your bedroom on Christmas Eve…"

Herman suspected everyone at the church was a criminal. The only exception was his half-brother, who was simply a fool for letting all these freeloaders in through the ancient wood doors.

"They're not freeloaders, Herman," said the Reverend Michael Jeffers with a smile. "Most of them have paid a heavy price to come here. They've lost jobs, homes…"

"Then they should have been more careful," replied Herman, urging his half-brother to hurry on past the people in worn clothes lining the pews. He could tell some of them were drunk and others were high on drugs, while a few were plenty enough disturbed without the aid of artificial substances.

"You shouldn't be so quick to judge," said Michael Jeffers. "Misfortune can visit us all. We can only hope others are around to pick us up when we fall."

"Every man should be able to stand on his own two feet."

"And if life were to chop off your feet, what then?"

"I'd sue. Can we get this over with?"

Michael Jeffers laughed and led the way out of a back door, across a dark patch of muddy ground and into a Portakabin serving as a makeshift office while the never-ending renovation of the rear of the church continued.

"I think you spend too much time in that shopping centre," said the Reverend, switching on a small, portable heater. "It's soured you to the whole idea of Christmas. You do know it's not really about tinsel and lights and buying as many garish presents as your credit limit will allow? It's about peace and goodwill to your fellow man—"

"And a baby supposedly born in a stable while shepherds watched their flocks by night," retorted Herman. "Do you know that means he was probably born in the Spring? This December 25th date has more to do with stamping out a pagan festival or guesswork about the day of creation than credible historical fact. Seems to me that lying about the birthday of the Messiah sets a better example for those hawking life-enhancing aftershave than it does for those who think everyone should just be nice to each other."

"Yes, well, Merry Christmas all the same, Herman."

The Reverend handed him a bottle of wine carefully wrapped in paper recycled from last year's gift-giving. In return, Herman produced a plastic bag containing a bottle of wine bought ten minutes ago at the local off-licence.

"Merry Christmas to you too, Michael, and you can thank God from me that it'll all be over in twenty-eight hours time."

Locke's nose dribbled onto his scarf and each drop felt like the last reserves of his life ebbing away. His whole body ached and his chest was wracked with pain whenever another rattling cough forced its way up out of his lungs. He wanted to curl up in a ball and die, but was reluctant to do so in the aisle of a twenty-four hour chemist.

He wiped his nose with the back of a hand and grabbed a box of fresh tissues from a shelf. It joined an armful of cold and flu remedies that he hoped would stave off death long enough for him to return the mitten in his pocket.

The girl behind the counter was wearing a red hat with a furry white bobble on top, but while her headgear showed festive spirit, her face did not.

“Wotcha, Mary,” said the short fellow queuing in front of Locke. He had a very high-pitched, sing-song voice and unusually pointed ears. “What do you say to me fixing some mistletoe to that bobble of yours?”

“I say I’m not kissing anyone until March unless they can show me proof they’ve had a flu jab.”

“Fair dinkum. Um, do you, err, get tinnitus at all?”

“What?”

“You know, ringing in the ears, like jingling bells. Some people get it especially bad this time of year.”

“The only bell I hear is the one that rings when that door opens. Fair sends a chill through me every time. Never know what sickly creature you’re going to be facing next. That’ll be four ninety-five.”

“Hang on, I think I’ve got change.”

The diminutive man fished loose coins from his wallet and promptly spilled some on the floor. He darted after a pound coin before it rolled under a vacuum-moulded Labrador collecting donations for the blind.

“You know the best cure for jingling bells?” said the man, returning to the counter. “Turn your TV up. Drown them out, works every time.”

“I’ll remember that. Merry Christmas, weirdo.”

The pointy eared customer left, the bell over the chemist’s door signalling his exit. Locke stepped up to the counter and then looked down at the floor.

“Talking of sickly creatures…,” said the serving girl.

Locke ignored her. Instead, he bent down and picked up a wallet.

“That must be Wally’s,” said the girl. “I bet if you run you can catch him.”

Locke slowly lifted his head and glared at her. Another life-sapping drip dropped from his nose.

Even with the curtains drawn tightly shut, Abigail could see the light from the display strewn around the house and garden seeping into her room. She unstuck posters from her walls and plastered them haphazardly around the window frame until the cracks were sealed.

These exertions left Abigail tired. She collapsed onto her

bed, but her body wouldn't let her relax. While her mind was making a stand against Christmas, her stomach was grumbling about missing dinner. She hit it with a fist. That didn't help, but at least it made her feel like she was in charge.

Then she saw it: green, slim and discrete; pinned to the rump of her rocking horse. Abigail leapt from the bed and snatched the stocking from its mooring. Her mother had probably gambled that she wouldn't see it until the morning. Even now she was curious to see what gifts bulged the fabric, but her curiosity didn't argue with the fist that carried the stocking at arm's length toward the door, which opened before Abigail reached it.

"Oh, damnables and botheration," muttered her grandmother. "I could have sworn this one'd be the toilet. Hmm, perhaps I could just go in a corner and no one would notice."

"Granny!"

"What? What? A witness?" She squinted at the little girl. "My sainted undergarments aren't going to like this, dear me, no."

"It's me, Granny, Abby."

"I know who you are, I was just wondering how long it'd be before anyone noticed you were missing. The way you've hidden yourself away up here, it could be quite some time. Yes, perhaps it would be worth—"

"The toilet's just across from the stairs. I'm going to flush this thing down it," said Abigail, holding up the stocking. "I can show you the way."

"No need, dear," said the old lady, "I'm quite capable of finding my own way." She turned around slowly in the doorway and switched out the light before leaving.

"Granny! I'm still in here!"

The old lady stopped and half-turned her head.

"Do you ever stop and think?" she asked.

"About what?"

"About how that shadow by the wardrobe looks like a man in a coat, watching and waiting for you to fall asleep?"

Abigail turned her head and saw the shadow. It looked exactly as her grandmother had described.

"Live in the moment, child. Play games. Build snowmen. Make believe." She edged out of the room, pulling the door shut behind her. "Just don't stop and think. Thinking's for those like me, whose moment has passed."

Herman walked briskly to fend off the night's deepening chill. These streets were not brightened by Christmas lights, making do with regular orange street-lamps that offered no warmth despite their colour. But Herman was almost home. Once he was safely inside, he could turn up the fire and content himself with his murder mystery DVDs.

The first flake of snow only prompted him to increase his pace.

"That'll be the country ground to a halt then," muttered Herman.

Within five minutes, the snow was falling heavily, swirling like swarms of Christmas fairies beneath the streetlights and causing him to bow his head and swear frequently.

He didn't see the couple hunched down in a doorway until he was almost upon them and only then when her wailing made him think a wild dog was about to attack.

"You've got to help us, mister," she said. Dank hair falling from beneath a threadbare woollen hat framed a face damp with snow and tears. The man cradled in her arms was buried beneath countless layers of coats and cardigans, but despite all the clothing, his lips were blue, his eyes lifeless.

Herman walked on. The girl didn't even register that he'd left. She continued talking with lips numbed by cold.

"Last words he said to me… last thing he said… was he heard jingling bells. Maybe he was right about Santa Claus…"

Thomas Locke stood outside a high-rise office. While the neighbouring buildings were dark, this one shone light from its high windows. This was odd, because Locke had circled the base three times now and was quite convinced there was no door. There weren't windows at ground-level that would allow someone to climb inside and neither were there stairs up to an elevated entrance or ramps down to an underground car-park. Yet this curious place was where Mary from the chemist said the pointy-eared Wally worked.

Locke backed away from the building into the empty road

and looked up. Chunky flakes of snow drifted down onto his face. Even if there were loose stones handy, he doubted he could throw one high enough to strike a lit window.

He produced a fresh tissue, wiped his face and blew his nose. Then he looked at the deposit left in the tissue, because that's what men do. It wasn't anything spectacular. His lungs were holding onto the green phlegm that infested them, leaving only watery mucus to soil the tissue. However, lining the edge of the tissue were the words of a poem:

'Twas the night before Christmas and all through the house, not a creature was stirring, not even a mouse…'

Why anyone thought it was a good idea to print poetry on a disposable snot-rag was beyond Locke, but he knew this was a sign; this was the beginning of a trail that would lead him inside that building. His talent for finding was as inexplicable as the reasons for the writing on the tissue. Locke knew only that he could trust its guidance and that was telling him to look for…

There! Scurrying toward that drain to escape the thickening snow!

It was a rat instead of a mouse, but that was close enough for Locke. He immediately gave chase.

Abigail held a pillow over her head, trying to blot out the noise from the living room below. She didn't want to hear her family's desperate attempts at playing charades. The intermittent laughter was almost as bad as the arguments that broke out whenever Uncle Maurice thought Aunt Ivy's mimes weren't up to scratch. It was the same story as every Christmas and that was the last thing that Abigail wanted to think about.

The sudden burst of 'ooh's' was new however. People began moving around below in defiance of the usual script.

Abigail threw aside the pillow. Her bedroom was dark, even though the light had been on. The hallway light had to be off too, because its tell-tale line of yellow was absent beneath her bedroom door.

She pulled aside one of the moved posters and opened the curtains. The strings of bulbs outside could be seen only as black threads criss-crossing a garden now pale and pristine in the moonlight. The snow reached halfway up the front gate, with more steadily falling. Her father was loudly blaming it for the power-cut. Abigail silently blamed it for returning the dark figure that lurked in the shadow of her wardrobe.

Herman blindly tried to find candles in the cupboard beneath the kitchen sink, but soon gave up and decided he'd go to bed early instead.

His tiny terraced house rapidly lost the heat the electric fire had pumped into it over the last hour and by the time he'd cleaned his teeth and climbed into bed, his fingers and toes felt nearly frozen. The accumulated weight of a sheet, three blankets and two duvets reassured him that everything would be warmed up again soon.

He closed his eyes and immediately saw the inside of the shopping centre, festooned with glittering streamers and tinsel stars. Faceless shoppers milled around him until he managed to wrest control of his treacherous imagination and clear the floors. Then, concentrating hard, he took great pleasure in erasing every piece of Christmas decoration and every artificial light until the picture in his head was entirely dark.

That was when he began to hear the jingling bells.

The stench of the sewer clung to Locke long after he emerged from the grate in the office basement. He ached even more than he had an hour ago, despite taking twice the recommended dosage of Max Strength cold and flu tablets. Worse, he was sure that rat had been laughing at him before vanishing at the mouth of a rising overflow. Still, he was finally inside the door-less building and able to set about finding Wally and returning his wallet. If all went well, he might even be able to give that girl back her mitten before midnight and then peacefully expire without taxing himself further.

His eyes had grown accustomed to the dark whilst traversing the sewers and this proved helpful given the lights here no longer appeared to be working. He guessed the snowfall was to blame. Otherwise, it appeared to be an office building much like any other. There were desks separated by partitions and kitchen areas at regular intervals. Locke found nothing untoward about the place until he brushed past a photocopier and knocked a piece off. He quickly picked it up to try and put it back, but found it tacky to the touch. Further inspection revealed he was a holding a length of candy-cane and the photocopier itself was made of the same substance. Locke looked around in confusion, before feeling compelled to experiment on other parts of the office.

The desk partitions were made of gingerbread, the desks themselves, marzipan. A computer tower was opened to reveal circuits traced in liquorice and transistors made of mint humbugs. The staplers were chocolate and tasted quite nice, but the pencils were regular pencils made of wood and less palatable as a result.

Locke ran up the stairs, his illness forgotten. He just wanted to return the wallet and be out of this place before he found himself eating a whole A3 printer made of Battenburg cake.

He exited onto the eighth floor. This was where he'd seen some of those lit windows. A moment of listening gave no suggestion others were here. Locke ventured forward. Wally had appeared relatively normal, but there was no guessing what other kinds of people he'd find in a workplace built from confectionary.

He passed an open door. A glance inside showed it full of filing cabinets. Unable to resist, he checked the nearest. It was made of strawberry cheesecake. It had also been locked until he broke the lock off to taste it. Inside were paper files. The foremost one caught Locke's attention. He pulled it out and began to read, while idly munching away at more pieces of the filing cabinet.

"Freeze!"

Locke looked round, then looked down.

The security guard was very short, with very pointed ears. His uniform was regulation black, but his shoes were green, with a toe that curled up and ended with a golden bell.

"You're a real, live elf, aren't you?" said Locke.

The elf duly shot him with his Taser.

"Are you all right in there?" asked Abigail's mother from the other side of the barricaded bedroom door.

"I'm fine," called back Abigail.

"Well, we're all going to bed now. Your father expects the power will be back on come morning."

"Doesn't bother me."

"You will be down for breakfast, won't you? And maybe to open a present or two?"

"No."

Her mother sighed.

"Suit yourself. We'll see you when we see you then. Night, night."

Footsteps retreated away along the landing, a door closed and then all was quiet in the Redwood house. The only sound Abigail could hear was that of her own breathing.

"I'm not afraid of you, you know," she whispered to the shadow by the wardrobe. "And I don't care if you're here because I said I didn't believe in Santa Claus, because I know he's not real and things that aren't real can't hurt you."

The shadow did not speak and did not move from its position by the wardrobe.

"I'm going to go to sleep now. You'll be gone when I wake up."

She rolled over in her bed and pulled the sheet up around her chin. She wanted to check if the shadow had moved while she wasn't looking, but didn't dare. Instead she closed her eyes tight and told herself she was safe as long as she stayed in bed.

Then she heard the faint jingling of bells.

"We'll have to kill you now," explained Wally, waving the file Locke took in front of his nose.

"But no one would believe me if I told them," said Locke. He'd given up struggling against the unnaturally strong silly string that held him to the chair as soon as he realised he was glad of the sit down.

"Oh, you'd be surprised," said Wally, pacing up and down in front of a crowd of elves that glared at Locke from beneath paper hats and sporadically menaced him with party blowers. "Those ridiculous rumours that people mock today have a nasty habit of turning true all too soon afterwards. We remember when there were only four elements and the world was flat and—"

"Was Santa ever more than just an advertising campaign?" asked Locke, nodding at the file.

"We do all of this so you people don't ask questions like that," said Wally. He gestured to his colleagues, before pointing at windows that looked out over the powerless town. "All of the money and marketing and lies, we do it all so you big people never learn the true meaning of Christmas."

Herman covered his ears, but it didn't help. He shouted at whoever was causing the noise, but if they heard, they didn't stop. He gritted his teeth and balled himself up in bed, holding tight bedclothes that were still as cold as when he first climbed beneath.

Finally, Herman snapped. He hauled himself out of bed and shoved his feet into his slippers. A dressing gown was brusquely pulled on over his pyjamas. He crossed to the window and flung it open. A blast of chill air swept into the room, carrying with it dancing crystals of ice. He leaned his head out in search of whoever rang the bells that denied his sleep.

The backyards and rooftops were lifeless; smothered by snow. Herman shivered. Goosebumps riddled his flesh. He withdrew, closed the window and hurried to the spare room.

The street at the front of the house was equally barren. The only light that fell upon the world came from a full moon gazing down from a clear sky.

Yet Herman could still hear that damned jingling. Was it coming from downstairs? He went to check, slippers flapping against his heels as he navigating the steps in the dark.

Nothing in the living room, but the bells were definitely louder. He closed his eyes and tried to determine their direction, but the origin seemed to fall within the bounds of his skull.

He stormed into the kitchen and threw open cupboards. He checked the oven and the bin.

Jingle, jingle, jingle.

He clasped his hands over his ears.

Jingle, jingle, jingle.

Herman snatched up a jam jar and hurled it at the wall. He saw it explode into glassy shards and globs of red, but heard only:

Jingle, jingle, jingle.

He staggered out into the hall and then back into his living room. It was then Herman knew the sound came from the chimney. With both hands he grabbed the electric fire and tried to pull it clear of the bricked up hearth.

The bells grew louder and louder, until the vibrations ran through his head and his teeth began to chatter. Twinkling lights appeared at the edge of his vision.

The fire fell away and he began scratching at the bricks behind. His fingers were blue and the veins standing proud on the back of his hands ran black, but Herman could not see this. He could see nothing but the twinkling lights and hear nothing except the jingling bells.

"Leave him be," said an elderly elf, pushing his way through the crowd toward Locke.

"But he's a human," protested Wally. "He was trespassing! He stole a file on the Santa account and he stole my wallet!"

"I didn't—" began Locke.

"Hush, both of you," said the elderly elf. "I know why he's here and I also know he's of The Office of Lost and Found."

This revelation sent nervous murmurs running through congregation. The newcomer walked up to Locke and then sat down cross-legged on the floor before him.

"You were asked to find Father Christmas, were you not?" he asked.

Locke nodded. "By a little girl called Abigail. She didn't believe."

The elder elf's shoulders sagged and he shook his head.

"I will tell you the secret of Christmas, Thomas Locke of the Office of Lost and Found, but you must know that we keep this secret only so others do not share the fate that will befall young Abigail this night."

Abigail did not want to leave the sanctuary of her bed. She had shushed as loudly as she dared, but whoever was jingling those bells either did not hear her or chose to ignore her protest.

She rolled onto her back, counted slowly down from three

and then opened her eyes. Her heart skipped a beat in anticipation of the shadow looming over her, but instead she saw it remained by the wardrobe, unmoved.

Abigail gingerly climbed out of bed. The carpet was cool beneath her feet as she crossed to the window. A glance outside showed the snow was now three quarters of the way up the front gate. The pavements were free of footprints and the cars parked by the kerb had not moved since the snow started falling. Every tree was dark and still. Not even a breeze could claim responsibility for jingling bells.

It must be someone in the house, thought Abigail. She turned and headed for the bedroom door.

"Christmas is about presents," explained the elder elf. "It's about crackers and the terrible jokes you find inside. It's about trees and the baubles we hang upon them. It's about churches and prayers and carols sung even by those who cannot sing. It's about the story of a child born in a stable and a jolly man branded by Coca-Cola and how a luxury fragrance can make you look handsome and witty and desirable to the opposite sex. Gross commercialisation, festive cheer and religious rites; Christmas is all of these things, because we made it so. Christmas is anything and everything that keeps us distracted."

Abigail stepped out onto the landing. A floorboard creaked under her weight. Her breath flowered as a faint cloud in front of her face, before gently dispersing. She hugged her arms tight about herself. The jingling bells sounded as if they were coming from the guest room at the end of the hallway. When she heard a booming "ho ho ho" in the middle of the night exactly one year ago, she had run to its source with unabashed excitement. This time she proceeded with caution.

"If we are not distracted, we might see how dark the nights have become and we might feel the chill of the winter in our bones," continued the elf. "Once our minds are open to such things, they are prone to noticing that which came before gods or credit cards and as we notice them, they notice us. And they come with their jingling bells and twinkling lights and bleed you dry of every happy year you've lived and have yet to live until all that's left is a life not worth living."

The bells grew louder.

Abigail could not feel her toes. She had her fingers wrapped up in the folds of her nightdress, but they too were turning numb.

She tried to speak up to tell the ringer of the bells to be quiet, but couldn't summon her voice.

She cast a glance over her shoulder. Was that shadow by the banister the one from by her wardrobe?

The bells grew louder.

"I just want them to stop," Abigail told the shadow. "You can come for me if you have to, but I have to make them stop."

She turned back to the door. She didn't even care if it was her father behind it, stealing away the magic of Christmas for a second year, the jingling was a pain in her skull that chattered her teeth and made the space behind her eyes hurt.

She pulled a hand free of her nightdress and reached out to the door. Her fingers were so pale they almost glowed in the darkness. She touched the handle. The brass burned against her skin, but she pressed down and pushed forward and the door swung open.

The room beyond was full of noise and colour. Abigail saw Christmas trees and gaily wrapped parcels. Children were running around, laughing and arguing. The smell of roast turkey filled her nostrils. It was a hundred Christmasses rolled into one, with each slowly bleached of colour by strands of black tinsel that criss-crossed the room like a bleakly festive spider-web. The memories fell from Abigail's grandmother, who was suspended in the middle of the room, convulsing.

Abigail stared in horror as twinkling lights began to crowd the edges of her vision.

Her grandmother managed to turn her head. The old woman's tears fell as crystals of ice to the floor.

"It'll be okay, dear," she whispered. "You just need to believe in—"

The words caught in her throat, strangled by black tinsel.

"But I can't," said Abigail, shaking her head. She could see the sight from a year before: the beard was fake, the fat belly a pillow; her parents puncturing age-old magic and mystery with a brandy-fuelled grope beneath the mistletoe.

Her grandmother finally fell limp. The bells ceased.

But only for a moment.

Then they returned, louder and deeper, chiming in time with the terrified beating of Abigail's heart. The black lines within the room shifted, melting away like wax before cutting a new path that led them closer and closer to the little girl.

She backed away. Her head was swimming; drowning in noise while the flashing lights all but blinded her to the fate lancing toward her.

"I can't believe in Santa," said Abigail, "but I can believe in shadows…" She turned her head. "You can come for me now."

The weave of black tinsel snatched for her, but the shadow from her wardrobe got there first.

The Reverend Michael Jeffers knocked on Herman's door for a third time. While he waited for a response, he stamped his boots on the doorstep to help keep warm. A few of the neighbours were already out with shovels, clearing snow from the pavement or trying to extract cars from the white mounds that covered them. As the Reverend looked around, he couldn't help but smile. There was something magical about a white Christmas.

The door finally opened.

"Merry Chri… Good Lord, Herman, you look terrible. And about ten years older. What on earth did you get up to last night?"

"Uh, nothing, I guess I must have just not slept very well."

"Staying up late waiting for Saint Nicholas? I always knew you were a big kid at heart."

"Yeah, that's me. Big kid."

"I was checking up on my flock after last night's power-cut and thought I'd drop by and see if you wanted to come down to the church and help—"

"Do I look like I want to help anyone today?"

Herman glared at his half-brother and then slammed the door shut. He cringed on hearing a defiant "Merry Christmas and Happy New Year!" make it through the wood.

"What on earth is merry about Christmas?" asked Herman, sloping back off to bed. "I swear one of these days it'll be the death of me."

Locke sat on the wall to the Redwood's front garden, swinging his legs back and forth so his shoes wore channels in the snow. He drew a deep breath in through his nose and grinned at the novelty. Then he watched Abigail finish off the construction of a snowman a few feet away. It had a long carrot for a nose and pieces of gravel formed eyes and a mouth. The arms were broken twigs and a battered old Fedora sat on the snowman's head. She patted his ample torso into shape with mittens restored to both hands.

"You didn't need to lie, you know," said Abigail, while fastening a school tie around the snowman's neck.

"About what?" asked Locke.

"About not finding Santa."

"So you believe he exists now?"

"I believe... Santa's not as important as people make out." She appraised her handiwork before gesturing toward the house. "Do you want to come inside? Mummy makes the best mince pies."

"No, it looks a bit chaotic in your house this morning."

"That's because Granny died during the night."

"Oh. I'm sorry."

"Don't be sorry. She saved me. And she wanted me to live in the moment and build a snowman, so that's what I've done. I think she'd like that." She turned to face Locke. "Will you be visiting your family for Christmas?"

Locke bit at his lip and shook his head.

"I'll be heading back to my kiosk. Maybe my business partner will be there... Would you believe he lost my flu and gave me socks? Socks. I suppose I should try and get him a Christmas present, but what do you get someone who—?"

He stopped and looked down at Abigail, who was standing in front of him with arms out-stretched.

"I think a shadow would probably like this," she said.

Locke hesitated, then smiled and accepted the snowman's battered Fedora.

THE END

Appendix II: Artwork

Author's note: What follows are various sketches and promotional artwork I created for the book, in addition to the original Anarchy Books cover. While Veronica and Locke appear, I don't consider anything I've drawn to constitute their definitive appearance; when writing, I see them only as fuzzy impressions, rather than a specific collection of physical features, which means any attempt to pin their faces down with ink ends up invariably inaccurate.

VERONICA DRYSDALE

THOMAS
LOCKE

"THE BEST DARK COMEDY SINCE DOUGLAS ADAMS..." - ANDY REMIC
The Office of
Lost & Found
VINCENT
HOLLAND-KEEN

The Office of Lost & Found
Veronica Drysdale
The Office of Lost & Found
Thomas Locke

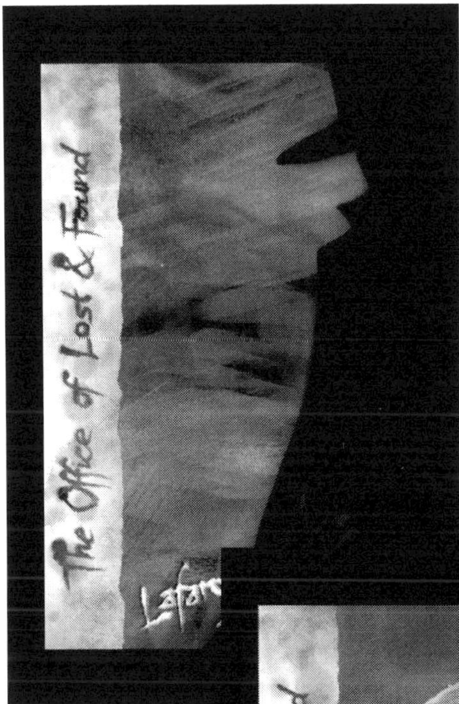
The Office of Lost & Found

The Office of Lost & Found
PRAY
FOR

The Office of Lost & Found
Roadworks Rule
The Office of Lost & Found

Appendix III: Written Notes

Author's note: The following pages are taken from my notebooks and show some of the planning that went into 'The Office of Lost and Found'. They show the genesis of ideas that formed the basis of the story, other ideas that were cast aside and even unrelated ideas and doodles for which I can offer no rational explanation.

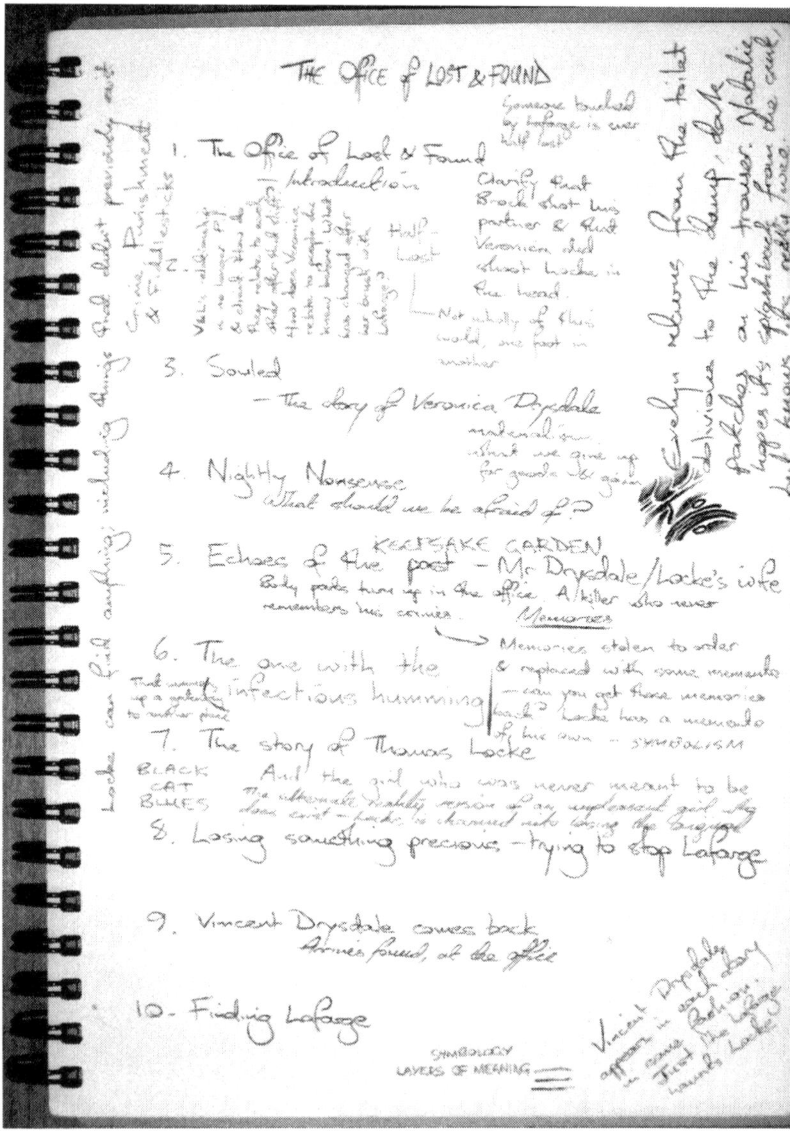
THE OFFICE OF LOST & FOUND

Someone touched by Lafarge is ever half lost

1. The Office of Lost & Found
— Introduction

Clarify that Brock shot his partner & that Veronica shot Locke in the head.

2. Crime, Punishment & Fiddlesticks

Half-Lost — Not wholly of this world, one foot in another

3. Souled
— The story of Veronica Drysdale
materialism — what we give up for goods we gain

4. Nightly Nonsense
What should we be afraid of?

5. Echoes of the past — Mr Drysdale / Locke's wife
KEEPSAKE GARDEN
Body parts turn up in the office. A killer who never remembers his crimes. Memories

6. The one with the infectious humming
Memories stolen to order & replaced with some memento — can you get those memories back? Locke has a memento of his own — SYMBOLISM

7. The story of Thomas Locke
BLACK CAT BLUES
And the girl who was never meant to be

8. Losing something precious — trying to stop Lafarge

9. Vincent Drysdale comes back
Armies found, at the office

10. Finding Lafarge

SYMBOLOGY
LAYERS OF MEANING

Evelyn relieves from the toilet oblivious to the lamp, Locke patching on his trousers. Natalie hopes it's ... from the cuk but he knows it's ...

Vincent Drysdale appears in each story in some fashion. Just like Lafarge haunts Locke.

Locke can find anything, including things that didn't previously exist

The arrival of the cruise ship. Mr & Mrs — welcome back.
Veronica in the back room, looking over the material of her life.
Veronica's parents are rich enough to buy back Veronica's contract, but they aren't interested — they want Drysdale's
Supernatural security at the auction house.
Veronica up at auction. Her only hope is for Locke to place the highest bid or for the paperwork to go missing.
Locke could do a deal with Lisforge.
Establish her ex-husband is linked to her parents.
The auctioneers inviting Veronica to the auction. We will come for you at 6 o'clock.
The auctioneers coming for Veronica
Veronica burning her things and as each turns to ash it turns up at The Office of Lost & Found.
REDLICH
MERCURY'S WAKE
REGENT'S WAKE
VOYAGER
CRUISE LINER
BLIND NAVIGATOR
daex
DAEX
DSX

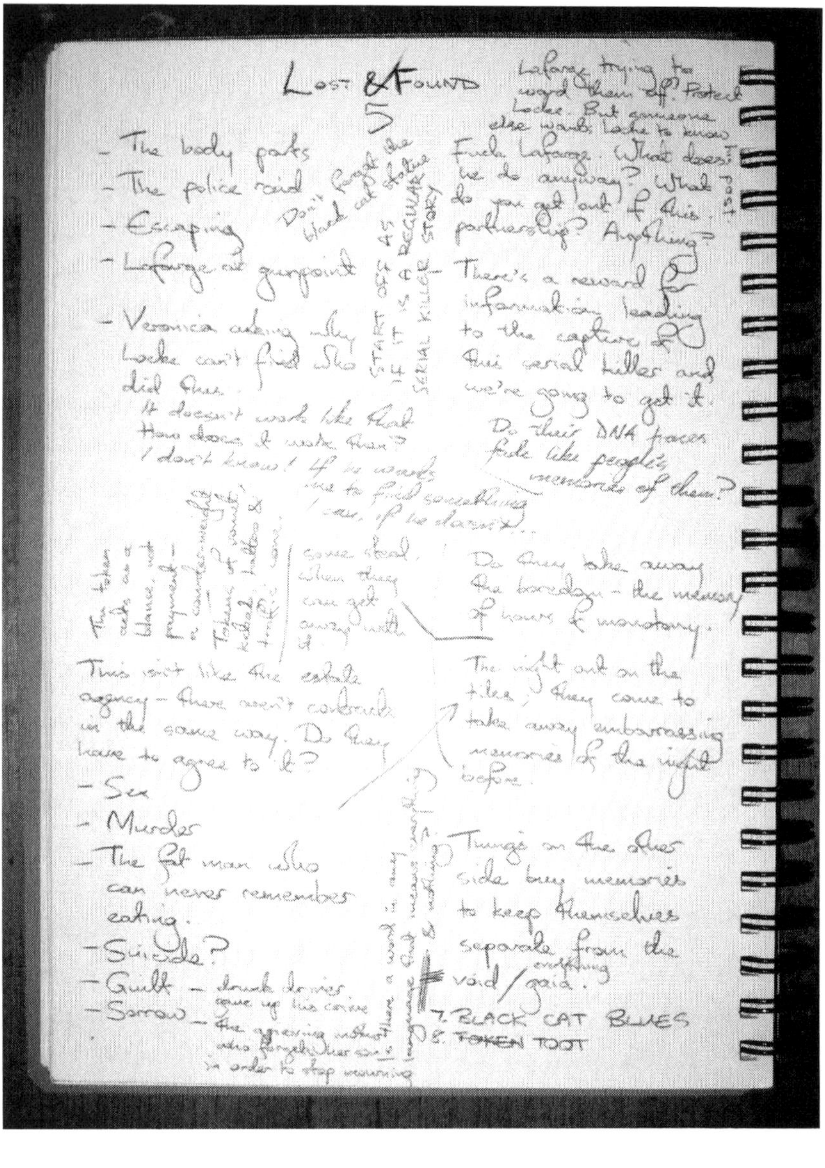
LOST & FOUND
5
Lafarge trying to ward them off? Protect Locke. But someone else wants Locke to know
Fuck Lafarge. What does he do anyway? What do you get out of this partnership? Anything?
- The body parts
- The police raid
- Escaping
- Lafarge at gunpoint
Don't forget the black cat statue
START OFF AS IF IT IS A REGULAR SERIAL KILLER STORY
There's a reward for information leading to the capture of this serial killer and we're going to get it.
- Veronica asking why Locke can't find who did this.
It doesn't work like that
How does it work then?
I don't know! If he wants me to find something I can. If he doesn't...
Do their DNA traces fade like people's memories of them?
Some steal, when they can get away with it
Do they take away the boredom – the memory of hours of monotony.
The night out on the tiles, they come to take away embarrassing memories of the night before.
This isn't like the estate agency – there aren't contracts in the same way. Do they have to agree to it?
- Sex
- Murder
- The fat man who can never remember eating.
- Suicide?
- Guilt – drunk driver gave up his crime
- Sorrow – the grieving mother who forgets her son in order to stop mourning
Things on the other side buy memories to keep themselves separate from the void / gaia.
7. BLACK CAT BLUES
8. TOKEN TOOT

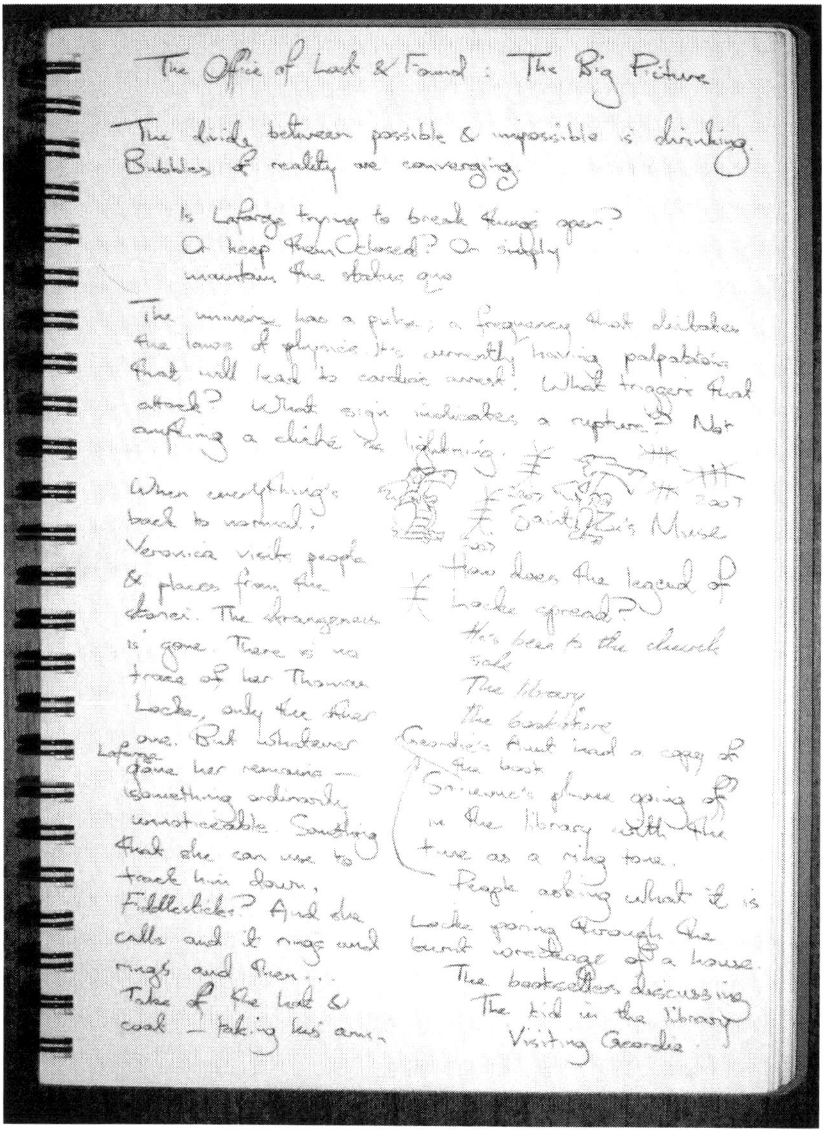

The Office of Lost & Found : The Big Picture

The divide between possible & impossible is shrinking. Bubbles of reality are converging.

Is Laforge trying to break things open? Or keep them closed? Or simply maintain the status quo

The universe has a pulse; a frequency that dictates the laws of physics. It's currently having palpitations that will lead to cardiac arrest. What triggers that attack? What sign indicates a rupture? Not anything a cliché like lightning.

Saint Zu's Muse

When everything's back to normal, Veronica visits people & places from the stories. The strangeness is gone. There is no trace of her Thomas Locke, only the other one. But whatever Laforge gave her remains — something ordinarily unnoticeable. Something that she can use to track him down, Fiddlesticks? And she calls and it rings and rings and then... Take of the hat & coat — taking his arm.

How does the legend of Locke spread?

He's been to the church sale

The library

The bookstore

Geordie's Aunt had a copy of the book

Someone's phone going off in the library with the tune as a ring tone.

People asking what it is

Locke going through the burnt wreckage of a house.

The booksellers discussing

The kid in the library

Visiting Geordie.

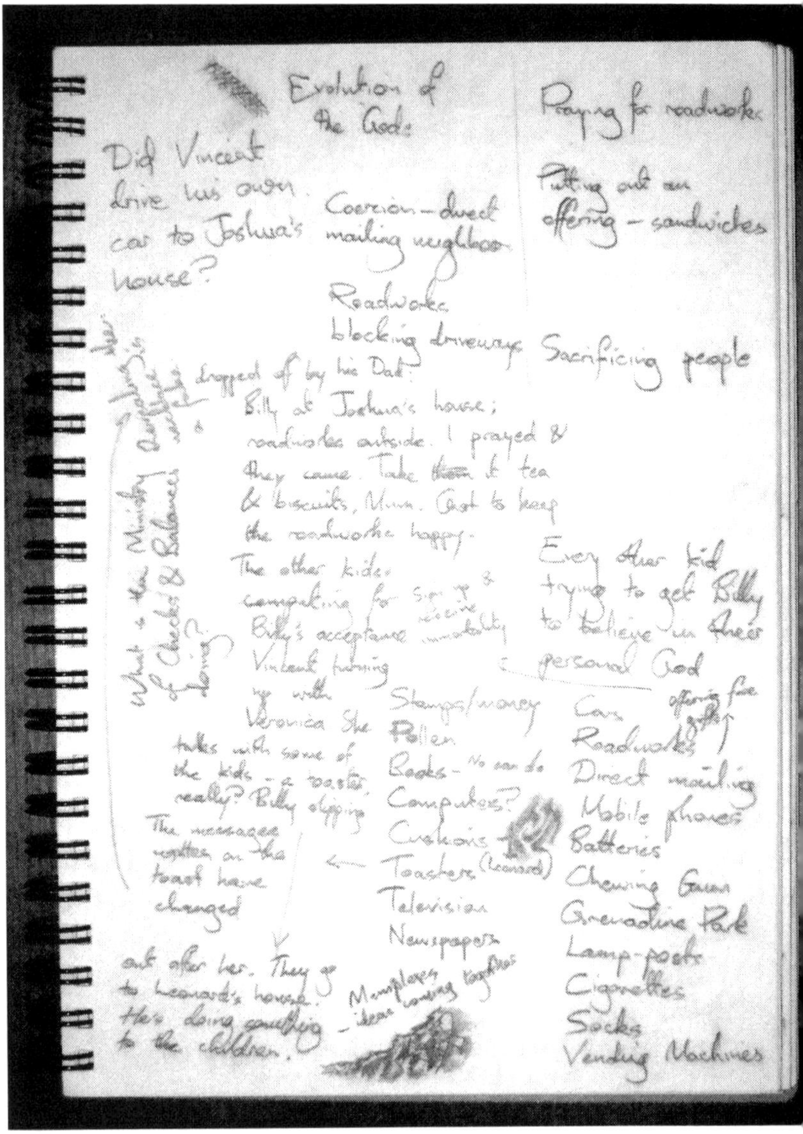

Evolution of the Gods

Did Vincent drive his own car to Joshua's house?

Coercion – direct mailing neighbour

Roadworks blocking driveways

dropped off by his Dad.

Billy at Joshua's house; roadworks outside. I prayed & they came. Take it tea & biscuits, Mum. Got to keep the roadworks happy.

The other kids competing for Billy's acceptance – sign up & receive immortality

Vincent teaming up with Veronica. She talks with some of the kids – a pastor, really? Billy slipping out after her. They go to Leonard's house. He's doing something to the children.

The messages written on the toast have changed

Stamps/money
Pollen
Books – No can do
Computers?
Cuckoos
Toasters (Leonard)
Television
Newspapers

Mumplaces – ideas coming together

Praying for roadworks

Putting out an offering – sandwiches

Sacrificing people

Every other kid trying to get Billy to believe in their personal God

Cars – offering for gifts
Roadworks
Direct mailing
Mobile phones
Batteries
Chewing Gum
Grenadine Park
Lamp-posts
Cigarettes
Socks
Vending Machines

54819131R00241

Made in the USA
Charleston, SC
13 April 2016